Malcor's Story

Look for these other great titles!

Dar Tania – October 2016, a 100 page story

Malcor's Story – November 2016

Bomoki's Gate – April 2017

Forsaken Isles "100 Page Stories" – May 2017 on

For more information about the stories set in the Forsaken Isles, its characters, author, or whatever else inspires you to contact Dar Malcor:

darmalcor.weebly.com

Send me an email and join my email list as well at darmalcor.weebly.com

Library of Congress: 2016919935

ISBN: 978-0-9981076-3-9

Table of Contents

Description

Malcor Kell'Tayris experiences Time as flashes of brilliance that help him enter the paladin trials. His dreams of knighthood along with this genius gift set him on a quest of legend. Seeing Time murder him, killing those he cares for and everyone he knows, he struggles to become a divine warrior. Watching Time's flow, he learns how to wield it to join the mightiest of Tania's paladin orders, to fight the strongest foes, to face the greatest of challenges. In his blood lays dormant berserker rage, a truce with shadow dragons, and a prophecy of the next king to be. Malcor struggles with fury to stay true to his faith.

Trials of pain, dragon fear, and a quest to slay a mighty foe take him into a head-on collision with necromantic gods that threatens the shadow dragons' return back from darkness and heresy. Malcor's passion and his allure to the shadow dragons threaten the straight path of faith and force a choice: will he remain true or fall to the shadows? When gods rage and Time slays, Malcor's choices and dreams drive his quest beyond even prophecy and faith.

Author's Preface

Writing is like a fiery compulsion burning in my soul. When I was young, like 5 years old, I remember this dream of being trapped in bed with a giant deer or moosehead mounted on the wall. I imagined it staring at me. I'd wake up late at night feeling alone and watched. One time, I tried to see if the animal on the wall stared back so I made a circle with my fingers and looked and looked. In the dark of the room, I know I imagined it – or maybe it was part of the dream – but a bloodshot canine eye I just knew belonged to a wolf, looked right back at me. It freaked me out but set the stage for my mind to put together a very important thing.

Our world is real, but our perception of that world creates a very unique experience for each of us. I choose to let my world include magic.

Later, as I grew up, I'd lose myself in books with fantasy and sci-fi taking up a disproportionate amount of my life. Having been raised in a very religious family, I felt challenged to make sense of it all. Malcor's Story comes from years of daydreams about how much cooler and awesomer our world would be if, all around us, magic lurked. I have found magic everywhere but most enjoy certain quiet moments in the cathedrals and temples of this world. Nothing can really compare to connecting with something as old and ancient and exposed as a mountain's peak. There is always something bigger out there reminding us that we are a part of something whether we focus on it or not. These temples stay with me and I felt very much the same in a very different way when my children were born.

As vast and overwhelming as the temples of the world can be when you let yourself open up to them, it is the vastness that brings with it magic. In the birth of a child, it's reversed. All that vastness of the world falls into your hands when that tiny life blinks its eyes into confusion and chaos. Suddenly, the vast becomes very small, singular, and important. Whether you believe in the divine or not, whether you see the world as I do, there are things that we will never individually understand. Meanwhile, unconcerned with our lack of understanding, those same things comprehend us.

I heard the roar of a thunderstorm rising up a mountain where I stood above the timberline. The wind swept the clouds up and I imagined that if I jumped, I would take flight and soar. It was July and I stood on Mytikas, on Mount Olympus in Greece. An hour later it began to snow. I will never forget the sound, even though I would be sore tried to describe it. In the noise of a hospital at my daughters' births, I felt very much the same way. I heard the same sound because all the noise of the hospital and chaotic activity that is a birth became this magical moment. I experienced it as sound. Another way I might say it is that Time moved *sideways*.

Malcor begins his journey at time in life when all of us struggle to confront the inevitability of adulthood. That transition is full of clichés and wise pithy sayings like, "You're going to make mistakes. It's okay. Learn. Keep going." My favorite, "Learn how to manage money." I wanted Malcor to have a different experience. Morbatten is a militaristic empire that knows and practices what we tell our children – they are the future. Given that this is true, Malcor is allowed to struggle into his dreams and is accelerated every bit as much as he can handle towards his dreams. Because magic is real, his dreams are shared. His partners help him move towards his dreams. Sure, he might fail, but so did they. Having been there themselves, they know when to back off for Malcor to have his moments of success. Having experienced heartache and disappointment, they know how to let Malcor fail in a way that the lesson and wisdom is not lost.

This is the empire of dragons who watch and have watched over humanity. Their god emperor, a fire breathing dragon named Alerius, considers the people of Morbatten his treasure. He has found that the real treasure is not gold and gems, but the free-willed humans of his empire choosing to serve and advance his dream. The life of a citizen is but a blink, but the bloodlines, the stories, and the impacts of heroes stay with the dragons far more than stackable gold coins ever could. Don't get me wrong; Alerius loves treasure too. Some of you may wonder at the archetype of a dragon like this being benign, even benevolent. Make no mistake. Dragons do not see the world the way we think they do. In Dar Tania, a wise ruler of the kingdom north of Morbatten explains it best when he tells Princess Alaura, "Dragons do not have friends. They do not see you as a friend. Your life is but a blink, and you were used as a tool to send us a message. Our royal prince is dead and taken by your dragon *friend*. Our paladins, though not killed, have been demoralized and humiliated. Your dragon *friend* bathed our city in terror. That message and this story will last for ages. You were used to deliver that message. Nothing more."

If you have not yet, or if you enjoy this story, I encourage you to visit my blog at darmalcor.weebly.com or pick up *Dar Tania*. Dar Tania tells the story of how Morbatten was founded some 1,800 years before Malcor's Story.

I dedicate this book to some of the best friends I could ever imagine – Dar Malcor and Tembri, the battle priest I have seen in my real life friends. To those who provided comments and critique, thank you: Mark F (and for helping with the map), Kenneth B, Sara I, Tony R, and my wife Ryann B who spent almost as much time reading this as it took me to create it. Also, special gratitude to Brian Mclean and Marsha Hairston who helped me with final proof editing.

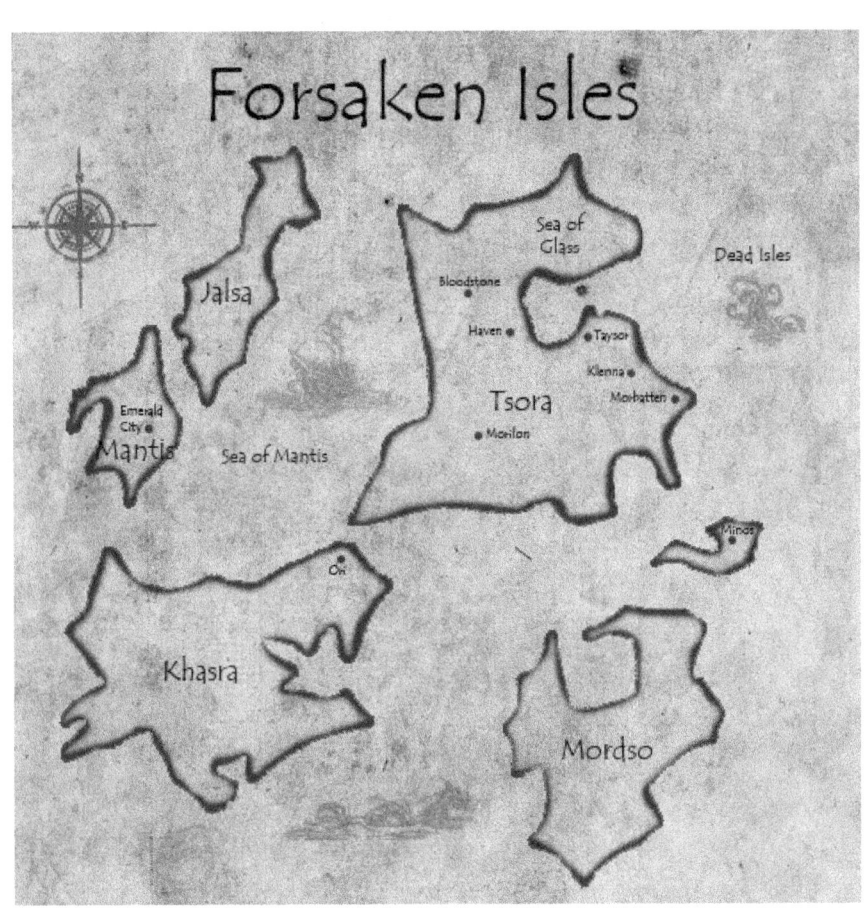

Chapter One: Coming of Age Ceremony

Malcor stood tall on the hill. It looked down on the valley he called home, the village of Klenna. The tavern, just there at the crossroads cut southeast to the capitol city of Morbatten and northwest out of the empire towards the wilderness and several small provinces between here and there. He found more and more, that he liked these high places. He could see forever and imagine his future waiting out there. His future felt glorious in his dreams, full of honor and might; very different from the day to day grind here. His nineteenth birthday would arrive soon and that meant another Coming of Age ceremony. Starting five years ago at the age of fourteen, he tried to attend. Each year, the foundry's owner, Tor, had conspired to prevent him. This time he would make it. Nothing would stop him. If he failed, he'd be too old and would be trapped as just a smith. Forever.

The wind chilled his face in the early summer day with just a hint of snow from the high mountains between Klenna and Morbatten. Tiny human figures maneuvered horses and other beasts along the crossroads and their various side branches. Far to the northwest, he noted a cloud of dust from what was probably a large caravan. He felt restless as if the world confined him. Leaving Klenna sounded so good. If only, if only,... if only he could find a way to actually leave! How many times had he stood here and imagined voices carried by the wind calling him, "Malcor! Come away with us!" No such voices today except in his dreams stirred.

Apprenticed to one of Klenna's blacksmiths when his parents died in the last war, Malcor had quickly become a favorite in the foundry and earned a small measure of fame. He had an eye and knack for alloying metals together that resulted in higher quality goods and repairs. Also possessing uncommonly good intuition and strength, he seemed to pick up more than his fair share of odd jobs. A lot of repair work, along with maintenance of adventure-worn gear, gave him time to listen to the stories and he yearned - *if only*. This year there had even been rumors of war stirring from the west. Stories like that usually flew through Klenna without lingering but this one had weight to it given the outpouring of knights from the capitol city Morbatten passing through Klenna heading west. The rumors suggested something with the Bloodstone Valley, a place often tied to such things because of continual warfare with hordes of undead for centuries.

He sighed and ran his calloused fingers through his hair, at least the parts not scarred over from a forge accident years ago. As much as he loved the stories, the knights posed a mystery to him. He often found them watching his work and whispering to themselves. Were they talking about him? Altogether different from adventures he and other children grew up on in Morbatten, the actual knights troubled and intrigued him at the same time. They clearly had a presence more than simple power and strength. Why they always ended up staring at him, he would never know. His master often joked that one day he would find himself talking to a knight and realize that all the religious posturing in the world amounted to zero mystery and just a lot of boring administration. Malcor noted this joking never happened within ear shot of a knight or anyone connected to the Temple.

Malcor's eyes followed the side road up to the shrine of their Goddess Takhissis. He preferred the name *Takhissis*. Wanting to be a knight, he appreciated that more warlike and actioned name than *Tiamat*, the Mother. Either way, their multi-dragon-headed goddess of the colored dragons would watch over them. The difference in names came from whether worshiped in combat and action, or in times of peace. Crowning a hill just a bit taller than his, the dark gray stonework and golden lines of script and art had a presence to them, similar to the knights but etched in immortal stone. His master had warned him to stay away from the shrine and all temples, but Malcor never listened. He liked it there. The oppressive weightiness of the religion, when viewed at a distance, was nothing like the warm embrace he had felt during his parents' funeral in that very shrine. Or, the times he snuck up the shrine's hill to watch the knights training. His nineteenth birthday at that shrine could change everything for him tomorrow. *If only...* if only the priest or priestess watching the Coming of Age ceremony took note of him and saw something different than a simple young blacksmith.

Still staring at the shrine, he noticed something and shielded his eyes from the sun to get a better look. Just to the side of the entry way column, a hooded figure appeared to be staring at him. The dark robes apparent in the column's shadow gave the figure away. "It's a priest," he thought and waved. He saw the figure pull the cowl back. Even at the distance, he could tell by the brilliant red hair that it was a priestess. She shook her hair free and waved back as a giant of an armored knight stepped to her side into his view. He felt the knight's regard even as he calculated that the knight must stand close to ten feet tall. Like the knights at the foundry, he suddenly felt the weight of a conversation about him taking place. Only Dar rank priests and priestesses would have a knight with them like that. Was it a dragon, a Dread Lord? And a priestess, one attended by a giant knight. So, not just a Dar rank perhaps one of THE high priestesses. He made a mental note to ask about the red-haired priestess. He hoped the pair would not be there at the Coming of Age ceremony. Still feeling their gaze, he returned to the Klenna path and started the walk home. Or, maybe they should be there?

Malcor slept in a small room just off the kitchen of his master's house. A few trinkets he had forged rested on a shelf by his cot. As a blacksmith, he had prepared carefully for the Coming of Age ceremony. He wanted something to show off that would give him the safety of the blacksmith career. But, what he wanted more than anything, was something new and different. "Tomorrow's my chance," he said as he picked up a black iron-wrought statue of a dragon. Over the past few months he had worked gold in to detail to add further dimension to the dragon. As far he could see, it was perfect though it always seemed to need just one more thing. Absently, he began to polish it - again - and wondered about tomorrow.

His other prized possession, a longsword he started forging when he turned 10 and had been re-forging ever since, rested against the bed. Like the dragon statuette, the sword appeared jet black wrapped in a matrix of scriptural text and artwork design. Though the sword had never met his own approval, many a knight had offered to buy it from him. The *apprentice's sword*, asked about by knights for several years now, had become something of a draw for the forge. He picked it up and drew it from the matching scabbard his master had gifted him. It drew out silently only the razor edge gleaming in the light in contrast to the tine's jet. "Maybe, just maybe" Malcor whispered. "My ticket out of Klenna." As he partially resheathed it, he thought he heard a whisper say back to him, "Your ticket to destiny..."

"Do you think the Queen pays attention to such hopes when not voiced as a prayer?" the blacksmith, his adopted father Ishan, asked from the room's doorway. "She listens. Perhaps to you, more than most." His Klennan lisp dragged the last part of the sentence out and turned it into a question.

"Does she?" Malcor replied drawing a small bead of blood from his fingers along the sword's edge. "I know we're taught She does, but if so, why voice it as a prayer? When I feel nothing, why bother at all Ishan? Except at the shrine or when the Temple is watching. Oh, I saw a red-haired priestess at the shrine today. A giant was with her. Is a Dar and her Dread Lord here for the ceremony tomorrow? That'd be more than Klenna's ever had before."

He heard the blacksmith sigh and rest his back against the door. "Aye Mal, we've heard rumors that Dar Shara, Lord of the Temple of Glass, is here. She's here to watch over the westward knights heading to Bloodstone or somewhere. Lots of speculation but no real reason for her being here. Some of the knights in her entourage came by earlier for some repair work. She hasn't left the shrine, though someone claims she healed old Marta from southside. You remember Marta?"

Malcor grunted and laid his sword on the bed next to him. "We fixed that steel circlet she wore as a necklace, yeah? I remember her. Didn't know she was ill."

"Stories are that she was *called*, she went, she was cured. No one knows of what though. Clerics," the smith muttered, "always have to be so cryptic. Cured of what? Can't be a miracle if nothing miraculous occurred now can it? Well, if true, I'm sure Marta knows. Said it was Dar Shara who called her," Malcor continued inspecting the scabbard and said nothing in reply. The smith added, "Speaking of which, do you know yet? You'd be a master smith you know, coming out of the Ceremony. Fighter, warrior, knight? You sure you want that really? There's a bet that you go fighter with odds of making it to the knights you know. Boy you'd be a blacksmith for the ages if you stayed."

15

Malcor listened as Ishan rambled on about how it had been years since so many knights had been deployed west. Rumors about war, Bloodstone Valley, the king, and even wild dragon sightings. Nothing particular stood out about any of it, and Malcor had heard much of it himself many times over, but all together? That made it interesting. His mind had long ago begun connecting these kinds of things and often allowed him an almost prescient ability to determine the flow and ebb of war. And it had made the forge a fortune. If it looked like war preparations and involved the military, then logically… his master cut into his musings, "I wonder if we're about to get into it with Taysor? The peace has held too long, no – that's not it."

Malcor thought about it though. Taysor, their strong and far more populous neighbor to the north, did some trading with Morbatten, but mostly the truce – ceasefire really – had been intact for ages. Morbatten and Taysor patrolled the borders in the mountain range that divided the two, but in winter when the passes became impossible, everyone knew that both empires fought a shadowy winter war there. The knights even had a rank medal for fighting in the winter wars. The medal featured a dark metal dragon coiled around a star, Morbatten's winter star. Every knight had one, and so did more than a few of the veteran soldiers. Taysor mirrored Morbatten, their knights having some variant of the winter war medal. Malcor noted, "The other night, at the inn, I overheard a group of Sorians. They seemed fine and relaxed. I doubt it's war with them." The smith nodded. "More likely that it is a common threat to Sora and Tania," Malcor noted using the two empires' more common slang terms. "Or maybe it's some big thing at Bloodstone. Wouldn't be the first time we've seen this many troop movements because of it."

Malcor settled on a final polish and began applying it to another handmade offering for the Aging Ceremony tomorrow. Klenna had just ten other children in this Coming of Age ceremony. A few were already spoken for by betrothal or by apprenticeships ready for contracting once the child crossed over to adulthood. The only real stand out this year would be Calvin, the magistrate's son. Though not friends, they were friendly enough for Malcor to envy the better education and martial training Calvin received. While Malcor made friends quickly enough, he always felt a loner in a crowd and Calvin always made this isolation feel worse. Probably because of his father's status, Calvin always had several girls with him and never wanted for friends hanging on his every antic. Malcor, while seeming to attract the attention of girls easy enough, struggled one on one. Like Malcor, Calvin had not yet declared his intentions, even though the Klenna's magistrate could buy Calvin's entrance into anything except the Temple's orders. Malcor refused negotiating and declaring he would stay a smith his entire life. He felt compelled to refuse, though he could not say why. In contrast, Calvin had often and openly speculated about his desire to join the knighthood. The owners of the metalwork operations had taken his silence as a negotiating tactic and had tried everything short of abduction and torture to learn what it would take to have Malcor stay on.

Though not required by the Ceremony, doctrine allowed a handmade gift to be presented within certain rules; bribes were not allowed. However, a gift made of fire, love, dreams, and an eye single to the Queen's glory could be presented to and accepted by a priest. The empire overflowed with stories of failed attempts at this. Malcor had a dream when he first joined the forge of presenting a steelwrought dragon statue at the ceremony, to a dragon, a black dragon. Since that time, he had worked on and off again to perfect this statue. Several months ago, he had felt it perfect and now only revisited it to apply polish. It had been hard to keep it a secret at the forge. In their all-things-dragon-obsessed empire, a piece of art from a prodigy like Malcor would have commanded a fortune and brought the forge fame beyond the Apprentice's Sword.

Ishan egged him a bit in this regard and summarized, "Your own foundry. Your own supply sourcing. Your first pick of next 5 year's apprentices! Damn Mal, why not? With war or whatever coming, you'd have work and wealth. Why not declare? Save us all the trouble… let me win my bet!"

The entire village seemed in on the "what would Malcor do?" bet, with the bets growing daily for what Malcor would do, and what the outcome of the Ceremony would be. Though stopping just short of saying it, Malcor had made it very clear that he wanted to be a knight. So, a betting pool around his acceptance into a knightly order had popped up. Calvin had told him in passing that he had bet against Malcor making it. Calvin was like that though always getting in Malcor's way, or trying to create real and, like this, mental obstacles to what Mal wanted. Like how Calvin had asked that girl to the village festival the day after Malcor had asked her if she had a date. She had gone with Calvin.

The polish applied, Malcor held the dragon up and checked it from all possible angles. "It's perfect," he said wrapping it carefully in fur. "As I have said, I feel compelled to go out there and find something. I won't find it with metalwork, no matter the quality of metal or the quality of the team. You are the best here but somehow, I keep feeling that I, me, *I am out there waiting to find me*," he emphasized pointing out the window. He knew his master would have that look and so added, "Quit giving me that look."

"And your friend Calvin?" his master, mentor, friend, and father asked suddenly all those things at once.

"If it's just the two of us *AND* we qualify, I can only pray they take us both." He and Calvin had different family lives. Son of the mayor, Calvin's life pulled him into the political world of his father's wealth and influence. Calvin, by now, had received the best training available. *Me?*, Malcor snorted at the thought. He had received his training through metalwork and a few actual fights when they visited the nearby mines. His training in heraldry, combat, sword technique, even manner of speaking was paltry and inadequate compared to Calvin, but then that is why, "I made the dragon statue, to give me an edge."

"It's risky Mal," Ishan said. They both nodded. Custom allowed gifts, but not bribes. Walking that thin line. "I hope you don't feel the need."

With several hours till bed time and nothing to do, Malcor picked up his armorer's gear and walked to the foundry across the way. His master fell in behind him. They would work till exhausted. His fellows knew that tomorrow was his day and perhaps sensing his distraction, gave him space to work. In the heat wash of the forge's cradle, he could see clearly that his dragon statue must have red eyes, like the glowing embers of a fire. Sweat dripped and rolled from his back and arms as he moved the statue to a dream state where somehow he saw HOW to make the eyes glow like embers.

His hands moved on their own and materials just seemed to be there and ready. Molten gold, already refined and ready to pour, right there. So too did crucible with mithril hissing silver steam as it rolled along the lattice cut into the statue. And the red eyes appeared as if blood had been frozen into rubies, uncut but rounded and smooth cabochons ready for insert. "It's perfect," Malcor whispered as he applied the final touches and then he collapsed unconscious into a deep sleep. His master Ishan had long before fallen asleep propped up in the corner.

A voice answered back from the darkness, "Yes, it is." Dar Shara stepped into the forge. Her pale white skin perfect and flawless as the forge's heat whipped her long red hair and spidersilk dress. "Sleep Malcor, in Takhissis' embrace. Show us your best tomorrow. The king will be here. Offer but do not give him your statue." As she spoke she crouched down by Malcor and ran her fingertips along his brow.

From the doorway, a sinuous baritone voice demanded to know, "This is the next king?" Shara looked back at Dread Lord Armageddon and nodded her head. He sniffed, "He stinks of meat. Does *he* know?"

"No, the king shall see for himself. And he resents a ruined surprise as much as he hates surprises. Let him be surprised. Tomorrow." She looked down at the boy. "He has a feeling of destiny about him no?"

"The Queen has plans for this one no doubt." Armageddon chuffed and walked over to the forge where he ran his gauntleted fingers through the hot fires still burning as coal red embers now. A shower of sparks rose where he stirred the mix. "Already the River parts around this child. He is strong, for a human…"

Malcor greeted sunrise already bathed, dressed in his best leathers, and with no recollection of having cleaned up at all. A memory of rough hands that felt like hot boulders had caught him, or something, and the red-haired priestess had said something. Bits of conversation lingered in his mind about rivers and destiny but, like a soon-forgotten dream, he saw the giant's eyes. He wished he could remember.

Ishan and his wife gave him a satchel big enough for his statue also packed with a breakfast and snacks for his trek to the shrine. "Did you hear?" Ishan asked from the small house's doorway. "That caravan arrived late last night with a regiment of knights and others. There's been some heavy partying downtown but there's a different cluster of knights up at the shrine. Just thought you should know as you will have an audience. And Mal, you look great! Don't remember you coming back from the forge last night. Hey, let me see your dragon statue…"

Malcor felt himself pulled aside and his dragon removed from the satchel. Soon the entire neighborhood gathered and more came from the nearby workplaces to see. "Malcor's dragon! It's amazing!" and other similar expressions. He used the time to choke back the knot in his gut at the thought of the Ceremony and all the knights that would no doubt be there to watch.

After some time, the commotion died down and Ishan called him out into the front courtyard. Stepping outside, their tiny neighborhood and all those in the area looked from the dragon standing on a makeshift table, to Malcor. A slight pause and then cheering erupted. Malcor found himself swept into the congregation with many a well-wished "good luck!" and "give that Calvin hell!" and "we will miss you Mal!" Who knew that such a small neighborhood had that much good will or even that many people in it?

Malcor came at last to the street he'd walk to the shrine. The owner and lord of the forge stood there in his fine nobleman attire. The medallion of the Merchant's Guild hung heavy and golden around his neck. "R'Dar Tor, good morning to you sir." Malcor bowed and held the bow until the owner acknowledged him. Most of the well-wishers had noticed the lord and hush fell over the group. Not as high ranking as a "Dar", the *R'Dar* title designated wealth and inherited status. The title could be bought and passed along to one's family, but it was always dangerous to interact with them. And R'Dar Tor had prevented him from the Ceremony for years now.

"Yes, yes. Malcor my boy, I understand but must ask just once more – are you really sure that you're NOT staying with us? Really? Such talent. I can't have you going up there and making us all look bad. We did not train you as a fighter. Your calling is to the forge. You. Must. Reconsider." That last part was a command and Malcor felt its nuances.

"My Dar, I must apologize. While not trained as a fighter, I feel there is something out there, that if I do not at least TRY, I will have violated some commandment. Violated something I don't know. Apologies but my education in words and Temple doctrine fail me R'Dar Tor. I feel a calling and will go to please the Queen." Bringing the Temple into it seemed the only way to get out of a nasty confrontation. Malcor hoped it would work. R'Dar Tor worshipped at the altar of wealth, not the Temple. But, like all Tanians, he paid his tithe and did his service to the Temple and Empire.

"Reconsider." Again, that command. In the empire, commands like these often carried legal weight. To refuse could be considered insubordination against the lord. The lord's eyes stared at Malcor as if daring him to disobey.

Malcor did the only thing he could do. "I shall re-consider in the ceremony." He tried a different tact, "Have you heard that a high priestess presides? The one with red-hair. Dar Shara. She came by the forge last night..." Malcor walked past the lord as if beginning the long trek.

"I think not," and steel blade lanced past Malcor's cheek. Malcor did not flinch, did not look away, and carefully did not do anything that could appear as a challenge. "Reconsider now."

Though reality only held the steel blade in Malcor's face a few moments, Malcor felt an eternity slide by moment by dragging moment until, without warning, the earlier group of friends and family reconvened with enthusiasm and singing. His friends and family swept Malcor into its midst and swallowed him out of that dangerous moment with the angry lord. "We've got you Mal," he heard his master's whispered assurance.

To keep Malcor safe, the celebration would have to continue all the way to the shrine's grounds. "Thank you," Malcor said to each and every person as they came past him. The traditional Klennan dance had a lot of combat-style whirling and twirling. Usually only done at marriages, births, or other particularly happy community events, Mal felt certain it had never been done from the village up to the mountain shrine. A normal walk would take just over an hour of fairly steep climbing. Men, women, and the children all dancing and all his friends committed to carry him or else they would all face R'Dar Tor's wrath.

He saw in a moment those he had argued or fought with, like that one young man and his one time rival for his position at the forge. Some girls he had loved and through time or idiocy had parted ways with, some now partnered with past enemies and now they all danced together to give him this chance. Somehow, the surrealism of it all filled him with gratitude and then he saw something he had never noticed before.

Glimmers of dust in dawn's sunbeams seemed to slow and vertical lines became visible through the air and dancers' movements. Though they still moved, something streamed past them washing over them and he realized his perception felt shifted, different somehow. A small girl, barely six years old, who often brought him food or water at the forge looked at him with unfiltered glee and love and her eyes. She appeared frozen to his perception in that moment of sunbeams, which spoke of childlike adoration for that one time Mal had found her in the streets, and brought her home. She had been abandoned in Klenna by some passerby. It had snowed that day. The moment was there in the background of her eyes – of a sister's love for a brother protecting her - and... then it all stopped. Malcor fell to the ground as the hands carrying him parted. The girl who had come to be named Klara smiled and gave him a hug.

The perception was gone and his friends, he found all of them staring at him intently. Some had bowed. The vertical lines in the air faded and with a rush of noise, the surreal feeling passed. Everything resumed its proper time and place and motion but in the eerie silence, Malcor licked his lips and started to ask the obvious question. His master cut him off, "No my lord Malcor. No. Say nothing. If ever I wondered before, I know now. The Queen favors you." The crowd around him bowed and made holy signs. He had another twenty minutes of climbing.

"My friends," Malcor stammered. "My family. I will honor what you have done for me here today."

The crowd, though no longer dancing or singing, followed him the rest of the way to the shrine. R'Dar Tor, stuck in back, could only follow up the mountain trail. Their committed celebration replaced with something else, reverence? What had just happened? He arrived a bit late, but in time for

Calvin's introduction.

The shrine sat on the eastern hill cradling Klenna. Its spires caught the sunlight and officially marked dawn and other times for Klenna as the shrine's bell ringer sounded out certain times of the day. The shrine itself was fairly small and enclosed but opened up to a huge outdoor courtyard ringed by large steps. Except for times like this, the courtyard saw only visiting knights and clerics training, pilgrimages, and the occasional official function like this Ceremony. Sermons and preaching drew smaller crowds and so occurred inside.

Today, for the Ceremony, the courtyard was packed. Calvin and another eight children stood in the courtyard. They looked nervous and small and tentative. Then Malcor saw it. A throne had been erected facing the great city eastwards. The red-haired priestess sat on it. She stared down at Malcor. Moments before the rest of the attendees noticed him, the armored giant leaned around the throne to regard Malcor as well. The regard behind the giant's eyes felt like a kick to Malcor's gut yet it seemed the giant looked at him more out of curiosity as opposed to threat assessment.

Then, the crowd of villagers already there caught sight of Malcor and began cheering him. His family and friends, who had walked up with him, moved into the courtyard and its dark stone steps to watch. Calvin's introduction was lost amidst the noise and shuffling and then Malcor was pushed onto the courtyard's sand. Someone's voice announced over the din "Malcor of R'Dar Tor's foundry from the merchant House of Tor."

But Malcor's thoughts remained with the armored giant. He could not stop staring at it. It dawned on him, "Of course," Malcor muttered. Of course the armored giant... "is a red dragon and a Dread Lord" Calvin finished his thought for him. They suddenly felt very small, young, and insignificant. Calvin felt it as immense pressure to succeed and impress his father. Malcor felt the same smallness and pressure to impress, but something in his soul told him he would be okay. He drew confidence from that even though he could not think of any stories of any dread lords coming to a Klennan Coming of Age ceremony, ever.

Chapter Two – The Ceremony

The two regarded each other. Calvin stood an inch taller than Malcor in fine spider silk clothing and fencing boots. That alone made Calvin recognizable as a nobleman's son. His finely oiled hair, his immaculate skin with not even a single scar – thanks to Temple donations as needed for healing, and his general demeanor all fit Calvin, son of Klenna's mayor. A rapier, no doubt worth more than all of Klenna, hung from his belt.

Though not quite as tall, Malcor had years of muscle and hardiness from working the forge. He also had his fair share of burn scars, luckily nothing very visible except on his scalp. The oiled leathers of his attire gave him a somewhat roguish appearance offset only by the lack of hair burned by the same years of forge work. The scar tissue on his scalp had faded but his hair never quite grew back. He had just a few tufts of hair that he kept shaved. Malcor's satchel and hand-forged long sword hung by a leather belt that looked downright brutish compared to Calvin's elegant attire. Along with the eight children, they turned to face the high priestess as she was introduced by the armored giant at her side. There would be a brief wait to allow any stragglers to arrive.

The armored giant Malcor had seen with the red-haired priestess finally announced in a deep and booming bass, "Assembled peoples of the empire! Dar Shara, lord of the Temple of Glass and I, Dread Lord Armageddon, preside over this Ceremony in this, the Imperial shrine of Klenna! In attendance are other great lords and ladies of the empire. Let them now come forth." Armageddon's voice overwhelmed everyone present causing an immediate silence.

Custom dictated now that the squires of any lord announce, in correct order of their might and glory in Morbatten. The first squire stepped forward and Malcor realized that today would be remembered for years in Klenna. Always a key moment, if multiple squires stepped forward, there could be a challenge, or at the very least a political faux pas. None did and then the presence of the first-forward squire caught Malcor's attention. Though always a spectacle, anyone could tell in Tania who really had power. Gaudy displays of wealth attempt to compensate for lack of might. This first squire seemed to have both in equal measure. He clearly fell into the real power category. Tall, broad, and with features possessing a keen intelligence, the squire seemed to stand in a different level of humanity than the rest. Then Malcor felt it. *This is no human. This is another Dread Lord. How many are there?,* he wondered.

"Assembled peoples of the empire! I am known as Blade, first son of Dread Emperor Alerius, here to present His Royal Majesty Dar Rojo, human king of the empire and Paladin Lord of Takhissis' Knights! Let all bear witness to his glory. He is the first human to serve as king, and let all see..." The first human king after centuries of rule by the dragon emperor Alerius.

Malcor doubted there could be a single person anywhere who had not heard stories and rumors about the King Rojo, or the dragon emperor. *And the King and one of the emperor's sons is here?!* Their names and stories worked their way into everything most every day. It had been only ten years since Rojo ascended the human throne and the ripples of his reign had reached out and changed so much for everyone.

At Rojo's command, the Temple had revealed the truth: that the god emperor Alerius and other dragons had been shaping Tanian culture and its peoples for thousands of years. The implications had been staggering. It had seemed a joke at first: that the dragons would allow a human to rule. Yes, it had ended the deadly civil war in the temple between the priestesses and their male cleric counterparts, but the biggest change was actually in this ceremony. The unreal focus on identifying and finding paladins, rangers, warriors, priests, and mages or anyone with skills and talents contributing to war meant that prodigies and heroes and legendary children were being swept into the Temple earlier and faster than ever. King Rojo had driven that as he had driven the mortal, human, and humanoid citizens into gears of the empire. Talented at something? It became your career. Skilled at fighting? The war machine waited with its hot breath.

The king is here! Word ran like wildfire in a breeze and except for that breeze no one dared say anything and then, as if a presence had touched them, all bowed fists on the ground as the king entered. Even Dar Shara stepped down from her throne and bowed. Malcor noted that only the Dread Lords did not. He quickly counted three other Dread Lords in addition to Armageddon and Blade. Each of the three Dread Lords stood by priestesses standing in the shadows behind Shara's throne, noted only because they did not bow. Calvin and Malcor tried looking for the king without looking and could see no one and then, there it was. A footfall landed behind them as a dominating presence sucked the air from their lungs. The air heated around them yet grew dark at the same time as the king's power, like a heavy weight, fell upon them.

King Rojo, *The Rojo*, the stories about this man and here he stood – right there next to him. Malcor felt more than saw Rojo's cloak brush him as he stepped between Malcor and Calvin. Without meaning too or even knowing why he wanted to touch it, Malcor's finger caught just a touch of the hem. Calvin stared at the hand wide-eyed and then perhaps wanting to also touch the legend, reached out and just missed it. Made of grey spider silk and hemmed with golden threaded symbols, the cloak felt luxurious and somehow alive. Rojo passed beyond their reach and walked to Dar Shara. They kissed, exchanged words, and then Rojo helped the high priestess retake her place on the throne above him. Blade's words came out as a roar, "Behold and bear witness, the crown serves the Goddess and our Queen is here with the people of Klenna!"

The other introductions proceeded quickly but Malcor could not take his eyes away from the high priestess and the king. While both appeared in their prime of life, they could not have made more a contrast. The sunlight fell on Shara's red hair and lit it afire with red and orange. Her pale white skin seemed luminescent in the sunlight. The spider silk robes she wore draped her in such a way that said Priestess but screamed Woman. Her golden threaded belt and jewelry hugged her hips and breasts spotlighting her curves and emphasizing that scream of her as Desire. Like a jealous lover, her Dread Lord stood just behind her daring Malcor and others to continue looking. Malcor imagined Calvin's father also looking at the priestess, probably calculating political gain. Malcor noted her staring at him staring at her and blushed. He forcibly turned his eyes back to the king.

Standing in front of Dar Shara's throne, King Rojo stood in the same sunlight but appeared wrapped in shadow somehow. His armor, his clothing, his demeanor, all of it came together to create a man ready for war. The golden thread hemming his cloak that Malcor touched, glinted in the sun but dimly as if also in shadow. Here stood a warrior shown to be king only by the crown on his head. The same sunbeams illuminating Shara's beauty seemed unwilling to touch King Rojo. Malcor wondered why. He also wondered why no one ever mentioned that the king was shorter in real life than he sounded in the stories.

Shara leaned forward and rested her hand on the King's shoulder to whisper something to him. The light followed her hand and dimmed on his shoulder pauldron. He nodded to whatever she had said. She smiled and sat back into her throne. Rojo's expression hardly changed and Malcor noticed that more often than not, the king appeared to be staring at the representation of the Goddess back by the shrine proper. Like Shara and most Tanians, he had pale skin but dark almost black hair. He had heard the king had blue eyes, but if anything they appeared gray, almost entirely so that Malcor wondered if his eyes had white in them at all. Unlike the other knights, the king carried no sword. At least he was not visibly armed but then, many of the knights could summon their weapons at will.

At last, the introductions ended and Calvin's father stood to offer an opening prayer. He looked nervous but his nervous voice quickly faded as he called out. "Mighty Dread Lords, we pray to your Mother, our Queen and Goddess..." When the prayer ended, and without a word, the king walked to the stand where the mayor was getting ready to introduce the Aging Ceremony. "We are honored to have such a grand audience," and then he stopped when Rojo's hand touched his shoulder. The consummate politician seemed flustered and only somewhat recovered enough to step aside and back for the king.

"Our goddess Takhissis wishes to see her soldiers open the Ceremony. Paladins, all of you - now." That command voice! Malcor felt blood boil his veins as if he had been called. "Veterans of the wars and priests, you may join as you will. We dedicate this to our five Dread Lords and the Queen's Priestess."

Rojo clapped his hands together in a rhythm, a beat quickly taken up by the other knights and then the shrine's bell-ringer added to the din, then the crowd followed. It created a strong drum-like rhythm. Rojo walked off the podium as paladins of all ranks moved into the courtyard to join him. Their walk synched to the beat and then a writhing, twisting, callisthenic dance evolved. Clapping was replaced with armored gauntlet smashing against the knight nearest. Kicks and spins rang against the warriors' armor all around as they moved. The veteran knights executed the ritual flawlessly and around them the less practiced made errors here and there, but the errors were mostly in timing.

Thousands of years ago, this had been an infantry kata, a memorized set of moves designed to engage multiple enemies. When set to actual music, it told of the empire's alliance with dragons and the rule of the priestesses, the fall of enemies, and the rise of the paladins. Starting with only nine paladins, the dynamic changed as war veterans joined and then the clerics joined. Gradually, the tempo increased as did the volume of the warriors' and crowds' chant. The dance and song and the movement of wars waged to the tolling of the shrine's bell.

The dance evoked feelings in Malcor. He wanted to join the dance; *am I allowed?* He wanted to fight for his life and take the lives of the Queen's enemies; *when may I?* His throat ached with a war cry choked back; *why not scream?* Dar Shara walked into the midst and with a prayerful wave of her hand, flames struck up from the ground and soared into the sky around each of the knights as she added the Queen's glory to the dance. The king and his paladins erupted into columns of red fire that rose from the ground into the sky. No one burned though all felt the heat.

Driven by the dance, the Dread Lords gave up control of their human forms, leaping into the sky as their carefully magicked shells collapsed in rapturous ecstasy, peeling back as dragon wings filled the sky. Malcor watched mouth agape at the size and glory and majesty of Dread Lord Armageddon in particular, who dwarfed the other dragons for sheer size and power density.

The king's flame column rose from the courtyard like a tornado and blew out from his movements like a shockwave across the crowd. It hit Malcor physically and with each wave, Malcor felt a fever growing. He looked to Calvin and the Klennans on the courtyard steps. They appeared joyous, singing and dancing in place, unaffected by the shockwaves that rolled through and over them. The king's column of fire finally rose to the ceiling of clouds drifting above and like a stone splashing into still water, blew the clouds apart. It was glorious and powerful and made Malcor's blood boil. The dragon silhouettes diving and swirling around and through the columns of fire transformed the Klennan shrine.

Malcor felt that subtle shift in his perception. The dragons continued to fly, the warriors and dancers continued their dance, but Calvin and the "normal folk" seemed to quiet and blur. In that moment, something tore past Malcor's face like a slap of fire and the normal folk fell into a dim blur as if they moved more slowly with streams of wind blowing trails of color off their movements. In wonder, Malcor looked at his own movements and fixated on his fingers wiggling, which seemed sharper in its color and focus. He imagined he could see his blood coursing through his arm. Something darkened the sunlight and Malcor looked up to see Dread Lord Armageddon dropping down from the columns of fire high above him. As the dragon fell, he shapeshifted into human form landing with a crashing blow that fragmented the courtyard around him in front of Malcor.

Armageddon stood up tall and stared intently at Malcor. His true dragon form and his magical shell of a human body seemed overlapped somehow, both vibrant with energy and power. Dark reds and lightning black torrents of energy raged around them in the dragon's presence. It took Malcor's breath away.

The dread lord leaned in close to Malcor's face and sniffed. "You see the River?" Malcor's expression conveyed only confusion. The giant grabbed Malcor's face and turned his head pointing him towards the villagers. "You see they move out of synch and some not at all, but they blur? Drowning in the River. The trails of light off this one," pointing to Calvin, "show the River murdering him with Time and Age. You see this with your own hand aging here and here. You are dying and do not even see it killing you. Time is killing you and you drown in its flow. We call this the River," he said bringing Malcor's hand before his eyes. The dragon let go of Malcor's face and Malcor gasped when he fell several feet to the courtyard. He had not felt himself being lifted.

"Behold the paladins, My Lady Shara, and your human King as I see him." The Dread Lord's voice boomed out the command and Malcor unconsciously stood erect and looked exactly in that order. "See them and then look back at the Innocents." Malcor noted the dread lord's use of the draconian term for "normal people", *Innocents*.

Some of the knights, just like the villagers streamed trails of light around them. It streamed over some quickly, others more slowly. The two knights closest to the king, like Malcor and Armageddon, appeared infused with energy and magic and colors. As he looked at them, the dread lord hissed, "Those are paladins. They thrive in the love and worship of their Mother. Do not confuse them with knights."

One of the paladin's colors reminded Malcor of a fiery sunset full of colorful reds and oranges. The other's aura appeared more like a lightning storm amidst thunderous storm clouds. The dragon extended an armored finger to point and then said, "The colors are their life experience and devotion to the Goddess. You see their intensity through your own life experiences. I see two knights devoted and enraptured with their Goddess. Both have earned glory and honor beyond your current understanding. One however has paid sacrifices in sorrow and pain. No doubt you see him differently?" Malcor heard the question and nodded. "Now, see Dar Shara. She plays with the River."

And so she did. Malcor saw her uplift her hand as if floating upwards in slow motion and then turn it over as she voiced her flame strike prayer. The effect appeared to be a slow spell followed by a decisive and sudden flame strike happening as if in the blink of an eye. Her hand sliced down as fire erupted from the ground encircling one of the paladins. The sound of her prayer spell echoed and boomed as he focused in on hearing her voice, both softly feminine and all-powerful sounding in this place. Her body's turning whipped her hair and silk dress around her creating a frozen barrier and then a cascade of movement quickly. Her beauty had been near overwhelming before. In this way of seeing her, Malcor could barely breathe. Desire tore at him, awe dazed him, and against it all he marveled at the many colors of her aura. Tornadoes of the dragon colors arced out of her heart to lance up into the sky and then crash back down into her, through her, and throughout those nearby.

30

She looked rapturous. Every so often, the color arcs would crackle along some invisible barrier and for a ghost of a moment, would outline fractions of a dragon surrounding her, as a wing here, a giant clawed arm there. Her breathing, like mist in cool winter air, exhaled tongues of flame and inhaled the trailing beams of light from the River pulling across the courtyard. Malcor asked, "The paladins are different than knights?"

"Yes," Armageddon breathed back at him. "Paladins are driven by faith. They are also knights and you humans refer to them by that term too often. Consider your friend Calvin and his father." Malcor cast his eyes about looking for them and saw them again. As he focused on them, their images paused and became clearer in the River. Calvin's father appeared standing next to Calvin. Part of his aura burned intensely towards Calvin. That part of his aura contained the only color at all between the two of them.

Suddenly, one of the priestesses attending the royals walked past Calvin. Malcor noticed how she drew the River after her. In that moment, Calvin's gray and pastel earth-colored aura burned brightly as she smiled his way. Malcor noticed the priestess' aura did not even flex. "The River…"

"Allows immortals and magic users to see these things. As you learn more, you'll be able to focus on someone like that boy," he gestured towards Calvin and his hand sent ripples and currents of arc-lightning through the River, "and see their past, who they are right now. Time is a moment by moment thing for mortals. Who your friend was, who he is now, who will someday be – these things are always changing. Only the past is fixed. The present is momentary and fleeting. The future is mostly unknown except during those times when something so momentous it affects the gods occurs."

"Will Calvin ever be able to see this? How do you see me?" Mal's suddenly became self-conscious again.

Armageddon stared at Calvin and then shook his head. "No. He lacks the force of will to break free of time. As for you, prophecy and destiny shroud you like a heavy cloak and it buries any future I might see in shadows. To tell you would displease my mistress Shara. I will however tell you that a trial is fast approaching. One that will set you on the path of being a paladin, maybe more. You must use the River. This place, through your force of will and focus on the Mother, can aid you. Right now, your body dances and just a moment has passed.

"Even though the River drowns you, you cannot yet exist outside of Time without paying a price. It exhausts your will. You can master it, but it takes time, experience, and a singular focus on either your Goddess, or magical studies. Because I brought you here, my strength sustains you. You see, for my kind, the River feeds us in this place, on the banks of this symbol of time's passage. Yes human. Those in the River are pulled through Time to their deaths. You see it as the passage of the day and seasons, in time and places as they erode, dim, and ultimately die. Your friends, even you, right now are drowning. Dying so slowly it is only apparent in startled fits of awareness, like when you see a favorite child years later and they are so big and *different*. You... are so conditioned to Dying, in this place, soon you will die unless we pull you back. For now, take it all in. Remember it. Speak of it to no one. This place, the ether on the banks of the River, gives you power over Time but you are too weak to survive it for more than a few brief moments on your own."

Malcor nodded, feeling suddenly concerned. *If I stay here, I die. If I go back, I die?!* Staring agape at the priestess, he noted the king's movements crossed in front of her, but unlike the many colored auras Malcor saw in the others, the king's was altogether different. He remembered scriptures and doctrines, stories of legend. It all came together. "Dread Lord, the stories and scriptures. I always thought the references to water, rivers, and the passage of seasons was a metaphor. It's an actual place though. It's real."

Armageddon gestured expansively with his hand and said, "Well done human." He pointed towards the king in that second and speculated, "I wonder if you see it human. The king is different, yes?"

The color auras stabbing out from the other dancers and Lady Shara fell into shadow the instant they came near the king. Even the column of fire from Shara's flame strike raged around the king like a tornado, but its colors were less vibrant and somehow slower the closer they came to him. *No*, Malcor thought, *not slower but different like looking through*

32

aged or warped glass? He looked harder, concentrating but it hurt his head, and then remembered the dread lord's hand gesture. For such an expressionless being, the gesture stood out, like a hint or perhaps a clue? With the king, he thought he might need to step back? Imitating the dragon's gesture, Malcor physically took a step back and forced himself to try to look larger, bigger, past the marvels and wonders around him. Knowing it was death and dying before his eyes made it no less beautiful.

Then he saw it, or at least he thought he did. He gasped. As large, as awesome, as dread-inspiring and beautiful as the Dread Lords' had been, they were nothing compared to the translucent barely-noticeable outline of a gigantic dragon looming over and surrounding King Rojo. The clear form dimmed and warped images behind and near it, and it moved approximately with the king's movements. It was the king's form, as a dragon, clear and colorless. Armageddon looked closely into Malcor's eyes and his face twisted in a rictus of a grin, "You do see! *LORD* Rojo. This one has found measures of favor with the Queen and she has claimed him higher than any before, even the dragon emperor her most favorite." He hissed and Malcor could not tell if it was a good or bad kind of hiss.

Malcor started to take it all in, to ask more questions, to... but he stopped and felt something pulling at him. His legs and hands felt suddenly cold as if pricked by an ice-laden wind and the air stuck in his throat. He tried to form words but nothing came though the ideas sat heavy and pregnant in his mind. Flashes of light from the fire and auras felt painfully bright and then a convulsion took his left hand. Malcor felt his fingers spasm into a reverse fist as his fingers twisted in on themselves. Then his stuck breath exploded just before he collapsed over backwards onto the ground. Dimly, he thought he heard Armageddon say, "The River has you now..." and then an explosion of light and sounds and pain as Malcor collapsed into nothing at all.

For a long moment, he struggled to breathe, to catch a breath. Gasp. Choke. Finally, he breathed and as air rushed into his lungs, Malcor felt the normal world invade him with its smells, sounds, and sights. Gone were the sparkling lights and the dreadful weightiness of the River and its

Time. Armageddon stood near but was watching the dancers still. All around, the throng of Klennans either danced, clapped, or pointed from one wonder to another. The blacksmith, his master danced on the opposite side of the courtyard doing a decent job emulating the paladins. R'Dar Tor had apparently made it as well though he stood back from the throne's platform watching either all of it or just staring into space. Malcor guessed he came only to stop him from leaving the forge.

Armageddon turned and made eye contact with Malcor over his armored gorget. "Food and respite will help you recover quickly. I wonder Malcor if you feel the River as the deadly disease we Eldar first saw it? Maybe you only feel the loss of glory. Tell me."

With their eyes locked together, Malcor suddenly felt naked as if his entire soul laid bare for the dread lord to sift apart. "You're seeing me in the River aren't you? The trails of light and tiny crack by crack, you see me dying right now?" he asked.

"Yes, I see you as you, bathed in the sickness of Time. I see your ambitions, your past dreams, your mantle of glory and shadow if you take it. Tell me Malcor, do you know Her Voice calling to you?" referring to the Queen Takhissis.

"When I was in that place - <"We call it the Ethereal, the place between the infinite realms and the River of Time," Armageddon interjected> - I felt overwhelmed and small but fascinated with everything I saw. Did I hear Her Voice? I have heard a Voice all my life calling me to be a knight, to be something more than a blacksmith."

The dread lorded nodded, "That is Her Voice. Next time you go into the Ethereal, listen for it. It will guide you and direct you." Having said that, Armageddon flexed and jumped into the sky transforming back into a fire dragon. Though the paladins and Dar Shara continued their dance, the sudden appearance of another dragon caught everyone else by surprise as they all thought Armageddon remained in the sky. Several fell down in shock as they lost their balance, or instinctively tried to run away. Such a large and ominous dragon could be terrifying. Malcor watched the dread lord rise into the sky amidst the columns of fire.

Every once in a while, a dragon would land on the hill outside of the shrine and tremble the ground with its presence. So too, every now and then, the dance's tempo would start to calm. Normally, it would have ended almost as fast as it started. But normally, Klenna lacked knights of this caliber and an audience this noble. On and on it went. Some of the villagers sat down. Younger children somehow fell asleep. As it went on, soon only the sweat-drenched paladins, Dar Shara, and the dragons continued. It was mesmerizing. At some point, Malcor and Calvin were waved into the dance by the priestess. Though they felt clumsy, Malcor grinned when Calvin collapsed after just a few seconds of the dance. Wanting to do better, Malcor focused and danced even though he felt as if his body would explode.

An eye blink later and the sun had begun to set. The dance ended. The dragons, as dragons, sat in a circle on the shrine's hill, their wings rising up over their fierce heads making a crown of living dragons around the courtyard. The king Rojo and those paladins who had lasted the entire day stood frozen still as Dar Shara collapsed the columns of fire. And there was silence while the fireball sun dipped below the western mountains and lit the sky on fire.

Chapter Three – Tor's Defiance

Armageddon, as a dragon, stretched forth his mighty claw and onto it Dar Shara stepped while the dragon lifted her up above the shrine. Looking down at them all, she spoke with a whispered voice quiet yet loud enough that all heard as if she were speaking directly into their ear. "A special day indeed for this Coming of Age ceremony and the people of Klenna! The emperor and King Rojo's armies move westward yet we pause here for this dance, to show you the Queen's love, to recognize this day for what the Queen decrees it. You few of Klenna who seek to rise up and become adults, we celebrate you and your families and your village.

"But that is not all. Long ago, prophecies foretold of a westward march when summer warms the day and stars bathe the night. A night like this one. Exactly this night." She paused and the shrine gradually fell silent. "When King Rojo selects his successor. When the successor will be revealed to us. Any of you here may claim this right though only one of you is destined to become the next king."

Like the crashing silence when the dance ended, her words quieted the shrine and its courtyard like mist and then everywhere, Malcor felt people looking sideways at Calvin. Shara waited a moment and then continued, "Are there any here who would claim a king's destiny?" Malcor looked at Calvin and saw his erstwhile friend blush, his hands clenching and unclenching. Calvin's eyes lifted and met Malcor's. It pained Malcor that he could not save his sometimes friend from the River. He imagined Calvin would be struggling with ambition and the distraction of the beautiful priestesses all around him.

Then a sound of creaking leather and metal armor as one of the King's paladins stepped forward from his dance posture. Fist on heart salute to the king and he spoke loud and clear, "My lord, may we assist? The queen has shown us who it is." A flood of whispers washed around the crowd.

Rojo's hand slashed down and he replied, "No, we may not. Destiny calls out the Emperor's need. If my successor cannot feel the Queen or hear Destiny…" and the king's voice reached the ears of all those present.

Malcor heard them and felt Destiny, he tried to understand but… he also heard footsteps approaching and then something shoved him, hard.

R'Dar Tor's boot slammed into Malcor's back and sent him hurtling through the air to land face first in the dirt at Rojo's feet. Malcor saw Klara standing and point open-eyed and scared for him back in the crowd behind Tor. The R'Dar saluted the king and keeping his eyes on Malcor said, "This one speaks constantly of destiny." His voice sneered as he said "destiny". The R'Dar's words and spittle rained down on him, here, in front of the king and a Dar Priestess… and dread lords.

Malcor rose up to his knees but so close to the king, he remained prostrate. His heart pounded in his chest and all he could think was how unfair it all was. He had given his life to that forge, had brought it business, had made it fortunes, and now to be ridiculed in front of his friends, his adopted family, the village of Klenna, and the empire's ruling elites and the king… it was too much. A rage began building in Malcor's heart, but unlike other times he had felt anger, this one had a cold hard edge to it. The fury threatened to overwhelm him, similar but altogether different from those times he worked himself unconscious in the forge.

The king's voice, now a whisper that still carried to all, turned like a slow-moving viper to R'Dar Tor and partially broke Mal's rage, "Your tone insults me sir. In the eyes of the Queen, all are as great as their Destinies allow. As any take for their own. The young, the infirm, the weak, it does not matter. It is up to each of us to realize our own Destiny. I ask for one who would be king and you kick this boy to my feet. What is your intent here R'Dar?" Normally a title indicative of inherited wealth, power, or status, R'Dar also meant hero of the realm. The particular inflection R'Dar Tor used always danced between the two. The king's inflection left little doubt that, in this case, it meant Dead Man.

R'Dar Tor blanched and stepped back, "No offense intended my Lord King. The temple asks about Destiny, and my ears are laden with talk that takes this boy out of my forge. If none here will answer, then please Dar, allow me to bring this boy back to my forge. He has incredible skill with metalwork – he is a prodigy - I do not wish wasted in some childish daydream of knighthood. There is not any king here other than you Dar Rojo." As he spoke, he slowly continued his retreat back from the king's steel eyes. The title Dar, in Tania, meant many things all superlatives higher than a R'Dar. Even though R'Dar Tor had said it perfectly to mean *Highest of the Highest*, he took another step back. The king took a step forward, which put him in a line with Malcor.

That viperous whisper turned to Malcor, "Is this true? Do you wish to be a knight? *Do you hear Destiny?*"

R'Dar Tor began snickering, but the King's regard cut him short. Malcor felt that searing feeling threaten him with tears, tears that he choked back before answering.

"My Lord King Rojo, I have long held a dream of being chosen to be a paladin. It is all I have ever wanted, and I have felt driven to create and show, no give, a gift of my own making..." he reached for the dragon statue.

King Rojo's whisper and a hand on Malcor's shoulder called him to stand. He rose and with surprise found himself at eye to eye level with the King's eyes. He almost did a double-take when he noticed flecks, many flecks of varying color embedded into those eyes, but not a hint of affection or mirth lay therein. "Your name is Malcor correct? Your words are true, but this is not what you feel. Turn and face your *R'Dar* – inflected as *slave master* – and tell him who you are. Impress me Malcor-who-dreams-of-being-a-*paladin*."

Just before turning to confront R'Dar Tor, Malcor thought of the correct politically-wise thing to do. But, he saw Armageddon give him a warning glance, as if a dragon had facial expressions. He felt that fire in his heart again and knew.

The courtyard's silence felt stifling. R'Dar Tor's expression, well known after years of servitude, seemed caught between deferred respect/fear of the King and disdain for Malcor. He could end all of this by declaring himself a smith, and returning to the forge. But, those days spent walking the hills and listening to wind in the grass and the knights' stories about town begged him to not be just a smith. If only... no, it was now or never. *This is my trial.*

"R'Dar Tor, I have worked with you since my master adopted me." Malcor drew the long sword from the scabbard tied to his bag. His hands shook and he saw Tor snicker at it. But the rage in his soul threatened to break him to pieces. In the silent moment, its keen edge resonated shrill and clear. He heard a murmuring rise up from the crowd, especially the knights nearby, *See the apprentice's sword!* "I have dreamed of being a knight, of serving the Empire, of fighting for the Queen. My destiny is not at the forge. It is out there, westwards." He pointed his sword tip at R'Dar Tor's forehead. "I am not yours. We are free."

A vein on Tor's head pulsed in the various lights of the shrine wreathed about by fire from lanterns, from the dragons themselves, and from the last fading rays of sunset. Faster than Malcor thought possible, the R'Dar drew a rapier and cut Mal's cheek… or at least that is what should have happened. Instead, Mal slipped out of the River for just a moment. There, in the relative calm and eerie silence of that place, a thunderous and deadly female voice roared in his ears, "Kill him my son and you will be a knight!"

The command hurt his ears and he dove back into the River somehow stepping below Tor's almost-attack and spinning around the R'Dar's body to the right. Crouched low at Tor's side, Mal saw the man wide open and then wide-eyed as he realized the youth had vanished and reappeared in the worst possible place for a counter or defense. The R'Dar tried to spin aside but as if hammering iron at the forge – *does the smith think about the pain of the metal as it cooks and melts or is struck by hammer blow upon hammer fell?* – Mal impaled his sword up through the R'Dar's rib cage, spearing the man's heart and exiting just through the left shoulder. Blood dribbled from the man's lips as his head and face stared at the exited blade point. He seemed as if to say something and then, without another thought, Malcor twisted the blade as he yanked it out. "I am not yours," he screamed into the R'Dar's dying face. The R'Dar's corpse collapsed like a bag of meat.

And silence… in the courtyard… not a sound and then one of the dragons leaned forward and bit the man off the ground. A slight head twist and the R'Dar vanished into a maw of teeth and fire. More moments passed, and the King spoke again breaking the silence.

39

"Not a very usual Coming of Age ceremony, but one we shall not forget. But for that fool of a merchant – what was his name? – we might have a king. But it has been revealed and the prophecy fulfilled! Dar Shara, let the Temple send word to the Merchant's Guild that," a scribe whispered to the King, "R'Dar Tor of Klenna is dead, slain in fair and witnessed combat before myself and all others. Make a note that the usual rules apply for belongings and deeded properties."

The scribe backed away scratching on the parchment and King Rojo stepped forward indicating he would like to see Malcor's sword. "Excellent balance. Where did you get this?"

"I made it my lord, with my master's help in the beginning. I have been refining and improving it ever since."

"Has it a name?"

Malcor shook his head no, "This is the first time it has been used to kill…"

"You did not kill him Malcor. The Queen took you as Her tool to end his life. Look." Rojo drew his own blade from his waist. Its keen edge resonated shrill and clear as it came free of its gold-inlaid scabbard. A bloodstone ruby glistened from the pommel's hiltguard. The metal, if it was metal, absorbed light as if the darkest hour of night. Nothing reflected from it. Besides those differences, it was identical to Malcor's handmade long sword. "This is my sword. My blade. My strong right arm. I name it "Twilight Fell on Her Shining Eyes". My life, my sword, my Destiny is to honor, to serve, to love the Queen Takhissis with all that I was, am, and shall yet be. How is it that your sword resembles my own? Have you seen it, read it, perhaps saw it as a drawing?"

"No my king. I saw the sword in my dreams and crafted it. I have never seen your blade until now. At the forge, working this blade, I always knew what I had to do, and have done it. It is a work in progress."

"Your father or master perhaps?"

Ishan stepped forward and bowed low, "My Dar, my son enters trances and does this work as if possessed. He collapses when done." The king nodded and Ishan stepped back.

Rojo presented his sword, "Attack my sword Twilight Fell. Show me what the Queen instructed you to build into your un-named blade." When R'Dar Tor had fallen, Malcor had watched his dreams of knighthood die. It seemed beyond belief that he should still be standing, let alone talking with the King. *Attack the KING?!* He dared not. "Go on - Attack. I order you." The king's voice, which had been jovial by comparison, went back to that very dangerous snake-like whisper. Malcor swallowed. No backing down now.

Mal raised his blade and for the first time since its making, he prayed to the Queen and said Her Words as he heard them in his heart, "*Let that which is created, come undone.*" As he spoke, he heard the Queen's voice moving as if he had lost control of his voice. The words sounded not like his own voice, but nonetheless, his. His sword pulsed in his hands suddenly feeling squishy like flesh but hard at the same time like a flexed muscle.

His sword had a name and Mal had heard it moving through him during those lost fugues at the forge. His pulse quickened and Malcor felt it was time. Though hardly a moment had passed, his perception ripped between the real world of the living and the ethereal realm on the banks of the River of Time. The King appeared split in half with his more glorious self apparent on the shores of the River. His real self, though it did not lack for glory, seethed with frightful power.

Malcor struck out with his sword, faster than he could believe, faster than he had ever wielded a blade or swung a hammer. Equally fast, the King lowered Twilight Fell and summoned a sword of lesser craft in its place. Malcor's sword bit into the edge of that lesser sword. In the realm of the River, Malcor saw this occur as if in slow motion knowing the King's intent to switch and the wide-eyed watching as small crackles of lightning ate away from that crack into the king's blade. A concussive blast rippled the river in circles around them.

All around, dragon wings dropped to protect the villagers and onlookers. In the real world, there was a fraction of a second and the King's blade's magic exploded in an outbursting of fire, energy, and hot color. It washed over and throughout the courtyard vanishing up into the air along the ramps of leather wings. The king's sword cracked at the small chip and then shattered across its length snapping the blade in half along its length. What remained, bereft of magic, was still a well-made piece of sword art but magic-less and shattered.

The dragons, the clerics, the knights all watched stoically as the blast's shockwave blew out over them. The villagers in the courtyard took a longer time re-adjusting their eyes from the bright explosion to the now near-dark night. "A well-made sword Malcor. Perhaps R'Dar Tor spoke the truth and you are a prodigy who should stay at a forge. Your blade has ripped, permanently it seems, the magic from my own. Though not Twilight Fell, that blade," he said kicking at the broken tip, "was made by a powerful trio of mages and highly skilled craftsmen. It is truly remarkable that your unnamed sword did this. You're nineteen? What do you want out of this Ceremony?"

Malcor nodded yes to his age and then a thought struck him. Straightening his back and standing in firm imitation of the knight's saluting, Malcor cleared his throat and asked, "My king, more than anything, I want to be a knight, no a paladin. I do not know about Destiny, but there is something I am supposed to do today. I have a gift I was supposed to give to you. But now I feel there is a different recipient for it, a black dragon. I know this in my heart and must." His satchel holding the dragon statuette felt solid and weighty. He removed the dragon statue as he said "black dragon". He noted Dar Shara's interest.

The king raised his eyebrow and, sweeping a hand around the area, said, "There are more than a few Dragons here, but none are *black dragons*." The Temple classified dragons by their breath weapon and then as a color. Black Dragons breathed acid instead of fire. All of the dragons here were Red, or fire-breathers. A dragon could actually be any color, but until very aged or until they used their breath weapons, a human could not tell what "type" of a dragon they faced. "Are you sure this is your destiny? Be careful of what you "want" versus what is actually your path. May I?" He took the statue from Malcor and examined it even as Shara walked up and touched it lightly.

That voice came to him again, the female roaring voice now softer and

42

more sensual, the one that had commanded him to kill R'Dar Tor whispered in his ear and he felt it in his heart. *Yes, this is what you must do my young dragon. Call out for Dar Kell, the Black Dragon. Stand strong. Be proud. He is your father. Of course there is yet another you might call out to, but be warned for I am a jealous god.* The whisper almost stole Mal's resolve if not for how strong hearing it made him feel. *Dar Kell – my father?* The voice whispered it but still, Dar Kell – THE high priest from the capitol's greatest temple? It could not be possible, yet the whisper made him know its truth.

Strengthened by the voice, Malcor answered the king, "I am sure My King. I must give this gift to my fa... – Dar Kell. The Black Dragon! He is here." Malcor looked around expectantly but not before taking note of the quickly hidden smile exchanged between Dar Shara and the King. While most Klennans had heard of Dar Kell – who had not after all? – just few knew that he stood as the highest ranking member of the Temple, and its first male priest. And he had a deadly reputation. The voice whispered to him again, *You do well to not declare him your father. Do not grow overly fond of him as a father. There is no love and no father for you there. I am pleased by your exercise of wisdom in face of great revelation.*

Chapter Four – The Father's Trial

Thirty years before Malcor faced Tor in Klenna, a young paladin stood at the Temple At Morbatten's altars, a priestess by his side. R'Dar Kell, heroic knight of Tania, asked his request for marriage to a young priestess of powerful and noble birth. Though Marshella had not yet attained lofty rank, she and Kell had found themselves lost in love while serving in one of the never-ending Bloodstone Wars. Though a priestess always could take any lover she chose and to birth any child with any man she deemed suitable – even paladins, paladins themselves were not allowed to exit their chastity vows except if they left the knighthood, or through retirement. As a young knight and of noble birth, leaving the knighthood represented too much dishonor. Retirement lay too far away to consider in the midst of a war notorious for killing and death. Their love and pride in honor held them there asking for this one exception.

The high priestess of the Temple at Morbatten declined to hear their request. "A paladin may not marry and remain a knight. That is the absolute doctrine of the Queen."

Kell and his fiancé bowed low and left. They wed anyways but were careful to keep a low profile. Seeking to work within the Temple structure, Kell submitted request after letter after audience seeking permission to become a priest. And, the Queen drove him to escalate his request. *I am the Goddess. I am the Queen of Dragons. I understand why my people have followed this matriarchal order, but my Children of Morbatten are not Dragons, not yet. My doctrine and my will never required only female priests. You will be the first my Son Kell.*

Bloodstone called them back time and time again to war and years passed. Kell rose to the highest ranks of knighthood. Despairing of becoming a priest and being free to openly wed with honor, he began teaching the Queen's will as a new doctrine, that all of Her Children could serve in the Temple. Quietly, he pursued the suggested revelation that Her People could become dragons. Taught by the Queen and blessed by Her, his teaching lit a fire suppressed for millennia. Morbatten would burn. The Dar Priestess named Kell heretic.

Time passed and Kell, finally wearing a priest's robes and symbols over his knight armor, ascended the road to the Emperor Alerius. Hundreds of paladins and priestesses and male disciples of Kell followed. Atop the mountain, in his throne chamber, Alerius consulted with the High Priestesses of the Temple at Morbatten and Bloodstone. Dar Ana of Bloodstone felt the change Kell brought and in prayerful deference to the Emperor and the Goddess, spoke in favor of allowing men to the Priesthood. Glass had said it best, "The gender separations of the Eldar dragons do not apply to us. Not necessarily. I feel that this is the Queen's will, to bind the male color with the female metallics and heal. Kell seeks marriage, not dominion. I will grant him this."

The High Priestess of Morbatten, most powerful cleric in the most powerful of the Temples, remembered her refusal of Kell's marriage four years ago. Her pride would not let her be shown to be wrong. The Emperor, shapeshifted in to his human form, put his hand on her shoulder. "After all, I am a male am I not? When the River first moved, my brothers and I gave the Queen our power, not because She is female, but because She is the Strongest. Though culture and practice, change is endemic to humans. Even the dragons see that Morbatten becomes stronger by allowing this. I could order you to allow this, but the Queen desires your free will."

No. Not Kell. Heretic.

As Kell entered the vast chamber and bowed before them, priestesses and paladins from the Temple At Morbatten loyal to the high priestess attacked, massacred, and slew Kell's entire family and hers too. Kell and Marshella had two children destined for great things. A seven year old boy, beautiful and endowed with the Queen's favor, fell to a paladin's sword and a priestess's flame strike. His wife, the love of his life, was put to mutlifixion; tortured death on the wings of healing to draw it out until the soul rips and tears. The broken vessel left behind fills with undeath and the multifixion continues until faith or magic fades entirely from the soul leaving nothing. Their three year old daughter, blessed with rare golden hair and bright green eyes clung to her mother as her death spasms ripped the poor girl's world to pieces. Stricken with madness, the child fled and was taken hostage, as a safety precaution.

Bowed low, Kell felt it. The attack had been timed impeccably. It could not be stopped. Kell looked up at the High Priestess and growled as he felt his wife's concern turn terrible as her soul began to tear apart in the first multifixion. As his children came under attack, he asked a simple one word request, "Stop."

No. You are heresy. My charge is to protect the Innocents from the likes of you!

Then his wife's death throes hit Kell. A life and mind brightly dedicated to the Queen's Glory and the majesty of Morbatten snapped and blind rage filled Kell's heart and soul. Not just the first male priest, Kell had studied with the Queen Herself. In that moment of his wife's first death, he dragonshifted reaching out for her the impossible oblivion left when a soul is multifixated. Overshadowed with anger, his first dragonshift turned red fire into darkest black. His human hands on the chamber's gold-gilded stones pulsed and morphed into giant dragon claws and his human skein burst asunder. The transformation caught even the Emperor off guard as Kell became a Shadow Dragon; the only dragonkind to not pledge to either the Queen Takhissis or Her Consort, the hated King of Dragons.

Kell's human voice slurring all-consuming pain through the shadow dragon's maw, "I will kill you and will not stop until you and yours are beyond death..." In his madness, he may have attacked all. The high priestess seeing the shadow dragon cried for guards to attack. There in the emperor's throne room, Alerius ordered them to stand still. It almost worked but when Kell sensed his daughter's terror and saw in the River she had been taken, he snapped. Spears of shadow slashed into the high priestess.

Alerius, turning dragon in an instant, clamped down on Kell's throat and ordered him to stand still. "Give me time to protect the Innocents Kell. You may not hurt the innocents!"

"My daughter still lives –" Kell growled. "Why?!" he raged at the priestesses standing by shredded high priestess. "WHY?!"

"I will find and guard her," Alerius promised. At his words, Ynt'taris raced

46

south to find and preserve the daughter of Kell.

The Kell Conflict began. Multifixion ensures no resurrection, no hope for reunion by either destroying the soul or trapping it in undeath. It is the ultimate Tanian execution normally held for capital crimes far beyond a love-based marriage between a paladin and a priestess. Kell would never see Marshella again. Mutlifixion denied her an afterlife. The son, Ynt'taris resurrected by the Queen's grace. The daughter required more time and healing, but under Ynt'taris' care, they were removed from the Conflict.

Kell's wrath knew no end as he lashed out at those who supported the high priestess and murdered his family. Those who participated in the massacre, he killed. Females, he captured and raped. *You will see me everywhere you look*, he seared into their fear-filled days of captivity. The Queen seemed to abandon those who had turned against Kell, and though they tried to surrender, when they saw Kell's hate and rampage, they took up arms. The civil war stayed mostly confined to the families of Kell and those loyal to the slain high priestess.

The Emperor ordered all to withdraw except the House of Kell and those loyal to the High Priestess of the Temple at Morbatten. Alerius sought out and found a knight, one of intense devotion to the Queen and Empire rather than a Temple – Rojo – and made him witness and enforcer of the Kell Conflict.

At some point, Kell began regaining his senses and was guided back by the Queen Herself. Dar Shara, an upcoming priestess in the Temple at Morbatten, fought against her own High Priestess and slew her. As a peace offering, she offered the position now rightfully hers, to Kell. The slain's great house almost continued the war as an internal temple one. However, Rojo intervened and with a force of paladins secured the situation by execution and new vows. Rojo witnessed the end of the civil war when Kell took the offered role of High Priest.

Kell became Dar Kell, the High Priest of the Temple at Morbatten, first dragon shifter, and Lord of the Shadows. The female priestesses were ordered to keep the children spawned by Kell to be raised amongst the Empire as foster wards held sacred by a prophecy that a boy and girl child would seed the next generation's heroes. Provided they did this, they retained their rank. Kell rebuilt the Temple and appointed Dar Shara as the successor to the High Priestess of the Lost Temple of Glass. The emperor appointed Rojo the first human king.

Very quickly though, it became apparent that the children of Kell possessed an alien edge, as Kell's insanity pulled him into the realm of shadow and anti-life. Wondering at what it meant, Alerius ordered the children abducted and placed in safety throughout the kingdom so that not even Alerius knew where they had gone. He knew Kell, even if he regained his sanity completely, would never forgive, never let it go. When Kell found and murdered the first child, it confirmed Alerius' concerns. Later, as the house of the fallen priestess realized what had happened, they commissioned death squads to find and kill the remaining children. Touched by shadow dragons, the children of Kell lived in secrecy and anonymity. Those with overt markings, died quickly.

The ending of the Kell Conflict should have brought peace. Peace ushered in a new era for Morbatten, one of unprecedented might, wealth, and influence. The doctrine of Matriarchy fell to the doctrine of Mighty; of the great temples, the Dar Priest or Priestess would be the mightiest regardless of gender. The priesthood remained a separate path from the paladins, but rather than paladins swearing to a Temple or even a Priestess, they swore to the Mother. The era of dragon shifters began and Dar Kell *the Black Dragon* wrote his pain in letters of blood across the Empire. And his story will never end so long as even one of his children worship the Queen.

And Dar Rojo's story as king began. There is a prophecy regarding his successor, a prodigy and the rebuilding of the Lost Temple of Glass. The Kell Conflict identified a weakness in Morbatten and, filled with undeath as priestesses and paladins warred, the Demon God of Undeath chose this time to attack, reclaiming much of Bloodstone. The Kell Conflict became the Jaden War. Kell led and drove the undead hordes back into the mines combing the Bloodstone Valley.

Chapter Five – Malcor's Path is Set

The King Rojo, the High Priestess Shara, the Dread Lords, and the Klennan villagers watched Malcor stand before the king. The moment drew out but Malcor stood firm. The dragons watched. No black dragon appeared. Again, that small voice from behind Malcor spoke. Klara walked up and touched Malcor's shoulder. "Are you going to be a knight yet?" she asked.

As the moment stretched, the King saw Malcor's resolute stance and asked him, "You intend to wait for the Black Dragon?" Malcor nodded. "There is not time to wait for that one. He comes and goes as he pleases. When you find the Black Dragon, you will give him the statue. Tell us about it."

As Malcor described the statue, the king's expression did not change in the least. Dar Shara's face though took on one of amazement. "Young man," she breathed, "this is amazing! Rojo," she added dropping pretense and title, "this looks like it came straight from…"

"…the tapestry in the Emperor's library. Yes," the king finished. He looked long and hard at Malcor and then noted, "There is no way you have ever been to see the Emperor, or visited his library? Of course not. Malcor, your statue is an exact match to a magical tapestry in Alerius' library. Only members of the Inner Council would have been in a position to see it, along with other Dread Lords." The king shrugged, "I do not know what this means, but there is certainly Fate and Destiny on you."

Dar Shara touched it, as if scratching a pet on the head, "Remarkable that someone so young could do this… "She turned to Malcor and eyed him more closely. Behind her, Dread Lord Armageddon swirled from his titanic dragon form through a whirlwind of fire and dark energy into his human form. He walked up behind her.

"The statue is in the likeness of the rebel king Cor'tanos, the shadow dragon patriarch who refused to pledge to Takhissis or the Consort. We also call him and the shadow dragons, 'the heretics'. The human mind, especially at such a young age, struggles with placing a color or type on the shadows. Black is suitable. The black iron wrought with gold and ruby eyes is a flawless likeness."

Dar Shara took the statue and walked back to her chair. As she walked, she suggested, "Shall we continue with the Ceremony? There are some here who will remember this with fascination, but the villagers need their rest. Dar Rojo, may we?" She sat down and placed the statue on the throne arm looking out over the courtyard. "I believe we have the matter of Calvin and the others to review."

"Yes, we shall proceed. Malcor, return to your place with the others. All other youth step forth and let the Ceremony continue." The mayor stepped out into the courtyard as did Calvin and the other teens. "Keep in mind that, the way the Emperor designed this Ceremony, it was originally three days of combat demonstrations, worship, and sermons while fasting." He laughed. "And, well long before that, back when we worshiped the dragon totem, Alerius hunted us looking for any who could resist the dragonterror. We've gotten so much better at letting families and communities self-determine this. However, we must see for ourselves if wise decisions have been made here in Klenna."

The Ceremony resumed its normal course. There were no surprises or exceptions. Each stated their desire and their acceptance, by blood through marriage or by apprenticeship, and were blessed by the priestess Dar Shara. At last, Calvin stood forward and declared what he had been prepared and trained for his entire life, "I seek entrance into the knighthood." He summarized his training and exploits. His father, the mayor, came to stand beside him as he wrapped up his qualifications. Lacking the show Malcor had put on, the customary endorsement or rejection by the shrine's prefect would take just moments.

This ceremony did not follow customary. The prefect stepped forward but Shara waved the old man back. Armageddon helped her step down from her throne and she slowly circled Calvin. "Strong back. Fair complexion. Well-rehearsed summary my dear Calvin. Tell me," she stepped closer to him with each word, "is knighthood what you really wish? Serving the Queen means long days soldiering, studying, seeking the mightiest foes, protecting the weakest of the Queen's vassals. Maybe you don't have what it takes to be a knight, let alone one of the most elite paladins, blessed with holy powers? Unless a priestess chooses you for love, you are bound to chastity and death. As a paladin." Her eyes scanned the crowd of villagers and noted some of the girls. "Do you have what it takes Calvin?" her lips brushed over his and he flinched. "To be a paladin, or a knight? Both would be glorious. Which path would you take?"

To Calvin's credit, he tried to answer but words failed him until he at last nodded his head affirmative. Shara looked him in his eyes and then to Malcor's. "Neither of you <indicating Malcor as well> have yet been accepted. I see a path forward for you both, into the knighthood. One of you into the paladin ranks, perhaps." She held out her right hand, "This path is easy. A test. Right here and right now. You pass – you are a knight. You fail; you die with the honor of trying." She lifted up her left hand and said, "But, this path, this one, it takes longer, requires sacrifice, but will surely put you into the knighthood, eventually - someday. To be a paladin, you must also be a knight... though there are many knights are only that. Paladins are special."

She leaned into Calvin to rest her cheek against his and made eye contact with Malcor, "Choose wisely."

In the silence of the moment following, Calvin's father could be heard saying, "You will pass. I know it. This is what we have been training for." No one counselled or encouraged Malcor.

Malcor remembered the many stories where the two terms "paladin" and "knight" seemed interchangeable. Listening to the high priestess though, he realized the difference as one of faith and servitude. He stepped forward and stated his choice, "I choose the path of sacrifice. I have much to learn. The more difficult path is my destiny. I would be a paladin."

"I choose to be...", Calvin said as Dar Shara turned from Malcor back to Calvin. "The same as Malcor."

Shara embraced Calvin and declared loudly, "Welcome to the knighthood young squires!" More quietly so that only Calvin could hear "You do not hear the Queen in this regard. This path will bring you pain

Calvin. Your destiny is not the knighthood. You are too easily distracted by beautiful things." He winced as he caught her gaze pass over the girls waving at him.

Applause erupted throughout the courtyard and at long last, the breakfast feast that would have happened with a usual ceremony became the evening feast. Several of the paladins and their temple counterparts had musical talent and music soon filled the courtyard. The dragons, not comfortable with so many normal humans, flew off to hunt leaving only Armageddon behind. He endured the curious stares and questions from Klenna's children with grumpy dignity.

Eventually, he felt a small hand tug on his fist. He looked down to see a small girl. She had a touch of prophecy about her and uncanny blue eyes similar to Malcor's. When her eyes met his, the eldar chuckled and knelt down. He held out his hand asked, "What is your name?"

She put her tiny hand in his giant armored one and said, "I'm Klara. I saw you dance with Mal. He is leaving with you and the red lady?"

Armageddon regarded her from the River for a just a moment and saw her small aura pulsing there with concern for Malcor, whom she viewed as a brother and protector. "Malcor, you love him."

She nodded, her eyes threatening to burst into tears. "He saved me. It was so cold and I was so lonely. He brought me to the warm place, his forge. They got me a job. He is always here. With him gone – "

Armageddon touched her forehead, gently for how strong his hand could be, and interrupted her, "Malcor goes to serve the Mother. You know the Goddess?" Klara nodded, her eyes wide. "By doing so, he'll be better able to look out for you and those like you. He'll always be here in your heart and dreams. Now, hurry, go give him a hug and tell him these things so that you never regret missing a good-bye."

The little girl smiled, sniffled, and then turned to run and find Malcor. The dread lord watched her run as the crowd seemed to magically part for her. She looked back over her shoulder at one point and mouthed a thank-you. Shara walked up on her guardian as he watched the small child hug Malcor in fiercely tight grip that almost knocked Mal over. "It's not every day you see a child make friends with an eldar dragon," she commented. "I may have to commission a piece of art for this moment."

Armageddon continued to watch not answering his mistress. "We must keep an eye on that one Shara. She is different. Special."

Shara turned her eyes to gaze at Klara from the river and nodded. "Do you think –"

Armageddon said nothing. Some children have a sense of potential and destiny about them but only when older does it show. Generation upon generation, Alerius' records had shown that this sense in the dread lords would offer Klara as a genius prodigy or an omen. "She is too young to tell," was all he said.

Chapter Six – Initiates to the Temple at Morbatten

The applause, the congratulations, the well-wishes, all had faded. Klenna sat as it ever had, three days behind them on the road to the capitol. Dar Shara had been most explicit that they travel quickly and unseen to Morbatten. In seven days, they must report to the Temple at Morbatten or forfeit their acceptance as knights, and thereby paladins too. Normally, the trip took seven days on the main roads crisscrossing the empire. Moving quickly but quietly proved difficult in the mountainous region around Klenna. Though the terrain would level out, the straight roads built over centuries would not serve their need for stealth. They needed to go faster to make up for any inevitable delays along a main highway.

Mal rather enjoyed this test of their resolve. His conditioning made the travel and the pack load easy. More than once, he carried Calvin's load. The difference between hard manual labor and the attention to detail required from hours in the forge gave Malcor clear advantage over Calvin's privileged lifestyle, even with Calvin's tutoring; nothing beat the kind of constitution developed by years of hard manual labor. Malcor crouched down behind a thicket from where he watched the main road. Calvin struggled off the road into hiding several hundred feet back.

Around the road's wide bend and a gentle rise, Malcor thought he had seen signs of travelers. *Be unseen*, she had said. Sure enough, dark shapes crested the rise and a column of infantry led by a knight came into view. Jogging in double-time, Malcor counted and realized it would take this regiment hours to pass. The knight drew parallel to Malcor's hiding place. Not just a knight of noble birth, the man bore the markings of a paladin. Malcor felt the weightiness of destiny and a tug from the River's current. Not just a paladin, a powerful paladin. The knight reached into one of his saddle bags and drew out a small glass vial. He held it up and Malcor saw the man's lips move as if whispering to the vial. He kissed it and then pushed it towards Malcor's location. The vial quivered in the air as if about to drop and then the push sent the vial hurtling to Malcor. He held up his hand to block it from hitting him and instead it landed in his hand.

As he caught it, he heard a whispered voice say, "You are safely unseen initiate. This potion will heal even dire wounds. Tonight you will be challenged. Beware. Only wisdom will save you."

An hour later, with the regiment still double-stepping past them, Calvin finally caught up to Malcor. He too had received a potion. Late in the afternoon, they finally dropped onto the main road and began running to make up lost time. Luck held them and no other travelers interrupted until hunger finally forced them to stop. Though late at night and exhausted from their travel so far, they both felt antsy with the knight's warning.

Not daring to make a fire, they ate dried fruit, bread, meat, and cheese and quietly discussed whether they should wait the night out and at least face this encounter as fresh as possible, or continue their travel. Though they prayerfully sought guidance, with no answer forthcoming, they readied themselves for a confrontation and waited. It felt awful, just waiting for something dangerous to happen. Malcor finally stood up and began pacing.

"I wonder if all paladins do this?" Calvin asked. "I've heard of initiation rituals but sneaking around for days and days to The Temple feels not like a paladin." It had grown cold and his breath's fog hung in the air around his words.

Malcor shrugged, "There was a knight at the forge once, a young one, just out of training. We talked. He had to do a trip to The Temple too. In his case, he was given a cup of water. He had to get it there from one of the western provinces – so, nine days on the roads? – without spilling and there had to be water left. It was summer." Malcor stared into the darkness around them. "I think it is a test to see if we can follow difficult if somewhat pointless instructions. It's how they weed out initiates who lack focus I guess."

"Well, at least he made it. Are we supposed to reach The Temple and not be seen? Morbatten is a crazy busy city and The Temple is continuously watched and very busy. Have you been there?" Malcor shook his head no. "It is on the eastern mountain overlooking where the river enters the harbor. We have to go through the city, or around the Emperor's Mountain," Calvin explained.

"Calvin, that knight with the water? I saw him at the forge later. He was an officer. He didn't make it into the paladin ranks."

"Do you know why?"

He shrugged. "Ishan said it is orders of magnitude more difficult to become a paladin than a knight. Harder still to be a knight than an officer. There are tests and things they look for."

Morbatten as a country lay along the eastern side of the huge land called Forsaken Islands. Where the island's center contained large forests and its own mountains, the eastern coast grew increasingly mountainous until dropping into a roiling and stormy ocean. The capitol itself, also named Morbatten but pronounced slightly different from the empire, meant "children of the father" and honored the dragon emperor's guardianship of the barbarian tribes that then grew into the people of Morbatten. The capitol nestled in a large valley with three mountain peaks straddling its northern edge. The tallest mountain served as the throne of the dragon emperor Alerius. It sat dead north of Morbatten's center. Fortified by artisans over millennia, its lower southern sections stretched out into the nicer estates of Morbatten's wealthy and nobility. The other faces and upper sections had been left in their natural state. The emperor had long ago transformed the interior into everything needed to rule and watch over the empire.

To the north and west, lay a smaller mountain capped by a fortress. The fortress served to overwatch the main road in and out of the capitol. The paladins, though based in the Temple itself, used it alongside the knights and military officers as their base of operations and training. As the military grew and the knights turned into the main command structure of the army, the fortress had taken turns as an administrative, then training, and eventually the guard purpose it now filled since the Bloodstone Wars began centuries ago.

Opposite the fortress and facing more east than north, stood a mountain divided from the emperor's by Tania's Great East-West road and a series of plaza fountains feeding the Cordabad River. Called simply the Temple At Morbatten, the largest and mightiest of the Queen's three temples looked out over the ocean, down to the capitol, and eye level with the

56

emperor's throne. These three mountains secured the northern edge of Morbatten as surely as a wall from Taysor. Off and on fighting between the two empires had yet to breach that mountain wall even as the winter war waged along it away from the nuances treaties and agreements.

"The mountain is not an option," Malcor said thinking about it. "We have to trust that our objective is to not be seen as we go through the City. If this is an obedience test, getting there is half of it. If we go around, we probably get caught by a patrol right? We cannot be late."

Calvin yawned and took a drink from his water skin. "You know, if "unseen" means unrecognized maybe all we need do is get there without being recognized or stopped."

Malcor sat down on a fallen tree and continued to scan the darkness. He shrugged. "Unseen. Maybe we just show up in the dark of night. Or without light... isn't there a scripture about dragon fire and other breath weapons in their relationship to darkness and light?" He reached into his backpack for his scriptures.

Calvin nodded, "Yeah, there was that story of the dragon patriarchs claiming their breath weapons, fire, acid, lightning, and so on. He tried to recount the scriptures "beneath the canopy of Heaven but cloaked in throneplanes of hell" or something. I never understood that story."

Malcor flipped through to the Book of Sparks, the first book and found a reference. He read, "The Queen reached up touching Heaven and proclaimed This Fire is mine and mine children's fire to light the dark of this new realm. This Fire shall never dim and my children shall wield its Light, each of their own destiny and shape, to create and guard a paradise for the fallen. This Light, this new realm, this sword against the dark is for the Fallen Unseen."

A gentle breeze swept towards them, heard in the leaves of the trees, and then rustled the scripture's pages. In the wind, Malcor heard a voice add, "...dragon's breath is an illusion. Dragons breathe Light. The Fallen and the Innocent of this world choking in the River, see it as fire or steam or lightning. To be Unseen is to cloak yourself in the Queen's power so that Innocents do not recognize you as different."

A quick glance at Calvin showed that he did not hear the whisper and Malcor pondered that too. Sometime later, Malcor startled awake where his head had nodded too far aside. Early dawn had begun but it was still very dark. Calvin had rolled up in his cloak. The road lay clear and empty. Mal woke his friend.

Making their way to the road, they did not notice the short figure standing right in the middle facing eastward to the City, until they almost ran into him. The figure did not move or give sign they were there. Mal and Calvin stepped back quietly and noticed the garishly bright clothing all mismatched. An odd assortment of different sized pouches strung along a bandolier. He, it, appeared to be a Halfling from the southern province of Home. They had emigrated to Tania with the promise of autonomy and their choice of fertile farm fields in the era of the first priestess Dar Tania almost two thousand years ago.

"I know you're there. Hi. I'm Kaia. I'm here to test you. I'm looking east so I don't see you. Malcor and Calvin right? I hope. This will be so awkward if you're not... well, are you?"

The Halfling had a high-pitched and excitable voice. Hearing it made the boys feel happy. Happy? No, wrong word. Interested? Excited? Calm but ready? Malcor could not quite place the feeling. Calvin said, "So what if we are? We already have a test..."

"At the Temple! I can get you there!" Kaia exclaimed. "I can get you to the Temple right now in fact, UNSEEN..." he opened his arms wide as he said the last part for emphasis. "I am the test. Well, sort of. What do you want?"

Mal and Calvin exchanged glances, "What do I want?" Calvin repeated. "I want to be a knight. What do you want and why are you here?"

"C'mon Calvin, let's go. No point wasting time here. We have a place to be soon." Malcor started to walk around the halfling.

Kaia added, "Sure, sure. Ignore the Halfling who wants to help with your test. Like I said, I can get you there now. If you try to go past me, you won't get past me."

They walked around Kaia. They walked past Kaia. After a few moments, they turned to look and he was no longer behind them. Looking east, there Kaia stood, same as before. "Told you. You won't get past me." The Halfling's voice had a mocking tone. "Why not let me help you?"

Off in the distance, Malcor noted the faint mist of a dust cloud, either a column of soldiers like before or a caravan. Either way, Malcor did not want to be seen. Calvin was about to say something but Mal grabbed his arm and said, "We need to get off the road."

"I'll come with you!" Kaia said.

The three of them sat in silence only occasionally interrupted by Kaia asking them what they want, could he help, or poking fun at something they wore or a facial expression. An hour later, a large merchant caravan accompanied by light infantry rolled past their hiding spot. Once past, Malcor breathed a sigh of relief. He had spent the time prayerfully contemplating what he should do with this Kaia. Nothing came to mind. The knight's gift of the healing potion and the appearance of this Halfling who knew their business must mean something. His offer to get them to the Temple, was it part of the test? If so, the choice of taking the help or not taking the help, after all the delays, really meant whether they would arrive in time.

Malcor turned to find Kaia staring at him intensely. It disconcerted him but he matched the Halfling's gaze and said, "Calvin and I were told to go the Temple at Morbatten unseen. I understood that to mean, travel…"

"…and I can take you there right now!" Kaia said excitedly. Clapping his hands, a dark rectangular doorway appeared as a slice in the air. "Step through this and you'll be there, on the steps. Right in front of the Order of the Shield!"

"…by my own means. I intend to walk. No doubt magic is a daily thing for people like the King or even Dar Shara, but I'm just starting out. I'd rather walk and be reprimanded for not taking your help than to get there early by magic and fail because of the magic." Malcor looked at Calvin who nodded his head in agreement. "We're fine. Thank you for the offer Kaia, but…"

The doorway vanished as if it had never been there. "Okay, so you don't want to get to the Temple early. Fine. What do you need though? I'm a member of the Circle and was told to come here and give you whatever you needed, by Dar Shara herself. There has to be something! Look at this from my perspective... I can't very well go back and tell the Circle that you refused my offer!"

Calvin questioned, "The Circle?"

According to Morbatten's long recorded history, the dragon emperor Alerius first appeared to the barbarians sixteen thousand years ago. The first makings of the current empire took several thousand years to appear in the form of language and the theocracy of dragon worship. Since the beginning, Alerius had ruled by proxy through the Circle. The Circle consisted of those heroes, citizens, and persons of such influence and merit that Alerius deemed them indispensable to the rule of the empire. While the emperor invited the elite to the Circle, they were also dismissed just as easily. Still, a few lingered on. The Halfling member of the Circle was part of Morbatten's legends. It was said that a Halfling appearing to a young hero portended great destiny, and the Halfling always gave a gift.

Kaia smiled and opened his hands. On the palms of each were tattooed half a dragon, that came together to form an image of the dragon emperor. A rune of sealing wrapped the image. The date key to the rune indicated it to be ancient. Kaia's smile grew wider as Calvin's face gave way his recognition of the date and tattoo's meaning. Kaia began laughing as Calvin noticed the Halfling's teeth were fanged. When Mal noticed the fangs, Kaia's laughter became belly laughs.

"Mal," Calvin said, "The Halfling came to us. The legends... "

"I don't care about legends!" Malcor's hand cut through the air between the two. He turned to Kaia and added, "My lord Dar Kaia. Please forgive our lack of respect. Dar Shara and Dar Rojo both gave us instructions to be at The Temple. We dare not disobey the King and Priestess. We dare not make a mistake in our obedience. My path is clear. I do not understand your interest in us."

Kaia flicked his tongue against his canine fang and chuckled a bit. "It is sooo interesting how things change when you humans recognize me. While I certainly do not outrank the king, it is doubtful the king outranks me. I am here. The legends are true. I want to help. What do you want? Ask anything. You, Calvin, you have something you want. I see it."

"I, I want..."

"Don't Calvin!" Malcor interrupted him forcibly by grabbing his shirt and yanking him face to face so that he could not see Kaia.

Calvin pushed back and said, "I want to know what my path is. Ever since Dar Shara said..."

Kaia nodded and finished, "...that the knighthood is not for you? Well, she is right you know. At least the knighthood and paladin order you are thinking about. I can help you with that. Just ask." Kaia looked at Malcor, "And I can help you too even though I see you won't ask. Foolish."

Malcor stared at Calvin. "She told you to not be a knight? It is all you have trained for." Even as he said it, he felt his thoughts turn to too many memories of working at the forge while Calvin went off with others to play, and later, girls to court. He remembered the dance at the Ceremony where Calvin lost tempo and had to stop while Malcor kept pace with the knights. Was Calvin really cut out for the knighthood? Malcor cleared his throat and recited a scripture that came to his mind, "In the mighty days of the children, their sons and daughters shall reach up to grasp the stars. They shall hold the stars and yet fail to see how the Queen orders their paths, and lose their way. The path of the lost leads to shadow."

Calvin nodded his head, "Yeah, um, what does that have to do with the Halfling Legend?" He stepped aside and re-addressed Kaia. "You can help me become a knight?"

Kaia winked. "Actually, I can help you both. Calvin, I will give you a shield recognizable to a certain group of knights who will take you as an initiate. Your choice as to whether you take it, or use it, or not." A templar shield appeared magically next to the Halfling. It radiated magic and power. It was beautiful. It was not a shield carried by any knights Malcor or Calvin had ever heard of in the empire. "Malcor, you want to be one of those knights known for being a knight. Like the king, you want people to whisper, "That is Dar Malcor! Look! See it IS him! Wow!" and you want your enemies to tremble at the mention of your name. This is a problem because what you want puts you at odds with your destiny. The king's name is not whispered because he is king. His name is whispered because, well, for other reasons less to do with rulership and more to do with the *who* and the *why* of his being king. One of you wishes to be a knight while the other wants to define what it means to be a knight."

Calvin walked over to the shield with Kaia's eyes following his hand. He appeared a bit tentative about picking it up. "Go ahead, pick it up. It is yours. A magical shield. Light as air. A glorious start to what will no doubt be a complete suit of plate armor. It is easily worth all of Klenna." Calvin picked it up his face changing from dubious questioning to wonder.

"I accept," Calvin said eyeing the shield. He traced his fingers along the bright insignia and blazed heraldry. They had seen it before but did not know it meant a paladin order.

Malcor watched Calvin and had to bite back another reminder to stay the course. "What you say about me Dar Kaia is true, but you missed out on the most important part – that my dreams change and grow. Just days ago, I danced with the king. Today I just want to get to The Temple and honor my king by so doing. Years from now, what I want matters not at all to me now because I hear Her Voice and every part of me aches to obey."

"But you do not hear Her Voice now." Malcor paused and then admitted he did not. "You do not hear Her Voice or have heard it tell you to not accept my help?" Again, Malcor admitted no. "Then, do not tell me what you want right now. Ask for something I can give you that advances your vision of your destiny."

Ever so faintly, Malcor felt a whisper run through his mind in this moment, "At last, now you can ask for what you need. Wisdom, the River, power…"

Malcor looked around and then up at the sky. "The great king Alerius smote my hands in the forges of creation and shaped them to be Her Hands. He bent my back with the weight of destiny and proclaimed the untamed world Her Throne. He tore my legs and with molten fire created them to pace Her Steps in the sand here at the river's edge." Kaia looked askance at Malcor who continued, "All my life, I grew up not knowing my father. Now I know. All my life, I read these scriptures and they stay with me. I feel their meaning, but do not understand them. I want to understand not just their meanings but the intent of prophets who recorded these as Alerius spoke them. However, my Dar Kaia, I do not ask for this as a gift. I do not want this as a favor. This is what I need to grow and progress. I do not believe these are gifts to be given."

While Malcor spoke, Kaia's expression had changed from one of amusement, like a child with a new toy, to a more serious and thoughtful if annoyed one. "I do not serve the Goddess Takhissis but abide here in Morbatten with her permission. I block her voice when speaking with children like you." His eyes narrowed, "What did she tell you?"

Malcor maintained his gaze locked with Kaia. "Nothing I have not heard my entire life. I want to understand the River." Calvin's blank stare told Malcor he had no clue about the River.

Kaia looked quickly sideways at Calvin and back at Malcor, "It is the flow of magic from where chaos creates to where chaos destroys. "Good", such as it is, aligns with the creation process; "Evil" with the destructive. Creation to destruction creates a flow, the River, and that is what Time is. They told me you had seen it. What you do not yet understand or see is that all our magic – ALL of it whether from mages and priests and gods and demons and all the powers under heaven for life and death – hate the River and yet are addicted to it. Even as you drown in it Malcor, you scream out for more. You humans always want the next thing. Like an addict, the River feeds you tomorrow, hope, the future. Sometimes even destiny. Even the priestess Shara when she resurrects a fallen child, she revels in its turbulence. Even the dragon king knows that without the River, you die, we all die. The disease of Time gives us the power we wield between our creation and death. You will only truly understand the River when you have at last drowned in it."

"Dar Kaia you asked. I told you. As I said, I do not need or want anything specifically right now."

"What is this River? Wait, you can see it Mal?" Calvin asked. They both ignored him.

Malcor continued, "I want to understand the River. Dying for that understanding is not an offer of help unless you intend to kill me...?"

Kaia's eyes grew wide and then the serious look faded back to amusement again. "If I did, they would be most unhappy with me!" He burst in to giggles, "Killing Malcor before he makes it to The Temple! They'd kill me for sure!" Some time passed before he calmed down enough to say, "Clearly, I cannot give you what you want young Malcor. Instead, I suppose I must magnify your capacity to understand." He stepped forward and touched Malcor's arm. The Halfling's touch felt warm and embracing and then like wind blowing smoke clear, the Halfling vanished.

Calvin asked again, "What is this River you keep talking about?"

"It is a metaphor within the Queen's doctrine. Think about it. But it's also a way of looking at Time, maybe even using magic to get around it." But, Malcor knew with sudden clarity that Calvin would not. He also sensed that it was time to continue on their journey. "I cannot describe it as I am just barely learning what it means. It has to do with how dragon's age and why some grow strong and powerful with each passing year while others wither and die."

Calvin was too distracted by his new shield to keep asking questions. "Check this out," he said disc-tossing the shield to Malcor. The shield felt barely-there light and though metallic in appearance felt more akin to wood. It felt wrong in his hands though and Malcor quickly gave it back with an appreciative comment. Not just that it felt wrong, but the symbol it bore felt wrong for the Goddess. It suggested protective might where the Queen's religion and its symbols exclaimed dominance, power, and ability to do anything with strength.

Though exhausted, they returned to their course and travelled for many hours before another sign of travelers caught their eye. Unlike the other times, Malcor felt it no longer mattered to hide. Unseen could mean so many things and clearly the Halfling found them. As Kaia had noted, he felt an increased ability to consider things and the obvious intent of being "unseen" clearly meant something other than to hide. He remembered the term *Innocent* and *Fallen*, but had never considered them as maybe being those people unaware of the River. His teachings always talked about the world as being "fallen" and that Tanians had a duty to protect the innocent. He wondered if they were the same things. If yes, then clearly Innocents meant more than just the people of Tania or even those consecrated to the Goddess. He made a mental note to study it out when time allowed.

A light cavalry patrol came around a bend. Morbatten routinely made its military visible in all places and this patrol bore all the correct signs but lacked veteran and other leaders. The lead rider nodded to Malcor and Calvin but did not stop. Over the next several days, the boys passed other similar groups where instead of cavalry, merchants or pilgrims or whoever passed by, each group leaving the Capitol on some mission with some sense of purpose or satisfaction.

Moving even faster, Malcor encouraged Calvin to keep up and skip the frequent breaks they had enjoyed while hiding from normal foot traffic.

Chapter Seven – Morbatten's Northern Road

Finally, late at night, they crested a hill offset by a glow in the distant horizon, and saw the Soldier's Fort. Hundreds of lit windows created a vague texture against the dark stone outline by lights atop its battlements. Even higher and behind, the eminent glow of the dragon king's throne chamber sat high in the night watching over the City. At the same height and to the side, the Temple at Morbatten radiated wondrous lights cycling through the different color representations of dragon's breath weapons. The lights had danced that way for more than a thousand years now. After what their history termed the First or Tanian Cascade, Alerius had ordered the children to rebuild the Temple. Since that time, the second temple's lights glowed continuously.

Calvin had been here many times with his father on government business. He happily pointed things out to Mal as they descended the road to the city's outskirts. Though Calvin spoke nonstop, Malcor rejoiced that he had picked up and maintained a much faster pace for nearly two days now.

"Soldier's Fort used to be a shrine but fell into disuse when the Temple was built... to our left is where the wealthy heroes and nobility live... this road will dead end at the great fountain in the Bazaar where all merchants do their business... Alerius' mountain is about 2000 feet taller than the Soldier's Fort. It is actually taller than the Temple, but the emperor's throne faces the Temple at eye level with the altar there... Morbatten is the only unwalled city this big here because magic and the dragons and other flyers allow us to secure the passes quickly and the emperor did not want to hedge his people in... did you know there are over a hundred thousand people who live here in addition to the 15,000 soldiers? ...did you know that when Alerius selected this as the Capitol there were only 300 barbarians living here AND that almost all of us are related through those three hundred to everyone else?"

Calvin excitedly talked and Malcor just enjoyed taking it all in. The Temple called out to him. If he had come here before now, Mal would no doubt be just as excited as Calvin. He tried to show interest but the magnetic draw of the Temple made it difficult. Soon, the outskirt road –

paved though it was – forked. The southern route continued to the Great Bazaar and Fountain. The northern fork rose into the estates and manors of Morbatten's wealthiest. A guard station serving as a shrine sat at the fork with guards paying close attention to those traveling north. The more travelled southern route not so much. "What happens if we go north?" Mal asked. "Will we get to the Temple faster?"

"I don't know," Calvin admitted. "My father and I never went north. He always said we needed special papers to go that way."

"Lets try," Malcor said as they turned out of the throng to the almost empty northern route. "There must be side access roads or something for service and the like right?" he wondered aloud.

Calvin nodded and gulped when two heavily armored knights stepped out from the shrine. The gauntleted fists looked menacing enough without holding a weapon and they waved the boys over. Calvin unconsciously let Malcor step forward first.

"We are traveling to the temple as knight initiates. Is this way faster than the Bazaar road?" Malcor asked as bravely and unflinchingly as he could. Somehow he knew that any sign of uncertainty would not bode well for them. Since they did not wear the clothing of nobility, their attitude had to make up the difference.

The two knights stared at the boys, one walking right up into Malcor's face till their eyes were scant inches apart. "Yes, this road connects to the Temple, but you see this road is not for anyone except those who live in the northern quarter."

The knight had a drawn out almost slurred way of talking. It caught Malcor's attention. The Temple healed most wounds received in war. The only time wounds were left to mend on their own was when dishonor, misconduct, or the nature of the wound itself prevented magical healing. Malcor could not tell. It seemed the wealthy would not want their estates' road guarded by dishonored and misbehaved castoffs. It had to be the magical nature of the wound, which meant undead, which meant Bloodstone.

"Tell me, are you so recently returned from Bloodstone that your wounds have yet to heal? I myself hope to serve there as part of my training."

The knight stepped back as if struck and stammered, "How did you know...?"

His comrade elbowed him aside and jokingly said, "Come now, how could you know something like that boy? We're impressed. Impress us some more and we'll let you be on your way."

Malcor looked harder. Normally, this would seem to be a situation for a bribe, but that felt wrong. Malcor stepped back, tried to step out of the River, and for just a moment see if he had missed something. He felt his perception shift and catch in his breath and then he felt his face break free of it just enough. The two knights before him were Bloodstone veterans. Their armor and weapons glimmered with the lighted auras of magic. The men themselves, no not men, they appeared as men but under scrutiny, their illusions fell aside to Malcor's eyes. They were both fire giants. Malcor rested his head back into the River as sight and sound crashed back in on him. As before, he felt the weight of the River as fatigue. He shook it off as best he could.

"Two of you to guard this place is impressive R'Dar Kerckhi <emphasizing the draconian plural of *fire giant*>. With hundreds if not thousands of travelers each day, any normal empire would place a garrison here. That two such as yourselves are here! It is truly our honor to meet you. I pray you find your quarry. We are not it. Dar Rojo and Dar Shara have ordered us to the Temple within two day's time. Will you let us pass?"

Calvin adjusted his gear so that his shield dropped down and became more obvious to the guards as well. Simultaneously, they burst into laughter, drawing more than a few stares from other travelers as well as the shrine's prefect, who stepped out to them. "What is going on here?"

Before the prefect could say another word, the fire giants each slapped the boys on the shoulder. Calvin went flying backwards from the friendly slap, though Malcor braced himself and took it. They said, "These two paladin initiates are on their way to the Temple. They are clear to pass!"

He looked at Malcor and with a wink whispered, "Kaia asked us to watch for you and tell him which way you went. YOU are the quarry." Both burst into laughter again.

After walking several minutes, Calvin said, "I cannot believe. How did you do that? How did you know?"

Malcor shrugged it off. "It was a guess. I just said the right things I guess. Your shield helped too."

"But how did you know to use that title? R'Dar Kerckhi? I don't even know what that means! They're all yelling at you and suddenly you sort of spaced out and then you're all best friends. What is with you Mal?" As they continued, Calvin's questions gradually turned back into sharing what he knew about the Capitol.

The road here, while as wide as the main road to the Bazaar, had almost no traffic. A swiftly flowing stream split the road through its center. To the right and left, estates arose. Some appeared as intimidating and dreadful as the Soldier's Fort. Others resembled grand palaces. Each had a main approach connecting to the road over a bridge. Like their appearance, some had extensive walls, battlements, or nothing at all. In front of one such, Malcor just stopped and stared. The estate appeared to be a well-tended park with trees, meandering paths, and statues depicting different monsters. He thought he saw a wall back in the forest, but could not be sure. "Do you know about this place?" Malcor asked pointing. Stepping closer, the façade wavered and then suddenly a deep ravine and impassable walls became clear. Malcor realized that most of these estates had probably been enchanted to hide their true nature.

Calvin stared for a second and thought. "I think it belongs to a member of the Inner Circle. Either an intelligent silver golem or a dark elf. I can't remember. My father and I never came here but we heard and I was told stories about a park estate like this. There are two of them actually. One is bright like this. The other only looks this way and is an illusion to hide what the estate actually looks like."

As they spoke, leaning on a bridge over the stream, a man came walking around a tree back on a garden path. He wore dark grey travelling clothes and stared intently at a scroll. His long fast steps drew him quickly to the road. When his boot stepped onto the white stone bridge connecting the park to the main road, he appeared to snap out of a trance and looked around. His eyes focused briefly on the two boys and then scanned up and down the street as if looking for something.

He stepped out to the boys and cleared his throat, "Excuse me but will you tell me who all you have seen in the past little while? I have a gold coin for you if you do," he said rolling a coin along his knuckles.

Calvin spoke up, "We've been here for about an hour coming off the Bazaar Road. Been here resting at this bridge for about – what, ten; no five minutes Mal? – and we have not seen anyone except you. We don't need your money. Thank you for the offer though."

The man, something about him more than the estate he just exited, pulled at Malcor. While the man continued what looked to be a brief conversation with Calvin, Malcor mulled it over in his thoughts. According to Calvin, this area served as home for the most powerful and wealthiest of the empire. The fire giant guards had been looking for them specifically. No one else took this road. Common citizens clearly did not use this road. They had not seen any other people the entire time and now here they stood, talking with a servant, no... this had to be someone like the fire giants.

The man kept looking sidelong at Malcor while Calvin danced around the issue of where they were headed. "Your friend is sure quiet. Is he always like this?" he asked turning to look at Malcor directly. His question caught Malcor assessing the man's clothing. Similar to Dar Shara and the king, his clothes draped and looked like the same dark grey material worn by the nobility. Even the boots, though trimmed with shimmering silvery thread, had that dark grey luster. Startled by the abrupt question, he looked up to the man's eyes and took note that the silvery thread briefly resolved as magical runes.

Malcor met the man's eyes and remained silent. The moment stretched and then Malcor finally said, "My lord, you ask who we have seen. We have seen only *you*. I am Malcor. This is my friend Calvin. We are initiates to the knighthood making our way to the Temple." He pointed in the Temple's direction. "So far we have had an interesting journey." He took a measured stare and then added, "You ask who we have met on this road." Maybe road meant more than this particular street. "I've met many interesting people on my road. If you would like to hear more, I'd be happy to come visit you here or you can find us at the Temple."

The man's face split into a grin, "Very good Malcor. You're starting to get it. I am Do'Larus, or Dar'Yx. However, I've been here long enough that most Tanias call me "Daryx". While I will not be calling on you at the Temple – they don't particularly like me there – you are most welcome to visit my estate any time. Either I, or one of my servants, will be able to assist you. Kaia told me to expect something uncommon from you. I see it." For a moment it seemed his eyes glowed purple and Malcor felt the rush of the River and the eyes. Calvin felt it too though not the same.

Malcor remembered the stories and legends about a dark elf who had been recruited by the dragon emperor eons ago, who chose to stay and serve the empire though not the Queen. So, this was *that dark elf.* Probably masked in an illusion like the fire giants.

Daryx turned and with a wave of his hand walked west away from the estate. The parklands seemed somehow dimmer, quieter with each step. The birds and water sounds vanishing in phase to each footfall. "What was with his eyes?" Calvin wondered. "For a moment, I felt like he was looking right through me like he knew everything about me."

Malcor kicked a pebble into the water under the bridge. "You know how these people are better than I do. They see things differently than normal people..." a distant sound caught his attention, a horse galloping at full speed.

Sure enough, a moment later, a heavy charger replete with Temple armor and adornments came into view around the gradually curving road. In contrast to the heavy armor, the charger's rider wore brown leathers and flailed a scimitar or a sabre – hard to tell at this distance – in the air. He was screaming over and over until finally they could hear him. Because the bridges could only be accessed at sharp turns off the roadway, Malcor and Calvin did not move. They just watched, their hands wandering compulsively to what few weapons they had.

Chapter Eight – Tor's Revenge

"Revenge!" the rider screamed and came at them galloping full speed. At the smaller cross-section the rider spun the horse and pointed the scimitar at Malcor. "You! You killed my brother! You are Tor's murderer and I will have your life!" Without a pause, he continued across the bridge from the other side.

Understanding at last what was going on, Malcor drew his long sword as did Calvin. Feuds, revenge, and duals played out frequently across the empire. So long as both parties agreed to it, they fell outside the law. If one party did not, then the law could intervene, though often too late to save the reluctant party. "The Law saves the dead" had evolved as an expression conveying how often these things resulted in the wrong person being killed. In this case, Malcor had indeed killed R'Dar Tor. If he pointed his blade and matched the accuser's movements, it would be a fight to the death. If he pointed his sword down, then it would be a fight to first blood. If he resheathed his sword and called for the law, he'd likely be killed where he stood. This street did not seem to have a heavy police presence. Malcor whispered to Calvin, "Witness," and then pointed his sword tip down.

The rider's eye narrowed and he screamed out, "No!" and charged.

Each hoof strike, each movement of the charger's armor as it rose and fell with the charge, caught Malcor's eye. He held his sword at the ready and squared his stance to the charge. A deep guttural sound rose from his belly and Malcor found the words spilling from his lips, "My Goddess, My Queen, for your glory… this foe. *Coming Undone!*" His words rose and inflected his sword's name. In spite of the tension, Malcor felt a prayerful and reflective mood fall upon him. It strengthened him and quelled his heart's pounding. Like the charger, Malcor felt his arms swell with blood and flexing muscle.

The rider brought his sword in to strike at Malcor's face. Malcor side-stepped and deflected the strike along his blade's edge. Where the blades met, an uncharacteristically non-metallic sound rang out as if a ceramic pot had broken. Small shards of the rider's sword shattered from contact along Malcor's longsword. Malcor finished his side-step and cut into the charger's hindquarters. His sword sliced into the armor and again, the sound of pottery shattering as the armor chipped and then shattered. It felt like he drew blood but the trained charger moved past him across the bridge and wheeled to turn on the other street's thoroughfare.

The rider's sword hilt retained a shattered fraction of what used to be a quality blade. The rider threw it to the side and held up his hand. The air above shimmered and a lance appeared in his grasp. He leveled it at Malcor and charged again. As before, Malcor squared himself to the attack. "My Queen, the emperor wrote that my children's enemies shall be Mine own. They shall fall as wheat caught in the dragon's flames. They shall fall and know not why the earth claims them to its face where My Chosen rise into the sky, full of glory and might. Let no fear, no wound, no poison, no magic, no harm, no dread touch those who wield Her Name in righteousness…" he prayed.

The lance speared for Malcor's center of mass, no elegant attack this time; the rider just wanted to strike a blow. At the last instant, Malcor saw the rider change the charge slightly so as to trample Malcor under hoof should the lance miss its mark. Not wanting to expose himself, Malcor kept his guard and caught the lance on his sword edge where it scraped with a high-pitched and annoying metal on stone sound. Small cracks followed the lance where it touched Coming Undone as it began to disintegrate. Just before Malcor would push back from the attack and attempt a counterstrike, the rider spoke a word and blue lighting shot from his arm into the lance and into Malcor.

The light and shock hit all at once and Mal temporarily lost track of what had happened. When he regained his sight and breath, the rider had reached the other thoroughfare and discarded the ruined lance. A crossbow shimmered into the rider's hand, nocked and ready to fire. He pointed it at Malcor. Malcor noticed the smell of cooked meat and part of him registered the grievous burns all over his body. If he waited too long, the burn wounds would become actual pain and he could tell it would be very bad. He needed to end this fight. Calvin asked if he wanted to switch and Malcor shook his head no.

Malcor drew a measured breath and attempted to fall into the River of

Time, even as the rider's finger pulled the crossbow's trigger. The bolt lurched forward and then Malcor rose out of the River. He saw his opponent slow and freeze, drowning in time. The mounted warrior's aura seethed with black tendrils of hate and greed. The crossbow and its bolt stood out plainly revealed as magical and bearing a poison of some kind. Even the charger bore the markings of magic and Malcor realized in an instant that R'Dar Tor had a powerful and wealthy family. This would not end without a decisive strike. He noticed something else. A darkness hid watching in the background. Malcor regarded the darkness and felt it smile back at him. *The rider can see me like this*, he realized. The bolt arced out of the River and began a slow path to Malcor. A spark of magic pulsed along its spine.

Malcor swatted the bolt back into the River with his sword and waded towards the rider. The crossbow itself flashed and a second bolt appeared nocked and ready to fire. The rider attempted to track Malcor but clearly struggled with keeping pace with Malcor's movements. Close enough now, Malcor immersed himself back into the River...

...and stabbed his sword at the man's offhand side. The charger, aware of the danger before the rider, sidestepped and Malcor's sword bit into the rider's thigh. A fountain of crystallizing blood erupted from the wound. Caught by surprise, the rider pulled back and the charger reared trying to kick Malcor with the steel-reinforced hoofs. The rider lost his balance and fell back out of the saddle.

Malcor found himself confronted by the opportunity to take this man's life. The fury of the temptation took his breath away, but he shook it off as bloodlust. His sword rose once and fell, slicing across his opponent's face. Like the thigh wound, an eruption of crystallized blood, bone, and eye fluid replaced the rider's face. And then Malcor sheathed his sword. Calvin ran forward to grab the charger's reins. The rider struck the ground, his hands rising to clutch his ruined face.

"You didn't kill him?" Calvin asked.

Both boys looked down at the man sliced across his eyes with bone visible across his nose bridge and left cheekbone. Malcor raised his sword, tip down, "You challenged me to a death fight and I countered to

74

first blood. My sword is down. Forsake your vendetta or I will honor your death challenge."

They could not tell if the man could even hear them through his pain. While Malcor had pulled his strike to not be fatal, the man clearly suffered from shock and could very well die from the pain and nature of the wound. Malcor's arms trembled holding his sword as the weight of his own wounds started to grow heavy with pain. "Yield?"

The rider continued writhing on the ground but he gestured as if to say something. Malcor leaned forward a bit to hear the man speak amidst blood gurgling, "Rathos, kill." Malcor dropped his sword through the man's shattered face into the stone pavement right as he heard the charger rear up to club their skulls. Too tired and wounded to really care, Malcor felt Calvin move quickly as Kaia's shield blocked the horse's hoof attack, and then was met with the sounds of a horse dying. Calvin had drawn and sliced the horse's unarmored belly as it reared up.

Malcor slumped back against the bridge railing and then slid down to the ground. A spreading pool of blood traced the pavement stones trailing out from the rider's face. A new one had started from the slain charger. Calvin wiped his sword clean on the charger's gambeson and looked with concern at Malcor. Mal smiled back as best he could but his arms and legs felt heavy and fatigued. He pointed to the man's face, "I think this is what she meant about "unseen". Ha," he choked referring to Dar Shara. He felt cold and realized his burned flesh had cracked and started to bleed in numerous places.

"You moved so fast Mal. How do you do that? When I watch you fight, I feel like I am at a concert or performance. There is something about it that makes me want to cheer for you. How?"

Mal coughed and winced, "You saved my life by taking out the horse… first time I have seen you fight. Have seen you train but never for real…" It felt harder to focus and his vision swam. "You –"

Calvin said something but Malcor could not make it out. He saw a bright flash of white light and odd sounds. At one point, through gray sparkles of light, a priestess looked down at him with concern and said, "He was an armorer? With less conditioning, he'd have died already. Turn his head." Other sounds, other noises and feelings rose and faded.

Finally, against great fatigue, Mal opened his eyes and saw a figure he would later remember as Calvin talking to a white robed person. The blinding light hurt his eyes. When he tried to move, everything hurt but he found he could push through the pain and sat up. Everything felt familiar but he did not recognize even a single familiar landmark. The figure turned to him. The robed person turned out to be a woman wearing ornate jewelry and white silken robes so sheer and close to her porcelain skin tone as to make her appear nude. Her mouth moved but all he heard was a loud rushing sound. Her mouth moved again.

Slowly her words resolved into, "What is your name?"

Malcor tried to answer but realized his name, though on the tip of tongue, would not come out.

"You had a close brush. Your friend over there, Calvin right? - says you're Malcor. Is your name Malcor?" He nodded his head yes. "Take it easy. I have healed your wounds. You technically died probably before the fight ended, but your force of will kept you going." She smiled at him. "My name is R'Dar Ora. I tend the Queen's shrine at lord Sai R'Dar's manor just down the street from here." She brushed the hair from his face and Calvin pulled up a bucket of water from the flowing river beneath them. She wiped his face and he started feeling stronger.

"Did I...?"

"Win? Yes, you killed your challenger. He is part of the Tor family, an influential one from the Merchant Guild. Your friend killed his horse. I have already questioned him and his witness stands. As such, you two are basically free to go."

"What about Tor? Will others...?"

"Come for you? Yes. Well, who knows. These things tend to burn themselves out quickly."

Malcor looked at her and felt there was more to tell. "What else? Is there a way to make it stop?"

R'Dar Ora looked carefully at Malcor and reached out her hand to help him stand. "Try to stand. You're healed and so are fine but will feel weak for some time. You need to get some food and rest."

Malcor stood up unsteadily. She was gorgeous. Not unlike Dar Shara, her closeness made it hard to think. It dazzled him. She continued, "As to the other matter, there are two ways the lords deal with these. The first way is to decimate the family so as to remove their ability to strike back. The other way is to convince them you do not need to be attacked, like a truce." She shrugged and Malcor fell forward into her embrace. "You know because either you are dead, innocent, or worth letting live. Any of that work you?"

Malcor touched his own arms and felt an electric tingle. He pushed himself back and tested his legs. Still wobbly, but he could manage. He let go. None of those really worked. He had killed R'Dar Tor. He looked at the dead body and the charger. "Is it too late to heal them?"

"The man is beyond healing. And resurrection is not something I can do without an edict. Or payment." She walked over to the charger. "The horse though. This is quality. It is dying but can be saved. Is that what you want?"

Malcor replied, "I want both saved but have nothing to pay you with."

"What is a horse like that worth?" Calvin asked.

"Lots. I've never had a need for a horse like this and a war-trained charger with this type of armor. Easily thousands of gold pieces. The armor could be magical and worth even more. Speaking of..." She held her hands out over the horse and prayed. Slowly, the horse's armor and then hooves began to glow. She smiled and turned her attention to the corpse. His boots, belt, something within a belt pouch, and three rings on the man's fingers glowed. "You know, I did not call for the Law and neither have you. If he did not..." she shrugged. "You could just take all this stuff." She opened the pouch and withdrew a glowing potion flask. "Healing potion," she said. "All the glowing stuff is magical. Collectively, this is all worth a fortune."

Calvin spoke up, "We'll trade you the healing potion in exchange for your healing the horse." He smiled trying to be clever and persuasive at the same time. Compared to the girls back in Klenna, this priestess was amazing.

"No," Malcor said. "We need to let this play out. None of these options free me from ongoing entanglement. It'll have to be what it will be. Maybe we can make this less than it has to be though. Can we send a message to the Tor family instead of calling the Law?"

The priestess thought about it. "Yes, all of these estates belong to wealthy and powerful members of the nobility. You could probably hire a servant to take a message."

"What about you?" Malcor asked.

"What about me? I serve Sai R'Dar. I'm a priestess, not a messenger. The Goddess favors you which is why you are healed. The magical item check is just a bonus because I was curious for myself. You'll have to get your own messenger. Maybe your friend Calvin here. I can tell him how to get to the Tor family."

"I don't think so. The message has to bring them here before the Law arrives. This only works if it saves them legal entanglements."

"Oh, I see. Clever boy." She looked at him again, noting his handsome and chiseled features. "I don't remember seeing you two here before. You must be something special to warrant this assault."

"Malcor and I are going to the Temple," Calvin said pointing over his shoulder towards the Temple. "Dar Shara sent us," he added trying to sound important. "Though, just before that, Mal here was challenged by a member of the Tor family and killed him. Mal won. Obviously."

"You're knight initiates?"

They nodded yes.

She pursed her lips. Malcor could not but help stare. Her lips suddenly seemed narcotic in their beauty, perfect, red, and curved. He tried to look away at anything else before she caught him staring and then it was too late. She noticed, and smiled. "Paladins? Well maybe knights. Dar Shara though. Give me a moment."

She walked off a few steps and closed her eyes facing to the sun. She seemed to be praying or casting another spell. After what felt longer than it was, R'Dar Ora turned back and with a gentler expression said, "I will help you Malcor and Calvin."

She walked over to the charger and touched it, praying. Her prayer came out as a softly whispered song and Mal tried to see it from the River, but was too wiped out to make it. The ragged wounds and strained breathing smoothed out as, before their eyes, the wounds healed into fresh hairless but healthy horse. It whinnied and stood.

"Put his body on the horse. I'm going to calm it." While she held the charger's head, her song changed and it visibly calmed enough for the boys to lift and secure the rider to its back. When done, they looked at her and she said, "Lets go call on a friend of mine at Sai's."

Though they only covered two more estates, it took almost 2 hours before they reached the estate of Sai R'Dar. The horse followed the priestess trailing a few steps behind. Its slow and steady clops gave a cadence to their two hour trek. Malcor, tired as he was, struggled to keep pace. After a brief period of silence, Calvin found his stride and began trying to engage the priestess in conversation. "You must be special to have attained R'Dar rank so young!" and so it continued as he tried to catch her attention. Mal had seen this behavior before but it struck him how childish Calvin seemed with this priestess. Things that would have had Klennan girls swooning, she barely acknowledged.

Her polite responses and the sound of her voice helped pass the time and then they came around to the front of Sai's estate. A couple steps before the main gate and the compound appeared to be vacant parkland. Standing right in front of the gate, the estate suddenly appeared as a baroque metallic drawbridge anchored by stone columns adorned with metal statues arching over a chasm of water. R'Dar Ora pointed and said, "This is where I serve. Please stay here. I'm going to consult with a friend and hopefully, that'll be that."

She turned and walked onto the drawbridge. A faint ripple of a magical barrier pulsed between the stone columns and then the boys saw the hundreds of metal statues turn to watch her. Two metal statues, larger than life, regarded her but let her cross unchallenged. An oversized statue of a bird, huffed and glared at them. When moving, the statues had a keen silvery appearance, but the instant they stopped, they took on a cast grey tone.

After a few moments, R'Dar Ora emerged along the drawbridge and passed through the shimmering barrier. A falcon statue of pure silver rested on her arm. "This falcon will summon a Tor representative to meet us on the road to the Temple. This way we can continue. They will not refuse a request from my master." She threw the statue into the air where it flew off south and east.

Turning onto the road, they resumed their trek. Calvin asked about Sai R'Dar. She explained that Sai was created by the dragon emperor and the mage's guild. "Though they have tried and tried, the true spark of life has yet to emerge. Sai is unique. He is a master golemsmith, the master if you will. That falcon is one of his creations. His golems are throughout the empire now. They watch over important places and guard the empire's most important secrets."

"And, you're a priestess and you serve there, for a golem? Does it serve the Goddess?" Calvin's follow up had a touch of incredulity to it.

"Sai does not worship anyone though he regards the dragon emperor as his father, the emperor's sons as his brothers. As a created being, neither he nor the emperor is sure how religion matters for him. By the way, he hates being referred to as an "it". If you ever meet him Calvin, you'd do well to remember that."

They continued even as the sun began setting behind them. The Temple appeared no closer than before though the road cut through the estates to the base of the emperor's mountain, which served as a useful landmark. Ora had said they would stop at a nearby shrine before nightfall. They had made progress, just not as much as it would seem. Soon, sunset turned to twilight. They passed few other travelers all of whom gave them wide berth and made it very clear they had no desire to interact. They had just started talking about Dar Shara and Malcor was wondering how much to tell, when a voice from the shadows of a side road called out. "Are you R'Dar Ora and Malcor?"

Malcor stepped forward his hand on his sword and replied, "I am Malcor."

"We received your message. I speak for the House of Tor. The message said to meet with urgent secrecy if we wish to avoid humiliation. I see my uncle's horse and a body. Is this the humiliation you wrote of?" A man stepped out of the shadows. Unlike the earlier combatant, this one wore the clothing of a merchant, a noble one, but a merchant nonetheless. Like R'Dar Tor though and the rider, Malcor assumed he could summon weapons and if not deadly, probably had not come alone. His words held a dangerous edge to them.

Malcor bowed to the man and said, "My lord, I served at the Tor armory in Klenna until my Age Ceremony. I was chosen by Dar Shara and Dar Rojo to enter the knighthood. R'Dar Tor felt otherwise..."

"Yes, yes. I know this. So, that corpse is R'Dar Tor's brother." The man sighed. "It would seem you are lethal to members of the Tor family young man. I may or may not have a grudge for this. How did it happen?" he asked pointing to the corpse.

Malcor almost answered when R'Dar Ora stepped forward. "I am Ora, of Sai R'Dar's estate and servant of the Takhissis. It is in the Queen's best interest that her paladins are not bound to the affairs of merchants, commerce, and politicking. I have asked and been satisfied that this boy was challenged, fought with honor and mercy, and won the duel. It was properly witnessed by this other here Calvin. My master wishes to repay a debt to House Tor by offering you this chance to keep your own losses from view. Both Tor and his brother were renowned for their sword skill. And their tempers. Malcor," she pointed to him, "was challenged by Tor before Dar Rojo and Dar Shara and the emperor's son Blaze. It was a fair fight and one much witnessed. The normal rules of vengeance should not have applied. To the extent these are still boys, the Law of

Innocence applies first." She pointed to the body on the horse, "As this one should have known."

The man nodded. "An interesting offer. The horse and the gear alone would repay Tor several times for that debt. And yet, this man and his brother are not well known outside the Merchant's Guild. I will have to consider if avoiding possible humiliation and Tor's recovered items is sufficient to repay such a debt." He stepped back and a figure materialized next to him from the darkness. They began whispering.

The priestess indicated that last year, the Tor family had redirected several shipments of raw materials to Sai and as a courtesy had not charged extra. "They opted out of receiving a premium fee but Sai has felt a burden of obligation since. They, of course, knew this would happen. Lets see if they bite. Either way, Sai's involvement will shield you Malcor."

"What is the Law of Innocence?" Malcor asked. It suggested a difference in governing between him and the House of Tor. He did not remember ever having heard that term before.

"At some point, in any heroes' journey, they reach an elevated place in the Empire. Wealth, heroic deeds, might in magic and combat, fame, glory – any of these can elevate your above what the emperor considers the normal people and citizens of Tania. For you, as a nineteen year old just barely finishing your Ceremony but not yet arrived at the Temple, you are an Innocent in the eyes of the law, as it applies to the higher law of the R'Dar and the Dar. The term literally means that you're Innocent of understanding the higher laws."

Calvin chimed in, "This was part of my studies. Yeah. For a Dar to attack an Innocent, it's a big deal. I didn't even think about that. It's one of the few times that the Empire really cracks down on the ruling class."

Ora nodded, "Indeed. Both the emperor and the Temple are particular about the affairs of the rulers not negatively impacting the Innocents. The emperor uses this separation to remind his rulers of their duties and obligations to the people. Too many times, our history shows the mighty becoming destructive. He's seen this play out over millennia."

"Because Malcor won, he could take the entire House of Tor and do what he wants with it, were he a R'Dar."

"He could, but doing so would elevate him out of the Law of Innocents. He'd be fair game to assassination, plots to overthrow him, the financial tools of the Merchant's Guild to lay claim on him, his property, and other "resources" like his family." Ora pointed to where the Tor representatives were talking. "Or, you could self-elevate and remove any thoughts they might have by attacking them now. It's what most Dar would do in this circumstance, but then I am no lawyer. So long as you only attacked their leadership and any of their retinue directly loyal to them, you'd be fine. Probably."

Magical glowing orbs of light ignited and bathed the street in a moonlit glow. The Tor representative walked over to them. "Very well, we accept your offer but on one condition."

"Yes?" Ora said back a bit more sharply than Malcor was about to.

"We wish to interrogate him," he said pointing to the corpse. "R'Dar Tor's will left explicit instructions for his wealth to fall to his brothers, but the King's message implied ownership of the armory going to Malcor – possibly. We just want to make certain. As a priestess, what is your price to assist?"

She smiled and deferentially replied, "A token of your gratitude equal to the value of the information retrieved and offered in Sai's name to the Temple is sufficient, but I dare not do this here. We must be on consecrated ground. Come with us to the Temple, it is where we are heading anyway."

Agreement reached, the representative and the figure from the shadows joined them. They refused conversation and kept to themselves.

Chapter Nine – The Shrine

Eventually, conversation returned to Dar Shara and their encounter with her. Ora hung on their every word and asked questions. Unlike the conversation before, her questions aimed at what the high priestess' personality and reactions were like. The presence of Armageddon struck a note and fired her interest even more as she wondered if the dread lord had feelings for the priestess.

"I dare not say," Malcor said. "Armageddon has a demeanor like that but when I was with the dread lord, all I ever felt was a direct and pressing agenda to do whatever the lord's purpose required. As her guardian, I would imagine that directness might be perceived as something not intended by either. The dread lord is awesome. My guess is that he is amused by Dar Shara and how we react to her, to him, to his guardianship."

This started Calvin asking questions and it occurred to Mal that Calvin had not even been aware of his proximity or time with the dread lord. "But, he is always with her right? And I have never heard that she took a lover... " Ora continued.

Mal cut her off. "R'Dar Ora, I can't! Should I see Armageddon again, my focus needs to be on other things. Each moment I was with him, I felt my life's worth being judged. People in my village couldn't even make eye contact with him. His power was so... and when he dragonshifted and leapt into the sky, it felt like an angel of death had fallen over us. Without the Temple and the knights there, that feeling of death alone might have killed us all."

She touched his arm, lightly, and then grabbed it more firmly to walk with him. "You're going to be a knight right? So, as a priestess, you really do have to do what I say. I want you to tell me EVERYTHING." She smiled at him playfully. "Everything Malcor. I want it all."

Calvin started laughing and Malcor flinched. The Temple appeared to be at least two more hours away. Though night had fallen, the Temple stood alit by magical lights and fires. "Everything? All right." He put his hand on hers. Her skin felt soft and small and warm on his arm.

"I was standing on a hill, the day before the Coming of Age Ceremony. Across the valley of Klenna, I saw Dar Shara and the dread lord standing in the shrine's entry way. I did not know he was a dread lord then. I assumed he was a bodyguard, probably a paladin." He described it all, letting it all come out except the River. He slowed his pace to allow the Tor representatives within hearing range. "So there I was, standing with Calvin before King Rojo. Dar Shara sat off to the side on the shrine's throne. Armageddon had taken to the sky. The priestesses spoke of prophecy and the king spoke of the empire's future. There, before the entire village, the shrine of Takhissis, Dar Shara, Dar Rojo, five dread lords…" he looked back at the Tor representatives and stopped so that they walked into his words, "…including the dragon emperor's eldest. R'Dar Tor kicked me in the back and mocked my desires to serve the Queen. I fell at the King's feet and felt so incredibly angry."

The representatives kept their faces passive and blank but Mal saw his words had registered and they were paying attention. The level of insult, not just to Mal but to the King as well and on such a public stage, would have triggered civil war between even the smallest of families. "Dar Rojo stood me to my feet. Dread Lord Armageddon landed and human-shifted to my side. I was commanded to slay R'Dar Tor. In my heart, within the River, the dread lord and the Queen's voice told me that my purpose, my destiny, would begin with his death." He stared straight into the Tor representatives' eyes without blinking or flinching. "Ora, truthsay my words. After all, how could a teen-aged boy be with such an august group or defeat a duelist of the renown held by my master? Or even have defeated my challenger there," he pointed to the corpse carried on the charger.

Ora nodded, "A truthsay is not required. We have a witness. We also know the reputation and heroic character of Malcor's attackers, both now fallen. How else but by the Queen's decree would a youth such as this be able to defeat them? I will not truthsay. The truth is that you're alive and they are not." She looked at the Tor representatives and sniffed, "But maybe House Tor plans on castrating itself on Malcor's blade and the Queen's will in this regard. You may find it cheaper and more respectful

85

of your House's lives to end this with honor."

They nodded. "We will think on it."

With some urging from Ora, Malcor began describing how the dragons arced through the fire columns during the dance. When she seemed to have exhausted her questions, he asked her about herself. "How did you come to serve with Sai R'Dar?"

"The Golem Smith, I was very young. He is a master craftsman and mage. I don't know how long he has served the empire, but his estate contains temple writings suggesting pre-Imperic Morbatten. He is a wonderful lord though he lacks devotion to the Queen, his loyalty to her son – the emperor Alerius – is without end. My family used to be a great house, but it was crushed out during the Kell Conflict. My mother had hoped to not choose sides and *his* view of that well, here I am."

"So, he..."

"No, no. I was barely walking when the Conflict happened. His faction took me in trust after my mother swore her allegiance to Dar Kell. He took many daughters of the great houses to bring up in the new teachings." She laughed. "My mother probably thought we were all heretics, but she has come around. My house though never recovered. I was given to Sai by the Temple in my own Aging as payment for work he provided the Temple. Sai has been, interesting, to serve." She laughed again suddenly self-conscious. "You were an armorer correct?"

Calvin, not used to gorgeous young women ignoring him, butted in. "Malcor was a blacksmith's apprentice, but in Klenna, he is a genius. He could do things with metal that the armory's best either struggled with or took many extra days perfecting." Calvin noticed that Malcor maybe felt the same about getting this much attention. "One time, my father - the mayor of Klenna, needed his sword sharpened. My great-grandfather's sword, a family heirloom from his stint in Bloodstone. R'Dar Tor wanted extortionist prices to repair it. Some of the masters did not think it was possible. It was a magical blade but rust had set in on the blade near the cross guard. They feared breaking the blade and losing the magic. Several weeks later, Malcor came by and said he would do it. And damn but if he did not do it that very night! It was a perfect repair."

The Tor rep spoke up and interrupted, "Did the mayor of Klenna pay Tor for the repair?"

Mal looked back at them and said, "Calvin, your dad confused the swords. Paladin swords do not rust no matter how old. My forge took in an antique replica of that sword and restored it. The mayor was invoiced and paid. The armory's ledger would prove this."

"We'll be sure to check," the representative said. Malcor knew that when they did, they'd find everything completely in order. Malcor had actually done work on both the replica as well as the actual blade just in case there ever were an audit.

Ora asked, "Is your sword the heirloom one Calvin?"

He nodded. "Yes, I'm the first since my great grandfather to qualify as an initiate. This is probably nothing to the sword Malcor presented at the Ceremony though." He removed the sword and scabbard from its frog and handed it to Ora. She drew the blade just enough to fully view the pommel and keen blade. Scrollwork art and letters describing its bearer and his exploits ran its length.

"A beautiful sword. I can see why your family would have made a replica. I'm sure many asked to see it over the years. Malcor, may I?" wanting to see his sword.

"When we get to a stopping point, sure. How much farther?"

"We'll be at the Fountain of Dragons in about another mile. That's a crossroads between this district, the road to the dragon emperor, the Temple, and the Great Fountain in the merchant district south. There we can either grab a room for the night, or continue. The Temple does not sleep so we can arrive at any time. You almost died and have been on the road continuously. Our friends here from House Tor may want to rest for the night as well?"

No one seemed willing to say they needed rest and so, in silence, they came to the Fountain of Dragons without a decision. The fountain represented each of the cardinal dragons worshipped. Pure water flowed into the fountain basin easily large enough to look like a small, if perfectly round, lake. Bridges arced up over the pool which in turn, drained southwards to fill the basin at the Great Fountain. In the merchant district, the Great Fountain became a play area for children. Here, in the wealthiest district and the most important crossroads of the empire, the pool sat undisturbed and mirror smooth. Looking down into it, Malcor saw the stars and moonlit clouds perfectly reflected except for occasional lapping from the fountain overflow.

Ora walked now in silence next to Malcor only speaking to point out some landmark or correct something Calvin said. Northwards, the road to the dragon emperor's throne glistened in the dark night sky lit by stars and a cloud-covered moon. A merchant's guild tavern straddled the road framed by a human incarnate form of the emperor holding hands to make an arch with Takhissis. The statues stood as high as a four story building. The tavern's windows flickered with light and from even here, the humming of many conversations carried to them on the wind.

Straight ahead, the Temple's road lay marked by a shrine on the northern side and a cluster of other religion shrines on the southern side. Though Takhissis and the dragons enforced an official religion, travelers, customs, trade, and excommunication held enough worshippers of other gods that their presence was officially recognized, even welcomed. The southern road followed the basin's canal to the Great Fountain in the merchant district. Merchant Guild offices as well as the Adventurer's Guild headquarters sat astride that wide boulevard. Malcor felt fatigue grow on him as his eyes traced the Temple road in a straight line up the mountain.

Seeing they had reached a decision point, Malcor finally said what he hoped the others were thinking. "My friends, I must apologize. Calvin and I have been on the road for many days and my skin and clothing reek of my burn wounds. Before arriving at the Temple, I would like to rest and recover as well as change. Priestess, since there are no paladins here, may I ask your permission to visit the Shrine and recover?"

She nodded, and seemed relieved. So did the others. The Tor representatives made a brief fuss over the charger and its deceased cargo before agreeing that Ora could take it. They left to the northern tavern and agreed to meet at first sun to make the climb.

When Calvin and Malcor crossed the arched entry to the shrine, a sob of relief almost escaped them. The shrine had been set out with a banquet of food, drinks, and a wash basin awaited them. Twinkling lights floated in the air and various functionaries bustled about while chanting an ancient hymn in the Temple's sinuous and raw dragon tongue, the first language dragons taught their human children eons ago. A young girl, probably an apprentice, came forward and held up a wash basin for Ora and then similar basins appeared for Malcor and Calvin. The water smelled faintly of roses.

After washing their hands and face, the apprentice sat Ora at the head of the table while Malcor and Calvin found themselves puled to a side passage and then into a bathing room. Their guides pointed to the flowing water dripping down from the ceiling and then to the steaming pool of clean water clearly meant for relaxing. They tugged on their clothing and when stripped, vanished. Suddenly, the smell of food and a voice saying "Don't make me wait" carried in on a breeze. The boys quickly cleaned themselves and were glad to see their clothing returned clean.

Minutes later, they sat down to Ora's side. She bowed her head and prayed thanking the Queen, the Temple, and the dragons for the bounty of food, the gift of fire by combat, and the Queen's justice in preserving and bringing them together. Though basic fare, the food tasted fresh and better than anything they had eaten since leaving Klenna. As apprentices cleared the table, Ora indicated she would like to see Malcor's sword. "I have heard of the apprentice's sword. Now that I have seen it drop a mounted enemy and heard the story of how you slew R'Dar Tor, I would like to hold it." She held out her hand.

Malcor drew the blade from its scabbard. In this place, it made a soft keening sound. Candlelight caught its razor edge and set the golden script work aflame with red and orange. As he did every time, he noticed something not quite right with it. "It feels a little top heavy since the Ceremony," and then turned it sideways for her to take.

Holding it sideways against the light, she bent forward and looked at the calligraphy along its tine. "No story of a great grandfather here. You chose to inscribe scripture, and in the dragon tongue?" She ran her fingers along the writings. "You chose a scripture from the first age's ending. Interesting." Seeing Calvin's questioning look, "A passage describing when Chaos tried to eat creation, and failed. It marks the beginning of Time, of death, of humans, magic, elves, and other races and monsters that fill this world. Of the gods."

"Oh yeah, I remember that," Calvin said, pretending to know.

Malcor just held the sword still for her scrutiny. "I always imagined it as a time of heroes, fighting against Chaos, but since meeting the King, the Priestess, and seeing the dread lords, I now understand that there is another meaning." Seeing Ora look up at him and testing, he added, "That Chaos was trying to stop the River, and before the River, all of creation was godly."

"I can't believe you made this. It is light and balances like one of Sai's best. Do you know magic?" He shook his head no. "Yet it is built with powerful magic. A gift from the Goddess no doubt." She looked straight down the blade and took a few practice swings. "Did you know that your sword, this sword, is famous? I've heard my matron speak of it with some of the paladins in her entourage." At last, she held the blade to her lips and kissed it. "Thank you," she said handing it back to Malcor.

A small statue of the Goddess wrought in a dark grey silvery metal and etched in Temple script looked over the room and a series of nondescript stone benches. Ora moved to and sat on one of these. Calvin and Malcor felt exhausted and finally freed from the hunger of travel could easily have gone to sleep. Instead, they found themselves sitting down and taking in the shrine's interior. To break the silence more than anything else, Calvin finally asked a question. It echoed more than it felt it should in the stone-chamber. "Can you tell us what happens tomorrow?"

Ora, who had been looking at the Goddess' image, turned around to face Calvin. She explained that when they arrived at the Temple, they would need to find any member of the knighthood and introduce themselves.

"Be careful though. There are multiple orders within the knighthood and they are quite competitive. In a way, this is how you select which order you apply for. That knight will take responsibility for your indoctrination, qualification, and training. Every year, around this time, many initiates come to the Temple. Most arrive as part of Temple service. The actual number of initiates directed to the knighthood is always, surprisingly, quite small. Still, it is so exciting!"

Doubly exhausted from his earlier combat and relentless travel and wounds, Malcor felt the room swimming. Ora may have asked a question of him, but when he tried to focus, he found instead an exhausted sleep.

He woke in a small room on a flat wooden pallet, what passed for a bed for low ranking members of the Temple. His clothes, all mended and cleaned to near new condition, waited on a chair. It felt disorienting to wake up naked, but he felt a thousand times better than the night before. He stretched and noted the areas of pink skin where the Ora's healing prayer had mended burnt and dying flesh just hours earlier. The Shrine sat quiet and from the dim light, he thought it might be pre-dawn. Across the hall, he noted Calvin's prostrate and apparently also nude form.

He stood up and stretched noting that even his boots had been repaired and polished. He heard a humming sound from the Shrine's main chamber and recognized the tune as a nursery rhyme common in Tania. It told the tale of how the dragons had pledged themselves to the Goddess and in turn creation had pledged to the dragons as protectors. He found himself whisper singing along as he got dressed and at last stepped out. Ora stopped when she heard him in the hallway. When he arrived in the main room, he looked but did not see her. The light grew and turning around he saw a patio open to the east where the sun had begun to climb through a low dip between the Temple mount and the rest of the mountain range. Ora sat on a stone step watching eastwards.

He debated joining her when she asked, "Is your friend still sleeping?"

"Yes. I don't think the mayor's son had to wake up as early as my master did me at the forge." An attendant came out with a small platter of fruit, cheese, and water. He took it and walked out to the patio.

Any second the sun would rise and the first ray of morning would shoot out. "There is often a mist over the city and the eastern mountains this time of year. The humidity and higher altitude here makes it happen. Then you get all the fires in the city. Look!" A spear of sunlight cut through striking Malcor's left hand where he stood. She looked at his hand and then added, "An omen. Watch," and lifted his hand so the spear would continue into the Shrine. It struck the Goddess statue. Somewhere a chime sounded. "Normally, blocking the first day's light is considered bad but for innocents who do not yet understand, there is prophecy for each to be touched by the light before the Goddess. I'd imagine that right now, all across Tania, your experience is repeating. For some, the light strikes their face, or chest, or leg before continuing into the main chamber. To touch the Goddess next, is an omen of good fortune. For your hand, an omen of strength of will and action. Go and look at the Goddess statue where the light shines."

Malcor went in and saw Temple script glowing in the sunbeam. In fact, the entire statue's every surface contained writing. "The Goddess breathed and Her Air burnt like fire, froze as ice, stung as venom, danced as lightning, and all but the darkest of shadow witnessed Her gift. Let creation bear witness that it is mine, she said, and I gift it to all My Children." Ora walked up behind Malcor and touched the script. "Speak the verse," she whispered. "My master Sai has granted you a gift."

Malcor read the verse with the odd draconian lilt, doing his best to inflect the Temple language. Ora held in her hand a gleaming silver rose cast of metal that reflected light as if water. As he spoke the words, small red script appeared in fiery letters along the rose's petals. When he finished, she let go of the rose and it hung in mid-air. It slowly began to rotate. Each petal and leaf in the perfect replica threw light from the sun in a prismatic spray. "It's beautiful. I've never seen anything like this. Why?"

Ora nodded and lightly touched the rose. At her touch it made a soft humming sound like crystal when rubbed with a wet finger. "Sai is a master golem smith. His best work is with mithril. But he has an artistic streak as well. He makes these for another House, the one you met earlier – Daryx. Sai gave me this gift when I finally passed my Temple rites. I want to give it to you." She blushed. "So you don't forget. Touch it…"

She took his hand and lifted it to the flower. A similar hum but deeper sounded out. She touched it a second later, and her sound rose up over his. "Every person has a different aura. I'm not a fortune teller, but I can hear one, were she here, telling you that this omen, this scripture, means you have all dragons balanced within you but you have a rebellious nature. Do you believe that?" She laughed. "The shadow dragons. I've heard Sai speaking with others that soon, even the shadow dragons will join the dread lords. When you study, look at the shadow dragons through the lens of prophecy rather than metaphor. They're real." She plucked the flower out of the air and placed it back in a leather-like pouch but padded. "Here."

Malcor took it and thanked her. Her face seemed bright and full of color, especially her eyes. When Calvin stepped out of his room rubbing his eyes and face, both of them broke their gaze and she stepped back. Outside, they heard two horses walk up and riders talking to the Temple attendants. The House of Tor representatives had just arrived. It would no doubt be a long day but Mal found him looking at Ora whenever he could. The butterflies in his stomach and the way he found her looking back at him made the morning breeze by.

Chapter Ten – House Tor's Fate

All too soon, they joined a growing crowd of travelers making their way to the Temple At Morbatten. Like Ora, some members of the group were obviously Priests or Priestesses. People afforded them lots of space. At one point, a young girl barely able to walk stumbled into their way and Ora caught her as she almost fell. The parents rushed up full of apology but Ora set them at ease. She held the little girl and whispered a prayer. To the girl's delight, a butterfly-sized dragon began dancing in the air just in front of her face. The girl turned to chase it, towards the Temple. "I hope that helps," Ora said to the parents.

The Temple looked close but Malcor realized that he had failed to understand how massive the structure actually was. When they finally reached the bottom steps, and he stood looking up the 100 steps to the grand entrance, he finally got it. The Temple had not been built for humans to worship the Goddess. Its audience had allowed humans to use it. Its audience was dragons. While Armageddon might have had to humanshift to enter, any of the other dread lords would have easily been able to walk or even fly directly in. Almost black columns held the roof, each covered in pictograms and Temple script that varied with the color and story by dragon type. A knight stood at the base of each column. The northern side of the Temple had a smaller door for those serving. As they climbed, their group joined many others at the entryway.

Calvin took out his shield and carried it proudly, "Malcor, you should do more to stand out. We don't belong with the normal supplicants. See? Look!" Calvin pointed to a knight walking towards them on Calvin's side. Mal thought about it and decided to not – "be unseen" stood out in his mind and he actually found himself wishing he could shrink himself. He adjusted his position so that Ora would block any of the knight's gaze that seemed to be in a position to spot him.

The knight reached Calvin and greeted him formally. "I am R'Dar Hess, Order of the Shield proctor, and you are?"

"Calvin of Klenna, initiate to the knighthood!" and he stepped away with the knight.

Ora did not indicate she noticed. The Tor representatives following looked concerned until they saw no one taking Malcor. They entered the Grand Chamber. What could have been a life-sized replica of the Goddess in her dragon form reared up in glory at the opposite end. Her dragon heads circled around to look at a raised platform on which rested a throne and podium. The platform appeared to be held up by the hands of the Goddess in her female human form. The noise of voices merged into a din against which a chorus of children, already slotted into the priesthood, sang hymns. As other Temple workers moved about, they also sang in perfect time.

Just below the platform, a knight stood at attention, watching over everything. Malcor knew at that moment where he would go. He tapped Ora on the shoulder, "R'Dar Ora, I have business here and must honor the House of Tor. I also see where I must go, to be a paladin."

She followed his eyes to the knight by the dias and then led them to a side room. She consulted with a priestess and then came back to them. "The Temple will enable questions. Tor will pay in silver, here." They did so. A scribe brought them a parchment and silver traded hands. The Priestess returned.

"This is not an affair of the Goddess or the Temple. However, for Her Children, she grants this request to question the dead." She raised her hands out over the corpse and prayed. Another acolyte entered with a paladin, who placed his sword above the corpse's ruined face. The Priestess wound her arm through the air as if reeling in a line and then pulled. What could only be a soul tore free from the corpse, or returned to it. The difference felt key but Malcor could not tell on which side the difference mattered.

"Brother, we have questions. Why did you attack this boy?"

The soul looked around as if listening and then replied, "I received a message from our estate in Klenna. This boy will destroy the House of Tor. My brother's words... "Should I die, the boy must die. Kill him."

The soul suddenly appeared agitated, its eyes darting around the room. The priestess looked at the Tor representatives and said, "We cannot hold the dead very long, as you know. The jade god watches us. Be fast if you have any other questions."

The man nodded and said, "Brother, did you ever discuss any other way besides killing Malcor?"

The soul's agitation had grown to alarm and Malcor imagined it would have been backpedalling away from them if it could move. It shook its head and then whispered, "Don't let this boy..." and then the whisper turned into a scream of horror. The priestess by the door quickly silenced it with prayer, and the head priestess cut the spell cord holding the soul present.

Malcor found his mouth had grown dry. The room felt darkened and several passerbys stopped and looked into the room was nervous glances. The paladin, his sword not having moved or quavered, swallowed. "That was close," he said.

Malcor found the Tor man staring at him. While the Priestess cleaned the corpse for burial and did whatever else needed to be done, the man said, "Do you hold ill will towards our house?"

Malcor met his stare and when he did not answer, the man continued, "R'Dar Tor made it very clear that you were to be treasured and accommodated and incented to stay at the Armory, no matter the cost. I did not know of any decision to enforce that by threatening your life. With their deaths, I am now the head of the Tor House. They believed you would destroy the house. Will you?"

R'Dar Ora walked up behind Malcor and put her hand on his arm. "He could," she said smiling. Her words smacked the man but he held his ground and looked waiting at Malcor.

"The Armory and the master smith Ishan... they are and have been my family. Even R'Dar Tor. I grew up there. None of them understand the business of the Armory outside the actual day to day work. Without a business person, it will surely be destroyed. Not by my hand though. Besides, I made my intent crystal clear to R'Dar Tor and even this one that I am to be a paladin, not a blacksmith, and certainly not whatever

96

this is." He paused and looked in their eyes and wondered if he should view them through The River. He added, "Unless it is the Goddess' will that your House fall."

That last part hit them again like a physical blow and before they could retort, Malcor drew in a deep breath and continued, "Consider this. R'Dar Tor, in the presence of the five dread lords, the King, and Dar Shara of the Temple of Glass plus who knows who else would be in such a place, sought to humiliate me. The KING ordered me to kill him. How can you put me in a position to defend myself from such humiliation and then also expect even a reasonable person to disobey Dar Rojo? Would you?" He breathed and let the silence stretch. "If House Tor is destroyed, it is because R'Dar Tor humiliated it beyond repair."

Ora squeezed his arm. Malcor imagined he could hear their resolve breaking like glass shattering in slow motion.

The man slowly bowed and uplifted his hands, the traditional show of obeisance. "On my word, House Tor will not and shall not pursue you. In express keeping with the King's command, the Armory shall remain Tor's but under the leadership of your master. We will steward it to their benefit. In exchange, I ask that you absolve House Tor of these two attempted death threats. And any lingering resentment from what happened in your Aging."

Malcor looked down at the man kneeling before him. It seemed like the kind of solution that would put this forever behind him. It felt off though and he could not explain how or why it felt that way. For just a moment, the River pulsed around him and he saw what looked like a hand sign flash from the man kneeling at his feet to the other.

He felt Ora step back and away from him as if jolted by energy. Against the magical silence of the room's barrier to sound, only their words shared between them. But, he heard another voice – a woman's voice and the same one that had told him to slay Tor – "House Tor is yours my son. Take it."

As the words came to him, he felt his sword somehow appear in his hand as he stabbed it forward into the top of the man's head. "…coming -" His

97

sword speared through skull, brain, and into his neck column. A second later, he removed his sword "…undone. House Tor is mine." The lifeless corpse dropped to the ground by his feet and he pointed to the other representative who had half-drawn a wand of some kind. "Tell your House Tor, it is my House. Let any who protest come and protest to me. I will be training. I suggest they come quickly lest they find themselves fighting against the Queen's chosen."

The servant, caught off-guard by the sudden violence, started shaking and murmured, "Yes…" put his wand away, and then fled.

Malcor wiped his sword on the man's cloak and resheathed it to find everyone staring at him. The paladin spoke first. "How do you know the Talon Strike technique?" referring to the head stab attack. "Would you join my…"

"My lord," he interrupted the paladin. "The Queen calls me to a different order. I believe my business is done here. Ora?"

She stepped forward as if commanded. She seemed a bit surprised by her unquestioning obedience. "I owe a debt to you and your master. As a gift, I grant a tenth of the Tor House's property to the shrine at Sai's estate. Will you administrate my gift?"

Chapter Eleven – The Order of Water

Their business concluded, Ora wished Malcor good fortune as she pointed to the central podium and noted all the other paladins all throughout the Temple complex. Malcor looked around at each, smiled and said thank you one last time. He had no interest in any of them except the knight standing atop the raised tower in the central chamber. He circled the tall podium so that he would not be in the gaze of the one near its top, watching as the guard's head turned side to side. With the crowds, it took some time, but at last he reached the steps. He would need to wait for any distraction and then sprint. Only luck would get him to the top.

He meandered with the throng of worshippers near the stairs for many long minutes before a commotion near the entrance seemed good enough. He lunged taking the steps two and three at a time. The stairs wound round and round the tower, but he knew his luck would not last long enough. Almost on cue, he heard someone shout "Look!" Fingers pointed at him and he slammed into the fully-armored chest of a knight. The impact almost knocked him backwards and out into space, but the knight caught his arm and steadied him.

"No one is allowed here. Leave." He immediately noted the guard must be female. He had not expected that.

Breathing hard, Malcor grabbed the knight's breastplate and heaved saying, "No. I want to join your order."

The knight laughed, too quietly for any to hear except Malcor. The knight lifted the visor on the armor's helmet and Malcor gazed in the scarred face of what would have been a beautiful face. Realizing his own scars and the hypocrisy of that thinking, he put it out of his mind. Activity in the Temple stopped as everyone watched. "They wait for me to throw you to your death. Do you know what Order I serve?"

"I know you serve Takhissis." He transitioned to the Temple language, "I pledge my life to Her Cause."

Her eyes narrowed. The crowd had started chanting, "Throw him! Throw him! Throw him!"

Her hand turned from his arm to chest and then a force blast blew him backwards straight off the stairs out over the throng. It really hurt, but he did not fall. After the disorientation and the excited gasps of the crowd, Malcor looked back to the knight. Her arm twisted with magical energy like a snake coiling out to hold him mid-air.

She addressed the crowd, and Malcor saw R'Dar Ora step out to see, and also Calvin with the knight from earlier. They all watched him twisting in the air, trying to get some sense of balance. "This boy wishes to be a knight!" She squeezed and the coils wrapped around him violently, chokingly. "Tell us why boy!"

Shame for another public humiliation warred in him along with the same growing rage he had felt in the sand at Dar Rojo's feet. He almost lost it. Somehow he fought it back. He could hear people in the crowd laughing and pointing. No one ever believed in him. Sure, the knights loved his work in Klenna, but while they shared their stories none had ever taken him seriously. "I am serious. I. Will. Be. A. PALADIN!"

"The Queen alone decides that, but for now, we might give you a chance! Why?"

"I have decided to follow the Queen, here, to you. To this Order. Don't make me fight – "

Laughter erupted. Finger pointing became clapping and wild cheering. "You would fight me?" the knight asked sarcastically. "You dangle above the crowd that wants to see you fall. Tell me why."

"It is my destiny!"

The knight signaled for quiet and in that sudden silence, the coils holding him relaxed and he felt the pull of magic bring him back to the stairs. "It has been more than a few years since any have sought out our order. What is your name?"

"Malcor."

"Your father?"

"Dar Kell," he said feeling it somehow right noting how she choked at the name.

His father's name did not seem to phase the lady. She pressed, "Profession? Skills?"

"I trained as an armorer and weaponsmith. I speak and write Draconian. I see the River."

Loudly for all to hear, she said, "Very well, you may try." Then, as applause and cheers began roaring out, she said more quietly to him, "You SEE The River?" The applause continued. "We'll talk more away from here. Give me your sword and kneel."

She lifted his sword straight in the air and a pulse of energy blasted over everything in the Temple. People moved their mouths still cheering and then looked around in alarm at the lack of sound. Kids laughed trying to scream but all had gone silent, except the lady knight's voice. The knight's voice proclaimed, "Malcor of Klenna. Kneel now, armorer by trade but rise up, Knight of Takhissis and initiate of the Order of Water."

Malcor noticed her eyes dance along his blade as if she recognized it.

Chapter Twelve – Interlude of Kings

Unseen, a man in dark priest robes sat atop the statue head of the Queen. Below him, he watched Malcor stand and receive back his sword. "You are certain that this is the one to succeed you?"

Dar Rojo also watched and answered, "Yes Kell. Even Armageddon saw it same as I. Though Armageddon later met a small girl, who may be the other. Her name is Klara. She is special and was present at the ceremony, so the conditions of the prophecy could be true in her."

Dar Kell nodded. "But the boy does not, yet, at least believe he can be king. I can see that he will be a strong addition to the Order of Water. It's almost a miracle that any of them survived. Looking at him, I cannot tell who the mother was. How do you think he will react to me?"

Dar Rojo poured wine from a crystal decanter into Kell's glass and some for himself. "He will try to view you through The River. No doubt. In his mind, he knows but any ideas he has of his father are likely warped. His adopted father was excellent by the way. He will want to understand if you are more than just a father, but a real father. He has a strong desire to please, but suffers from near berserker rage, like you. Kaia helped with that, a bit."

Kell watched Malcor climb the podium with the knight. When they reached the top, she pointed to the Goddess statue, right at Dar Kell, and bowed low. Malcor followed though he did not see the two men talking atop the statue. "He will be very strong. Rojo, to be king of Tania, he must be ready before you ascend."

"Yes, my lord."

"Instruct the Order to speed his rites, and then you are to take him to Bloodstone. If he is destined to fall in Bloodstone, let his fall be like the epic heroes of myth, and baptize this boy in the blood of heroes."

"Immediately. To be clear, you wish Malcor baptized in the blood of heroes, as per the prophecies?"

Kell nodded his head. "…Let the blood of heroes flow forth and in them, shall LORD's successor, be drowned to rise up. Brought forth by blood and serpent wings shall bear him back to life and to Her Love. So shall it be known that this is the one to lead the children to the last bright Temple."

Malcor's name had just been announced as Malcor Kell. The applause and cheering was deafening, likely audible down in the city.

"It's been almost ten years since we had an initiate in the Order of Water," Rojo noted. "The blood of heroes may be premature. Perhaps a different test first is called for."

Kell just stared. "I'd like to be kept informed of progress. You were right. He has an air of destiny about him. I wonder why he does not sense it. You know, the prophecy does not necessarily foretell your doom Rojo."

"It doesn't matter. My time here feels stretched. All I hear anymore is the Queen's voice urging me into the next. When I stand on Her Throneplane as LORD, and the Lost Temple is reconsecrated, it'll be a glorious day." He stretched. "It is remarkable that your son went undiscovered for so long. Your doing?"

"No, Her doing. The sister too. Our enemies have hunted down and slain all the girl children before their Aging Ceremony. His mother must have either been a sympathizer, or someone placed in my rampage by the Queen for this very purpose."

As they spoke, a light footfall and a whispered apology interrupted them. Without looking, Rojo gestured the newcomer forward. "So, you've already heard. Or maybe were waiting. Who else knows Daryx?"

"All of them my lords. I greeted the boys on the East West Highway. The other was of no consequence. That one though," pointing to Malcor, "deserves special consideration. Long have I waited for just the right type of paladin. If he is, it changes many things."

Daryx stepped in line with Rojo and Kell. His shorter but more graceful elven features stood out against the blocky and grim features of the two humans. "He must pass a hastened initiation..." Kell said.

"…and the Goddess requires the blood of heroes."

Daryx looked askance at them both. "How much hastened?"

"Before the first snowfall, he must be done and ready for Bloodstone. The time of prophecy draws nigh. I will not have time to manage the prophecy and fight the Jade God should it arise here in Tania." Rojo looked at Daryx noting how bright and white his fanged teeth always appeared in dim light. "I ride for Bloodstone whenever the first snow falls here in the valley. You have until then. And Daryx…"

"Yes?"

"Do not interrupt his Order of Water training. He will need to be a full paladin, unquestioned in the eyes of both our allies and enemies."

Daryx nodded. "My lords, by your leave, I will go and ready my teams and start tomorrow."

Daryx gave a traditional farewell in Undercommon, answered in same by both Kell and Rojo. Rojo called back, "By the first snowfall Daryx. No waiting."

From the darkness, Daryx's words floated back with a touch of echo, "Even if he dies, it shall be done."

Kell looked back at Malcor where he walked down the platform. The crowd still cheered. For just a moment, Kell shifted to the River and looked at his son. "Do you know who the mother might be?" the king asked.

"No, but his aura is like Cor'tanos. The shadow dragons will be pleased. I wonder how the Mother will see it?"

Rojo chuckled, "She remembers. I can feel Her wrath whenever the topic of the shade dragons comes up. Should Cor'tanos submit and ask forgiveness, She will seethe but ultimately allow their return. I doubt She will forgive them though, ever. Their departure left our Mother too un-balanced against the Consort to truly seize dominion over all dragons. She hates Cor'tanos for that, even now."

"Who can blame Her for it? They left at a critical moment when the River might have been changed by the eldar. I wasn't even there, but I see it as Cor'tanos' memories and visions and the doctrine of it, it hurts to see. In our terms, it'd be the greatest act of treason imaginable."

Rojo nodded, "And this all means of course, that the prophecy draws nigh. I wonder if Bomoki is out there, looking for that gate in Bloodstone."

"You know he is. It's what he is damned to seek for all eternity," Kell said and turned to leave.

The prophecy had been recorded by the emperor after the last undead war. In that vision, Alerius had seen a human mage, Bomoki most likely, exploring in the Bloodstone Valley. There he had crafted a portal when the Abyss was still young. As Chaos often did, it reacted to creation by spawning around the portal, and hell had come to Tehra. Though Chaos had failed to destroy creation, the jade god had vowed to destroy the sapphire jewel of this world; this one world where creation spawned limitless potential and free will. The emperor had seen the jaden god rise up from a pool of dead heroes and rampage from Bloodstone to the very gates of the capitol. For this, the emperor had prepared Tania's three greatest weapons: the Temple, the Mages, and the Knights. And their northern neighbor Taysor had been poked and prodded by this trident until it too had become at last a shield for Tania.

For hundreds of years, the dragon emperor had nurtured his trident and augmented it with recruited and hard-won allies so that no magic, no weapon, no skill, no talent would be absent when the day came. "Do you think Daryx will break the boy?" Kell wondered.

"No, the boy will not break. I have seen his mettle. He has everything the prophecy requires. More will come with experience and wisdom. For now, I suggest we preserve his bloodline, and watch the sister-candidate, Klara."

Chapter Thirteen - Order of Water

Malcor had been walking for some time into the chambers carved into the mountain beneath the Temple. The lady knight from the Temple walked with him and explained the Order's name. "Water, when calm, reflects everything. No dragon breathes pure water as a breath weapon. Steam, frost, gas, venom… all of these almost-liquids, but not water. Even fire can have a liquid component to it when it burns hotly enough. Water, in nature, is one of the most destructive yet enduring elements. It is also one of the most difficult to control with magic as it cannot be created from component parts. For these and other reasons, we have named ourselves this Order.

"As an initiate, you must become like Water. Ahead of you, is our chapel, our sacred place of meditation. While there, none shall disturb you. You may find visions and you are commanded to record them. Our scribe holds these in a library.

"Your initiation will not be public like the others, though you will participate in those to be seen by the King's order. Tomorrow is a big day for you. You will either become a paladin, or you will die and be lost in the River. Yes, we discuss it openly here. Instructions have come to hasten your training."

Up ahead, Malcor could see an area of light, bright by contrast to their passageway. "Hastened in this case, means what exactly?" he asked.

"It means that where a normal initiate might take months or even years, you are to do it in weeks. As fast as your constitution and health can tolerate. There are normal rites, the ones you have heard of. For Water, the rites are far more intense. We accept only the best."

They entered the chapel and Malcor instantly felt a prickly heat dance along his skin as he crossed its threshold. Stained glass capturing daylight from mirrors above illuminated the dragon emperor's story and his pivotal role creating the religion of the Goddess. Malcor stared at the stories he had grown up to illustrated here in daylight and grinned.

Gray stone benches rose up like a bowl around the large center stage on which a small gold and bejeweled representation of Takhissis stood, the Goddess' human form wrapped about by her many-headed dragon form. She looked rapturous. They walked down steps to the center stage and Malcor noted the stage had written runes all around its edges.

"A combat rune. It allows us to simulate and fight illusions for training purposes. You are welcome to use it. The Order of Water, while not obvious about it, is the best. We serve as the King's and Priestess' honor guard and tend to the dread lords when called on. We have a sacred calling to intervene directly against the empire's greatest enemies. And, I'm not referring to some nation-state like Taysor. Think enemies on the god-level, like necromancy. As such, we watch but are not often seen within Tania. Do not expect the Order of Water, as a name, to bring you fortune and fame. Only you will bring yourself those things.

"And Malcor, while every other Order no doubt tells their initiates the same thing, for us, it is real. You are not to hold yourself to their lower standards."

She stepped into the combat rune and tapped a giant red jewel gleaming opalescent in the room's light. The runes all around flamed into light and a bell rang. "Come, show me what you have. Our fight here will not be illusionary but I have summoned healers to tend you as we fight."

Like a panther with prey, she attacked - her gauntlet slamming into his chest. He imagined he felt ribs crack and then worse when he slammed into the stone benches around the stage. He could not breathe and then a hand touched his face and healing warmth spread through him. His vision cleared and R'Dar Ora smiled at him. "You'll need to be on your guard Mal. The Order of Water is tough and they don't train or play by rules or a code. To die here, is to actually die. No knighthood easy out if you fail."

He drew his sword and re-entered the stage. "You know, I don't know your name yet," he said as he made a defensive thrust to test her guard.

"Wound me and I'll tell you." Her sword ignited with a brilliant ochre fire. The heat washed over him burning his hair and then another strike as

107

the flat of her blade crashed into his collarbone, breaking it. The force knocked him to his knees and as he fell her knee caught his chin. His head cracked back and then healing warmth restored the shattered face, neck and collarbone. "You're dead twice now boy. Come on, show me why you're so special."

Malcor held his blade trying to breathe through the pain and healing and disorientation it all caused. *I must focus*. He began the scripture reference that empowered his sword and felt it respond. At the same time, his opponent began a prayer and the crimson fire along her sword snapped and pulsed and coiled like a ribbon. He charged and stabbed, and her sword struck like a viper wrapping itself around his sword and then his arms and then down into his neck and chest cavity. Instantly, the healing surged holding him on the brink of death as the fire viper of her sword uncoiled and retreated. "Another death," and Mal noted that Ora had been joined by 5 other healers all chanting and directing healing at him. He had yet to even scratch her.

He struggled through the dizziness and fell back into the River. As he lifted his face from the River, he saw her standing there, like darkness in shadows at twilight. The facial scars and signs of age gone, she stood as a twenty-something woman armored in power and wielding an elemental sword that appeared to shift from water to fire to air to earth faster than he could see. From the River's banks, she smiled at him and then struck her aura igniting that place in a rainbow of color that blinded him after that initial dark.

Only vaguely aware of the healers drowning in the River alongside him, Malcor barely parried her attack this time rolling far from her deadly sword, and attempted a counterstrike. She blocked it with a second sword that materialized in her hand and then skewered him with both blades and threw him back into the River.

Life and sound exploded as he laying seizing against both blades, one spearing through his sternum and the other his pelvis. Slowly, he slid down the blades to the stage floor. The flood of healing energy flickered as a priestess collapsed unconscious. And then another. The knight pulled her swords out and took his face. He saw her lips move and then healing from her hands brought him safely back. His first breath of air

108

had never felt so good. His senses were all tangled up between pain, terror, anger, and the ecstasy of healing.

Ora staggered to the stage, scowling at the knight. "No wonder you haven't had an initiate in years!" She took Malcor's body and held it relieved to see he was okay. Blood drool oozed from his mouth and he tried to smile.

"You see the River. Your sword is powerful. But you are not trained. We will correct that." She looked at Ora, "We train like this all the time. To the very brink of death. You must lose your fear of death and replace it with a healthy respect. We stop when the clerics can't keep up with the damage. He's all yours, for tonight at least. My orders are to have him through first rites by tomorrow. Daryx will be coming for him as well. Soon."

Ora's eyes widened. "Daryx? Why – oh, I see. So, he truly is Dar Kell's son?" The lady nodded. "But that means – "

"Yes, time is short and the first rite is, as you know, brutal. More so than perhaps what you have seen as a priestess. Ready yourself."

One of the lady healers lay on the ground still seizing from trying to keep Mal alive. She was carried out by the other four. Ora helped Mal stand. "I've never been asked to heal under these circumstances, but those were battle healers. I must have done well to keep up." She laughed. "Come on Malcor, let's get you cleaned up." Her voice had an excited tone of anticipation.

The hallway leaving the Shrine was huge and decorated with portraits of knights starting with its founding centuries ago. Ora recognized Malcor's opponent as the most recent addition to the gallery. As head of the Order of Water, her name stood out as Dar Kendra of Kell. Kell's sister? Malcor focused on keeping his footing. "What happens now?" he asked.

"We clean you up and ensure you go into the knighthood with a clear head and no regrets." She hugged him close to her for emphasis.

The portraits told the story of civilization and refinement as well as the life stories summarized for the honored dead. Doors opened off to either side and Malcor could hear a restaurant or dining hall at the end, brightly lit. At last, Ora stopped and opened a door. "Your room," she pointed. Though spartan, the quality and craftsmanship stood out. A raised bed platform against the far wall sat near a large table. A bathing pool in the corner and a small pantry full of food all caught his eye.

Ora led him past these to the bathing pool. "Tomorrow you become the Queen's. Tonight, you must recover. And tonight you are mine." Seeing his look, she added with a seductive grin, "Don't worry, the Queen won't mind…" and kissed his forehead. She eased him into the bathing pool, which immediately clouded with blood and then went clear. Placing a platter of food and drink next to it, she urged him to eat. After checking that the room had everything needed, she turned to see him looking glassy-eyed and exhausted. The gashes and wounds, though healed, mixed in with the wounds of his youth. She joined him.

Being underground, Malcor had no idea what time it was when he startled awake to Ora's gentle tapping on his arm. Their time had passed in a blur and at some point, he must have dozed off. "Mal, they're coming for you. For the first rite. This one will be difficult, but I have faith in you. If they let me, I will greet you at sunrise."

Outside, Mal heard soft footsteps of people trying to be quiet. Then, the entire room went magically dark. A sack found its way over his head, but overall except for a whispered apology for disturbing R'Dar Ora, no noise and no clue as to who had come for him. Suddenly, a cold gush of air hit him and he was pushed. He fell, into snow. Gasping, he ripped the sack off his head.

The hooded man they'd met just a day before, from the estate of Daryx, stood before him in knee deep snow. The cold air and snow immediately hit him almost taking his breath away. The starless night masked by clouds failed to tell him where he had been taken. Five others stood around him and a dark black rectangular slice hanging in the air swirled and then vanished. The hooded man, he had originally guessed to be a servant, turned out to be Daryx, the man they'd met on the Great East-West Highway just two days ago, or was it longer?, before.

"Good evening son of Kell," he said. Dark shimmering purple gleamed in his eyes shaded by an oversized cloak. Five others stood in silence around them. Daryx pulled back his cowl and shook his silvery hair. He had more than a few feathers tied there. His jet black skin framed his dark eyes except for dancing purple fire therein. Some kind of leather armor covered his entire body. He smiled and Malcor noted the brilliant white fanged teeth. Malcor remembered that Daryx was a dark elf serving the empire long enough that the name "Daryx" had entered myth and legend.

The others remained hooded. "I'm Daryx. You probably have questions. What you need to know, for now, is that you are on the northern slopes of the emperor's mountain. If you do not reach the summit by sunrise, you will die. You will face dragonterror."

He pointed towards the summit. Something massive moved through the clouds above him. The cold hit him again and he felt keenly aware of his nakedness. His teeth had started chattering and his body shook in the snow. Daryx prompted, "What would you like to ask?"

Malcor looked at them and took his first step up the mountain. A scripture came to mind and he spoke it as he took his next. "By my love, I guard those that are Mine. By their love, shall they be guarded for Mine are precious and I know every one." He started shaking and not knowing what else to do, took another step. His bare foot sank to his knee in the snow.

The five figures touched the glowing feathers by their ears and one by one, they vanished. The massive form hidden in the night's clouds above suddenly felt more dangerous. Daryx opened his hand to wave farewell and called out, "Malcor, run."

And, Malcor ran. Each step sank to his knees or worse, gave way to things masked by the snow. Sharp rocks, branches, soft grasses and leaves, all sensation faded as his feet froze. When he could no longer run, he stumbled and then crawled. The lady's words ran through his mind about replacing a fear of death with a respect for it. The faster he went, the warmer he felt but the growing presence above pressed him down threatening to steal his courage. Fragments of memory, of his night with R'Dar Ora came unbidden to his mind as did a strong desire to stop and sit still.

The summit taunted him, above but hidden and then something swooped down and battered the snow into a drift that washed over him. He clawed his way out of the drift choking on snow. It had to be a white dragon. Supposedly, white dragons were the dumbest and most ferocious of the Queen's kin. Their breath could manifest in any form of winter weather, but – Malcor realized – the dragon's color mattered not at all. *I'm alone, naked, freezing to death, and a dragon is hunting me.*

He felt that massive shape looming near again and for the first time in his life, dragonfear washed over him. He had heard about it, but after spending time with the dread lords and feeling only awe, had dismissed it as rumor maybe even propaganda. Now he realized that the dragon's intent governed that fear. This meant for Malcor to feel it, to be paralyzed by fear and to freeze, the dragon's intent was to kill him. He choked almost laughing at what this would feel like were Armageddon to hunt him. Would it be the same as this white dragon? He looked up blinking into the snow cast by the dragon's flight but could only sense the massive beast somewhere nearby.

He wondered, *how many knights had faced this trial? Surely, most – some had made it. How*? Out of nowhere a cold wind came rushing down the mountain with a torrent of snow. As cold as it felt, Malcor shivered uncontrollably and realized it felt warm. *I'm freezing to death. They say you feel warm as you die.*

When the blast of ice ended, the clouds tore apart to reveal a white dragon hovering in the sky looking down at Malcor. The dragon gleamed white like Daryx's teeth, or white like the whitest thing he could imagine. His thoughts felt sluggish. Unlike the red dragons, this one (maybe all whites?) looked more serpentine and less blocky and ponderous. Its wings beat to hold it there and then it pointed at Malcor with its fore claws and shrieked. What the dragon lacked in mass, its oversized and disproportionate claws made up. Mal could not guess the distance, but the claws definitely appeared to be as long as the dragon's head. Its wings were also disproportionately huge. The dragon, framed by clouds and illuminated by moonlight, appeared beautiful.

The claws closed one at a time till just one remained pointed at Malcor. Its mouth appeared to move and then a single line of ice shot from that finger towards Malcor. Held by fear and paralyzed by cold, Malcor knew he would die. "How, how did they make it?"

Chapter Fourteen – Malcor's First Rite

With that question barely crossing his cold mind, Daryx appeared out of nowhere and touched Malcor. At that touch, Malcor stood on the River's banks. Daryx looked the same but more vibrant. Malcor could tell that Daryx worshipped some other god, but held respect and positive intent to Tania and the Goddess. He, by comparison, looked horrible. He saw his life's thread flickering and though murky in the River's flood, he saw the white spear of ice reaching out slowly towards him.

Daryx shook his head. "You never asked even a single question. Many fail and die in this test. The normal test, you do this with your entire class with some preparation. If you are to survive, you must wrap yourself in the Queen's love. Look at yourself in the River. Do you really think there is any difference between cold, fire, blades, electricity, poison, whatever it is that changes the Queen's appointed time for your life to end? Your life flickers and what holds you here in this place? Hope, fear, fear of failure, fascination with your own death maybe? It isn't you! It is the Queen's place to decide when you die, not some sickly monster. Your scripture is correct, but you must take it literally. As Her Paladin, you must Love your Queen, or die. She does not want you to die. She wants you to live and love Her, and serve Her with your life, not your death." Daryx stepped forward and touched his hand to Malcor's heart. "You must do more than believe. You must know - here. You. Are. Your. Queen's. Knight."

Daryx shoved Malcor back into the River. As he cleared his senses, the bar of ice struck his heart. Still recovering from the River, Malcor felt it touch, then burn, then pierce his skin and spear his heart in slow motion. His heart spasmed as it tore through his back and struck the ground. His body shook threatening to die held upright. He grabbed the pole. His lips moved and frozen, they split and cracked bleeding. "My Queen, my love for you. My dream… to serve."

He labored to breathe and willed his heart to beat. "I am yours." His hands found strength and squeezing, he shattered the bar of ice. The dragon reared up, and the end connected to its claw began falling, twisting and shattering by section. Its wings beat three times and Malcor counted each saying, "I am Yours."

The dragon plunged and rolled, its massive wings folding around as its entire body shot towards Malcor. The length in his heart slipped out and back as he leaned forward and fell to his hands and knees. The dragon's head reached out from the folded wings and its mouth opened, crackling with the terrible power of its breath weapon. "My Queen, I live to serve. I am yours. My dream. Is to love and serve."

Strength and pain shocked through him as suddenly, his deadened limbs came alive. The cloying snow became firm like stonework. He stood and looked up into the onslaught. White dragons breathe winter weather and this one unleashed a blast of razor hail. The deadly cone followed by the dragon itself would no doubt slay Malcor if he did not move, but "Like you, I serve Takhissis." He stood unflinching and the cone of razor hail slammed down all around him, but did not touch him. The dragon fell like a comet, but pulled his maw back at the last instant. The wings opened like a whip and the dragon landed around Malcor. Except for the snow blinding his eyes, Malcor choked back the fear and stood trying not to flinch.

The dragon stared at him, slowly lifting its head back from his. It hissed, "Well done little egg. What changed for you? I saw you die a thousand times and then you enervated... and lived."

Malcor saw cruelty but also the beauty of a world blanketed in clean white, the snow revealing prey tracks, and the infinite chaos of crystalized ice. All this and more, Malcor saw looking into the dragon's eyes. "I serve your mother and love your beautiful dream."

The dragon began wheezing and it took moments for Malcor to realize it had started to laugh. "You? Love my dream? What do you know of my dream? You humans – so arrogant - but you do not know." The dragon opened its claws and looked at Malcor. The dragonfear slammed into him and overwhelmed him. Malcor realized the dragon was testing its own boundaries with the Goddess. Those razor claws turned to him and a malevolent smile creased its white face. "How could food KNOW what a dragon wants?!"

He stood firm but the fear had taken root and his faith shook. Not knowing what else to do, he ran. His first steps stuck in the snow, but then he remembered his faith and how the snow had firmed under his feet. He sprinted. Behind him, the dragon swiped at him, halfheartedly or else he'd surely be dead. He felt its regard and the fear wracked him again, and then nothing as the dragon jumped back to the skies.

Freed from cold, fear, and the sinking snow, Malcor ran straight towards the summit as best he could. His legs above his knees ached and tore with agony. Below that, and his lower arms, nothing. His skin had turned pale gray-white, and multiple lacerations tore bleeding only to then refreeze. He did his best to run, but his feet dragged on the now-firm snow leaving behind a bleeding calligraphic signature of frozen blood. The dragon's mountain towered much higher than the emperor's throne room. The thin air made him pause frequently. He stopped to catch his breath and then proceeded more slowly. After what felt like an eternity, it occurred to him that physical exhaustion or even breathlessness should not impede him any more than a dragon's breath weapon or weather would. He steeled his faith and renewed his sprint to the top.

When sunrise touched the peak, six black rectangles opened in the air from which Daryx and his knights stepped onto the snowpack. Malcor sat crouched down in the snow. They thought he had fallen asleep but he was actually studying the three inch ice-packed hole in his chest through his heart. His cold-dead feet and unresponsive hands had withered to bone poking through the skin on his feet. All was quiet as they listened to the wind and the wheezing sounds of Malcor's breath, as he struggled to stay alive.

Dar Shara embraced Malcor in prayer. For him, he felt death had finally taken him. He'd felt warm since before his encounter with Ynt'taris. Suddenly, that warmth exploded throughout him as red hair, sunlight, and pain lanced through his heart and into his legs. His roar of agony from the healing echoed and then he collapsed into the priestess' arms who stroked his head and whispered, "You're safe now. You survived."

One by one, the knights with Daryx removed their cloaks. Dar Rojo, Dar Shara, Armageddon, the lady knight from the Order of Water, and a fifth he did not recognize all began clapping. "Well done sir!" Daryx

116

exclaimed. Pointing at the unknown, Daryx said, "Malcor, may I introduce Dar Reznor, head of the Mage's Guild?"

While Reznor stepped forward, Armageddon grabbed a handful of snow in his massive fist and squeezed. Steam burst from his gauntlet and then he opened it. A white ring of crystal ice sat there. Daryx took it and stepped to Malcor and Reznor. "This is a ring given to novice knights who reached the summit. Most do not even try. It is specific to this test and bears the name of the dragon you stood against." Daryx grinned. "I, we are all impressed."

Reznor whispered a spell and stabbed the ring through Malcor's ear. As it magically sealed, Reznor said, "Your ring commemorates your match with Ynt'taris, patriarch of ice breathers."

Rojo stepped forward now and Malcor noticed that the king had an identical ear ring. In fact, except for the dread lord, all of them did. "Malcor, you have passed your first rite. A process that often requires months of training to overcome dragonfear alone. And, then months of physical conditioning to survive and overcome with faith the trial here that would kill a normal person. We have great expectations for your progress." He looked at Malcor's legs and arms. "You lost your flesh but faith and resolve carried you through this. The Queen will always guard you, and in the end, it is your faith and trust in Her that kept you from dying."

The king, Dar Rojo, stepped back and bowed to Malcor, as did the others. Dar Shara stepped aside and Malcor saw R'Dar Ora rush forward and prayed for healing to continue what Shara had started. He had turned himself off to the cold and fear and pain. Though still cold and freezing, he tried to stand but his legs betrayed him and once again, Ora helped him.

The lady knight from the Order of Water stepped forward and bowed low. "Squire Malcor, you have passed your first rite. You have received the Knight's Ring," she touched the cool ice ring through his ear, "and stand here on Morbatten to greet the sunrise." She switched to draconian, "Does not the Mother look after Her Children?" She withdrew a pair of boots from the folds of her armor and, kneeling, helped Malcor step into them. "These will protect you from Nature's wrath. Wearing them, you will always feel perfectly at ease whether in a place like this, or in the hottest desert."

They felt warm. In fact, even standing there naked, the chill vanished completely. Aware of the cold, but unaffected by it, he expressed his thanks. The King stepped forward again and held out two rings of dark grey metal. He placed one on each of Malcor's hands. In draconian, he said, "Her Children shall wield Justice in their left hand and Righteous Might in their strong right arm." He took Malcor's left hand and raised it up to the sun. "This will summon or dismiss your armor. The ring is linked to your breastplate by the Temple." Same with his right arm, "This is linked to your sword, Coming Undone. You will learn how to summon without conscious thought. Until then, squeeze your fist and say either Justice or Righteous Might. Give it a try. Dismissal is harder than summoning so for now, focus on summoning."

The king stepped back. Malcor squeezed his left fist and said, "Justice." Within a second, dark grey plate armor bearing the Order of Water's crest framed him, fitting perfectly. Its chrome silver gleam and Temple script sparkled in sunlight and snowy white all around. "Righteous Might!" and his sword leapt into his hand, ready.

Dar Rojo smiled, "These gifts are tools. You do not own them. They are the Queen's."

Reznor now stepped forward and placed his hands open near Malcor's temples. He began to chant and Malcor felt something enwrap his head and then take on the leather feeling and weight of a helmet. A nose guard and visor covered his face in the same dark grey metal and then vanished. Not quite vanished, he realized, the helmet's weight was still there but it was invisible. When Reznor finished chanting, he took a deep breath. "This helmet is separate from your armor. The Emperor desires all knights of the Order of Water to have special protections. It responds to physical and magical attacks. Its limitation is that it can only protect against one or the other, but not both at the same time. When masked and near invisible like this, it protects against magic, particularly the type that would influence your emotions and thoughts. When in physical form, it completes your armor and serves as an actual helmet."

Armageddon now stepped forward. "Human, you have much to learn. Do not let all of this go to your head. Hold still." Armageddon removed one of his massive gauntlets. His hand skin showed black and red tinged reptile scales but the end of his index finger elongated into a dragon claw and burned red hot. Without warning, he stabbed the claw into Malcor's heart.

Malcor choked and though he tried to retain his posture, he failed and writhed twisting on the burning claw. "This," twist, "is to remind," twist back, "you always that," twist up, "you live by," he lifted Malcor off the ground by that single burning claw and roared "our permission!" He ripped the claw out and caught Malcor to his feet as he fell. And, Dar Shara had somehow come from behind with another healing prayer that held him for a moment on death's door and then fully revived him. He felt Ora choke as she barely caught him adding her prayer to Shara's.

The dread lord stepped back and Dar Shara came around. "You'll have to get used to this. The Queen has no use for knights who fear pain or death. We will continue to kill your fear of death until all of it is gone from you." She smiled and the seduction in her smile stole his breath away.

She stretched her arms up to the sky and three times said the Queen's full name in draconian. On the third time, she placed one hand over the torn hole in his breastplate and other on the pommel of his sword. Golden light followed by flashes of the prime dragon colors – red, blue, green, black, white, and then darkest blackness. Where she withdrew her hands, the Temple symbol of the Queen adorned his mended breastplate and the pommel of his sword. "These symbols will allow you to channel the Queen's power, as if a Priest, when there is no member of the Priesthood with you. They also proclaim to all that you are a Knight of Takhissis. You are instructed now to return to your quarters and rest. Eat. Heal. Many initiates fail this first rite, either by dying or losing heart when presented with these gifts. You have done well. Our Mother is proud of you Sir Malcor!"

Each of them stepped back raising a weapon before their face in salute. The king and the lady knight raised their swords, Reznor a wand, the two priestesses their Temple maces, Daryx a scimitar, and Armageddon a dragon claw. Malcor raised his sword and returned the salute. Black doorways opened at Reznor's command, and stepping through, Malcor found himself with the others in the main room of the Order of Water.

Eleven knights sat in full armor in the chapel and stood as they appeared on the stage. Healers, battle priests, and others sat behind them. The lady with Malcor turned and addressed them, "Fellow knights of the Water. Meet Sir Malcor, our newest member!" The sword salute was repeated by each who then withdrew their helmets and greeted Malcor with their name and title.

At last, the lady knight who had brought Malcor in and then beaten him, stepped forward. "Sir Malcor, for now, you are my squire and I will mentor you in the Queen's Grace. I am Dar Kendra, eldest sister to Dar Kell. I guess that makes you my nephew. Don't let it go to your head. I was the first priestess to crossover to the rank of paladin. I have fought in three Bloodstone Campaigns and currently serve as special advisor to the Circle. I am a dragonshifter."

She turned to the others and said, "Let it be known that last night at second bell, Malcor was taken to Morbatten's peak, and naked on the northern face, summited after facing the white dragon Ynt'taris. Having achieved his first rite, he has been ordered to complete all three rites before first snow. He will need all of our help to do this. After careful thought and consultation with the Temple, I have decided that R'Dar Tembri shall serve as Malcor's battle priest. Let him come forward."

From the back of the chapel, Malcor heard a slight commotion that sounded like congratulations being whispered. A middle-aged man, strong, and covered in scars walked boldly down to the stage and bowed low to Malcor. "Sir Malcor, may my faith be your shield and my strong arm the beam on which our enemies shall break." He stood and Malcor realized the scars were actually barbarian tattoos reminiscent of the northern wild tribes the emperor kept mostly separated from the rest of the empire.

Kendra added, "R'Dar Tembri has been groomed to serve the Order awaiting a new initiate for five years. Because our Order rarely has new initiates, we actually have a number of battle priests ready." She looked out at the area in the back from where Tembri had stood. "To you still waiting, patience. A time is coming when you will serve the Order of Water. And, we will require your skill in the days of Malcor's second rite.

"As I just noted, Malcor is to be hastened. The next rite requires combat. Knights of the Order, we will be outnumbered and so you will each receive an additional battle priest. Battle priests, step forward and be chosen now! Daryx will share with us the details of the next rite."

Daryx stepped forward and began, "So, our southern trade partners at Ori have requested our assistance. They asked Taysor first but my sources say Taysor has dispatched a group by boat that will not arrive in time to make a difference. Intervention and contingency is what I do for the Circle. So, I met them on their way to Taysor and offered Tania's help. As you all know, Ori is a small fortified kingdom on the northern bay of the island of Khasra. They are also an important trading partner and do not restrict the Queen's worship amongst its people. Their culture and martial arts hold a special place in Dar Rojo's heart.

"A party of adventurers there recently uncovered an ancient ruin beneath a mountain. While mapping it, the adventurers came under attack and were forced to retreat. The attackers followed them back to Ori's southern wall, which is now under siege by all manner of foe. Of particular interest is the appearance of a lich who is either leading the attack or is fronting the actual power behind it."

At this point, he asked Reznor to activate the combat rune and an illusion of Khasra appeared. The southern gate of Ori then came into view and Malcor noted the Imperic appearance of its architecture. The illusionary view of the gate then opened out to a road heading into Khasra's center. Malcor remembered from his studies that there are two paths to immortality. One is Ascension where a hero transcends the real world and enters the realm of the gods. The other is through undeath. To preserve free will against the immortal gods of necromancy, especially the jade god, transforming oneself into a lich – that is, a vessel for magic devoid of the soul, is the only other way. In Tania, early experiments by the Mage's Guild had proven it could be done but the Emperor had removed its study along with all necromancy many centuries ago.

"The lich is not known to us nor does it appear in our recorded history. It

121

must therefore predate even our tribal founding. To have survived this long, free of the Jade God's influence, is notable but creates a risk that the jade god will try to claim the lich and make it a Hellhound. Our forces at the Bloodstone Temple report that all hellhounds have been either spotted or slain recently. As such, the risk is low of the lich being taken.

"How does this matter to your newest member and the Order, you may wonder. Malcor, the second rite is to face a mighty enemy. To stay in this Order, you must defeat a vampire or stronger undead, convert or slay a dragon, or serve a Bloodstone campaign. Usually, for other Orders, an undead is summoned in the Temple and defeated there after many months if not years of training. You will train for three days and then we leave for Ori. During those three days, you will accomplish your second rite. You will not face a strong undead in the controlled safety of the Temple. You will face and defeat the lich. The Order will create that opportunity for you. Any questions?"

Tembri laughed and clapped Malcor's back, "By the Goddess, a lich! A mighty foe indeed!"

One by one, the rest of the Order came forward and introduced themselves and their battle priests to Malcor. By title alone, he noted that they were all Dar rank. He also saw that all of them including their battle priests bore the Bloodstone ruby ear ring given to veterans after their first campaign in that valley.

As they spoke, a space was cleared and a table set with a late breakfast. Though full of questions, Malcor found the combined late night activities, encounter with Ynt'taris the white dragon, and spending so much time in prayer to save his life from his wounds and the bitter cold, had left him exhausted. Very quickly, he began struggling to stay awake. Much to his relief, he felt Tembri's hand on his back shoulder and felt a surge of energy. He still felt exhausted but remained alert. During a moment, Tembri carefully whispered, "An enervation prayer to hold onto awareness for long watches and battles."

Dar Kendra led them in a prayer and then they sat. Daryx and Reznor each dismissed themselves. Dar Shara arrived and joined them with her dread lord watching impassively into the shadows all around. The conversation turned to news from Bloodstone with Shara fielding questions about the Temple there and her counterpart Dar Ana. At some point in the conversation, Lady Kendra leaned over and whispered to him. "You are probably exhausted. While you may stay, if you would rather not, you are dismissed. I believe R'Dar Ora is waiting for you in your chambers." She looked at him and winked. "Were I you, facing accelerated training, I'd leave and go be with the soft and beautiful priestess who is obviously so smitten with you."

Malcor nodded and hesitated wondering if she tested his resolve. Seeing this, Lady stood and tapped her goblet. "Order of Water, Malcor will be leaving us to rest and prepare. We are to help him defeat an ancient lich, possibly an eldar. Each of you will be receiving training instructions for him and Tembri as well as a schedule." She raised her goblet in salute as did the others. Malcor stood, smiled, and then Tembri pulled him away.

Chapter Fifteen – A Brief Rest

Once away from the main chamber, Tembri said, "I thought you would like to know that Calvin is firmly joined now with the Shield Knights. They are an honorable but lower level order often joined by wealthy children of Dar and House families. His first rite is scheduled for the next festival. Unlike your meeting with Ynt'taris, Calvin will face a fallen white dragon." Tembri smiled and then added, "The Order of Water... is powerful. It is amazing you found your way here Sir Malcor. I joined the Temple when I was fourteen and finished my first Bloodstone campaign before Dar Kendra would even consider my application. Even still, I did not face Ynt'taris until after I had trained here for several months. I hope you understand how remarkable all of this is. For myself, I hope to be the battle priest recorded in Tania's stories who served the knight prodigy of the Order of Water."

They reached Malcor's room and Tembri bowed and left. Entering, Malcor saw Ora had brought in extra furniture and stands. A large desk adjacent to a crackling fireplace had a few pieces of official looking paperwork on it. She helped him remove his newly-gifted armor and hung it on the stands. The gleaming silver rose she had given him just several days earlier, she started rotating near the desk. Purple flecks of light gently fell from it. She smiled back at him. Stepping out of her robes, she took his hand and pulled him to the bath. "Let's talk about your next three days."

Much later, he stretched and pulled on some clothes. "So, Ora... I see forms on the desk and you want to talk about training?"

She nodded. "Do I look like I want to discuss such things?" She pulled him into the warm water and wrapped her arms around him. "The forms are to take control of House Tor. Now that you are officially a member of the Order of Water, you have legal status you did not yesterday. As you requested, Sai R'Dar will take a tenth of the Tor profits to the estate shrine. I will administrate. You do not need to review this now, but it must be signed and presented. The longer you wait the more time you give to Tor to rebel or challenge you if they wish. I suppose the real question here is if you trust Sai and my intent in this."

"I will read it now," he said but she pulled him back down and he found her embrace far more exciting. Some hours later, he sat down and began scanning through them. Ora walked to the door and whispered into the hallway. A few moments later, servants began quietly bringing in other items to fill and personalize the space. Malcor looked up and saw several tapestries, one with an image of the shadow dragon just like his statue, as well as some sitting chairs and privacy screens.

Ora's scrolls were adorned in dragon art. He touched the runic calligraphy wondering if Ora had written it by hand. He wondered if all contracts in Tania used the Temple's draconian script. He could not read normal commoner writing. No one in Klenna ever wanted special inscriptions done in Common.

Reading went slowly as he was not used to reading at length and was glad when something caught his eye and he looked up to see a minotaur walk in carrying a forge anvil. Several dwarves followed the minotaur and the far corner of his room quickly took the shape of a personal forge and armor works. The minotaur, he had never seen one this close, wore leather armor adorned with their god. The dwarves spoke with it in Tauran, the minotaur language, and after some time, they all stepped back and filled the forge's cradle with small green gemstones. The minotaur retrieved a small rounded hammer and metal scribing tool of some kind.

"The minotaur is a runesmith Malcor," Ora explained. "I thought you might appreciate having access to a forge here. The Order has its own, but you have a particular knack that may exceed even the Order's best. They're going to ignite the gemstones to burn magically and contain the heat to the cradle there. Then, they'll connect a portal on that wall to the Order's quartermaster for any supplies you may need."

"I'm stunned that you would consider... how..."

"Daryx and the Lady Kendra asked me to make your space more personal, given that it may be some time before you have a chance to notice such things."

Across the room, the minotaur stood back and one of the dwarves placed a metal rod in the green gems. It immediately glowed red hot and started to turn molten. When they pulled it back from the forge's cradle, Mal heard its heat sizzle.

"The Tor papers, they're in draconian…"

She nodded. "That was not my doing. My master's scribe received word yesterday to rewrite the papers, all of them, in draconian. I don't know who sent word."

Malcor nodded. "So, someone knows I don't read Common." He sighed. "I have some observations. I hope they aren't too annoying. The first is that I want my father Ishan to own control of the Klennan armory. I don't have any issues with Tor advising and representing but whatever they call it, it is Ishan's to own and operate. I couldn't find anything that reflected this." She nodded. "Also, what is left of House Tor, I want a date set for all of them to come to Sai's shrine and pledge fealty. Any who do not show up, are to be cast out." He continued, "and I don't know how to do this next one, but isn't there some kind of compelling magic that can reinforce correct behavior? The elders, the leaders, whoever is nominally in charge of House Tor, can we bind them to good behavior?"

Ora thought and replied, "There is geas magic that can prevent certain behaviors, but at a certain point, unless you have trust, the contract would need to be written to define correct behavior. It gets painful to administrate as each new guideline highlights a boundary and thereby makes it easier to cross, break, or get around. Most of the elite here choose instead to create magistrates with total authority. Like what you want to do with Ishan. If you do not trust their fealty pledges, well, you already killed two of their leaders."

He sat down and stared at the minotaur as it rearranged the anvil and tools around the gem cradle. "Lets trust them until they prove themselves untrustworthy. I do not want to hold them to the same standards as those who challenged me. Also, one last final point, Ora, I trust you. Please update these so that you, not I, have final authority. In your absence, Ishan leads. I sense that the Queen wishes me to focus on my paladin tasks, not commerce and business."

The minotaur had started inscribing additional runes on the cradle's opposite side while the dwarves had started placing and fixing with mortar white pre-shaped stones along the wall framing a doorway against the stone. The tapestries had been hung, each depicting moments Ora likely thought interesting to Malcor. One showed Klenna's valley framed in winter mountain snow. Another showed King Rojo's ascension and his sword Twilight Fell. His favorite showed the emperor working in a forge, hammering the first divine scriptures out onto metal plates – the Book of Flames. The picture showed the emperor's human form striking the open metal pages of the Book of Flames with hot plasma surging from the strike and exploding out into draconian scripture that then framed the tapestry -"By my love, I guard those that are Mine. By their love, shall they be guarded in Mine," read the verse on the tapestry, that had connected him to withstand the white dragon.

A different tapestry, really a map, also hung by the desk showing the general locations and layout of the empire. Tania was oversized to provide detail against the large island that held it, Tsora. The elven empire of Morilon, the boundaries and general city locations of Taysor, the Sea of Glass – a deadly desert of burning sands, the Bloodstone Valley, all of it stood out and for the first time in his life, Malcor saw the shape of the world he lived in. Ori's location on Khasra stood down in the south just to the western side of the island named Mondo. Coming back to Tania, he noted the general locations of Home, where the Halflings lived as an autonomous part of Morbatten, as well as the minotaur port island just off Tania's eastern shoreline. And there sat Klenna, on the road to Bloodstone.

Ora dragged her fingernail from Morbatten to Ori, and tapped on Ori. "This is where your second rite will be." She pointed up to Bloodstone in the northwest. "Normally, this is the second and final rite for initiates. After that, you're a fully-fledged paladin of Takhissis." She leaned against the wall and stared at him. "There are always exceptions though and I guess you'll be exceptional throughout." She traced her finger back to Morbatten and tapped the mountains crowning the city. She moved it down to the south and said, "This is where I was born."

A knock on the door interrupted her, and Tembri stepped into the room.

"I'm here to discuss training." He saw them looking at the map and walked up and pointed to the area north of the emperor's mountain. "I'm from here, the tribe of the winter wolf brought me into this world."

"Training," Ora said. The word sounded flat and dull compared to everything else that had happened.

Malcor nodded and they went over and sat down in the new seating area. Tembri placed a leather book on the table and turned it to a page showing a drawing of a lich. The skull head was half bone and half emaciated flesh. Phylacteries and other magical objects adorned it. Tembri asked, "Have either of you encountered a lich?" They shook their heads no. "Neither have I. My second rite as a battle priest is actually going to be this test. Even in my Bloodstone campaign, I never encountered a high enough ranked undead to qualify." He chuckled and rubbed his bald head. "It wasn't for lack of trying though! I'm excited to face off against a lich. I pulled this as a reference just in case. Here is what I found in the archives."

Malcor recounted the basics. "A lich is a sorcerer of great power who trades their soul for prolonged life and enhanced powers in undeath. While any evil or abyssal god can enable the exchange for prolonged life, Tania views lichdom as dangerous and heretical." He went on to add that liches gradually decay as they age over thousands of years. Eventually, the magic holding them together disintegrates leaving behind a shadow of the lich, but still dreadful.

Tembri approved, "Glad you didn't skip your Temple education while working as a smith. You got the basics down. The point here is that you have to imagine someone very powerful, like Dar Reznor or Sai R'Dar. Imagine then that they exchange their soul for additional powers. Then give them hundreds if not thousands of years to become experts in those powers while also continuing their sorcery. There is a chance this lich is an eldar, which increases our danger many times over."

They then discussed the hellhound possibility. Malcor had never heard of hellhounds. "They aren't dogs," Ora said. "They are disciples of the Jade God and serve undeath. They can seize control of any undead they encounter, even this lich. Anything they kill rises in undeath. They are free-willed and entrusted with that god's malice and hatred of life. A lich like this, as a hellhound, would be a nightmare. Not to be confused with normal hellhounds, which are actually devil-spawned dog creatures from the Hells. While there are no artifacts of the Jade God in Ori, there is nothing that stops a hellhound from learning of the lich and going there. Typically, the lich will be offered gifts for its fealty to the Jade God. As undead, the lich is already part of the Jade God's dominion, the lich just doesn't realize it yet."

"So, this word – hellhound – why that name?" Malcor asked.

Tembri turned the pages of the book to a picture of a skeletal wolf standing behind a human-sized figure for scale. "This is the hellhound's state when it comes into this world. It takes a while for them to consume enough living souls to alter their shape. In the Jaden War, a powerful hellhound naming itself Mauler, took possession of a low level priest and within months, Tania fought a civil war of the living versus the dead. The western provinces all but fell. Dar Rojo and Dar Kell, with new doctrines and teachings, marshalled a counterstrike that killed the hellhound and the priest. After that, it was a mop up job. Their bones are likely the closest artifact we have besides Bloodstone itself."

Ora added, "Oh, and liches don't trade their souls until death. Part of the ritual is the transfer of their soul into an object to keep it anchored to this world. So, killing the lich without destroying the soul "gem" – it could be anything – allows them to return over and over." She pulled Malcor's face to look at her. "Malcor, this is important. If you kill the lich, you pass the rite. BUT, the glory is many times more if you destroy the soul gem." She let that sink in and then bit her lower lip. "And, if you capture the soul gem, and the lich has not yet been destroyed, you can take control of the lich for even more glory."

Tembri nodded. "I agree. The objective here is clearly for Sir Malcor to pass the second rite. In so doing, I will pass my rite as well. But, to capture a lich and its soul gem. To take control of a free-willed lich, perhaps even an eldar. Can you imagine?" The sparkle in his eyes and Ora's interest also came through loud and clear. "The rest of the Order will be working to create an opportunity for you to confront and destroy the lich. However, as your battle priest, I will be in the fight with you. Our secondary objective is to become a single fighting unit, united in faith. We must become mighty. I am ready and I have faith you will be."

Malcor pressed, "We have three days to get ready to capture a lich's soul gem. I doubt we will be able to wander around freely looking for it."

Ora chimed in, "You have three days to get ready to defeat a lich and pass your second rite. Remember though, it's a lich and you're still new at this knight business. No matter the training. No matter the plans. When we get into combat, who knows what opportunities might present themselves? However, you can bet that an ancient lich is not going to leave its soul gem lying around for the taking. It did not last this long by being sloppy. I get it is either nearby or retrievable. The trick will be to not engage the lich so much that it retreats, or abandons its body. Instead, we will want it to betray the gem's location. Well, maybe we are too far ahead. Mal, what do you want to do?"

Malcor looked at them both. "I'm barely nineteen. I just faced down a white dragon. I've never faced undead. This all seems a bit beyond me. Maybe I can do it, but is it wise to make plans when we don't even know if I can survive the battle? Above all else, I must defeat the lich. If the opportunity is there, I think I should take it. That is what I need to prepare for. Maybe if we had several months to plan, but we have three days. And that assumes the second rite goes well. Tell me about it."

"Leave the lich plan to me Lord Malcor. If I cannot identify some possibilities by the time your moment comes, then we'll just follow the Queen's will. Have faith," Tembri winked. "About the next three days."

"Tembri," Malcor cut him off. "I'm not very comfortable with you calling me Lord. Malcor, or Mal, works just fine."

Tembri shrugged. "Okay Malcor, so let's start with the basics. Kendra basically killed you on the stage when you first came here. I understand that Ynt'taris essentially killed you on the mountain. So did Armageddon. You know, through this and your forge work, how painful life can be. We may not get to choose the circumstances of our pain, but as a paladin, you must be able to make decisions with faith-unwavering and clear from pain or death as a possible consequence. The fear, even anticipation of being caught in that moment can make you lose focus. You must have faith that the Queen will save you. You must be wise in combat and help save yourself. Too many knights, especially in these more powerful elemental orders, they get addicted to that moment "on the edge" as some call it. Your training these days is all about this. Measuring you."

Ora interjected, "It's also about understanding how much pain you can take Mal. Not all paladins can take as much as the healers can heal. If Kendra matched you well, Tembri is the perfect battle priest to augment your combat skills with healing."

Tembri nodded, "So consider this. A newborn child, in fact, any innocent, would have died on that mountain. You did not die. In fact, you lived through it. So, you're hearty. And you have faith on a level most Tanians do not. Yet, there are things that will kill you dead quickly, slowly, and some not so obvious. As you train and work through your second rite, you, me, all of us will see what it takes to kill Malcor. Understanding that will allow all of us to better support you."

Ora took his hand and traced her fingers in it. "Some things only come with experience. You must become more powerful than you are now to face the lich and win. Your second rite, it will be brutal. You will train. You will fight, past death, past exhaustion, past all possible hope of rest. We will sustain and heal you so that you may continue. It won't make sense until later when you've had time to digest it all, ponder on it, and learn from it."

Chapter Sixteen – Killing Malcor

Tembri recapped the first rite. "Not all paladins face the white dragon you did. Some are required to face fears drawn by a priest from their very own thoughts. At the end of the day, fear is an emotion. Tania does not want its heroes make decisions based on fear avoidance. Cowards are ruled by fear. Tania wants you to be ruled by the Goddess. You cannot serve these two very different gods."

He went on to explain how training for and serving in Bloodstone takes the place for most knights of the second rite. "For ease of discussion, lets call these rites what they are - phases. There is the trial of fear and pain with a dragon; because the Queen can heal you, you must learn that there is no pain, not even unto death, that you should fear. While the loss of your arm, should it be cut off, will hurt, part of being a paladin is overriding the pain and functioning anyway. Her power can regenerate your lost arm, or limb. On that note, only decapitation cannot be healed normally. Resurrection handles that and other more extreme deaths. Just remember, you can only be resurrected so many times, so try to avoid death okay?"

Tembri's trial of pain of involved working in a stone quarry without food, water, or healing. "First, I died of thirst struggling through the lack of water. Then they healed me but did not give me water for days and then weeks till I died of hunger. They kept healing me until starvation rather than thirst took me. My skin wore away to my bones. Without nutrition and care and surrounded by other first rite initiates, we fell prey to disease. I began to dread the healing because it brought back pain.

"We failed to quarry any stones worth anything, but I learned that pain from thirst, hunger, and disease is much worse than the types of wounds suffered in combat. When the trial ended and I regenerated, I found that knives, fire, destructive magic did not phase me at all. It took almost two months to feel normal. Your friend Calvin will have something like that though abbreviated and much less so.

"For battle priests, we have to be ready to heal you even knowing how much pain you might suffer because of it. Trust me, it's harder than it might seem to heal someone when you know they're just going to die again. For you though? There isn't time. It'll be something else."

Ora added, "He'll be multifixed, essentially." She squeezed his hand and tried to sound reassuring. "Healing someone over and over on the brink of death is beyond belief Mal. I'd heard about the Order of Water being harder, but not this. You experienced it a bit when you died on the mountain yesterday. But," she looked at Tembri, "there are other ways to create pain. I wonder." She grew a bit downcast and grim as she thought and then said, "You'll be spirit wracked. That has to be it. The problem here is that *you know*. You know that you'll be okay. With you Tembri, it took so long because you had to move beyond hope of relief until you not only stopped fearing it, but stopped noticing it. New initiates in the other orders often take the Temple and healing for granted. The Order of Water though trains to not take relief and healing for granted; it is always life and death. Malcor, you have a battle priest. Your experience with the Temple is somewhat limited and Tembri isn't exactly thumping his chest and bragging. So let me...

"In any other order, Tembri would be a Dar rank priest. Already. He is also a veteran of Bloodstone. The fatality rate in Bloodstone amongst priests and priestesses in combat is two-thirds. The surviving are offered positions within the knight orders. It takes a special candidate to be accepted into the knighthood, let alone the Order of Water. When you look at Tembri and the other battle priests, you should see yourself. Prodigies who beat the odds and bring with them special gifts and talents, along with a singular determination to overcome the odds.

"Consider also the number of battle priests in this order. Most other orders are lucky to have a small handful. The Order of Water though has them because they are needed. By the time you reach R'Dar rank Malcor, Tembri will most likely have two or three other battle priests supporting you. By contrast, the Shield Order your friend joined, has only two battle priests in the *entire* Order."

She took a drink and in the silence, Tembri spoke. "I wanted to be a knight. I went into my Aging Ceremony to request it. The priestess there, without even asking me what I wanted, told me to be a priest." He laughed. "I told her she was crazy and for that, she slapped me down.

The odd thing though, I saw it happening and moved... through the River. The next thing I knew, a member of the Order of Water, sent by Dar Kendra, stepped forward and offered me a position. Well, there had been a lot of conditions on that offer. My training as a knight stalled during preparation for the first rite. I stubbornly continued though and only during the second rite did I realize that priestess had been correct. I should have started as a priest." He laughed again.

"I will be spirit wracked or worse," Mal pondered. "I was often burned in my work at the forge. I got past it without magical healing. In Klenna, magical and divine healing are considered miraculous and rare events when they occurred. You both seem so casual about it. I can do it. If She says to kill the lich, then she will give me the pathway to the lich's destruction. What else?"

They explained and discussed that as part of the rite of pain, "You'll be taught a combat technique. You'll spar at first with that technique until Dar Kendra deems you have mastered it. You'll then be tested on that mastery against a real enemy. In other orders, they use criminals. The more you master, the more you'll be taught. BUT, there is no rest, no recovery time. You'll have breaks for food and water, while you train. The healers will keep you on your feet, but you must trust us and fight with all your heart. Training will end when your heart fails from exertion, or Dar Kendra deems you have reached your limits."

Ora opened her scriptures to the Book of Flames and held it to Malcor. She pointed to a verse there. "My Children, my children. Let your hearts soar as the dragons. The winds may blow but they fill your wings and carry to Heaven. My Children, my children. Let you not fear the grave but take hope in your hearts; the River does not have you yet and you are Mine now and always. Though the River may take you, let it fill your hearts and soar to my Heavens. In the beginning were the dragons not the mightiest? Are they not My Children? Remember remember my children, that you are also mine."

As she finished, Ora whispered just barely, "Do you understand this?"

Malcor shrugged, "I am to fight like I am a dragon? There is a suggestion here that humans can serve beyond death."

Tembri raised his eyebrow, "Most initiates read this to mean that the Queen and the dragons are above us. You read this to mean you should face the trial of combat like a dragon?" He grinned an approving smile and added, "By the Goddess, this will be a hero for the ages!"

They continued to talk about training and the lich quest. Eventually, Malcor felt a presence and the three of them stopped. The minotaur towered over them and nodded his head. When he spoke, his voice had a deep baritone and guttural quality to it that felt like he was being insulted and condescended to at the same time. "The forge is completed as ordered. I am required to seek your approval?"

Malcor stood and had to step around the minotaur, who did not move. The beast acted like he wanted a confrontation with Malcor. Reaching the forge, the two dwarves bowed low. A few steps thundered and then there stood the minotaur again. His clawed finger pointed to a rune. "This rune is elemental fire from that realm. It heats the green gems, a type of diamond we cull from Bloodstone. Do not touch the green gems when they glow. They glow when as hot as the hottest fire you can imagine *Sir Knight*."

"And these other runes?"

"They contain the forge's magic." The minotaur pointed to the door. "This will always be stone unless you touch your hand to the center rune." Malcor put his hand on the rune in the center of the archway. "And speak your name. The wall remains but you will be able to pass through. Go ahead."

Malcor spoke his name and felt the stone under his hand vanish as if not there. His eyes still saw the wall. The minotaur smashed his fist into the wall making a loud cracking boom. His other hand shoved Malcor, who stumbled through the wall into a large supply room. An elderly man sat at a table covered with papers. He smiled up at Malcor, "Welcome young master! I am Quartermaster Felnar. A pleasure to meet you." Malcor noted the archway glowed faintly behind him. After exchanging a greeting, he stepped back through.

The minotaur had stepped back by the anvil, arms folded across his

135

chest. "Tools are there," pointing against the wall. "This rune here allows heat to escape the cradle in case you need warming." He picked up the large blacksmith hammer. "This is enchanted to repeat whatever blow you last made." He lifted the hammer and smashed it down on the anvil. The force of the hit made the hammer face glow red hot from the force of the strike. He tossed the hammer to the stone floor where it clanged loudly and bounced a few times before resting by Malcor's bed. The minotaur then said, "Hammer, repeat" in draconian. The hammer flew across the room into position as if being held and then smashed down onto the anvil with the exact same arc and strike, as if held by the minotaur. "It will only move to the anvil and strike this anvil, but don't be caught between the hammer and its path to the anvil. Hammer, stop." At his command, the hammer fell bouncing off the anvil in a shower of sparks to rest on the floor. "Hammer, repeat" and it leapt back into position to strike. He stopped the hammer and asked, "Do you have any questions?"

"Thank you," Malcor said. He walked over and picked up the hammer. It felt solid and heavier than his old hammer in Klenna. He could feel magic moving through and around it. "This is amazing. Thank you." He rested the hammer down carefully on the anvil.

He turned around to see Dar Kendra leaning in his doorway. She smiled, turned, and left. The minotaur and its dwarven helpers bowed to take their leave. Tembri waited until they had left and walked over the forge by Malcor. "If I hear anything, I will let you know. I suggest you rest. Some feel like they need to prepare by exercising or practicing. There is no point. You will experience pain till death and combat until your internal organs fail. The important thing is that you learn. Not even this Order uses healing to accelerate training the way you will be. Rest. Calm your mind. Find your center. When all was pain and death, I watched many around me die out because they could not find their center."

He bowed low and left. Alone, Ora and Malcor eyed each other. To his surprise, Ora bowed low as well and left, taking the paperwork for the Tor House with her. She kissed his cheek. "I am not a member of the Order of anything. I'm a Temple priestess. As such, I do not know how long Dar Kendra will allow me to stay. I have never been in combat like

Tembri. I doubt I will see you very much. Remember, look for me when the snow falls. You are wonderful." She kissed him and in that embrace, Malcor had that feeling of his destiny out there, stretching into the distance and he stood firmly on that path. He held her tightly.

"I will look for you. I promise." So much had happened. Malcor sat down and exhausted sleep took him. And, the River flowed on.

Something struck him in the head. He faintly registered pain. It him again. Then again. His body felt weightless, as if floating, but trying to wake up everything seemed ponderously heavy. He tried to open his eyes. Nothing. It hit him again. His mind registered that he needed to wake up. Something was hitting him.

Harder than it should be, he finally opened his eyes and saw Tembri dump a bucket of icy cold water over him. It felt distant and heavy, but woke him up enough. "What time…"

Tembri smirked, "It's really early. You've been asleep at least 13 hours though. I'm surprised they left you alone so long. Kendra sent me to bring you to the combat rune. As you are. Now." Tembri lifted Malcor up to his feet and pushed him to the door. Mal's stomach growled.

The path to the main chamber would take a few minutes to walk and Tembri used it to brief Malcor. "Three of the paladins are there. They are to start you on basic hand to hand, agility, and signaling. Signaling is a hand talk Daryx brought with him from the dark elf realm. You will use it to tell me what prayers you need as well as your intentions in the field of battle. The Queen's divine might should be no different than your sword or shield as tool for combat. Once you master the basics, you'll move on to sword and shield and more complex signaling. So long as you do not quit and demonstrate proficiency, your training will progress until you either exhaust the healers – all of them are there – or reach your current mental, emotional, and physical limits. Remember, you must find your center. This part of training took me five years and my Bloodstone campaign."

They entered the main chamber. Three of the Order stood on the platform with all of the battle priests and a few healers he did not recognize sitting in the theater around the stage. They walked up on to the stage and it began.

One of the knights raised his hand and made a sign that appeared to be a summon to challenge. However, one of the battle priests stood and immediately cast a spell at the knight. The knight seemed to swell with power and confidence. "I am Verit. This is the signal to boost your defenses and awareness in combat. It is a basic blessing even the newest priests can use. You try." He showed Malcor the signal again.

Malcor copied it and Tembri immediately did the same sending vitality and energy to him. As the prayer washed over him, he felt a surge of confidence and loving protection. It came with a fire in his belly that made him feel ready to take on any foe. "Excellent," Verit said. He moved his arms in counter circles. "You might recognize this from the War Dance. It is a basic self-defense posture. In armor, your bracers can block swords and other weapons. In hand to hand, it keeps your front safe and your fingers free for signaling. We will attack you slowly. Once you have it, we will go faster and faster. We expect you to improvise the parry and use the Bless signal to augment when you tire."

The three came at Malcor, and similar to the war dance, it started slow and then went faster and faster. He quickly lost count of the parries but soon the knights attacked so quickly he could barely follow their movements in spite of signaling and feeling the boosts. Faster and faster it went until he could only feel their strikes.

One of the knights made some kind of a signal and Malcor noticed a priest touch a rune on the edge of the stage. Immediately, the stage vanished and they now fought in a heavily wooded forest where downed trees, leaves, and a stream made footing treacherous. Caught off guard by the transition, Malcor signaled for a Bless, and took a blow to his chest. It hurled him back into a tree which cracked from his body's impact.

"The field of combat is always changing Sir Malcor," one of the knights said from somewhere behind him.

Another added, "You cannot be distracted by illusions, or pools of blood and bodies in your way."

The third said, "What starts out clean and obvious becomes impossible to anticipate after enemy contact. The only thing that matters is the mission."

Malcor parried as the tempo increased again beyond his ability to see and several struck him hard from opposite sides so that he remained standing but unable to breathe. He signaled and then stepped out of the River. From his new ethereal perspective, he saw the knights moving and signaling to each other. He blocked reflexively. One of the knights used a signal that enervated the knight and accelerated his movements. Malcor made the same sign and felt Tembri's approval. Power coursed through Malcor and suddenly he did not need the River's perspective to fight. After several minutes, the knights stopped.

"Excellent Sir Malcor. We will now show you how to parry with your legs and turn your body into a counterstrike. You have correctly used the Hastening signal. This is the symbol for Healing. This is the symbol for Growth. This is the symbol for Strength. As your size grows, your Hastening will slow but Strength increases. We fight this time until you die. And the field will change every minute. Like last time, we start slow and increase the pace."

His training continued. He fought giants on a plain for lava. He fought nimble assassins on a glacier of ice. He fought the knights under pouring waterfalls amongst slippery rocks. Somehow he kept pace though his breathing became labored and his body went numb. He fought on and on and on. When he felt as if he would burst apart from the strain, they would take a brief rest to review new signals and techniques. At some point, they transitioned to sword techniques, then sword and shield, then dual swords.

When the pain became too great, Malcor stepped out of the River again and watched himself fight with blinding speed. The knights' choreographed attack looked beautiful from the River. He could see his life's thread fraying strike by slicing attack though even he struggled furiously for his life. He signaled for Healing for the hundredth time and one of the healers near Tembri collapsed. Tembri flashed a hand sign and another healer stepped forward shakily.

A voice near him in the River's space said, "You need to counterstrike harder. The knights are waiting to see you begin to hurt them before they allow you to progress." Malcor looked downstream and saw Tembri's visage there. "There are prayers that can help but you must do this by yourself, for now. Center yourself on killing them. Hate them. Spite them. Whatever works. They are your enemy right now. Focus on their deaths and pray to the Queen for victory!"

Distracted, Malcor dodged a sword cut too late and parried the blade with his arm. His arm sliced off from his elbow and went spinning to the side in a spray of blood. The shock unraveled his life's thread and tore him back into the River. Choking and dodging another attack, he screamed out "Regenerate!"

Tembri's power stabbed into his arm stump and his sword rose up to counter. He registered Tembri collapsing, but focused on fighting. Using his sword like a hammer at the forge, he found a rhythm of slice, stab, block as bone and tissue too slowly regrew. Parry and Heal sign but it lessened his grip on his sword and a knight smacked it away from him. He summoned it back with his ring Righteous Might just in time to parry and attack. He knew he would die but he had to… Malcor returned to the River and focused his attack on just one of the knights. Raised in a forge and strengthened by the Queen, his blows struck like a hammer and finally, his sword found blood. He looked in grim satisfaction as the tip of his sword pierced plate armor and drew blood from the knight's forearm. Too late for Malcor though, it felt odd to see three sword points explode from his body as dual swords stabbed into his torso and another through his neck.

The blood mist and shadows of dying made it hard. His vocal chords choked on the blade through his neck as he prayed. Against his death seizure, his hand struggled to form Heal. As the healing prayers held him dying, the knights withdrew their swords and the one he cut smiled and counter-attacked. His almost reformed arm stump slammed the flat of the blade and prevented it from becoming another fatal blow. It cut like an ax into his hip though. The pain of his heart, lungs, spine, and brain registering death but not dying exquisitely tried to dominate his senses, but against it all he remembered a hand sign the king had made at his ceremony. The sign had been followed by Dar Shara flame-striking the knights. Malcor made the signal. A female screamed out, "No! He can't...!" Was that Ora's voice or Kendra's?

The ground at his feet pulsed and the knights behind him jumped back. Malcor signaled for Heal and Strength and caught the sword buried in his hip. The pulse followed by hot crackling of energy as a circle around him erupted in dragon fire rising up and outwards.

The sword he held in his hip, melted into slag. The knight holding the sword jumped backwards. The flames rose up before his eyes and he burned. He knew that above all else, he must kill his enemy. He tried to pray but ash filled his mouth. His eyes and senses spoke only of fire, burning, pain. The fury in his heart matched his suffering and he yearned to break free, to fly above and away from it.

He stepped forward his feet grasping for sensation beyond the burning. *Coming Undone* clenched in his fist felt slippery and he squeezed it hard mindful of the need for healing but if his death proved to them his worth, he must make it count.

From the River's edge, he saw the knight diminished somehow and awestruck. He swung *Coming Undone* down in an arc that sliced through the knight's sword. It cut into the knight's magical armor with the sound of shattering glass and the knight blinked, vanishing and reappearing some distance away. He signaled and something happened. Malcor noted a charred skeleton held his blade. A mist of ash and embers hung in the air around him. He turned back to Tembri and asked, "Am I dead?" and then collapsed.

Tembri stumbled forward and caught him. "He is past normal healing. He is dying."

"Save him," Kendra ordered. At her command, a trio of Dar priestesses came forward and blessed Malcor with resurrection and healing. As they did so, Kendra said, "It will be a several hours before Malcor recovers. He is to immediately resume fighting. His combat training is sufficient, for now. I want to see how he fares against the undead. Make yourselves

141

ready."

Verit and the knights bowed and took a break. They still eyed the boy warily. "How can he be so damaged, but stay in the River so long?" Verit wondered aloud.

Kendra shrugged as she stepped back from the healers. "He is Kell's son? I can't say, but he is surprising in this and other ways."

Chapter Seventeen – Memory of the Necromancer

Dar Rojo stood before a golden throne. The dragon emperor Alerius watched Malcor's fight and collapse. "Father, as the prophecies tell, my successor will rage beyond death. His fight is worthy of a dragon."

Alerius, patriarch of the fire dragons and god emperor of Morbatten, watched the fight. "You humans are amazing. Look, he almost unleashed his dragon there. I cannot see if he will be a fire or some other type. He has the fury of a Red but rather than burning, he berserks like a Shadow with no thought to his destiny. It makes him powerful, but creates risk that he needlessly sacrifices himself when destiny requires him to not. This tendency makes him untrustworthy for epic quests."

"So that flamestrike, it was him? I have not seen a paladin ever do that."

"It is a trait passed down from the Ancients, from their earliest days when the dragon crowned their totems. It is quite rare, but not surprising given his father is Kell," the emperor twisted the view to see the columns of healers who had collapsed supporting Malcor's fight.

For sixteen thousand years, Alerius had guided Morbatten. Of all the dragons, he alone had seen the potential of these lesser creatures. Before the River, he had nurtured a tribe of them in the mountains here. As the River began to flow, he protected and then began shaping them - into dragons. His fealty to the Queen Takhissis had triggered the Dragon Wars that ended the age of the Eldar races.

"Rojo, I saw creation burn and nearly fall back into Chaos. I held stars in my hand and pondered ascension to godhood. The Queen commanded me to follow and I almost did. I chose to stay here. Though the River stinks with decay, I will hold this treasure to the ends of time. Tell me LORD, when you stand by Her side in your next life, will you miss these wonders?" The image shifted back to the column of fire that had lashed out when Malcor rebelled against death.

Most of the dragons, when they spoke had a tendency for a reptilian slurring of certain sounds. So long among humans, Alerius had long ago perfected his Common speech but still inflected certain words oddly. Words linked to fire and the Queen and his memories of the Eldar times especially drew it out.

"No Father, I will not. Since I first saw Her standing by the River, She is all I see." He looked up at the dread emperor. "It is too early to call me LORD. If you continue speaking of the wonders and treasures here, maybe I will change my mind."

Alerius did not laugh, ever. But when amused, the heat aura bending the air around him would shift. It did now and he smiled down at Rojo. "Perhaps we should speak of the River's stink then. The Queen may come here personally and have my death if you renege your destiny as LORD."

Rojo stood and asked, "You are reflective today oh great king of kings."

Alerius humanshifted and together they walked to a large opening in the side of the mountain that looked eastwards to the seas. "I look forward to your ascension Rojo. Too long have I labored against my kind's innate tendency to dismiss mortals. Except for Armageddon and my two sons, too many fire dragons see Morbatten as a jewel ripe for the taking of treasure. The greatness of the Eldar has died in them and left only a desire for power and its trappings of wealth and veil of fear. The blue patriarch my children have named Spark and the other patriarchs alone share this view. That the other dragons, the metallic and so-called "good" dragons, innately view Tehrans as I do, makes it difficult. The Queen has been too long absent this place. When you become LORD and join with Her, I pray your humanity is not lost. It makes you more precious than all the wealth of Tania. But, *even IF*, you will make a fine partner for Our Queen."

Dawn creased the far distant horizon over the eastern ocean, the start of a clear new day. High up in the dragon emperor's mountain, the air was cold but neither felt it. Rojo spoke, "Father, I dreamt a dream last night. The ram came with throngs of our people enslaved to war against Heaven. The Temple itself rose up. The Jade God spoke to me and commanded me to serve it. In the dream, I refused and attacked and died. The empire fell and then stood back up in the Jade God's image. I

144

was taken by the two-faced demon and revived to watch undeath freeze your children... these dreams are becoming more vivid and real-seeming."

Alerius stroked the air in front of him and the mountain opening pulsed with magic and a scene opened. Rojo recognized the early empire, back when its people came solely from the tribal barbarians. Like Rojo, they had pale skin but dark almost black hair and broad shoulders. Alerius controlled the image with his hand and said, "This is the first incursion of the Jade God, when I learned about Bloodstone. Watch and see how this happened the first time almost two thousand years ago."

Leather hides stitched together made rough armor and clothing. A flowing river split the Dragon and Temple mountains flowing south through the heart of the then Capitol. Rojo noted this because, in his time, there is no river except a fountain. It must have been destroyed in some cataclysmic event. Tania's histories did not mention it. Large tents had been erected all along the river with their openings facing north to the dragon. A small boy, barely eight years old, struggled along a well-traveled section of ground carrying a heavy burden wrapped in animal hides. He had a manic sort of look on his face.

Alerius pushed Rojo and he physically entered the scene, standing there besides the boy. He noticed a ram's horn protruding from the wrapped burden. No one reacted to him. He heard the boy whimper and then stand as if against his will. He stumbled onwards to the large tent. Rojo followed.

The large tent served as a tabernacle for the early Tanians. The female priestess stood before a stone statue of a dragon and prayed. The stone carving, a version of the totem, showed wolves, horses, and then griffins, priestesses, and then the dragon emperor. A wild sorcerer stood nearby with other females. At this time, there were no knights. Females served as priestesses or shamans depending on their education. Rojo remembered that writing, swimming, and other basics of Tania's education system would not yet to be implemented for several centuries.

The boy stumbled into the tent and fell on his knees. Several priestesses looked annoyance at him and a large man smacked the back of his head for interrupting. He caught his breath and then moaned as something compelled him to pick up the bundle. He lurched forward and made it within ten steps of the high priestess. A worshipper reached out to smack him again, but just before the blow landed, the boy dropped the ram's skull out of the bundle. A noise rose up from his throat as if being ripped from his lungs by talons. "Orcus....!"

The Jade God loved its name. Everyone knew never to use it ever. The ram skull pulsed a sick green light. Those nearest the boy scrambled away from him as terror and fear and an ill-wind swept through them. The high priestess turned and began summoning the Queen's might to turn and dispel the apparition. Rojo had seen this before and knew it would not work.

The boy's eyes melted to goo and his body twitched as, like that cursed word, his soul tore free into the ram's skull. The high priestess banishing prayer struck the skull and nothing happened. Had this been an imitation, it may have. This was the sceptre mount of Orcus' wand. It needed a body, which it took from the boy's spinal column. The floor nearby collapsed as a tunnel opened by zombie hands. A vampire rose up from the hole and grabbed the wand. Warriors had entered the tent now but a casual wave of his other hand blasted them back through the tent as if leaves in a strong autumn wind.

The dread wand fully activated as the souls of those warriors streamed into the wand. The vampire grinned as the priestess attempted to turn it with the Queen's might. He stood there. The radiance of the turning struck it and the ram's skull laughed maniacally back at her. "My turn," the vampire said.

The wand rearranged itself to face the priestess and commanded with the voice of a thousand nightmares, "Kneel before the one true eternal god!" Green rays of light arced like lightning from the ram's eye sockets to the priestess' and she screamed in agony.

"No..."

"You will kneel," the vampire said and again the wand's monstrous voice – KNEEL. Every bone in the priestess' body below her knees shattered and she fell to her knees. A whirlwind sucked the tent away to reveal the valley floor being struck by fireballs as a meteor shower exploded overhead and rained death down on the tribes. "You will all kneel," and the vampire struck the wand to the ground. Like a stone dropping into a pond, the earth rippled outward in a wave as bones shattered when the ripple reached the people. When the ripple touched the dead, their bodies twitched and reanimated.

Rojo heard Alerius' voice moan, "At this time, all of my children older than 10 would come back as ghouls or stronger. The suffering of the Innocents haunts me still. Only the very young or sickly would have become zombies. I have since allowed less strength into my children as it increases the population and odds of prodigies such as you and my Circle."

Ghouls, ghasts, wraiths, and mummified corpses stood upright and turned on the survivors. Combat broke out across the valley. The vampire laughed and the wand shrieked its glee. The whirlwind overhead swirled with green lightning and then a titanic cloven hoof stepped down from the sky.

Alerius whispered, "The First Cascade starts…"

The vampire morphed into a hellhound and attacked the crippled priestess. Somehow, she fought it off. But Rojo's attention remained on the Jade God as his head peered down from the clouds. Its pestilential breath struck the birds and insects in the sky which fell like wet spider webs of tearing flesh to the earth. "You offend me," it screamed. Even the undead cowered against the words. The living turned and ran in terror. Rojo, watching this, felt a part of himself respond; all at once and at the same time he wanted to apologize for the offense, to stand rock still, to beg forgiveness, to curry favor, to change whatever it was that offended the titan… and in his heart he understood that Life itself offended the Jade God. The implied reaction to the statement was suicide.

Chapter Eighteen – The First Cascade

Alerius in human form gated a legion of fire giants into the battle around the priestess. The familiar kerckhi armored warriors tackled the hellhound and pulled it back from the priestess. Alerius pointed to her and ordered, "Rally my children and let Takhissis' might guide you. Destroy the wand." Her wounds instantly healed and divine might filled her being. Kerckhi armor appeared around her as did a column of fire that burst from the ground and rose up around her. Her flames washed over the Dathraki and charred the vampire to a crisp, leaving the sceptre to fall shrieking to the mud.

Alerius lifted his arms and dragonfire erupted around him burning the undead to ash and healing the living. His dragonshift put him into his powerful form, but he appeared miniscule to the titanic demon. Rojo's heart leapt with pride as his god emperor attacked. As he raged dragon fire at the demon, other dragons answered the patriarch's summons as other reds, blue, white, black, and green dragons appeared from nowhere and attacked. Not to be outdone, the so-called "good" dragons appeared as well and silvers and golds joined the fight.

Alerius spoke to Rojo, "This is the only other time so many of my kind have gathered together since before the Dragon Wars. Our last great alliance. You'll notice there are no shadow dragons. And now the cascade begins. This much magic and might in one place next to an abyssal power..." The emperor at last cleared the area around the wand. A surviving zombie had grabbed it and began running away. The emperor's exhalation of white hot fire slagged the wet mud, which washed over the zombie. "In my pride, I thought I could destroy the wand." The wand sustained the zombie.

The Jade God tore into the dragons with its fanged maw and spat out undead dragons. As any creature fell, it immediately rose in undeath. Alerius himself barely avoided such a fate in a desperate maneuver to open a gate inside Orcus' mouth. The gate to the elemental realm of water filled the demon's mouth to overflowing. Meanwhile, the combined might of dragons scoured and then severed a massive leg and the Jade God fell to its hands and knees. It screamed but the water gushing forth masked it as a gurgle. Alerius swerved into Orcus' mouth and shapeshifted at the last instant. His human form passed inside the fangs and a moment later a gate to the realm of fire and then earth opened. Orcus reached for his wand, his Tehran instrument and embodiment of power but a kerckhi grabbed it up just out of Orcus' reach. A swarm of undead gave chase.

A moment later, a volcano erupted inside the Jade God's head. At the same time, Alerius chewed his way in dragon form out of one of the Jade God's eyes. The gore and violence took Rojo's breath away. "My god, I have read your histories and heard the stories but this... Father. You do us proud to name us your children."

"The volcano was the Queen's idea. It is now the Soldier's Fort. I've always been fond of the purity of the elements as a weapon."

The death of a gold dragon triggered it. As the gold rose up a dracolich, the powers of "good" sent a heavenly servant to fight. The angel appeared in a flash of sunlight and then more appeared. The green cloud maelstrom darkening Tania cracked open and natural sunlight scorched the undead where its columns touched them.

Across the plain, the wand shrieked, "Master! Master! Your Hellhounds come!" The dathraki holding it had fallen under its spell, driving the wand into his chest cavity to feed it more power more quickly.

Across the field of war, gates opened and Orcus' Hellhounds sprinted forth fangs and claws tearing into the living. In answer to the Hellhounds, other gods sent their servants. And so the fight escalated. Alerius said, "Watch Rojo, the River..."

The scene shifted and Rojo gasped. With so many alignments and powers clashing, the River had stopped flowing and instead twisted in on itself. Rojo saw Alerius step to the black hole of nothingness at the center. "Behold Anti-Life. This is not even Chaos, not even anything. It is oblivion and nothingness and nightmare and terror. I was naïve and thought I understood but the Jade God already knew. See there."

A hellhound ran along the banks of the River with a brown-robed eldar human on its back. Ignoring Alerius, the human enchanted a spell and flew into the void. "That is Bomoki. He seeks to affix Anti-Life in my children's home."

The knotted twisting River tore open and the battle scene in Morbatten suddenly opened in the River. The battle's participants began moving in and out of time chaotically, and from the blackness all around, demons from the depths of the Abyss surged forth as nightmares that terrified even the undead. "As you know, I moved this to Bloodstone where Bomoki succeeded in opening his portal." Back in the vision, Alerius slew the rider's hellhound and returned to the battlefield.

When the gate shifted with Bomoki, Orcus left. Without Orcus there to maintain the demonic pressure, the battle quickly shifted. Across the valley floor, undead crumbled to ash in sunlight. Angel feathers soaked in blood and burning blew in the wind. Blood mist hung in the air still raining down from fights high above. The idyllic plain had turned macabre. Of all the tribespeople originally gathered there, only twenty-five had survived rallied and protected by the priestess, the dathraki, and Alerius. There were a few tense moments as the forces of dragons and heavenly beings eyed each other. In that tense moment, Alerius reached his head up to the sun and howled. His wings encircled the survivors and all there, bore witness to the red dragon patriarch's tears as he cradled his twenty-five. The god emperor's howl turned to sobs and all there heard, "My children, my children…" He turned his wounded head to the sky and roared his anguish so that even the servants of Heaven trembled.

The vision ended and Rojo startled to himself held in place by the emperor's hand on his shoulder. His face streamed tears and he wept. Alerius' grip gentled and then the emperor spoke, "I turned my attention to fortifying my Morbatten. Those twenty-five, I removed to the northern mountain plains. The rest of my empire came together that day. Painful as it was, you humans are driven by events like this. Your lineage Rojo traces back to that priestess, the first Dar priestess of my mother's first Temple At Morbatten. Within 30 years, and by my own labor, Morbatten was fortified but lacked enough soldiers to defend her. I opened my borders, sent out recruiters like Daryx, and within 100 years I grew tired of waiting. We marched on Bloodstone."

Rojo's grief calmed in the silence that followed and wind blew through the mountain. The sun had started rising and gleamed golden orange out in the sea. "Take note Rojo that, when your destiny comes, you are of that priestess and she withstood the Hellhound in direct combat. At the feet of the Jade God, she rallied my children and guarded over them. You have already withstood Hellhounds. This time, you will stand before the Jade God and it will be different. My children must strike this time. It is your time. You, not I, must stand against it. Unlike your ancestor, you are armed with centuries of knowledge, training, and a war machine unlike anything conceived in Tehra, ever. With LORD and now LORD's successor here, the time is nigh for you to unleash this beautiful war machine. This grand spearhead is almost ready to destroy Orcus."

Rojo watched the sun rise and the white clouds drifting in the air. Down in the valleys below them, he could just make out the openings where the progeny of those survivors now lived as the "barbarians", the pure bloodline of the humans Alerius had preserved for millennia. His human father had been chosen by Alerius to come into the Capitol. There he had fallen in love with a Sorian woman and opened a trade route to Taysor. While not exactly "typical" behavior for a barbarian, Rojo remembered his father had always been a stand out. He had a gift for strategy that most of his kin did not. It made him stand out from the warrior stock. Though a powerful fighter, his father had shunned typical hand to hand combat and had proven a savant for defeating his challengers in unconventional ways.

In Taysor, he and his wife gave birth to Rojo and then to a daughter. By the time Rojo could walk, he and his father attended a dojo set up by Imperics worshipping the god Imperius. By his eighth birthday, his father had achieved their highest martial recognition. Had he converted, his father would no doubt have become a powerful priest in that religion. However, he remained true to Takhissis. His conviction to the dragon queen caused no end of problems in Taysor, which prided itself on the worship of the so-called "good" gods. It had orphaned him but not before his father had taught Rojo and ensured the Temple of Imperius knew Rojo. The martial skills learned there had always served him well. Rojo had brought it back to the knighthood and the Temple order. Proficiency with Imperius' religion and fighting techniques had been added to the Empire.

Rojo clenched his fist and turned looking up at the dragon emperor's eyes. "I will be ready Father, and will do the Queen proud."

Chapter Nineteen – The Lich's Ultimatum

At a different overlook far southwards, a dire figure shrouded in grayish shadow-shifting armor glowered over a battlefield. The southern gates of this human city called "Ori" had yet to fall. He felt out of time and place. While magic readily came to his call, it felt sluggish as if it suffered from too many chokepoints. Something about this place resisted his will to reshape it. He could, but it took far more effort than he remembered. Everything about this place felt like he walked against a current of wind and water, slowing him down and tripping his thoughts. The language and names and places, even the land all looked blighted and sick to his eyes. He turned his back on the carnage spilling forth in front of Ori's southern gate.

Two revenant warriors dragged one of these strange humans into the chamber. The human had a shaved head and wore loose-fitting clothing. His body from ankle to wrist to neckline bore a tattoo telling the tale of this new god, Imperius and probably some scripture and some other dribble about the human's own achievements. As ordered, the man's hands and feet had been amputated and a heavy head cage fastened around his upper body. The revenants tossed the man into the room, his wounds smearing the floor red with fresh blood and the heavy head cage shrieked against the stone. The revenant held forth a hissing and steaming golden symbol. Where its desiccated hands held it, small sparks of golden fire burned.

The lich stepped forward and enjoyed the man's increased quivering. He asked this Imperic, "Talai qkival?" The lich shook its head remembering that none of these new creatures understood the eldar languages. "Would you live?" The revenant tossed the symbol to the lich who caught, felt it begin burning into his hand, and held it before the man's face. In shock and writhing in pain, the lich sensed the man's death and touched his forehead. His black fingernail dug into the skin and hot burning magic and the lich's will that he not die bound his wounds together, trapping his soul in its dying body. "You will not die, not today. But, tell me, who do you serve? What is this token?"

The man took several breaths trying not to choke on the pestilential aura filling the space between the lich and revenants. "I serve Imperius."

"Yes, you serve this so-called god Imperius. I've heard this before. Do you want to die here, forsaken by your god? I need a messenger." The lich grabbed the metal head cage and lifted the man off the floor. "To take a message to that city. It's your lucky day. You'll be my messenger whether you wish to or not, but I know you'll say yes because it's the right thing to do." The lich rasped an evil chuckle. The lich held the man up to look out over the plain of combat and the southern gate. Life-stealing chills ran down the metal head cage from the lich's hand. "What is your name?"

"Toshiro Daikune, monk of Imperius," he coughed out blood and the words.

While they watched, the lich whispered and the flow of magic enwrapped them both. They vanished in a flash and reappeared several hundred yards before the gate. Corpses and rivulets of blood ran back from Ori's raised walls. Though the sun shone brightly overhead, the lich's daytime army worked siege engines and hurled stones, decaying flesh, and molten heaps of cast off armor and equipment into Ori. Holding the human in one hand, the lich pointed at the gate and its forces in line parted. More eldar words and the ground pulsed and rent as a crack ran towards the gate. Golden robed priests along the wall had already alerted to the lich's appearance, but moved into high tempo as the crack reached the wall. Golden spears of light and shields either tried to deflect the magical attack or to reinforce the gate and walls around it.

The lich chuckled low and wickedly as the gate held and cheering erupted from the wall's defenders. The cheering, after a minute, turned to jeers and taunts. "See how naïve they are?" the lich said to Toshiro. Someone used a catapult to launch a stone at the lich. The aim appeared dead on but the stone crumbled to dust that blew down and away from them.

"You will be my messenger now Toshiro. Tell them of dust and ash and pain." The lich dropped the hand and footless monk to the ground. The head cage pulled him off balance. "Crawl and give them this message. Either your god Imperius or your ruler shall meet me here tomorrow at noon to discuss Ori's surrender. Failure to respond, will result in more of this."

The lich lifted the head cage and turned it to the southern gate, "Watch."

The gates rippled and then turned molten. The walls around the gates did as well. Burning creatures leapt out of the liquefied stone mess and attacked the gate guards. Whatever touched them fell apart into oozing fire, like some kind of amoebic but elemental fire monster. Spells and prayers slowed the creatures a bit but then the gates trembled and fell completely into an oozing wave of glass. What had been the walls, puddled and began draining into the torn earth. The lich dropped the head cage and its weight clanged loudly on the stony ground as Toshiro fell on his face and arm stumps. "You'd best start crawling monk."

Toshiro tried to move forward and only sheer will made it happen as he whimpered in agony. A voice behind him whispered, "and Torment. Tell them they will serve me either way."

Another few lunges forward and he coughed choking on his own blood. Each movement hurt, was a lightning storm of agony. The creatures left him alone though. After what felt an eternity, he made it to the gate.

Chapter Twenty – Morbatten's Ambassador

Bereft of his hands and feet and weighed down by the heavy metal cage around his head, Toshiro crawled on his bleeding knee and elbow stumps. As he crawled, he prayed to Imperius but something about the head cage prevented his prayers. He could feel it as a different pain from his maimed body.

The gate was not safety. The lich's armies milled about laughing at the molten goo and splashing it at the Imperics across the way. Toshiro's pain and his wounds mocked him as he struggled on over the field littered with everything but bodies older than the night. As night fell, any corpses left would rise up and join the lich's host. The ogres commanding the day forces spit on him and laughed, being joined by the chattering of the other goblinoids. Overhead, the siege barrage continued in both directions but no one and nothing touched the monk as he wormed his way forward. The molten ground cooled to his touch and he began working across the oddly-colored lava.

He must have reached the front line because something kicked his head cage and then a gruff ogre voice swore and the obstacle blocking him moved. An eternity later, he felt the ground grow warm and he knew he must have reached the beginning of where the gates' foundation sat. Too far away, he heard his people cry out "Look! Look! What is that?" Some minutes later, the ground started to burn his already abused body and he tried to sit up. Someone cried out that he appeared to be a monk. At that, the ogres behind him barked a series of commands and the host retreated to let the defenders come forward.

He sat, praying, counting, trying to stay conscious. At long last when gentle hands and kind words spoke, "Oh god Toshiro! What did they do to you?!" he collapsed sobbing.

It took several mages and priests to remove the head cage. While they did this, Toshiro recited the lich's message. It created a flurry of activity as messengers ran to and fro. When they at last pried it open and off Toshiro, and the first healing spell kissed his body, Toshiro passed out from the relief.

He awoke propped on a cushioned divan that had been placed in the royal audience chamber. The high priest of Imperius and several kensai – expert skilled weapons master – adjutants stood in attendance around the daimo's throne. A healer knelt by Toshiro's side and offered up some tea. "Here senpai, you must be thirsty and hungry."

While Toshiro sipped the tea and fought back nausea, he learned that his message had been conveyed to the daimo who had called this emergency session. "Besides Imperius [referring to the Temple generally], the military and our allies have been called. Morbatten should be arriving shortly as well," the healer added.

Toshiro looked at the healer and wondered why Tania rather than Sora would respond first. The healer shrugged and held a rice cracker to Toshiro's lips. "You know how they are. They love a good fight. I doubt they are here for us, probably the fight draws them."

Sure enough, and after everyone else had arrived and started making introductions, and after the palace guards had sealed the royal chamber's doors, a hot breeze blew the windows open and the Tanian ambassador strode into the room from a black magical gate hanging two dimensionally in the air.

Walking into the circle, he stopped just before the daimo's personal space and bowed low. "All hail Ori and the mighty Temple of Imperius! I come with the dragon emperor's authority and tidings of support for our trade partners! King Rojo and the Queen of Dragons send their blessings and prayers that Ori emerge triumphant in this time of challenge. I am Dar Itain." The words rolled off his tongue in fluent Imperic, but the steel in the ambassador's eyes held no warmth. All present struggled to hide their annoyance but took note of the ambassador's rings, signs, and tokens of achievement and power. Without doubt, here stood a man highly decorated by Tania, a paladin of the dragon queen, and a veteran of what appeared to be no fewer than three campaigns in Bloodstone.

The daimo's magistrate answered politely and greeted him. Dar Itain turned and paid proper respect to all present and then took his seat. They quickly discussed the siege and noted the total destruction of the southern gate. Rebuilding, even if magically hastened, offered no guarantee that the lich would not casually destroy it again. Imperius observed the lich must be an eldar to which they asked Toshiro to recount his experience and observations.

Toshiro tried to stand on crutches but was gently restrained by the healer. His ruined feet and legs would require months of healing before he might ever walk again. He told his story pausing frequently to answer questions. "Yes, there were two revenant warriors. I saw them but there could have been more. No, I did not notice if the lich reported to anyone or thing else. It was in command. No, I saw no signs of worship or markings. Yes, the lich appeared fully in control of its armies, but also confused by our world."

On that last point, the conversation turned to ancient myth and legend. The Isle of Khasra had not been a center of any eldar empires or beings, at least not that anyone knew. No ancient legends fell on Khasran soil. If anything, the Imperics had been the only major thing to ever happen to it. Its proximity to the monster and demon wasteland of Mondsa Island tended to overshadow what few things happened here. Agriculture, some small mining operations, and vast uncharted territory from which monsters occasionally harassed adventurers made up most of Khasran lore. The daimo asked Imperius to come forward, "Will the great god come to our aid? Is it even an option?"

The Temple priest representing the Imperic Temple spoke now, "We have sought guidance and believe the great god Imperius would intervene. However, the Temple believes it is too hasty to seek at this time."

Dar Itain added, "Imperius is a mighty and powerful lord," the Temple frowned at the implied lack of godhood in title selection, but he pretended not to notice, "but in this case, I agree. The appearance of a contemporary (we must be clear about the eldar versus newer gods) god to an eldar creates too much risk. There is a risk that the lich is powerful enough to ascend but is not yet familiar with its capability to do so. There is also the risk of a divine cascade, which would bring unwelcome attention to such a creature. It would also be destructive to Ori."

The daimo interrupted him, "So Our Lord Imperius will not be involved

158

now?" and the Temple confirmed. "So I must go. Very well. What thinks the council of my speaking with the lich?"

Everyone present spoke against it, except the Tanian ambassador. The risk to the daimo, to it being a trap, to so many other things began to hurtle back and forth as arguments against action. At last, Dar Itain stood and stabbed his sword into the stone floor. The resounding crack quieted the chamber. Speaking almost too quietly to hear and in flawless Imperic he said, "This debate gets us nowhere. Either present a military option or accept that, for now, the lich has an upper hand. Might I add, it is not like a true lich to allow you to recover your fallen and give you an unasked-for cease fire to speak with it. Consider your own stories from Bloodstone heroes. The fallen always augment the necromancer, yet this lich gives you time to reclaim your own. He knows you are healing them."

A general presented a bold plan to rebuild the wall, send a decoy that would appear to be the daimo, and to attack the lich with all the forces of the priests and mages and warriors. "If we ignore the goblins and focus on the leader, we can eradicate the true threat."

Itain spoke, "The lich is not necessarily a threat. Just because it attacks you now, does not mean it could not become an ally..."

The Ori general drew his katana and in the blink of an eye flashed it between Itain's eyes. "Our people suffer and die and you say it is NOT A THREAT?!"

Itain did not flinch, and in fact did not even regard the man. "The dragon emperor stood in these islands during the eldar times. There were no liches, nor undead, well not like what we face now. Necromancy and especially the kind that would touch the elemental realms used on your gate... these things did not exist as eldar concepts. Life, death, various forms of life beyond death, time itself... these were playthings to the eldar, tools of creation and destruction.

"Consider Toshiro's report. The lich's confusion at our world extends, it would seem, to its failure to understand that there are gods in opposition to undeath and chaos now. The symbol of Imperius, for example... it burned the revenants and the lich but they did not care. Why? In other

159

words, does the lich even understand or care about your opposition? Because the lich is unaffected, its necromantic creations are not affected. To be blunt, the lich is not in opposition to your Imperius - YET. He stands in the sun, burning, and does not notice or appear to suffer. How is this a typical lich? I recommend you cease use of the term "lich" and instead find its name and use that, or the term 'eldar'. It is their term from themselves after all."

He made casual eye contact with the general and said, "You hear the term lich, but the lich has not said it. This eldar did not have a soul created here and then trade it for immortality and power. It has always had a soul and it has only ever known power and force of will. This is eldar, not undeath, not a sorcerous trade to the Jade God for an extension of life."

The general withdrew his sword at the daimo's express command. Itain continued, "I think we should speak with it. For Tania, I will be happy to accompany you my lord. I also think you'd be foolish to not rebuild your wall. Even if the lich smashes it down a thousand times, your people's morale requires action. But, really, what you most need at this time is first, for the attacks to end and second, for a brave group of heroes to step forth and neutralize the lich so it no longer menaces Ori nor can pose a threat through the Jade God. In short, you need more time. Talking with it may give us that. The longer term one, tell me, does Ori have such heroes?" Itain's eyes locked on the general's as he added, "Who is not scared of an eldar lich?"

The general quivered and then drew his sword against Dar Itain again. In a blink, Itain parried the attack and said, "Only a great coward would attack a friend." In that heartbeat and with Itain's words goading him, the General raged, too furious to listen to the calls to stop. Itain stood his ground and parried the wild attack. A lucky thrust reached in and scratched Itain's cheek tracing a thin red line. The daimo screamed for the general to stop and the Temple priests looked confused, not wanting to stop the General, not wanting to disobey the daimo.

"You are the coward!" the general screamed as he unleashed a lightning attack through his sword at the ambassador. Itain raised the Queen's symbol on his sword and unflinchingly stood as the lightning slammed

160

into him.

"I ride the hurricane of Chaos and stand untouched," he recited scripture from the Book of Fire. "I am the hurricane." The bolt sizzled and pulsed and Itain stood there, completely unaffected. When the blast and noise ended, Itain said, "Dar Rojo holds your religion and culture in the highest respect daimo. The empire of Morbatten stands by Ori," he looked at the general readying for another attack. "I am the hurricane!" Itain said in draconian and his sword crackled to life with the Queen's energy. His avenger, unsheathed, gleamed in the room's light and Itain observed, "No wonder your southern gate fell so easily, if men such as these guard it."

The general lost it and threw himself at Itain, who stood there, his blade poised and ready. At the last moment, a monk of Imperius side-kicked the general away from impaling himself on the ambassador's blade. The general crashed to the side whirling on his assailant. That the side-kick came from a high priest and grandmaster of Imperius did not seem to phase him, or perhaps his rage blinded him. Itain stood still, like a statue, and remained poised to strike. As the general started to scream a challenge, the daimo's sword cut through his arms and the general's sword fell to the ground. "Remove and imprison this... thing" the daimo ordered. "I have no room for generals who turn on our friends while real enemies ravage our borders."

The general was dragged out of the room and Itain relaxed his stance. His holy avenger, his paladin sword, calmed and was resheathed with a whispered prayer. The grandmaster of Imperius bowed and expressed gratitude, "My lord daimo, I apologize for interrupting but did not wish to continue insulting our northern friend. Dar Itain withstood shameful behavior far longer than most of his people. Consider his king for example." He bowed lowed to the daimo and then to Itain. "Our apologies Dar Itain."

The council resumed discussion, this time around preparations to secure the daimo. After some time, the daimo stood signaling the end of discussion. "Grandmaster, you and the Lord Ambassador shall accompany me. Generals, make ready for full attack and prepare the walls for defense." He bowed. The others, kneeling, returned it and then one by one left until only Dar Itain remained with the daimo.

After ensuring they were alone, Itain bowed again and whispered to the daimo, "The dragon emperor sends the Order of Water. Our objective tomorrow must be to extend the cease fire. The Order of Water will be the heroes I spoke of and will find and neutralize the lich. Even if a lost eldar, Tania cannot risk a Hellhound rising up in Khasra. We cannot afford it, neither can Ori I think."

The daimo looked into a brazier's burning coals and lost in thought asked, "Why is it that Tania not Sora responds to our request for aid?"

"Is it your intent to suggest that we planned it this way?"

"No," the daimo said. "No, not at all. Just that Sora could if it wanted to. I have heard stories. I find it odd that our more closely aligned-in-spirit allies to your north" referring to Taysor "always offer to send aid that arrives after Tania. And again, Morbatten is here and they are not."

Itain smiled and bowed, "Tania honors its commitments lord daimo. Surely Taysor has mages that can send their ambassador here, or like Tania, maintain a gate. Dar Rojo still desires formal establishment of an Imperic dojo at our Temple mount."

The daimo breathed in the brazier's incense and then sighed. "I wish to see your great city before I die. Rojo was an amazing student. I remember him never smiling, never laughing. But his technique and focus. Unparalleled. Please..."

"It shall be done my lord," and Itain bowed low. "The dragon emperor himself shall greet you and tour the Queen's temple with you. If I may, the Order of Water is led by Dar Kendra, the sister of the High Priest Kell. It is the strongest paladin order. They and their entourage will arrive soon and I have preparations to make for the Order's arrival."

Alone now at last, the daimo sat back and thought on his eighty years of life... and his fallen southern gate. "I will not be remembered as the daimo who lost the south, but who saved it."

162

Chapter Twenty One – Malcor versus the Undead

Malcor dodged to the side as a ghoul threw itself slavering at his face. Though his sword connected just fine, the ghoul barely noticed its oozing entrails and readied to jump again. As he had just been taught, Malcor stood tall and firm, almost defenseless and presented the Queen's symbol on his sword. A crimson light kindled there and then sparked as Malcor commanded, "Hear me now, and obey, or die!"

The ghoul retreated a step and eyed Malcor ferociously. Malcor's fellow knights stood around them in a circle. Of them all, Mal presented the easiest target. The ghoul readied to jump attack and Malcor repeated the command, "Hear me now, and obey or die!" The crimson light reached out and struck the ghoul's chest appearing to lock there and a battle of wills ensued. It had been like this since Malcor had opened his eyes and realized he had died. Before he could even ask about it, Tembri had shoved him back into the combat rune.

Tembri spoke from behind Malcor, "The ability to control or even destroy undead is a power granted to divine servants of any god. Our Queen allows us control, but it is a fragile thing. Too much control and you destroy them. Not enough and they attack you. Focus on bending it, like a green twig, but do not break it.

"Obey, and kneel!" The ghoul shook and as if an invisible hand pressed into its back, it kneeled. A look of hatred, confusion, and then berserker rage fought across its fanged jowls. "You will remain kneeling and take no action!"

Malcor thought his voice sounded tenuous and unsure, even panicky. One of the dead corpses arose as another ghoul. The strain of holding the one ghoul's obedience while fighting off a savage attack resulted in Malcor almost losing control of the one and getting killed by the other. Bleeding and covered in drool, Malcor felt the telltale feeling of paralysis from the ghoul's numbing attacks, but stood firm. Like the other, he created a space and raised his symbol. He also signaled for healing.

Lack of sleep and overall healing fatigue had quickly caught up to him. Healing Fatigue, a problem suffered by combatants healed too many times over a short period of time, sapped vitality and energy and focus. Healing could mend wounds and restore mental acuity but used too much, the toll on the body added up. Malcor guessed he had died and been healed at least a hundred times since training started yesterday. He fought while eating and drank while healing. Foe upon foe came at him until, with shock, he found his sword had cut apart a human criminal... who then became the first ghoul. Eventually, even if healed, the human body shuts down. It could still be healed but the mind, heart, and soul needs rest and eventually it asserts that need with unconsciousness. His training would take him beyond.

The room swam and Malcor struggled against it as the healing spell mended his wounds. "Hear me now, and obey or die!" he commanded. The second ghoul clawed at its own face and pranced around Malcor on its knees, whimpering at the other ghoul as if urging it to break Mal's control and then break Malcor.

"Stay focused Malcor. Think of the ghoul obeying as you would your arm. It is part of you. You are tired. Think. What can you do to retain control and also deal with your enemy?" Tembri's deep voice barely registered with Malcor, but somehow he turned his attention to the obedient one and ordered it to defend him.

The kneeling ghoul leapt and attacked the other ghoul. It gave Malcor time to marshal his will and try again. Tembri's lecture continued, "The healing fatigue you feel is similar to the feeling many undead attacks have. Shadows, wraiths, vampires, and other more powerful can drain your vitality. Some do it by touch, others can do so as a form of ranged attack. When you feel this fatigue, and you don't know why – like frequent healings or lack of sleep, you know you are being attacked. As a knight, your power will grow quickly until you can resist such attacks. For now, you feel the ghoul's paralysis. You will feel lethargic, but you can't let a feeling win. All warriors suffer from battle fatigue. Know it. As a knight, it is your choice to be paralyzed. Do not let the ghouls win!"

Malcor caught his breath and regained his footing and composure. The ghouls fought ferociously nearby, just out of arm's reach. He steeled his will on the one he controlled and renewed his command, "Defend only, do not attack."

"Very good Sir Malcor. You cannot turn a creature that is being attacked by your will."

He pointed his dragon symbol at the other ghoul and boldly ordered, "Obey me, or die!" He tried again, "In the name of Takhissis, I command you to obey!"

The ghoul, like the other one, grew confused and then clawed at its ears. Malcor felt a tenor of control assert itself. The ghoul calmed and sat back on its haunches. The other retained its defensive posture though still kneeling. Malcor, ordered both to stand at attention and then to hold hands and then to play leapfrog. The hatred burning in their eyes never left but his control felt absolute.

His legs, no his entire body, felt shaky with exhaustion. He looked at his hands and it trembled so badly he could barely see it shaking. It just kind of blurred back and forth. Dar Kendra walked up to the edge of the combat rune and commented. "You are doing well, but to defeat a lich, you must do better. As you can see, the ghouls obey you, but their hatred for you grows the longer you enforce that obedience. Eventually, it will break and they will turn on with all that pent up hatred. However, we need to test your boundaries Malcor. Ghouls are the highest form of undead that lack free will. What is the next highest?"

"Ghasts, they organize ghouls into hunting packs, like an alpha wolf with a pack. If you see a ghast, ghouls and other ghasts will be nearby. They are larger than ghouls and will often acquire armor and weapons. They lead from behind, usually."

"Indeed. And higher than that?" Malcor responded with "wraiths", "mummy", "shadow", "vampire", and lastly "lich". Dar Kendra looked at the ghouls as their hatred threatened to overtake Malcor's control. "And is this an absolute hierarchy?"

Malcor looked up at her, taken aback by the question. "It is the hierarchy I have been taught. That everyone knows. But, I suppose hellhounds and the Jade God himself would top out that hierarchy?"

Behind Dar Kendra, three hooded figures appeared. They walked forward into the pale light of the combat rune's circle and pulled their hoods back. Each looked like a powerful if older man but had a pale complexion, way too pale for their dark hair and midnight pools of blackness in their eyes. Dar Kendra said, "Malcor, allow me to introduce you to the three vampire generals of Bloodstone. Crea, Malcom, and Nineveh. Though vampires rank lower than liches in terms of undeath, these three are examples of how there are ranks upon ranks of power in any level of undeath. These three are free-willed, and at one time they commanded the hellhounds. Now, they are wards of the dragon emperor."

The three of them bowed slightly. Malcor remembered something about vampire generals but his vision swam and he gratefully welcomed the break to eat and drink. The one introduced as Crea stepped forward. He said, "I was a priest and a mage in the service of the divine god Pha Rann when an eldar vampire took me. Malcolm," he gestured to his side and the other, "served as the high priest of the worship of Braden the Healer. Nineveh was a mage on the brink of ascension. The Jade God took us and we were controlled much like you have those two ghouls. Never forget, in undeath, the dead retain some measure of their mortal power. Nineveh, as a zombie," they all laughed, "would be a terrible zombie to have to fight."

Malcor hoped to buy more time and said, "It is an honor to meet you. Thank you. Thank you so much for coming to help. I'm curious though. How did the Jade God take you? Braden, if I remember right, is the super good god of healing? I also don't understand the hellhound thing."

Verit started to answer but Crea nodded and said, "The Jade God's primary tool here is the Sceptre bearing his name. It is a magical artifact that, unlike a god leaving its throneplane, does not weaken. The sceptre can take any creature and possess it. Even us. Bearers of the sceptres are called Hellhounds. Unlike all undead, Hellhounds are free-willed. Think of them as the generals, avatars, perhaps even angels of the Jade God. The Jade God created it here in this world and it copies itself into a weaker form we call Wands of that god. Any of the three of us could have destroyed the wands. But the sceptre is a different story. Having been taken by it, we guess it could take a god."

Behind him, Nineveh agreed and Mal remembered that Nineveh was the one 'close to ascension'. "So you were all hellhounds?"

Kendra interrupted, "Malcor, we have to know the extent of your favor with the Queen. The ghoul challenge is usually not attempted for several years after the second rite, and then only in Bloodstone. These three are here to test your limits. I know you're tired. I know you are exhausted. Make yourself ready and signal when you are."

Malcor shook his legs and arms. Looking over at the ghouls, he re-seized active control and felt their hatred spike. At his command, they fell back to their haunches. Their finger claws spastically reaching out to Malcor and then falling back in confusion as he directed absolute obedience at them. He heard Kendra order Tembri to refrain from helping.

Chapter Twenty Two – Malcor Climbs the Undead Ladder

Crea walked into the rune and with a casual wave of his hand, the ghouls charred to dust. "Obedience requires a higher level of focus, as you have experienced. Combat, other things that distract, and the undead will seek to break free. They hate that you're controlling them. I'm sure you feel it," Crea said. "As a paladin, the pain, suffering, rage, perhaps even fear, or love... all of these become weapons to either help you control or destroy the undead. More powerful undead though can manipulate your focus. If you use love as your driver, as a vampire, I can sense that and project fear of losing your loved ones against you. These battles of will are deadly. You will almost always be better off destroying them rather than controlling them.

"There are levels of undead that you cannot even imagine Malcor. Entire worlds in the Jade God's realm are full of them, waiting to come here and feast. The Hellhounds, like their god, want to freeze this world in decay, and stop the River. Tania's philosophy is not to categorize or organize the undead, it is to slay them all. Permanently. Disintegration by magic or fire, or beheading does the trick."

A knight brought a chained prisoner to the combat rune. The prisoner looked petrified with fear. After removing the prisoner's shackles, the knight shoved the prisoner into the rune circle. He immediately fell to his face and began begging for mercy. "I will show you," the vampire said to Malcor, and also the audience that had come to see the famous vampire generals. Crea pointed his finger at the groveling prisoner and said, "Why do you tremble? Put your fear aside. I am your friend. Do you fear execution based on your murder of that little child last month? Look, as your friend, I get it. It wasn't your fault. Shhh, there now. Listen, it's going to be all right. No one is here to execute you. Far from it! The emperor has decided to give you a second chance!"

Crea's voice had an echo of magic behind it. It suggested pleasure, comfort, and safety. The man looked up. His eyes still held fear and terror, but his face relaxed and he asked, "You are my friend?"

Crea nodded. "Come stand by me." The man stood and practically danced to Crea's side. He looked relieved and happy, like a convict released from jail to a dear friend's welcome. "Malcor," and that same spellsong called to Malcor, "Come stand by me as well."

One of Malcor's legs twitched and he stepped forward. Though he tried to resist that charmed welcome, he started another step. Crea's eyes bore into Malcor's. "Why do you resist Brother Malcor? You are tired. Wounded. Why keep fighting for your dreams when I can give you relief. Your dreams are here with me. Don't you want them now?" His body lurched forward. Thoughts of relief, of a hot bath with R'Dar Ora, of food, of sleep filled his mind.

Crea's voice pulled him forward another step, "All these things are yours, just a few more steps and you'll be here with me. Such a good boy, such a good warrior. You are exhausted. That girl, Ora, she wants you. This training, this test takes you away from her love."

In his mind, Malcor knew this to be a test of his will but Crea's voice and that power... the test felt suddenly unfair, everything about it. He just wanted to be a knight. What did any of this so-called "training" have to do with being a paladin? Calvin surely was not training himself to death right now. He knew Ora was watching him and he knew she wanted to be with him. He could feel her hands remembered touch from the day before. He wouldn't have to fight a lich of all things... his body smoothed out a bit and he took a normal step forward and then stopped.

"No..." Malcor felt he screamed it but the word barely squeaked out of his mouth.

Crea smiled and suddenly, Ishan his old master from Klenna stood before him. "Well Mal, you've had a hard day's work here. Good job. Lets go grab some food and celebrate! You did it!" A strange man stood next to Ishan, probably a new apprentice or helper. The newcomer said, "C'mon, you had your first perfect day and look beat. And you finished your second rite! Way to go! I bet a kettle full of meat stew is what you want! Ora made it."

Suddenly, the image vanished and Malcor found himself back in the blood-soaked combat rune. His feet rooted to the stage, unmoving. Crea's eyes bore into his soul and Malcor knew what he'd see if he went to the River. "Dar Kendra, his force of will is sufficient for the lich, for a short period of time, provided he is not exhausted and near death like he is now."

She nodded. "Good, lets start at the beginning then."

Crea's hands abruptly sprouted talons which he buried all five in the prisoner's chest. Amidst a blood spray, the man said, "But, but, you are my friend..." and died. The lifeless body slumped, held by Crea's talons.

Under Crea's flat and emotionless stare, unholy light filled the corpse. While Malcor did not understand what Crea did or how it happened, when Crea spoke, he understood well enough. "Slay the knight," Crea ordered the still impaled body.

The zombie corpse pulled itself from Crea's fingers and turned to attack. Like the other zombies he faced, Malcor raised his symbol and ordered obedience. As he felt the zombie's will slip away, Crea did something and the zombie's will surged. Malcor fortified his own and it surged again, morphing into a ghoul. Just as Malcor took control of the ghoul, Crea flooded the ghoul with necromantic magic and it morphed into a wraith, then a desiccated mummy, then a shadow. The shadow spun free in the combat rune and a tendril touched Malcor, who fell to his hands and knees.

Dar Kendra said, "Shadows cannot be controlled. They are too connected to the anti-realms. Stop trying to enforce obedience and focus instead on destroying it."

The light from the Queen's symbol finally connected with the shadow and he appeared to be making progress, when Crea did something else and the shadow became corporeal and a vampire rose up. Dar Kendra ordered Malcor to slay it while Crea whispered to the vampire... "All this pain, all these changes, it is this human's fault. He imprisoned you. He chose you to come here to die and die and die. You'll never see the sun again. Your loved ones will curse your name and spite the day they heard your name. Your crimes are unforgivable because of this man. Kill

170

him! Kill. Kill."

The vampire, goaded by these words and whatever images came with them, turned a berserker flurry of attacks at Malcor. For a moment, all Malcor could see was a tornado of bladed fingers and then it withdrew just enough for Malcor to appreciate how wounded he was. The vampire licked the blood from its claws and, like Crea had, "Malcor, you look weary. Let me give you rest! Just relax and notice the blood from your wounds, how it drips and pools. It is warm. Let me warm you."

Without meaning to, Malcor realized the vampire had taken his head and tilted it back to expose his neck from the protective edge of his gorget's steel. Razor fangs opened. His mouth would not move, so Malcor prayed in his mind to the Queen and with every ounce of his power, called for Righteous Might. His sword lay dropped several feet away. It twinkled and reappeared in Malcor's hand, spearing the vampire through its head. He let the vampire fall back with his sword embedded in its skull and then, freed of the attempted mind control, stood and commanded it back to his hand. In a smooth stroke, he decapitated the vampire... except that as his sword struck, Crea did something and the vampire transformed to dust. The dust coalesced and flew back over to Crea, and then began reassembling itself. Unlike the cold hate of the vampire, or the dispassionate hunger of the shadow, this new form regarded Malcor with an insane intelligence and murderous intent. A sword and shield materialized on the form's hand and arm as Crea said, "He is responsible for all your pain and humiliation, Revenant."

Without word or hesitation, the revenant attacked Malcor. Dar Kendra must have allowed healing because Malcor felt what had to be the last healing he could tolerate and then fully joined the fight. Malcor found that even with the River's help, he could barely parry the creature's attacks. The more tired he became, the more the River's abrupt shift in perspective became a disadvantage, and somehow the revenant was there too. "Like a shadow, revenants and wraiths aren't entirely of this world. As such, the River does not really advantage you. Their lack of free will hinders them being entirely effective there though."

Cut, slice, and bruising wound after strike and then Malcor knew he was done. He had been thrown backwards spinning on his back on the blood slick floor. The revenant stalked him and had somehow acquired Malcor's sword in his other hand. If Malcor had wounded it, he could not tell. He knew he would die. The revenant raised both swords and made ready to take his life. The madness of its glee unnerved him. Though he had died before, this time seemed different like he had failed a test and in front of so many others he wanted to impress. Like R'Dar Tor, he wondered where the rage and fury was that would drive him to somehow win.

He felt nothing. The swords sliced down and Malcor's world went black. Crea looked down at him, standing where the revenant had been. Dar Kendra walked over and looked down as well. She smiled. "The true test of a revenant is that they most want you to suffer like they do. Every second, you are called by their madness to take your own life in despair and futility. That you fought with no such indication means we are done with this part of the test. Later, when there is more time, you can do the more deliberate and controlled test at the Temple."

Crea added, "Each undead inspires a different kind of fear. Lower level undead inspire disgust at the after-death state of decay. It is so nasty. This horror of seeing one's own decay can overwhelm normal humans. Ghouls and their like inspire dread at the savage ending of life. Vampires urge you towards a beautiful death and the beauty of immortal youth despite the consequences. You just experienced the revenant. They want you to ache for your own death to end the horror of living. The lich, well, they are all about subjugation and saving your life through pleasing the lich. All of these stack up until you reach the Hellhounds and the Jade God. Though demons and devils can use the same influences. As a paladin, you can become immune to these, but it begins with learning and recognizing these for what they are – lies. But, just like a weapon, those lies can kill."

Tembri helped Malcor sit up. His body felt cold and frantic. Tembri realized he could not move even his fingers. "My lady Kendra, Sir Malcor is done. Right now, a chill breeze would take his life."

Dar Kendra turned and said, "Thank you all for enduring these five days of training and fighting. We had planned for three, just in case. No one has ever lasted longer than three. Malcor lasted five days and taxed all

172

of you almost as much we tested him. You have all done well. A special thanks to Crea, Malcom, and Nineveh for their help with this last bit. Tembri, please assist Malcor with recovery. In fourteen hours, we gate to Ori."

Tembri carried Malcor to his room. Malcor asked, "Has it been three days?" Except those words came out as unintelligible garble. "I couldn't even berserk," he tried to add, but Tembri shushed him.

"Mal, you lasted five days. No one has ever done that. Your healing tolerance is –" but Tembri's words also turned to fog. It all passed in a dizzy haze, but at some point, he was cleaned and bathed, and fed. When he at last awoke in his bed, hunger struck him and he stood to grab some food, and collapsed. Ora tried to move him but he fell asleep on the floor, and after struggling, she let him be.

Some hours later, Ora screamed to Tembri sleeping on the couch. "He's not breathing!"

Tembri jumped up and ran towards them. Malcor, beyond fatigue from days of combat and healing, lay unmoving but also unbreathing. He face, lips, and skin had taken a dark greyish cast. A trail of spit rolled from his lips. Ora had begun praying, "I had a dream Tembri, of his death. I think this is recent." Amidst her prayers, a tear fell from her eye and dripped on Malcor's face.

Tembri half-expected a miracle and her healing prayer to work, but Malcor was so far beyond healing; he had drained all of the stand-by healers during this trial, and taxed Tembri and the other battle priests too. Tembri elevated Malcor's legs and anxiously waited to see if the boy would respond to Ora's blessing. "Ora, he won't take anymore healing. Try a blessing or fortitude prayer instead. His constitution is gone." Stepping to the River, Tembri saw Ora there cradling the tiny spark of Malcor's aura. It pulsed chaotically threatening to blow out. Dark snakes of black ink reached across the River towards the boy, something Tembri had never before seen. The aura had a feeling of dragonterror to it, but there was no time to study it. Being dragonterror, Tembri prayed to the Goddess and hoped for the best.

"Ora, there's a technique we use in combat. It will restart his heart and maybe save him. It's very violent though. When you are done, you must let him go and not touch him." After a few more moments of prayer song, she reluctantly let Mal's head go and scooted back. Tembri closed his eyes and began chanting in draconian, something from the Book of Lightning but Ora struggled to make out the words. Tembri was mispronouncing them and she understood that he changed the blessing. First one and then many arcs of red lightning swarmed around and through Tembri's fist until the buzzing sound of energy and power was all she could hear. Dimly, through the River, she saw Verit and his battle priest enter Malcor's room and lend their strength to Tembri.

Suddenly, mid-syllable and dissonant song, Tembri opened his fist and slapped it against Malcor's chest. The red lightning electrocuted the young knight. From the River, it looked like a firework show of light centered on Malcor's twitching and seizing form. Tembri raised his hand into a fist and then slapped it down again, and again. "Once more my Queen!" Tembri screamed and he drew all of his own and Verit's priest into his fist and punched it into Malcor's heart. Ora winced seeing his ribs crack. Holding it through, Tembri injected electricity into his heart in a pulse-like rhythm. She saw his aura respond, still weak and flickering, but the chaos calmed and began mirroring Tembri's rhythm.

He held it for a few minutes and Ora felt and saw Verit's priest collapse, just barely caught by the paladin. Somehow Tembri held on and Ora gave her strength to him. She felt another source of strength and noticed, for the first time, the extensive tattoos along Tembri's side. From the River, they were laced with bloodstone dust and seethed with power. That's how he held on. "You have a bloodstone?" she whispered as he latched onto her offered power.

Verit set his priest to the side and ran out calling for help. Tembri held onto Malcor's pulse minute by minute as more battle priests from the Order arrived. Watching Malcor's heart struggle, she saw Tembri's aura weakening as the electrical storm in his hand kept Malcor alive. As priest after priest gave Tembri their might, and fell, despair clouded her heart and she resigned herself to watching this knight's death. "I will not be a deathwatch," she whispered to the Queen.

"No," a sinuous dragon voice answered her back from the other side of the River. "The boy will live. He is mine." Dragonterror came with that voice and for the first time in her life, Ora felt what others must feel around the dread lords. A black tendril, she focused and saw it as a claw, reached through the lightning and touched Malcor. The electricity stopped, everything stopped. Tembri frowned at the voice and the dark energy, but when it let go of Malcor, his heart moved on its own and a ragged gasp of air moved through his body. Grey energy suffused his aura and then the ragged breath became deep gulping of air. Ora fell back weeping. Even Tembri choked and then quietly sobbed.

Much later, Tembri shook Malcor awake in his bed. Ora stretched out next to him and he tried to smile. Something was off in both their faces though and he frowned. The dim light in his room was too bright. Concern and sadness mingled with hope. Was that what he saw? "You had a rough night," Tembri said. "We almost lost you." He held up his hand where capillaries and veins had ruptured throughout his skin. "Don't worry Malcor, your entire body and face look like that. Too much combat, exhaustion, and healing fatigue caught up to you. Your heart stopped. If Ora hadn't caught you right in that moment."

His whole body hurt. Hunger and nausea tore at him and vertigo made the room spin. He tried to focus on Ora.

Her bright eyes gleamed at him, and he saw she had been crying, and she said, "It's time for you to leave me. You look awful, we look awful, but Malcor, our time together was wonderful for me. You'll hear about priestesses taking knights for any number of reasons. I'm not like that. By the way, you excelled. To last five days is a new record I believe. As a Kell, they thought you might beat the record and set the target at three days. We actually delayed our departure for your test!"

Ora helped him stand and Malcor looked at himself in a mirror. His veins stood out black against the all-over purple bruise of his body. His eyes appeared wet and red where his whites should have been. He looked at his hand in the light and marveled at how clearly the individual muscles, tendons, and even bone shapes could be made out. Compared to Ora's flawless and nearly nude body, Malcor looked like a zombie.

Tembri walked off to get some food and said, "You fought for five entire days Sir. Healing Fatigue and continuous action like that melts all the fat and water right out of you. I'd guess that you're at least half sustained by healing magic right now. You'll flesh back out, but it'll take weeks." Tembri put a goblet of milk in his hand and walked off to retrieve his clothing and armor. "You'll be prone to dizziness and will likely fall asleep - a lot. Based on what we saw, I expect that it will be at least three weeks before you're near peak again and maybe months before your body recovers its full weight."

Malcor sipped the milk and ate some food, finding that his hunger knew no bounds. "I feel like I could eat an entire feast!"

Tembri chuckled, "You'll probably feel that way for most of your recovery. Don't worry. This is a known thing that happens with Healing Fatigue. You'll have food, rest, and if you fall asleep don't stress it. Even if you're talking to the King. Even the king went through this. You will not offend anyone."

Tembri checked Malcor's gear, making adjustments here and there to account for his emaciated form. At last, he indicated the time had come. Malcor summoned his armor and sword feeling too tired to walk over and remove it from the alcove in the corner. He noted it had been cleaned, mended, and polished to like new condition. Tembri hefted a large backpack and slung a duffel bag over his shoulder. He passed over a smaller duffel bag, carefully designed to not interfere with armored movement and sword play. Tembri explained that the duffel bag contained the minimum essentials Malcor would need to survive for about three days if separated from the group.

Walking to the chapel proved almost too much for Malcor and he had to stop several times and catch his breath. "I feel like I just climbed a mountain..." he sighed. Eventually, they walked into the chapel. A mage's guild representative, at least the robes made it look that way, and a few others he had not met before stood on the stage along with the entire Order of Water and each of their three battle priests. Malcor and Tembri's support priests awaited. Though only five steps mounted the stage, Malcor had to steel his will to ascend and struggled to mask his exhaustion.

Tembri whispered to Malcor, "Everyone here who participated with you is also trying to hide their fatigue. Don't worry. It's normal."

"If that is true, then why are you trying so hard to appear unaffected Tembri?" he snapped back harsher than he intended.

Chapter Twenty Three – The Order at Ori

Tembri grinned and pointed towards Dar Kendra where she walked onto the stage. A Dar rank priestess walked beside her along with two other healers. With interest, Malcor noted that the other two were not clerics of Takhissis. Dar Kendra walked into the center and said, "It is not often that so much power is assembled together for an epic quest. Let us pray."

They all turned to the goddess statue, and Malcor noted the gleam from his statuette in the same alcove. Kendra began but a sinuous male voice overspoke her. Dar Kell walked from the alcove and raised his hands over the group and prayed to the Goddess, speaking to Her as if She stood amongst them in the group.

"Mother, your children have come together to bear your name to the southern kingdom of Ori. While Ori does not serve you yet Mother, they honor the ways and might of your children. They steward part of your throneplane and do well in the eyes of the dragons. They are beset by a lich and an army that threatens them and they have sought our aid. With dragon fury and fire, we alone have the ability to help them with such great deeds as to shake the foundations of Heaven, we ask you to bless us with strength and might..."

As Dar Kell prayed, everyone felt their skin tingle and heard whispers of approval and promises of power. Malcor saw himself standing triumphant and glorious against hordes of goblins, kobolds, and ogres and then faithfully defeating the lich. As Dar Kell's prayer ended, a roar of wind encircled them with the beating thunder of dragon wings. All present felt the favored regard of dragons and then the prayer ended.

Dar Kell walked up to each and pressed his hand to the dragon symbol on the breastplate of each warrior, priest, mage, and others. For those not faithful to the Dragon Queen, he wished them well and that their god would watch over them. When he came to Malcor, he met the boy's gaze and said simply, "You did well. Be honorable and strong. We will talk on the other side." Those words, so unexpected, caught Malcor off guard and he felt his heart catch in his chest. He nodded trying not to smile or worse look confused.

Dar Kendra then introduced the newcomers. Dar Reznor's apprentice would join them from the mage's guild along with another mage more studied in combat tactics. Tembri explained that no one knew the man's name and he was simply called "Apprentice". The Thieves' Guild provided two "thieves" to aid with scouting and any other stealth functions they might need. Lastly, Kendra introduced a cleric of Krentismar, the patron god of the islands and the thri-keen race, an insectoid underground collective. With him, an elven ranger stood forward and greeted the party. "All together, there are forty-five of us. And, we have two goals with this quest. The first goal is to safeguard our friend and ally, Ori. The second goal is to place our newest member Sir Malcor in position to defeat the lich."

Malcor did not see where he came from, but suddenly Daryx appeared and said, "We have received a report from our ambassador Dar Itain. Please clear the combat rune and let us see."

An illusion of Itain appeared and Malcor noted his stoic if pleasant expression as he explained the situation. "They are demoralized. Tomorrow, I will accompany their daimo to parley with the lich. The lich offered to speak with their god Imperius, but – of note – the lich is either unaware or unimpressed with their god."

Daryx asked, "Can you qualify that the lich is an eldar?"

"He may only be an eldar Lord Daryx, and not a lich at all. As you know, necromancy and other specializations were somewhat fluid for the eldar. It has the appearance of a lich. Watch." Itain laid his cloak out and magically presented Toshiro's memories of the head cage, the revenants, the lich not touching him, and the destruction of the gates. "The lich shows mastery of necromancy and elementalism, and fuses the two together effortlessly. Note the sunlight scalding its flesh, but the lich does not even notice."

While he spoke, the image of the lich suddenly changed and a chill dread reached a skeletal hand out of the cloak grasping at Itain, who danced back from the cloak. He smiled, "And apparently, the lich has mastered scrying magic as well, though this is three steps removed from the lich." Itain closed the cloak's image and the dread left. Maybe for comfort, maybe for good measure, Itain stabbed the cloak and ignited his sword's fire to burn the cloak. Malcor felt he could smell the burning cloth through the illusion.

Daryx spoke and said, "You have done well ambassador. Be safe. The party will begin gating to Ori shortly. Their orders are as we discussed. Please let the daimo know. Dar Kendra has lead on the party backed by her battle priest and then Dar Reznor's apprentice. Itain, the emperor has asked dread lord Blaze to stay ready to intervene if needed, at your discretion." Daryx turned and left with Dar Kell.

Tembri whispered to Malcor, "Blaze is the common name of Alerius' eldest son."

The mage identified as Reznor's Apprentice turned and began casting a spell. In no time at all, a black slice of a magical doorway opened in the air. Into the center of this, the other mage projected an orb that looked a bit like an oversized human eye, and sent it through the gate. After a moment, the mage confirmed it safe. Group by group, they walked through the gate...

...and stepped out into a courtyard surrounded by flying red silk pinions framed in gold that glinted in the morning sunlight. All around them, cheering erupted and flower confetti filled the air. A divan chair carried by servants held aloft an elderly gentleman who regarded their arrival. Dar Itain stood to the side of the divan chair. After they had all arrived and stood blinking and adjusting to the morning light, Dar Kendra approached and bowed to the daimo and Dar Itain. "The Order of Water, first of the knights of Takhissis awaits action King of Ori and Lord Ambassador Dar Itain!"

The cheering erupted again. Exhausted and starving, Malcor held his composure as best he could but felt relieved when all but the party's leaders were dismissed to make ready. Tembri had water and food ready for him as they walked to a section of the southern wall. Though repairs looked well underway, Malcor pointed out the large circular portion of glass smooth ground that extended into the courtyard and fused up the walls around the gate. Tembri told him about the report he had slept through where the lich had melted the gates and southern wall, essentially undermining the foundation. "This is why the ambassador and others think the lich is an eldar. According to the emperor, the eldar could shape and reshape matter at will, just by thinking about it. This is a form of elemental disintegration that shows the lich was not sure what it was. So he melted it to its most raw form."

When Malcor arrived atop the wall last, he felt an eagerness in his bones when he finally looked out over his first actual battlefield. Except for the siege engines, it looked nothing like he would have thought. For one, there were no corpses, only blast marks from magic and siege/counter-siege weapons. Large stones littered the ground here and there and what might have been bloodstains, colored the ground in places. Missile-shielding barricades stood at angles in front of the siege engines and Malcor noted the small forms of what must be goblins or something similar moving around their base. Then a smaller creature came into view and Malcor realized that what he had thought goblins must instead be ogres. All of the siege weapons appeared cocked and ready to fire. He counted at least eight trebuchets and maybe twice as many catapults.

"Tembri, shouldn't there be debris and bodies?"

"No Sir Malcor. This is a fight with magic and necromancy. The dead rise up and if not recovered, even their body parts become assimilated into the undead army as tools and bits and pieces of weapons. Wood and metal are either recovered by the living or recovered by the dead. I should have forewarned you. Necromantic battles look quite clean in the light of day. However, like your second rite showed, they are quite gory and liquid during."

An Imperic, perhaps a monk, nearby said they had recovered only a handful of bodies in the morning. "It was odd Tanians, the lich released some of the undead and they fell with no trace of undeath at all. We have placed them under guard on holy ground." The young man bore the signs of many freshly healed wounds and he noticed the bruise of Malcor's face under his cloak. "Your face, what happened to it?"

Malcor started to pull his cowl over his face but decided instead to pull it back. The ruptured veins through his skin and the blood in his eyes' whites must look even worse than he had thought. The monk stepped back reactively. "Dear lord, what are you?"

"Hungry," Malcor replied. "My training schedule did not stop just because of this war."

The monk eyed Tembri and Malcor and then he shrugged. "I have never understood your people. Were you beaten for disobedience, or worse?"

Malcor shook his head no. "It's part of becoming a paladin. A trial of pain by combat." Tembri moved over and brought Malcor a wineskin and urged him to drink as his voice was fading to a hoarse choking sound.

"Your goddess is cruel to try you in this manner," the monk said indicating no offense. He turned his attention to the distant armies gathered just out of range. "Our lord Imperius requires us to prove step by step, skill upon skill. Isn't that what you do?"

While Malcor sipped the tea laced with healing herbs and plants, Tembri leaned on the wall by the monk. "Our Mother recognizes our potential very early. We then test our own against that potential. As such, the earliest rites are a test of young resolve – can they reach their divine potential. After that, it is similar. Skill up on skill."

A courier arrived and noted that the talks were about two hours away. Malcor fell asleep to Tembri awakening him. "Sir, the lich has arrived."

Chapter Twenty Four – Truce with the Lich

Malcor stood and looked out again. The Order stood along a section of the wall giving excellent view of the battlefield but would hide them quite well. Their goals did not involve direct assault or participation in combat, not yet.

A gate, similar to the one they had arrived in, but pulsing with purple lightning had opened just out of the city's range of siege weapons. Into the bright sunlight, a tall thin figure in full plate armor stepped. The gate swirled closed behind it and the creature folded its arms and remained standing. Its armies cried out screaming and hammering their weapons and feet on the ground. Malcor noted that this sound was what an army estimated of twenty thousand must be like. He imagined Armageddon would be able to destroy them in a single pass of dragon fire, and it made him feel better.

Looking at the lich, Malcor felt a chill cross his spine and saw Tembri feel it too. For some reason, it gave Malcor comfort that even someone as powerful as his battle priest felt that dread chill. Malcor tried to shift to the River to see if the lich appeared any different but found he could not. He tried again and Tembri put his hand on his shoulder, "It's a force of will Malcor. You can't River step when you're still on the threshold of death. Give it time. You can't see anything anyway. We already tried. The lich has magical defenses in place. There's nothing to see there."

The daimo, unwilling to risk any attendants, walked out of the city gate with Dar Itain at his side. The lich did not move until the two of them stood about 5 paces away. Itain bowed and appeared to introduce himself and the daimo. As he finished though, the lich interrupted with a voice that pierced the entire city and surrounding area.

"Know thy place. I know not what a Dar Itain is. Nor this frail old man. My messenger instructed you to bring your fool god Imperius, or this city's ruler. I see only meat."

The daimo replied, "I am this city's ruler." He pointed to Dar Itain. "This is our ally and friend, my advisor."

The lich nodded, "Very well, Daimo. I do not wish to shed any more life than is necessary. Are you ready to surrender? My terms… are absolute surrender. Don't be a fool. What kind of god would I be if I did not reward and cherish the people of this city?"

The cold dread of the lich's tone, that struck them with fear, suddenly became that of a lover willing to do anything to protect his love from harm. Like before, its voice carried throughout the city. Some of the Ori guards near them murmured, "Yes, yes, he won't kill us! The daimo should surrender!"

Dar Itain appeared to bow and stepped back from the lich. When he was some 15 paces, he jumped and his body surged, transforming into a green dragon. While not as large as any of the dragons Malcor had experience with, the green dragon sparkled in the sunlight and then dragon fear crashed down over the city overcoming the seduction and offer of love. In draconian, the green hissed down at the lich, and its words silenced the lich's voice.

The lich looked at the dragon and Mal noticed Tembri holding his breath. Tembri explained, "The lich is checking to see if this is an illusion, or maybe if the ambassador is a mage of some kind. If we are right, and he is eldar, he will not recognize this type of divine intervention. The eldar had no gods, no religion, no doctrine. Ah, yes, the lich is intrigued."

The daimo spoke with the lich for some time, at one point, the old man even paced. The lich however, never moved. They appeared to reach some kind of agreement, with the lich nodding its head. The green dragon opened its claw and the daimo stepped onto it. A second later, the green dragon soared into the sky. The lich barely turned its head to acknowledge. All around, the siege engines relaxed on the enemy line.

The green dragon landed in the courtyard behind the repaired gates and gently set the daimo down. Itain, in dragon form, then leapt back into the sky. In spite of how gentle dragonshifted Itain had been with the daimo's body, dragonfear swept over the entire city causing panic everywhere. Like his fellow knights, Malcor stood tall and proud as every other person in the area quivered in fear or dropped down covering their heads. Some younger soldiers actually dropped their weapons and tried to run, but lacking a place to run to, they cowered trying to look unaffected. The daimo and a few others stood their ground but Malcor could tell the fear had affected them too.

The dragon left the courtyard pin-needle quiet. The daimo spoke, "My people, the lich has agreed to extend the cease fire. I agreed to some terms. Let this edict be sent forth to all our peoples. The lich will walk the streets of Ori unchallenged. He wishes to see our city. He has promised us no ill will, but will no doubt defend itself. As king, I require that all of you respect and honor the lich. He is not to be harmed, mocked, threatened, or antagonized in any way during his visits... on pain of imprisonment.

"Should the lich retaliate, the deaths and damages caused shall fall on the heads of those provoking him. Provocateurs will bring great shame to their families, and to me. I gave him my word. Though a powerful creature of evil, he comes from a time where "evil" did not yet exist. Concepts like "good" and "evil" mean nothing to him. Your lives mean nothing to him because death, in that time, meant a transformation into Chaos and a new life. He has started to understand our world but does not. Lastly, he mocks our god Imperius, and does not understand nor care to understand the ways of honor and honorable combat. He will visit the temple of Imperius, and we must comply! Let it be written as law.

"Also, he requires tribute. I have agreed to pay this tribute in the name of holding the cease fire. A tax shall be levied on all citizens. I expect full cooperation, beginning tomorrow! Let it be written as law."

The Order of Water retired to a barracks below the wall, to prepare.

Chapter Twenty Five – Out of Time

The lich walked into a chamber he had begun to use as his place. Melted rock glistened as if frozen all around. As he entered, his revenant bodyguards took up positions to either side and then enlarged to tower over the assembled group of ogres. The lich looked over them and smiled. Though magic felt sluggish in this new place and time, he had been able to summon these easily enough. Though they lacked the majesty of the ogres from his time – some new god named Grimsh or something – had corrupted them, he had been able to magically enhance two into magi, his army's generals. He considered transforming all of the ogres into magi, but experiments had shown an unacceptably high fatality rate. Only a few of them appeared to have the spark of intelligence required to carry and use magic.

The two general magi knelt before him. One commanded the siege line and the other commanded the main attacking force. "I have reached an agreement with the city," the lich said. "They will bring us tribute. A small amount tomorrow I will personally collect. After that, you two will be in charge of meeting them and collecting it. You will each take four of your own. Those four each are to take as much as they can carry, no more, no less. Any questions?"

One of the generals bowed his head. "Great one, when we have collected this tribute, what shall we do with it?"

The lich loved this about these magi. Straight to the point without being insulting. He could feel the other questions burning in their minds, but they chose this one. "For two of the four, distribute to the captains. The rest is to go into the treasury. We will drain this city dry of its wealth." The ogre magi smiled. It felt wrong that they were all so easily motivated by the promise of treasure. He continued, "Have the army begin practice skirmishes for a mountain invasion by small groups. But note, I want them monitored and challenged, not killed unless they are weak. The strong are to be allowed to continue. Set the strongest defenders at the treasury, with traps, ambushes; impress me." The lich twisted his hand and a golden and gemmed cup appeared floating over its hand. "Give this cup to the captain you deem most worthy to stand up a third army, a defensive one. I believe that the humans will shortly attempt to enter this place. We will try them and see how they do."

The other magi bowed his head and spoke. "The dead have all been retrieved and are laid out as per your command."

"Perfect. I am pleased with you both." The lich spoke louder for the rest of the captains to hear. "We have a cease fire with the humans. Use this time to repair and build new siege equipment. Bring more of those barking lizard creatures into the army and train them to scale ladders and attack the walls. The magi will begin a series of skirmishes, which are not to result in deaths. The winners of these skirmishes will receive plunder from the city. Until my order, none shall enter within sight of the walls. Each of you, take a squad and place a line of stones around the wall so that the army may know not to cross it." The lich turned back to the magi, "You two come with me."

When they left, the revenants stepped forward and glowered at the captains until they left. Boasting and challenges had already started and a group of ogre captains had started shoving each other. One drew steel and went to backstab his fellow. A revenant shrieked, causing all of the captains to scream and cover their ears. The captain drawing steel paralyzed and then roared in agony as the revenant tore its soul free from its body. The roar went silent as the soul's connection to the body severed. The captains watched in dark fascination as the soul continued to scream silently, trying to escape the revenant's grip. The ogre's body fell, and caught itself mid-fall, lurching back upright. Purple fire sickened in its eyes and the zombie turned, leaving the group, and walked with slow intent into the mountain tunnels.

The revenant pointed the terror-stricken soul to the group, holding it aloft so they could see. The soul pled, begged, and then began tearing apart in the revenant's hand. Many of the captains dry swallowed or licked suddenly dry lips. At last the revenant said something but none of the ogre captains could understand though the intent came through. Its harsh consonants vocalized by one long dead, conveyed a certain brutality. As the soul tore, what might have been spirit blood showered down from it. The revenant pointed to the exit and said another sound. To the captains, it might have meant "Go!" and they took it to mean such as they all hurriedly exited.

In a different room, the lich and the two magi looked out over linen-draped corpses. Laid out in neat rows, the magi noted two hundred and eighty-six had been recovered where the bodies met the lich's criteria. The lich uncovered one, noting the human had been killed by a single sword stabbing into its heart. "Perfect," he hissed. Though most of the corpses were from his own army of goblinoids, the lich looked over each of the humans noting the odd tattoos of this "god" Imperius. "What a pathetic god, to force its thralls to tell its story on their bodies, and then to let them die."

"Look here Great One. This one has more of those markings than any other. We found this one ringed by fallen captains and a pile of our own dead. We recovered the dead, and you'll see that all of them are in perfect condition. Somehow this human slew them without cutting or smashing."

The other magi added, "We fought ones like this before you came to us Great One. They are called "monks". They fight without weapons and use their bodies to kill."

Intrigued, the lich commanded, "Impress me. Bring this one back, as I instructed you."

The ogre magi stood over the monk's body and clasped their hands as if praying. Though they clearly despised each other's touch, the spell required it. As the lich instructed them, the ogres recited words they did not understand but had memorized in the eldar language of the lich. As they recited, the lich corrected pronunciation and form here and there. Purple, green, and other sickly colors of light swirled up and around the lich and, like serpents, struck the dead body. The magi began to sweat and then shake as exhaustion began to affect them. At last, the spell ended. "Very good," the lich said. "Lets see if you performed well... for your sakes, lets hope so..."

For too many moments, nothing happened and the magi began to fear for their lives. At last though, the monk blinked its eyes. Like the lich, only purple fires showed there. The monk sat up and looked at its hands confused. The magi grabbed the monk during this confusion. The lich pulled a vial from within the folds of its robes and armor. "Welcome monk. You will drink this."

The monk, finally noticed he had been grabbed and began struggling to break free. As it struggled, the purple fire in its eyes arced into its body. "You are weak monk. This drink will give you power."

The monk noticed the lich. "You... I was fighting..."

"Yes. Yes, and you fought well. You are surrounded by those you slew. Look at them all laid out. Magnificent battle. But in the end, you too died. You are dead. Your soul might remember bits and flashes of it, but you are my creature now."

The monk finally broke free of the magi and fell forward. He dug his fingers into the stone floor and then jumped back as the stone broke and shattered around his hand. His jump would have taken him into the ceiling had the lich not caught him mid-air. "I gift my servants with power. What you used to be, is no more. What you are now, is mine. I am your god now. I am your Imperius." The lich placed the monk back onto the ground. "While your old self would likely view this as a curse, it is not without its benefits..." the lich pointed to the shattered stone. "Strength, speed, regeneration, and immortality... these come with a certain price. In this case, your old life burns away and I become your new god."

The monk noted its teeth had sharpened to fangs. "What am I?"

"You are a vampire." The lich shook his head remembering, "No, not a vampire the way your old self would have understood it. In the eldar times, vampires were simply creatures that fed on magic through blood-drinking. The act of blood-drinking was a metaphor for acquiring magic. If you want to, you can and will be stronger for it. But, like my two generals here," he pointed to the magi, "you can draw directly from the wellspring of Chaos, the source of magic." The lich held forward the vial. "I command you to drink."

Compulsively, the monk grabbed the vial and drank the dark ichor inside. Purple fire immediately suffused throughout his body. The light became blinding and in that light, the monk saw the lich standing lordly and proud and very much alive. The monk noted that far away, almost too far to see, a ribbon of energy and light moved from searing brightness to twilight shade. *Is that a river over there?*

The lich's voice hit him sounding awesome and glorious. "You see this place and how magic flows through it."

When the light faded and the monk returned to the room, the lich looked like before, but brighter. The magi appeared smaller more diminished somehow. Monk tried to remember his life before and stared at the tattoos on his arms. The script there told his story of training and devotion to Imperius and the martial arts. "My name was Shiniba. I barely remember. We called that energy flow, the River. It is Time and magic and energy moving from creation to the end."

"It doesn't matter. I would rather you serve me of your free will. Though I can compel service, it is not how I do things."

Shiniba nodded. "I will serve you, for now."

"Good enough. Come. Your first task is to organize defenses for this, our place of operations. It is too close to the city of this god Imperius. We will either move into that city, or we will find a better base. For now, I need defensive fortifications and a plan to repel attack. I foresee several groups attempting to come here and either try to kill me or steal the source of my power, my soul gem. You are to be my last great defense against that."

The monk looked up and surreptitiously asked, "Is there a source of power that can be stolen?"

The lich laughed. "No, I am my own power. While I am not concerned about whatever attempts they may try, I do not want them thinking that they can walk into my place with impunity. In particular, lets make this interesting. I entrust the details to you. All of these," he said pointing to the corpses, "are yours to command and start with. In particular, I want this room and pool of water secured at all costs. It is to be your first priority."

"Master, what shall I call you?"

The lich did not answer and walked out of the morgue. One of the magi said, "We call him 'Great One'. We do not know his name either. The master said to know a being's name is to have power over it."

Not knowing how he did it, Shiniba summoned the dead to follow him and one by one they arose wrapped in purple fire and followed him into the mountain's depths.

Chapter Twenty Six – Preparations Made

"Wake up," Tembri's knee nudged Malcor's shoulder where he had sat down and apparently fallen asleep again. The barracks were too small for all of them. In Imperic fashion, they slept on straw mats. The heat and humidity of Khasra made it impossible to feel cool but so exhausted was he that any slowing down in the pace of activity made him fall asleep. He stretched and sat up.

Dar Kendra stood speaking with her battle priest and a member of Ori's royal household. The black haired man bowed deeply and ran off. "We have been granted use of the throne chamber to plan our activities. We start in thirty minutes."

Tembri handed Malcor some more food. With barely a day of recovery, Malcor still looked like a walking skeleton with too-stretched skin. Most of the Imperics gave the boy wide berth and more than a few stared openly at him, their eyes darting elsewhere when he met their stares. The other knights offered verbal encouragement, but for the most part gave him the space and time he needed to not feel self-conscious about how exhausted he felt. It made him feel a bit lonely though.

Walking out to the courtyard, Malcor saw heavy chargers dressed out in Tanian armor as well as light sprinting horses used by the priesthood in support of the knights. Tembri led Malcor over to their two healers and explained, "After we gated in, Apprentice brought in all our gear. Until you've had training, you'll be riding one of these lighter horses if we need them at all. I doubt we'll be doing much riding where that lich is."

Two healers came forward and bowed, greeting Malcor warmly. Though they had met formally, there had been no time for in-depth discussions or conversations. Malcor learned that, unlike Tembri, these healers had just passed their second rite, which qualified them for official combat support. "The next rite for a priest is to earn glory in combat. Brother Tembri has is order mixed up!" They had applied and been wait-listed for the Order of Water for years. "We probably missed many chances, but are thrilled to work with you Sir Malcor. My sister entered an order that is often involved in logistics and movements. She is already at her sixth rite, but..." and he chuckled, "...she'll have nothing on me when we defeat this lich!"

It dawned on Malcor that these healers would support Tembri supporting him. It made him feel humbled and more than a bit insignificant. The two healers had been friends for some time and watching them banter back and forth made Malcor wonder how Calvin fared. He asked how the Order of the Shield worked. Though both Tembri and Ora had explained it to him, he finally got it when they explained it this time. "The Shield Order is protective, especially of the mages. The mages are not often put in harm's way, but when they are, it is usually in anticipation of some attack that might overwhelm the front line. They train for guarding the mages and recovering them before they can either be killed or captured. Think of the mage as a fortress and the Order as the wall around that fortress."

They walked to the throne room. To get there, they passed through immaculate gardens of raked pebbles and pools of soft-flowing water. An elderly man played a koto, its dissonant twanging completing the feeling that Malcor, most certainly, was not in Morbatten anymore. The rhythm followed him through the garden and into the shaded steps before the throne room. Dar Kendra had changed from her armor into more comfortable dark steel gray silk attire Malcor noted many of the elite seemed to wear. Like most Tanian clothing, it had a certain flair but allowed for total freedom of movement. Like Malcor, the others kept their armor on. Mats and cushions had been set out for them and they all sat kneeling. Steaming cups of tea and snacks had been set out by each mat. Actual benches ringed the area and on these, the battle priests and others sat. Apparently, only the knights would sit with Dar Kendra.

Once everyone had arrived, Dar Kendra bowed to the empty throne where the daimo would normally sit and then turned to face her party. "Fellow members of the Order. Welcome to Ori. The extension of the cease-fire, though not anticipated came as no surprise to those of us familiar with Dar Itain. We have an unknown amount of extra time. My plan is simple. Our stealth experts and ranger will look for possible entry points to the lich's base. The rest of you will remain quiet and low key. The lich will be walking here in Ori. My orders are for each of you to avoid the lich at all costs. Understood?"

A priest, and a higher ranking one, signaled a question. "With the lich here, in daylight, this group should be able to easily turn it. If the lich is too powerful for turning, we could certainly attack and slay it. May we understand why we are to avoid it?"

Kendra looked out over the group. "This is not Morbatten. Expediency does not rule Ori. Honor does. The daimo gave his word. We must respect that. Also, defeating the lich is not the objective of our party. It is Sir Malcor's objective. We must create that opportunity and a fight here in the city, besides putting Ori's citizens at risk would not guarantee Malcor that opportunity."

Another hand signaled and Kendra said, "Ask."

The priest of Krentismar spoke and asked, "I do not understand the objective. Sir Malcor appears to be just a boy, against the lich. Surely defeating the lich is a higher order objective..."

Dar Kendra cut him short, "Our orders from the dragon emperor, and our agreement with your Temple, is not open for question. Sir Malcor is my squire and the emperor himself has made this decision. It is to be one of his rites."

Undeterred, the priest said, "Defeating what may be an eldar lich? For a rite? Am I hearing this correctly? Defeating a powerful foe, but - I still do not..."

"You are not required to understand," Kendra interrupted. "Look, I know this may not make sense to you but consider that nothing about your religion or your worship of a god limited to the Forsaken Isles makes any sense to us. Yet, you do not hear or see us railing against these things we do not understand. I ask that you take this on faith and may the Queen of Dragons bless you with insight."

Reznor's Apprentice signaled and asked, "The Order's request to the Mage's Guild was vague on several points. Are we here for combat, support, or other purposes?"

Kendra smiled and said, "Other purposes that include combat and support. I do not wish to go into combat with a lich without my own trusted mages. As you know, the Order's assigned mage recently crossed over into Temple service, leaving us absent a key post. Reznor felt you may have interest in this quest. Do you?"

"Honor and glory to you Dar Kendra. Yes. I would submit my application and prove myself worthy of this Order. It is long overdue that I serve outside the Mage's Guild."

Questions turned to more general tactics. Because only three of the other knights had ever faced a lich, Dar Kendra established some basic tactics. "The paladins will stand in front with the healers in the back. When not healing, the healers are to focus on turning. At distance, this should confine the lich to an area. The mage will keep the lich from leaving magically. Our resistance to magic, our divine gift from the Queen, should protect us from magical attacks. The real challenge will be Sir Malcor's fighting ability. This lich, it seems, carries weapons and is adept at both combat and magic."

"I will be ready to play my part," Malcor said as eyes turned to him. "I will not let you down." Tembri and his healers called out their support. "I have a question though," Malcor added. "If we engaged the lich's armies, this group alone would devastate it. Would it not be easier to confront the lich as part of the overall war, than to seek it out and manipulate it into being alone?"

Some of the knights chuckled and one said, "You come to us with dreams Sir Malcor! What would it be like for this group to come together and fight an army! It'd be glorious! Alas…"

"…since Bloodstone, Tania must be careful about full scale confrontation with necromancers. It tends to draw the attention of the Jade God. In this case, with a pre-Hellhound lich, we must find another way. However, once we have better intelligence about the lich, its armies, and the layout of its home, I am willing to allow any of you to fight alongside Ori for a time. Should our plans change to allow it."

Verit quietly noted to Malcor, "And the Order of Water does not draw attention to itself. You'll see. Daryx and the Empire prefer to keep us out of sight and out of mind. It gives us agility, mobility, and flexibility to engage strategic enemies, like the Hellhounds."

Tembri agreed, "Like all of us Malcor, you'll be given official rank in one of the other Orders. Only the Order Generals, like Dar Kendra, know who all of the Water members are."

Questions from there wandered back and forth between strategy and tactics and what-ifs. Malcor found himself paired up with two other knights, the other mage, and the elven ranger. "This group will be responsible to explore any potential openings and determine defenses and likelihood that we might find the lich. I want all of you ready to roll at a moment's notice."

Other groups were formed as well. One to shadow the lich as he wandered in Ori. Another group to explore and map the battlefield. "My group," Kendra said at last, "will be tasked with drawing the lich to the location we desire. As such, we must find something of utmost value to the lich, such as its soul gem. As you go about your tasks, keep your eyes, ears, and inspiration open to such items of value."

The next several days passed by in a blur. When not working or making preparations or moving to avoid the lich as it wandered through Ori, Malcor slept and ate. He started to show signs of recovery and the horrified stares sent his way changed to a normal curiosity at their foreign appearance and attire. Malcor heard stories of King Rojo having come and trained here as a young paladin, and having done well "for a foreigner". They always added that.

When not otherwise pre-occupied, Tembri and the healers sparred with Malcor teaching him new signals and practicing basic maneuvers intended to allow the knight to protect the healers and vice versa while exchanging healing and other spells. "Compared to us Sir Malcor," Tembri said at one point, "you are a battering ram. We are defense heavy and this basic tactic allows us to propel you forward. This creates space as enemies die or retreat. We then step forward to cover and heal you. Ram, step, heal, advance. This technique is called 'The Ram'." They practiced The Ram over and over. It meant three prayers Malcor had to open himself to. The first made him fast. The second changed his body's size. For an enemy line, they see only an increasingly large paladin charging them with unbelievable speed. "As you cross into their lines, we will flame strike you. The flame creates a zone around you of dead and dying enemies." Tembri explained it as the most basic Tanian squad tactic. So that he would not have to signal each, The Ram had its own signal.

They had drawn a crowd of samurai, monks, and others watching. Tembri ignored them. "They are familiar with Tanian tactics. Focus here. Sometimes, it helps to not be a giant target. The armor and weapons of the Order make you an easy target for powerful foes and spell-casters. Of course, you seek out such foes and welcome the attention. It is what makes you who you are. However, strategy sometimes requires a different approach. As a paladin, you are most effective surrounded by enemies. Look at this current situation as an example. All of the knights want to kill the lich, but you Sir have it as your sole objective. This means that, even if you see a prize far greater than the lich, you must refrain. A fellow knight could strike a death blow, but must not. So, The Javelin technique. May I?"

Malcor nodded. The two healers began praying and Malcor watched with interest as the three of them grew very large, but Tembri more than the healers. Suddenly, when Tembri picked Malcor up, he understood. They had strengthened and enlarged Tembri while shrinking Malcor. "We have also boosted your agility my lord." He made ready to throw Malcor, "This is why it is called The Javelin technique."

Malcor soared across the courtyard, and a fellow knight's battle priest caught him. As he landed, he grew back to full size. The two nodded at each other and Malcor walked back. He had travelled easily two hundred paces. When he made it back, Tembri added, "In combat, you would armor up and land on your shield. Hopefully, I throw you well and the bodies of your enemies cushion your landing. When you are more powerful, I can also flame strike you and that column of fire will burn back your enemies and also show us where you have landed."

"What do I need to do to withstand the flame strike? Tell me about that attack."

197

"You must be baptized in the River. By a transcendent servant of the Queen. Dar Rojo, Dar Itain, Dar Shara, Dar Kell, someone like that. By tradition though, it is not done until you have completed the fourth rite. In your case, I heard a rumor that yours would be the blood of heroes." Tembri sat back and gestured for Malcor to eat and drink. "Flame strike is our summons of dragon fire from the Queen's throne plane. It opens as a column of divine fire that reaches up into the sky. A novice's flame strike is typically four men tall and one man wide. It lasts seconds. As the cleric grows in favor, the strike becomes more malleable. Though I cannot yet move my strike, mine is fifty men tall and ten men wide. I can maintain it for about one minute and call upon the Queen's favor for it six times a day before it exhausts me."

Malcor remembered Dar Shara and how she not only held her columns for hours, but had multiple columns that danced with the knights and reached up into the sky above Klenna. The healers looked impressed at Tembri's description. "We have not been trained in flame strike. Our focus is healing and support. We'll learn it someday after we have mastered our core."

"Tembri," Malcor asked before they went, "the blood of heroes, is what exactly? I've never heard of it though it's a term I have occasionally overheard since coming here."

Tembri looked as if he would ignore him, but others expressed an interest in learning as well. He sighed and signaled for food and water. "We'll take a brief rest. So, look, you have seen the River. You can move in and out of it. As you know, it presents an overwhelming advantage. You might wonder, why not always fight from the River? I'm sure it has crossed your mind."

"It has," Malcor replied, "but I have also had times where I could not access it or was so abruptly pulled out of the River that it broke my concentration. It seems arbitrary."

One of the healers chimed in, "It does. Our healing is more powerful from there too, but my instructor told us to never trust the River."

Tembri took a long drink of water. "The thing about the flow is that it's made up of fragments of magic and major events from the entire realm of all worlds and universes. What is happening to us right now, is not reflective of what is happening everywhere. Just before right now, something amazing or horrible may have happened. It creates tides and currents. The longer you stay in the River, the more power you use there, the more likely you get caught by one of these. Those are random.

"The other issue is that not all those who access the River are like us. We live in Time. Each moment flows to the next moment. This flow of Time will eventually bring us death by old age. However, for undead, for immortals, for gods, Time does not quite work that way. Linearity only exists when they are in this world. One step to the River and linearity only exists when they engage with us in our time. Another step and another, and as they get closer to their own throneplanes or whatever passes for their home, and different rules begin to apply. For gods, like our Mother, there is only truly cause and effect, action and consequence. There is no Time.

"What this means for you and all of us is that when we enter the River and alter Time, we invite scrutiny. As you grow more powerful, you'll invite more and more. It'll be easier for enemies to find you if you're there splashing all about, metaphorically speaking."

They discussed this for a bit while snacking though they had to bring more and more food to Malcor. "And the blood of heroes is what – another metaphor?"

"No, it's literally the blood of heroes, taken from the River."

"So, heroes go to the River and bleed? I still don't get it."

One of the healers said, "You've heard about cascades right? And bloodstones?"

"I've only heard that bloodstones are rare, they're mined in bloodstone, and it's a big deal. I have not heard of cascades."

Tembri looked at Malcor, "But you know the stories about Dar Kell, for instance, when he fought in Bloodstone against the hellhounds and suddenly angels, dragons, undead, powerful beings joined into the fight?

The songs call it the War of Angels I think." Malcor nodded. "That's a cascade. Kell's fight with the hellhounds disturbed the River to the point that other gods chose to intervene. Your baptism will be in the River, during a cascade."

Chapter Twenty Seven - Lich Game

More days passed in training and doctrinal study. It was not until the fifth day that Malcor finally ran the battlement stairs without wanting to die for exhaustion. The Ram and Javelin had become second nature. Malcor sat in the garden listening to the koto and watching two monks spar when a commotion caught all of their attention. Conversation around him dealt with the lich. The lich had been busy, visiting Imperius' temple, visiting the libraries, and speaking with several of Ori's artists. Such interactions came back as reports to the royal household. After the lich visited the Imperius Temple on his first day, Tania had removed the shrine of Takhissis entirely, choosing to destroy it rather than have the lich enter it.

He saw a courier come running, waving a paper to enter the throne room. The lich had distributed papers throughout Ori. It announced a fabulous prize, set in a maze of traps. "Conquer the maze and receive the treasure!"

When the courier entered the throne room, the daimo and Dar Kendra stopped their conversation, listened to the courier's report, and dismissed him. The daimo said, "The lich grows more and more bold. He knows this will draw out adventurers. Perhaps he seeks to test the true mettle of our people on his own terms."

Kendra replied, "It is a test no doubt. Will you allow it?" The daimo looked out in the courtyard as Malcor stood and engaged one of the monks in basic sparring and foot movement. He looked pensive and she continued, "Your empire has benefited greatly with King Rojo's understanding of your ways. Do you still resent the Queen's knights studying these techniques?"

The daimo watched Malcor quickly pick up the basics. "I do not resent it. These fighting techniques were perfected by Imperius and became part of his glorious ascension. Your king would have made a great kensai." He referred to the reserved title for weapon masters who transcended weapon mastery and took it to an entirely higher level. "He would also have been the first Tanian to serve Imperius."

"The Queen has other plans for Dar Rojo. No doubt, the Queen has plans for you and Imperius as well. We all serve the Goddess."

The daimo grinned, "Indeed. I will allow the adventurers to gather and go. Perhaps your scouts could join one of the parties. Have they returned?"

"No, and they are overdue. If they do not send word or return by dawn tomorrow, I will attempt to scry and perhaps recall them. It depends. So far, the Queen provides no guidance. I feel the time we buy here gives us advantage, though I could not tell you why."

The daimo took of a sip of tea and continued to watch Malcor sparring. "He is young to have joined your Order no? If I recall, the last initiate was well over forty years of age when he joined. He is truly Kell's son?"

Kendra nodded. "Your sources do you honor. That one there - Malcor, well, he found his way to us on his own. He is a rare breed of paladin. And, he is Kell's son. Tell me my lord, have you met Ynt'taris during one of your visits to Tania?" referring to the white dragon.

The daimo thought and said, "Too many years ago when I was still young and foolish enough to think I could debate a dragon! After meeting the dragon emperor, a party was held. At some point in that, I was introduced to a dread lord who radiated an intense cold. Later, I was told I had met Ynt'taris, specifically that Ynt'taris had wanted to meet me. On my voyage home, my ship fell into an ocean blizzard that coated the ship in ice. Imperius had asked the dragon emperor to look after us. Ynt'taris pulled us from the ice storm and saved our lives. Though I often wondered if the dragon did not cause the storm in the first place."

"The dragons often surprise us. Ynt'taris does not leave the icy heights of his mountains unless the Queen requires it. That he did, tells me you either made quite an impression or you indeed have a destiny for the Goddess. The dragons care about what they care about. I have often seen the dread lords deviate from expected and planned behavior, even the emperor's commands. In soaring the heavens, they are closer to the divine. Ynt'taris seems to take special pleasure against the emperor's will. Fire and Ice do not co-exist well. However, Ynt'taris did tell me to

202

convey his regards. He also wishes to renew his invitation that you come visit."

The daimo laughed. "Many thanks indeed Dar Kendra. I will give you a letter for the white one. Lets speak of this lich now. Ori and this lich's forces do not co-exist well. I received a report that the lich had a conversation with a young boy coming out of dojo study. The lich wanted to know if the boy truly worshipped Imperius. We do not expect a boy that age to have developed faith yet, but the boy said yes. The lich wanted to know why and said something like, "If I do a miracle, would you have faith in and worship me?" The boy said no." The daimo chuckled and finished, "You are too scary to worship, the boy said." The boy ran away and the lich let him. He actually appeared amused by the exchange."

Another courier entered. He told them the lich had requested a tour of the royal gardens and palace the next day. "Well," the daimo said to Dar Kendra. "I expect you'll be moving your soldiers. I must make the palace ready." His eyes still followed Malcor.

"Daimo, may I ask that Malcor attend with you tomorrow? We can have him dress as a servant here in the palace. While he is much bigger than…"

"Excellent idea. I will have our largest warriors present as well. Maybe the lich will enjoy a sumo tournament. Sir Malcor will appear very small."

Chapter Twenty Eight – Dar Kendra versus Ori

The lich walked through the streets of Ori in what looked like a poorer more run down part of the city. While clean and pleasant looking, the paint and roof tiles and wood work looked a bit worn down. Scrolls bearing the god fluttered where statues stood in other parts of the city. To the lich, the whole city looked like a garden where people had been planted and cultivated instead of plants. Colored silk pinions snapped in the wind. The organized chaos appealed to the lich as he began to understand how it all worked together to create a society and a city.

Small children and curious onlookers followed the monk guards walking some twenty steps behind. For the most part, people avoided his gaze and withdrew behind door and window. At last he waved one of the Ori guards forwarded and asked, "Why does everyone turn their gaze aside?"

The monk took a deep breath and then looked into the lich's eyes. Trying not to let fear or anything show, the monk said, "In our world, in this time, a lich like you can steal souls and possess people's will through eye contact. It is common knowledge to our people."

The lich noted the man's accelerated heartbeat and fear-dilated eyes. "I see," he said. Every once in a while, someone would meet his gaze and he would try to call them to him. Though most of these attempts were pointless, the monks scared them off, every once in a while he found himself in a conversation. He sensed such an opportunity when they rounded a turn and a bald old man sat meditating under a manicured tree.

The lich walked straight to him and affected his best imitation of their odd language. "Are you in good health?" the lich asked. The monks, he could tell, were trying to shoo the man away, but when he replied and turned his head towards the lich, he saw the empty orbs of eyes long blind.

The man shivered as the lich drew close and its shadow fell across him. The monks realized the man's blindness and took up protective stance around. A small crowd drew close to watch and listen. The lich sat down copying the man's seated leg-crossed position. The blind man did not say a word but smiled to the sunlight as the lich's shadow stopped blocking the sun on his face. "May we speak?" the lich asked.

The man nodded. "It is a warm sunny day, though with a chill wind. Have you any news of the armies on the south gate?"

The lich grinned at the monks. "I have heard of a cease fire and tribute being paid, but other than that, the City of Imperius has rebuilt its southern gates and walls. The leader of the City's enemies apparently walks the streets of Ori. Have you heard?"

"What I don't understand is why we have an enemy at all? Did Ori do something to this lich? I mean, back when I was a soldier, we fought wars of self-defense. There'd be a gathering of orcs, they'd attack, we'd repel them. The orcs wanted plunder. What does this lich want so badly that we are attacked?"

The lich stared at one of the guards who happened to have met his gaze and answered, "Maybe the lich is simply fascinated by the chaos that comes with war. Plunder is not interesting. This god though – Imperius! Imagine how that must sound to it."

The blind man retorted, "Only a fool would challenge a god…"

"What if the god is the only conquest, or plunder as you would say, worth taking here?"

The blind man appeared visibly upset and said, "No no no, you must not question the Shining Lord Imperius, righteousness, justice, fairness in combat, these are principles that endure through the ages!" While he said this, he reached out to touch the lich.

"You don't want to do that old man," the lich said. "I would also tell you that these human concepts live and die with the human race. They are not godly principles."

The man's fingers stopped just shy of the lich's armored arm while several of the monks rushed forward calling for him to stop and trying to restrain him. The man's empty eyes opened wide as he realized, "This

205

painful chill... are you the..."

"Yes, I am the leader of the armies at your gates. If you touch me, in all likelihood, you will die."

Curiosity crossed the man's face, for a moment, and then he withdrew his hand. The monks reached him and started pulling him back, but he stopped them. "I am fine. Leave me alone." He shoved them away and smoothed his shirt down. "You do me honor, to talk with me," he said to the lich. "Had I known... oh well. You know, when I was young, I fought my fair share of monsters and others. But, I don't recall ever fighting one that had such intense cold surrounding it. What are you? May I ask?"

The lich looked at the sun blistering and withering his hand, even as it repaired itself. Had he breath, he would have sighed. Instead, he said, "I watched the sun take shape in the void of the realm, and I fought against the being who claimed that bright star as its own. I stood on this land when it seethed as an ocean of chaos, magic, and matter. Always, I railed against that which tried to limit me. Eventually, I found my life burning away and found magic to prolong it."

"Are you divine?"

"Divine? I'm sorry, I do not understand. Do you mean that I have worshippers like your god Imperius?"

"No, I mean to ask – are you a god?"

The lich thought for a moment trying to understand. "I am not used to being confused and not knowing. I imagine gods are not confused. I have enjoyed our talk, but must go before something bad happens. I leave you this though." He dropped a metal disk the size of a coin in front of the man. "Should you find you want to continue this conversation, on my terms, pick this up and touch it to your forehead. Good bye." The lich stood and walked away down the boulevard.

Though the monks followed him, he noted one stayed back and looked at the metal disk. The lich paused and turned to say, "Monk, I gifted that to the blind man. It is cursed for anyone else... to unleash an ancient pestilence. Heed my words and leave it be."

The monk jumped back, and a small group of onlookers who had rushed forward to hear what the old man might say, stepped back alarmed as well.

The lich chuckled and continued his stroll. He had some more hours before whatever this "sumo tournament" would occur.

When the lich had safely moved from view, a group of soldiers came forward with runners and a wheeled wagon. The old man and his disk were placed into this and they ran to the royal palace. The old man found himself dragged/ushered into some kind of cool and soft and sweet-smelling room. In his blindness he waited until someone said, "Old man, you stand before the daimo, and other nobility."

Flustered and increasingly alarmed, the man fell to his knees and bowed low. "How may I serve?" His keen ears heard someone whisper about his blindness.

The daimo asked, "I understand you had a conversation with the lich, the leader of the armies attacking us. He gave you something. Tell us."

The man pulled the disk out of his pocket and placed it on the floor in front of him. He heard the swish of robes and then a gruff Tanian accent speaking passable Imperic said, "There is no curse on this. It appears to be a disk of metal inscribed with eldar runes. While I can't speak for the metal, the runes predate anything held in our archives. Perhaps the dragon emperor could read it." The voice asked the blind man, "The lich said that if you put it to your head and..."

"...our conversation would continue on his terms. I have already been asked and said that I do not understand any special meanings in any of this. The monks were there too. They overheard everything."

Apprentice walked around the old man and looked him over. Finally he said, "Our doctrine tells us that all eldar controlled chaos, what we now refer to as magic, by thought and will. The only thing I see here is an old man who spoke with an eldar. The disk certainly contains large amounts of magic." Before anyone could say anything, the mage pressed the disk to his own forehead. A collective gasp filled the room, but nothing happened. The mage shrugged. "I had to know."

Without another word, the mage slapped it to the old man's head and grabbed the man firmly, skin to skin. The daimo and others cried out and several monks leapt forward. The mage touched the old man's fingers to the disk and then both of them vanished. The leaping monks fell to where the Apprentice had just stood moments before. The daimo whirled on Dar Kendra, "You will answer for this! Ori does not view its citizens as tools and experiments!" and stormed out.

Dar Kendra looked at the tense and uncertain looks from the monks and samurai guards turning to follow their daimo. She stood and bowed, "Daimo, how long can Ori afford to pay tribute?"

The daimo whirled, anger in his eyes. A samurai at his elbow swept his hand to his katana. "As long as it takes!" He turned but Kendra called out.

"And how long can Ori afford to have its southern borders tied up by a rising army? And an eldar walk its streets, challenging your god?"

"You speak heresy…! If you were mine…"

"I am not yours, but am here as a friend. My scouts have not yet returned nor sent word. The mage operated on his own, and so the risks are his own. I did not condone nor forbid this brash action. Turn and face me daimo!"

The daimo whirled and drew his katana. It pulsed brightly with the golden light of Imperius. Dar Kendra's holy avenger ripped into existence as if retrieved through the tearing fabric of space itself. Malcor had never seen it this way before. Her sword roared out a challenge that was part metal grinding on metal and part dragon cry. "We are here to help. There were no restrictions!"

One of the samurai stepped between her and the daimo but the daimo ordered him to move. "You draw steel against me, in my own house! You should all be killed for such insult." He stepped towards Dar Kendra death gleaming in his eyes.

Behind her, Dar Itain materialized and asked, "Kendra, this is not our mission. Sheathe your blade."

Malcor saw pride and anger and intelligence burning through her face, but with the daimo's sword crackling for battle, she could hardly be the first to back down. "I cannot leave this challenge unmet."

Itain said, "Of course not. The Mage's Guild does not answer to you the way the rest of us do. You do not have to defend such reckless behavior." He paused. The daimo did not retreat and made no sign of backing down. He stepped between Kendra and the daimo. Facing the daimo he said, "We will withdraw lord. Should the mage not bring your man back, I will honor our alliance and provide restitution, such as is allowed." The ambassador put his hand on Kendra's blade hand and pushed it back towards her sheathe.

The daimo finally moved. In a blink, his sword rested against Itain's chin the tip fractions from Kendra's face. "I accept your withdraw. Take your shameful selves out of my city."

Chapter Twenty Nine – The Camp along the River

And, just like that, their stay in Ori ended. Less than an hour later, all of them stepped from a gate in the barracks onto a windswept plain near a flowing river. The mage and the old man both sat against a fallen tree. As Malcor stepped through and saw them, he noticed how much cooler the air felt here. A small camp had been set up. Small game roasted on the fire and one of the thieves stood chatting with Dar Kendra. Malcor started to ask about it but Tembri pulled him aside.

"The Tanian alliance with Ori is mainly one of trade. The people of this country are obsessed with honor, etiquette, and keeping their word. In some ways they are no different from Tania except that we are not so patient. Later tonight, Itain will tell Ori that we have withdrawn to pursue our own solution to the lich and that they can wait on the Sorians' arrival. This will give them time to cool down and time for us to do our own thing."

"So, Tania considered a successful outcome the same as honorable conduct, where the Imperics feel that honor is all aspects of the work…"

"…is the only thing that matters. Life or death, they don't care so long as it is conducted and achieved honorably."

Within an hour, the entire camp stood ready. Malcor noted the temporary nature of the setup and then walked over to join a conversation Dar Kendra had with the mages and the thieves. One of the thieves spoke, "There is a western facing chasm that dead ends in a box canyon. We found a series of barely-crawl-able caves that lead into what appears to be the main fortress. Like Bloodstone, there are undead… true undead, not just these eldar variants."

"So, we have an entrance." She looked to the mage, "The disk, what happened?"

"It would have taken the old man to the lich. I redirected it elsewhere but the lich scried us. I know he saw me. He seemed amused? I took us several places before Daryx arranged a diversion. The old man is of no more use to us. I erased his memory. He will remember that he travelled with me back to Tania where we asked him questions about the lich, gave him some food, and promised to restore his eyesight should he pilgrimage to the Temple at Morbatten and convert. Dar Itain can take him back whenever you are ready."

"Relatively, how strong is the lich? Can you tell?" Kendra fingered her sword hilt.

Apprentice thought about it for a moment and then replied, "No. The weakest eldar we have ever encountered was so completely different that you can't really get a sense. Then, you have the dragon emperor and others – we have no foundation to measure their power. Consider Alerius; one of the strongest. We also have Lord Marshal Jisandra. She has helped us understand some aspects of the eldar, but she herself is so far removed from her eldar self that she is not that good of a gauge. Still, I have no doubt Jisandra could best any of the Order in single combat, even you Dar Kendra. But, from what we see, I'd put the lich somewhere below Jisandra as a fighter and perhaps near myself for magic, at least the way I use it. The difference being, of course, that my magic stems from study and talent where the lich – well, his comes from the fabric of creation itself. The eldar, they are magic. They are really only limited by their imagination. The fact he manifests as a "he" and as a "lich" suggests that he found his own identity and his own solution to the River long ago."

She kicked a rock by her feet and sucked air through her teeth. The wind blew chill and she caught sight of Malcor. "Big changes from working at a forge eh? What do you think of all this?"

He paused before asking, "It seems like a lot of effort for me to face off against a lich. I do not want to risk my fellow knights and their teams for some accelerated training protocol."

The Apprentice bowed and stepped away, leaving Kendra and Malcor alone. Kendra walked towards the creek and indicated he should follow. "What is happening here, is how each of us came into the Order. The simple truth is that this Order cares far less about individual honor and glory than other orders do, certainly less than the myths and stories tell.

211

While I did not fight a lich, I faced an enemy far above my abilities. The Order saw me through. We will help you. We will judge you. We will teach you to trust us and, as an Order, we are all stronger for that trust. Look at the water flowing. What do you see in this creek?"

Malcor looked noting its difference but similar features to the River of Time. He saw the swell and fall of water as it moved over and around rocks, some above and others below the surface. He described it.

"You have the River on your brain too much," Kendra laughed. "This river, right here, is like the Order. We go where the emperor commands. We fight as a single unit. We have never been defeated in battle. While wars have been lost around our Order, we have never failed in our objectives. Like water, the emperor uses divine and magical power to lift us up and place us where needed. Like this river, our Order flows over and around our objectives and leaves behind a smoothly flowing current. With enough time, we level mountains and divide the land. Everything about "us" has been refined by the emperor and the Queen to be the epitome of Tanian warrior culture. You're not just another paladin Malcor. You are also a priest, a healer, a missionary, a dragon, a shield, and a weapon for your faith. Where we pass, we leave either cleanliness or destruction."

She skipped a stone across the river and reached for another. It struck Malcor as odd that so mighty a warrior would do something so mundane. "This Order, you, continually surprise me," he said.

Another stone went sailing across the river. "Kaia blessed you with wisdom," Kendra stated. "Why are you here?"

He looked towards the mountain where the lich supposedly waited. "It is odd to think that right now, the lich is viewing a wrestling tournament. On top of that, no doubt, "heroes" from all over Ori are scrambling into teams to claim the lich's treasure. Our Order stands here already having found an entrance. I am here to be part of the Order's legend."

Another stone danced across the river. "And what is that legend Sir Malcor?"

"What else can it be but to see the Queen take this place as Her throneplane?"

A long silence ensued. At last Kendra broke it. "A good, wise, and safe answer Malcor. Doctrinally correct. Certainly the kind of answer any proctor would be pleased to hear her student say. About Tania, Alerius, about the paladins in general. Not the Order though. What is the Order's legend and your role here?"

Malcor shifted uncomfortably and picked up a stone to skip as well. After more time had passed, he finally admitted, "I don't know. Until I met you, I had never heard of the Order of Water. Knights always passed through Klenna, but I don't remember even a single knight, priest, or healer from the Order coming through."

She nodded. "We usually don't travel openly like other Orders. The emperor prefers us to be like this water – here, flowing, appreciated, necessary, but not necessarily something our enemies are aware of. We do have a legend though Malcor. When you figure it out, come to me." She put her hand on his shoulder and looked him in the eye. "It may take a while but it's right here all around you."

She walked off leaving Malcor by the river's bank. He stared into the water as they swirled by and realized how profoundly hungry he felt. He tried to ignore it. Like magic, Tembri appeared with food and drink. "You're fleshing back out quite well Sir Malcor. I was talking with some of the other priests and there is talk of another group going after the lich's soul gem. Are you okay to talk?"

Malcor said, "Yes, I'm feeling stretched out though. Dar Kendra was talking to me about the Order's legend. I guess I gave her the wrong answer." He held some dried meat in his mouth and sent a rock skipping across the river. "I never felt the soul gem to be our priority Tembri."

"The Order's legend? Hmmm, I have not heard of that one before. She, her predecessors, usually ask similar questions. I spoke with one of the thieves – Marcello – he and I served in Bloodstone together for a time." Seeing Malcor's expression, he added, "Don't let the term "thief" throw you. The Temple, the Mages, even the knighthood all have a vested interest in the skills our "thieves" bring to us. Don't confuse an official "thief" with the pickpockets you'll find running away from the city guard."

"We support them? I don't get it. Klenna had thieves. Every once in a while, we'd even have a thief executed."

Tembri sent one of his own rocks skipping. "By the emperor's decree, thieves are tolerated. The ones who get caught, are of no consequence. However, the official Thieves' Guild monitors those people of special skill, daring, agility, or intelligence. Like the rites here, the thieves are eventually guided to a test. The ones who pass are recruited and put into specialized training. The ones who do not pass, continue their thieving ways until captured by the civil authorities or join adventurer groups. This way, the guild always has a new generation of candidates coming in. By comparison, the knighthood and the Temple are at a disadvantage. Thieves can demonstrate their proficiency at any age. We have to wait and therefore run the risk of marriage, accidents, or other distractions."

"I get it. It's like when I first started dreaming of becoming a knight. I was maybe eight years old, but did not know what it meant. I had not even started at the forge yet. How would anyone have known that I'd be here, today. With the Order of Water. Tembri..."

"Yes Sir Malcor."

"Why is that I have never heard of the Order of Water?"

Chapter Thirty - Calvin's First Rite

"In preparing for your first rite, you must approach it with the utmost level of faith and devotion. Many initiates fail because they are unable to adapt to the extreme environment, or they forget – in the face of dragonfear – that they serve the dragons. The dragon is not going to eat you, though it will feel that way. Yes Sir Calvin, you have a question?"

"Since we and the dragons worship the Queen, why are we affected by the dragonfear at all?"

"Remember that dragons began as an eldar race. While some have diminished, like the "monster" or "wild" dragons you hear about from time to time, the ones you will encounter here in the Isles are all either aligned with our Queen, or with the immortal dragon Bahamut. As such, they have an aura of majesty. They predate our own creation and so we, as mortals, feel their aura. We were their food. We have some primal instinct that the dragons touch in us. Any other questions? Paladins, to your point, are immune to dragonfear at a certain level of faith and experience."

A young lady next to Calvin asked, "So, when the dragon emperor and the other dread lords fly over the city, or the villages... why do we not feel dragonfear?"

"Excellent question," the priest teaching the class noted. "Would anyone like to answer?"

A few answers were voiced here and there in the class room. At last the instructor said, "All good attempts, but the real answer is that the dread lords have so mastered every aspect of their being in this world that, in the absence of anything they deem threatening, they hold that fear back. There are a few dragons on the emperor's mountain though that have not yet reached that level of control. Now, tomorrow, a dread lord will be coming by to meet you all. I have not yet been told who, but remember, all of you. Best behavior. The dread lord may expect you to ask questions. All questions must be approved in advance. We do not want to risk angering the dread lords nor do we want any of you to come across as unworthy. I will be in the dining hall tomorrow morning, bring me a question – each of you. You are dismissed."

Calvin stood and quickly joined a group of friends he had made. They spoke about their studies, the things they were learning, the rumors they had all heard about Bloodstone and some threat south against Ori. Calvin's master was leaning against a column down the hallway and stood at attention as Calvin approached. The other sponsors of Calvin's friends came forward as well. Their next course, combat training, would be starting soon.

Arriving at the arena, Calvin saw an old man stood in the arena, bright sun streaming down around. In the late summer sun, it made them all sweat. The old man introduced himself as a retired paladin. "I served in Bloodstone for three campaigns. I fought in two foreign wars. I served in the Order of the Lance, heavy cavalry for those of you who do not yet know, for three decades. In my last Bloodstone campaign, I was wounded beyond divine healing and now work here as a teacher. You will each face me and receive a grade. The grade will determine the level of intensity and training you receive towards the Rite of Pain. Who can say – what is the Rite of Pain?"

An initiate immediately replied, "It is a test for how much pain a knight can endure Sir!"

The instructor looked around letting his face turn increasingly grim before asking, "Is that correct?" Silence answered him. "If true, you would expect the Rite of Pain to be one of... torture? Pray tell, how would we measure an initiate's passing or failing? Do we torture each of you the same, or just jump to the level of what we might think is agonizable? Oh, sorry. You died during that. You failed. Oh, look, this one survived and remained conscious. You pass? You think that is the Rite of Pain?"

Calvin's mentor said, "The Rite of Pain is an endurance test through combat. It is a test of how many times a knight can be healed before their spirit, their souls, and their flesh itself collapses. It is called the Rite of Pain because the healers must keep the knight alive, and the knight must continue fighting through dire, fatal, and maiming wounds the like of which any of us might expect in total battle. The healers must know, and

216

the knight must know, at what point continuing the fight would result in permanent death."

Calvin felt his mentor touch his shoulder. "My squire here, Calvin, volunteers to go first." He shoved Calvin hard and propelled him down to the stage's edge.

The instructor nodded and without missing a beat continued, "The Rite of Pain. You are each worthy to have been sent here as a candidate for the knighthood. However, if you cannot endure at least five hours, then you will be sent to the military for officer evaluation. You will not continue as a paladin. You must last five hours to stay as an initiate. Sir Calvin, draw your weapon and attack me."

Calvin leapt to the stage and attacked. The old man easily dodged and began counterstriking back at Calvin. From all around, priests and priestesses began entering the arena. Calvin thought he heard one of the Dar priestesses say, "Healer initiates, the ability to heal is a basic divine gift from Takhissis. If you cannot be counted on to successfully pray for this, you are not fit to serve. Today, knights are being evaluated. You will be called upon to heal the knight until you can no longer sustain it. Form a line here by the stage."

As he spoke, the instructor cut deep into Calvin's leg, crippling him. He had never suffered such a grave wound before and he felt his vision swim. The instructor jeered at him, "Come now, a dragon claw would inflict far more damage than this! If your first serious wound takes you out of the picture…"

Calvin steeled his will and tried to defend against the instructor's next attack. Steel raged against his blade and then the instructor's foot slammed into his face. Bone crunched and teeth flew as the force lifted Calvin up into the air to land on his back. The instructor paused a moment, maybe to give Calvin time to recover his breath. The instructor appeared to be speaking but the words came slowly to Calvin. "…the basic signal for healing is this. Are the healers ready?"

Something happened and Calvin felt a warm embrace wash over him, removing the pain in his leg and face. It energized him and he stood back up on increasingly firm legs. He saw a young priestess, barely his age if that, praying hands pointing towards Calvin. Too fast for his eyes to follow, the instructor's blade pierced his throat and severed his spine through the back of his neck. He barely had time to register shock, surprise, or even the pain when that warm embrace started and then abruptly ended as the young priestess collapsed into a seizure. The next healer in line prayed for Calvin and as the instructor's sword pulled out through his neck, he felt his body reknitting itself. He wondered where Malcor was and if he had to go through this test too.

This time, Calvin immediately attacked and almost scored a hit. The instructor parried and made several obvious attacks of his own. Calvin defended those easily enough but again, that kick to the face got him. This time the force of it spun him around in a circle and he fell back off the stage. Before he hit the ground though, the warmth of healing cushioned his body's impact. He leapt back into combat and after several minutes, Calvin's mentor took the instructor's place. All around them, mentors engaged their pupils in combat.

It was nothing like any of the training Calvin had experienced back in Klenna. The Rite continued relentless and cruel. With some grim satisfaction, Calvin noted several of his classmates collapse. Their mentors dragged them off and then joined combat with others lacking mentors. Calvin fought through hunger and dire thirst. At some point, he felt his sweat stop and his body began cycling through hot and cold flashes he knew meant dehydration. Someone nearby said, "It is called the Rite of Pain because, for healers, to enable someone to continue fighting like this, causes them pain."

Calvin shook it out of his head and renewed his attack against his mentor. He tried everything he had ever been taught but felt too slow and sluggish to make any of it work. He wondered how Malcor fared. His instructor slapped his face with the flat of his sword. It made Calvin's head ring. His master said something about a drink. He could not tell. A cup pressed into his hand. It was water. He drank it greedily but a sword cut his hand in two through the cup. He barely noticed his ruined hand, only the waste of the water where it fell mingling with his blood. The healing spell that began pulling his hand back together barely registered.

218

At last, Calvin fell to his hands and knees. Everything swam. He felt ponderous and yet could barely feel his sword in his hand. His body, as if not his own, did strange things. He felt himself lift up and watched with disconnected fascination as a pile of blood vomit poured from his lips. "I... must... fight...." The words sounded like a scream to him. He lunged forward slashing wildly with his sword. And then blackness.

He came to no idea how long later. A healer leaned back and said, "Well done Knight of the First Rite. Well, almost."

His mentor put down a goblet of wine and looked at him as if appraising an item of questionable value. "You did well Calvin. You could have done better. But still, all things considered. Over half your group was sent to the Soldier's Keep for military assessment. You still have a chance at becoming a paladin. How do you feel?"

The room swam and he felt so hungry. "I'm starving. I never imagined it'd be like that. Is that what combat is like?"

"No, it's worse. Eventually, the healers fall and a knight who cannot recognize his and his team's boundaries will also fall. When that happens and there is no healing, you die. The empire does not invest much in dead men walking. When even the healers fall, there is no return. There is only failure. You must not let your pride cause your team to fall. No forgiveness. No atonement. No afterlife. No glory. Do you understand?"

Calvin nodded. "Yes, I understand."

"Good. Your understanding will be tested. See that you pass. You did well today, but don't let it go to your head. You still have much to learn."

Calvin sat up, eating and looked around. His quarters had changed. "You're in the initiate barracks now," his mentor said. "You get your own quarters and an increased food ration. When you get to a mirror, you'll see that your Rite of Pain has caused you to lose a lot of weight. Until you're healthy, you'll be reviewing doctrine and history and eating like a king. I'll see you in a few days. Regain your strength." With that, Calvin found himself alone.

His new quarters were about the size of his old room back in Klenna. Not much bigger than a normal bed but with privacy and a closet. His shield gift from Kaia hung proudly on the wall by the door. His clothing and armor had all been cleaned. He noted a new outfit, similar to the robes and breeches worn by lower level Temple workers but bearing the Order of the Shield's blaze. He stood but found vertigo too hard to overcome and sat back down.

"I wonder how Malcor is doing. I haven't really seen him at all since the Temple. No matter, I did it!" He steeled himself and stood. Once dressed, he stepped out into the corridor and heard the sounds of a busy mess hall just down the way. The smell of cooking lulled him there and he entered recognizing a few of his former classmates. Most looked down-trodden, beaten, and skeletal. He caught a glimpse of himself in a reflective window and realized he looked the same.

An orderly came over and asked him how hungry he was and took him to a seat. The girl he had sat by before the Rite was there and smiled coyly at him. Some kind of pastry bread had smeared along her face and she self-consciously wiped her mouth. "So you made it," she said. She tried to smile and put energy into the comment, but it came out flat and exhausted sounding. She noticed and blushed.

"It's okay. I feel the same," Calvin said trying to smile and finding his face felt numb. "I'm Calvin by the way, from Klenna. What's your name?"

"Seline," she replied. "I'm from the Dutchy. Do you..."

"Yeah, I'm familiar with the Dutchy, but only from maps. Southernmost territory on the south wilderness right?"

His food arrived and they made staccato conversation back and forth as they ate. Eventually, a knight in full armor entered the hall and approached their table. "Lady Seline," he said. "Your retinue is ready and awaits." He bowed. "Doctrine begins in just under an hour."

She looked sideways at Calvin and then nodded. The knight withdrew. Calvin watched the whole thing trying not to be impressed. "Lady... are you part of a noble house? My family..."

When the knight was some distance away and the mess hall's din would mask their conversation she said, "Yes, you're the Klennan mayor's son right? My family used to be noble, but fell out of favor long ago. I'm the first to enter the knighthood since."

Calvin thought for a moment and then said, "I remember hearing something about a trade dispute but that's the only news to have reached Klenna about the Dutchy in ages."

Seline laughed. "So word of this has reached Klenna. I'm not surprised. Though it was not a trade dispute. My great-grandfather led an expedition into the wilderness to verify rumors of ancient treasure. He found it. There was too much to bring back, so he brought back what they could and left guards behind. Before reinforcements could get back, the guards were attacked and another rival house laid claim to it. They also spread rumors that they had been the first. Long story short, my family lost the claim and were forced to pay reparations. But I am going to change all of that." She stood and excused herself to go get ready for their doctrine class. "See you there."

Chapter Thirty One - Instruction

Doctrine class focused on the Rite of Pain, healing, and how the Queen grants divine power to mend wounds, even overcoming death, to those deemed worthy. "In the absence of apparent worth, the Queen has entrusted the person's "worth" to the healer. As knights, you will be assigned a healer. They will protect and heal you and you must protect them. Why does the Queen allow this?"

Several answers were given but they all centered on how the Empire's purpose is to safeguard the dragons. Something felt wrong about that answer to Calvin but he could not quite say why. The instructor asked several clarifying questions about this answer and organized a debate. While different sides tried to explain this objective of safeguarding the dragons, orderlies brought food and drink. Everyone still suffered from the wounds and healing. But, as the conversation progressed, something remained about the objective that did not sit well with Calvin.

At last, Calvin could not take it anymore and he signaled desire to speak. The instructor allowed him. He stood and said, "Given that dragons predate humans, and that the dragon emperor has safeguarded us for millennia, how can our objective as an empire be to safeguard the dragons? The entire alliance for the Forsaken Islands was created by Emperor Alerius and set with the deity of the Isles. As such, the number of dragons are limited. Humans, and humanoids, and other monsters have threatened the empire in its history but nothing except the Jade God has ever actually threatened the dragons. Am I wrong? The objective in the Queen granting healing must be something besides protecting the dragons."

"And, Sir Calvin," the instructor prodded, "What do you think that objective is?"

"The only thing I can think of is that She allows it to serve as a reminder that She is part of our lives. Not just a Goddess watching us from Her Throne. Not just some disconnected Mother we talk about. She is here, with us. Other deities allow healing, even amongst those who serve the Goddess. So, even if the Queen took it away entirely and did not allow it, we could still find healing when and if needed right?"

The instructor beamed. "Well said Sir Calvin. At the heart of the Goddess' doctrine is a core notion that we are preparing this world for the Queen. It is Hers. As such, we have a duty to serve as caretakers and stewards. Sometimes that means we build glorious Temples. Other times it means we engage in battle to remove stains from Her Throneplane. So, Sir Calvin, continuing with your idea... tell us. Why does the Queen's claim of this world as Her own matter to the doctrine of healing?"

Though Calvin remained standing, Seline stood and spoke. "It matters as a function of math. The dragon emperor's scripture notes that fewer than one in a thousand are capable of becoming paladins. One in a hundred of either wielding magic or divine might. The Book of Generations further noted that raising offspring surrounded by paladins, mages, or priests had no bearing on this. The dread emperor called it "Prebirth Destiny", I think."

The instructor nodded indicating she had the term correct. "So," she continued, "for Prebirth Destiny to matter, Tania needs lots of citizens. If we want there be one thousand knights, we need a population of families having children that is one thousand times that. Healing helps preserve members of the population that would otherwise fall to disease or accidents. It also preserves the dragon emperor's investment in the training we receive here."

The instructor turned to the others and said, "Witness. This is the real reason why the Goddess allows healing. The dragon emperor's intercession ensures the Temple and even paladins the ability to heal, even beyond death. While there are teachings about how various doctrines touch on other points of Imperic life, as a paladin, we want you to have a firm grasp of two things. The first is that you will hear teachings and variants of teachings that may not be correct. By decree, it is to be tolerated. As a paladin, you are to respect those differences. After all, you never know... maybe that person or priest's different understanding is actually how their Prebirth Destiny plays out.

"The second is the giving and receiving of healing honors you and the healer by continuing this great purpose. While training and skill and talent may help you overmaster your foes, each of us has foes far beyond our ability. Remember, your enemies are not just those you fight. You fight for the Empire, for Tania, for the dragon emperor, for the Goddess. As of right now, you can add the Jade God, its hellhounds, and all the enemies of Tania to your personal list of those who want to hurt and kill you. Receiving healing is not dishonorable. In point of fact, if a healer sees a knight in need and fails to heal them, the healer can be punished. The same holds true for a knight who refuses healing. It is a gift and a tool and a weapon. We will now have a demonstration."

A priestess walked into the room. Her bearing and attire showed her high rank and when she looked over the room, her gaze drove home the point she said, "You are all beginners. You passed your first Rite - of Pain. Congratulations. Who cares? Half of your class failed and are now trying to impress the soldiers enough to become officer candidates. Think on that for a moment because there are other tests before you become a true paladin. I need a volunteer. It will hurt."

A few tentative hands went up, but Seline stood and boldly volunteered. In that instant, Calvin knew that he should have volunteered. The priestess nodded and Seline walked down to stand by her. The instructor added, "This is Dar Niss, a high priestess who has come to see how you all fared with your first rite."

Not missing a beat, Dar Niss continued, "Healing can work both ways. It can restore vitality. Reversed, it can take vitality. It is only limited by the imagination of the priestess."

The instructor brought over a scroll and the priestess referred to it briefly. "I see you survived the Rite of Pain for seven hours and suffered mortal wounds requiring the healing skills of fourteen initiates. Impressive. Your name…?"

"Seline! Of The Dutchy!"

"Lady Seline, I apologize in advance. This is going to hurt." She bowed her head and began praying in draconian. As she did so, priest initiates filed into the room behind her. The draconian words, often chanted by

224

the priesthood, this time sounded dissonant – somehow wrong. A golden light enveloped her hands but crackled with gray-rimmed black lightning. A wash of heat lifted the priestess' hair and she opened her eyes, which also crackled with gold and gray-black power. She made a hand sign and the energy cracked outwards like a broken tree and just barely touched Seline. For such a violent but glancing touch, the audience expected Seline to simply dodge. She tried but the whip touched her. Disproportionate to the apparent force of the blow, Seline fell backwards clawing at her face and skin. Her cloak and robes shredded into bloody gashes as her skin melted and boiled blood erupted through her skin. Her screams of agony and choking cries of pain brought fresh memories of the Rite of Pain to everyone present.

The priestess twisted her hands into another sign and Seline's body convulsed in death throes, her seizures twisting her gory fingers into claws as she writhed on the dais. The sound of a bone in her body snapping resonated and echoed. Then the healing light from the priest initiates touched her, pulling her back by degrees to life. The room fell completely silent except for the soft prayers of healing that barely kept up with the priestess' horrible spell. The priestess spoke. "Lady Seline, a true paladin would stand and endure the pain. Though it feels real, with healing, it is no different than an illusion. Push it aside. Conquer it. Call your sword and make me stop!"

Seline shook and trembled on the brink of convulsing again but knelt back, her fists supporting her on the ground. Though blood fell from her torn face, she drew her sword. Using it as a crutch, she stood. The priestess twisted her hands into a new sign. Seline choked as pustules full of slime erupted all over her body. She held her sword and took a step forward. Another step and the trail of blood following her advanced another to the priestess. If anything, Seline appeared to strengthen. Another hand sign and the flesh withered from her body, skin stretched across bone cracked and tore. She lifted her sword point, palsied though it was, to the priestess' throat.

The priestess ended the torrent of pain and caught Seline as she fell. "Well done child!" Behind her, all but two of the initiates collapsed, utterly drained. The priestess noted the two standing and said to them,

"Excellent!" Her hand brushed Seline's ruined face, strands of her once beautiful hair sticking in clumps. The priestess helped her stand and lifted her head to her classmates. "For Takhissis, there is no sacrifice too large, or small. The Goddess will use us as she sees fit. This one – Lady Seline – will be continuing her studies at the Temple. For those of you with ambition, or talent, or even simple desire… remember this. The pathway to glory will not be found sitting out there in your classroom while others boldly volunteer to serve."

The two remaining healers stumbled forward and took Seline. She blinked and looked around dazedly. The priestess leaned forward and kissed her forehead. From that kiss, skin mended and tendons and sinew branched back together. The snapped bone rippled and healed. By the time the priestess ended the kiss, Seline had fully restored with even her clothing looking new and clean. She looked at her hands in wonder and then dropped to her knees in formal salute.

The priestess kissed each of the two healers and restored them. Seline remained bowed. At last, the priestess came back to her and said, "Stand Lady Seline. You are advanced to the Second Rite. What is your current Order?"

"Order of the Rock my lady."

"I am Dar Niss. I am lifting you into the Order of Fire. Are you familiar with this order?" Seline nodded. The priestess turned and asked, "Is anyone else here in the Order of Fire? Any of the elemental orders?" A young man stood. Dar Niss looked at the symbol on his cloak and said, "The Order of Earth. Very good. I expect to see you shortly." She turned and swept the class with her eyes. "There are four elemental orders in the knighthood. Fire is the second most powerful. Acceptance into an elemental order is the prerequisite for advancement into the most elite of all the orders. Unless you each own your training and take a more active part down here, you will stay where you are. The classroom is a poor substitute for knighthood. There is no "classhood of knights". Come Lady Seline of the Order of Fire. Be joined by your two healers. Follow me."

They left. Only the blood and gore from Seline's ordeal remained. Calvin took another bite of bread and thought about Malcor. Since seeing him dangling in the air at the Temple, he had heard nothing about his friend. Clearly, Mal had joined an Order but not one that studied with this group. He made a note to find Malcor as soon as time allowed.

After they left, the instructor gave them a break. Calvin waited till most had left and asked the instructor, "I wish to be chosen for whatever comes next."

The old man grinned at Calvin. "After seeing that, you want to sign up huh? Let me give you some advice." He looked at Calvin squarely and continued, "Your mentor has a reputation for being harsh, but those who survive not just the Rites but him too, they do very well. Tell me, do you know of the River?"

Calvin shook his head, "No, but I have heard of it. I came here with a friend who talked about it sometimes with a priestess. It's the flow of magic. At least, I think it is."

"It is the course of created energy and matter flowing through our world to destruction and chaos and inert oblivion. While it is magic, and you are correct there, it is specifically Time that is flowing. If you can access the River, bend it to your will, harness it, you'll do very well."

"My friend, when he fought, he moved so fast I could barely see him. It was like a blur. Is that what you mean?"

"Your friend. Who is he?"

"Malcor of Klenna."

Calvin saw his words have an effect on the instructor. "Ah, so you came here with Malcor. I see. Come, sit. Relax. Let me tell you something Calvin." As Calvin sat down, the instructor took a long drink of water and encouraged Calvin to do the same. "Once in a generation, Prebirth Destiny creates a prodigy. This is your friend. I served with one of these in Bloodstone. They have a gift for combat, revelation, or something else. It is hard to know them, to see them operate on such a different level. You will be tried with envy. As a paladin, I urge you to never ever judge yourself by Malcor."

Calvin realized that the instructor knew Malcor. "You know him? Already? We've barely been here a few weeks. Tell me. I've been hoping to see him here."

"Your friend has already passed the first and is well on his way to the second rite. He currently serves the Empire in a mission of great importance. There are rumors he might even one day rule here."

Calvin's mouth gaped open. "How is that possible?" he whispered. "He was just a blacksmith's apprentice."

"No Calvin, not just a blacksmith. Remember, prebirth destiny. Remember, we each have a role to play in the Queen's grand design."

"What is my role then?" Calvin asked but other students had started coming back and the instructor left to speak with them. "Tell me," he called out to the instructor, "how many hours did Malcor survive in the first rite?"

Looking back over his shoulder, Calvin could barely hear now but distinctly saw the man's mouth form the word "days".

Chapter Thirty Two - Lich Takes in Sumo

The lich forced his face into a smile and sipped the rice wine, or *sake*, that these humans kept offering him. A priest of some kind in elaborate and brightly colored robes officiated a wrestling match between two huge men. The objective looked clear enough. Whoever pushed the other out of the circle of salt or knocked the other to the ground won. The leader of these strange people, the daimo, sat next to the lich, wary guards nearby on high alert.

Everywhere he looked, other members of these people looked at the lich and then looked away quickly when they felt the lich might be regarding them. Apparent to all, the wrestlers followed some kind of a ceremony for purification, cleansing through combat, and blessings to the community through honorable victory. They had a glow to them, something of the divine but the lich saw it as a forced form of magic. He smirked.

Maybe noting a change in his demeanor, the daimo asked, "Do you have any questions about the tournament?"

The lich shook his head, enjoying how his silence caused discomfort to the daimo and his guards. Instead he retorted, "Will you be endorsing any of the parties attempting to reclaim your generous tribute?"

The daimo blinked feeling off guard and forced a laugh in his reply. "We have seen the groups and several have asked for help. I have not yet decided to risk ourselves in a cause like this. Rather, I hope you will reconsider your position and move south. If territory is what you wish, most of this large island is wild. Or end this conflict. You clearly do not need treasure, or even my people. Ori is the only – "

"You labor under a false assumption. You do not know what I want."

The daimo bowed and returned his gaze to the sumo tournament. The lower level initiates had finished and the larger and more veteran warriors performed their warm up ritual. "These paladins have each endured combat and trials for the Great God Imperius and have mastered basic tenets of our faith. This tournament is like a prayer to

Imperius."

The lich watched the warm up and withdrew a scroll from his robes. He opened it and then passed it to the daimo, through the hands of an over-eager monk who inspected it first. "This is a list of the names of those who have organized parties and responded to my challenge."

The daimo reviewed the list and the lich asked, "Do you notice anything about these names?"

"Only two of these are known to me..."

"That is correct. Neither you nor your people take my challenge seriously. Tell me Lord of Ori. How long will you be able to continue purchasing this cease fire? Rather, how long do you think I will be content to take your wealth before I take what I really want?" The daimo stared at him, unsure of a correct answer or intentionally choosing silence. The lich stared at him and when the daimo missed a signal from the priest, everyone turned to watch the two of them staring at each other. The lich felt a ripple in the fabric of chaos all around him and sensed the daimo's gaze represented some kind of a challenge.

Intrigued, the lich called his vampire servant Shiniba to mind and telepathically asked, "What is this that is happening?"

The daimo is gauging your will in a spiritual way. It is part of this people's tradition that through the eyes, the true mettle of a warrior can be seen. If you watch, the sumo do it as part of their face off just before the fight begins.

The lich continued his gaze with the daimo but felt no challenge at all. He smiled at the daimo, never breaking the gaze and for just a moment, the lich opened his soul to the primal chaos that rages through any of the eldar. The daimo flinched when that raging storm hit him but maintained his gaze. *How interesting*, the lich thought. He let the chaos bring forth images of the eldar world, the time when there were no gods, or at least the time before the gods knew they were divine. Sweat beaded on the daimo's head and in the entire arena, no one made a sound. The lich felt several of the priests lend strength to their daimo but it hardly registered.

230

"You see my world Lord of Ori. There is no Imperius in it. I have made a decision," the lich said holding the daimo and those now lending the lord their strength in the challenge of wills. "You do not take my challenge seriously. As such, I am going to increase the stakes of the treasure."

The daimo trembled feeling the gathering of terrible energy within the lich. Others felt it to and protective spells flooded the arena. Those nearest the daimo drew weapons. "I will take your soul, and the souls of any who attack me."

A monk hurled himself in a flying kick at the lich. The kick slammed into the lich's armor and jostled the lich. Hissing steam from the lich's armor and the monk's foot sizzled and crackled in the room. Then, like a branch in a hot fire, the monk's foot and leg withered into dust, rushing away from the lich in a breeze of power. The blowing ash of the monk's foot ate up into the monk's leg and then a sharp katana cut the monk's leg. The lich opened his hand at the monk and the samurai and a force explosion blew them backwards into the arena. Though one of the sumo caught the monk, the lich spoke an eldar word, "Yinta'ryx kor!"

Whiplash tore at the monk and all there bore witness to the shattering of the arena's sacred circle as the monk's soul ripped free of its body and howled in agony into the lich's hand. A second later and the daimo's soul began tearing free. Priests, holy knights, mages, warriors and all others present rushed to the daimo's aid... some by lending strength and power and some, like the daimo's family, grabbing to his body and crying out for mercy.

Armor befitting paladins swirled in around the sumo who leapt and attacked. Their large size belying their fast charge to aid their lord. The lich seized control of time, the eldar's most potent and dreadful power. Of all those present, the daimo, several priests, and a handful of warriors shifted themselves somehow and retained freedom of movement. All the rest froze into barely noticeable movement.

The lich turned his attention to those still resisting. "Yinta'ryx kor!" and the daimo's soul swarmed into his hand. A samurai cried out for his lord and spun a dancing attack of razor cuts at the lich. Barely thinking, the lich deflected the attacks when a sumo berserked into him. The strange armor worn by these over-sized warriors stuck to him and the lich felt himself lifted and then slammed into the floor. The part of his mind that registered this affront filled with horrible energy. The lich breathed into the sumo's face, which iced over. The cold-induced blindness did not stop the sumo from slamming the lich into the sword of eager samurai.

Somewhere, off to the side, a priest held forth a symbol of Imperius and screamed something about being banished. The feeling that came with the command felt annoying and the lich ripped that priest's soul into his gauntlet. The samurai's sword chunked into ice that then froze up along the blade towards the warrior's hand. He let go and reached for another weapon. The scream of the priest's soul as it passed through his form sent dread chills down his spine.

The samurai grabbed his short sword and summoned a shield, a bright flash of light caught his attention. In a blink, the blind sumo held only armor and the lich appeared on the other side of the room clad in sorcerous robes. Still unable to see, and apparently breathe, the samurai stabbed the ice near the sumo's mouth and winced as ice tore flesh from his friend's face. He had been correct though when he heard the sumo wrestler take deep bellows of air.

"Return our king!" the samurai firmly commanded the lich. A quick glance around the room showed that only he and the sumo remained standing though reinforcements would no doubt arrive any second. A second that would never come as frozen Time held everyone motionless.

The lich swirled his arm in the robe and brought up the strange gauntlet used for capturing souls. "I think, hmmmm, no. Organize your heroes and come take him."

The samurai firmed his resolve and readied to attack again. As the samurai charged, the lich's gauntlet flashed and then a cold icy hand grabbed the samurai from behind. The attack already started, the samurai swung around and tried to strike behind while calling on his god's might for aid. "Too little, too late," the lich hissed.

That icy hand snapped and cold seared through his neck. All was pain and then nothing. The samurai's momentum carried his legs up and forward and then he fell back on his back. His vision bounced and swam but he felt nothing at all. Somewhere a fire burned and cast flickering lights all around. Then two pits of chaotic purple looked down at him. "I'm sure your fool god can mend that wound. My message – your lord and priest and three others are added to the spoils offered. However, if they are not recovered by the full moon, I will add them to my armies and renew my conquest of this land."

The samurai tried to move to say anything but could not. Those eyes! He felt his body and will teeter on the edge of the abyss, and then he passed out.

Chapter Thirty Three - Countermeasures

Rojo entered the empty throne room and ordered maps, histories, and Tania's generals to attend him. His battle priestess Dar Jeri, loyal and faithful to him since that first Bloodstone campaign years ago, noted the dark haunting in her lord's eyes and saw how his hands trembled. "My Dar, how long has it been now?" Rojo sat at the base of the throne and leaned his head back, "Three, four days now. I think Jeri." He met her concerned eyes and smirked. "Does it look that bad?"

She took his hand and let it rest on her own. "My Dar, to me it does." She leaned back and smoothed her silver white hair. Her eyes betrayed the only other visible sign of her tremendous age. "We have been through too much together my lord. Please, let this wait…"

Rojo laughed, the sound hollow and exhausted even to him, "There is no time. Something strange moves in the south. Destiny calls us and the Queen will sustain me." She handed him an herbal tea laced with calming herbs. It often removed the trembling in his hands. This time it barely worked and he asked for more to be prepared. "This foul-tasting drink and the Queen, day after day."

A general and his aides entered from the far chamber and bowed, moving to take their place. Others began arriving and gave the king no special regard. Rojo often sat on the stone table at these meetings with his battle priestess nearby. Servants brought in the maps and books requested and arranged them before the throne. When all summoned had arrived, the greatest of the generals stepped forward, "My Dar, we are present as you requested. How may we serve Tania?"

Rojo cocked his knee up and rested his hand and tea there. "General D'Rath, do you feel Destiny calling us this glorious night?"

Shak D'Rath, Lord of the Griffin Riders, nodded. "My king, I felt something amiss several hours ago and came here anticipating your summons as did the others. It will come as no surprise to you that Daryx had sent a messenger as well. I have pondered this in my heart but cannot yet see the meaning."

Rojo looked them over. The seven commanders of Tania, men and women, knights and professional soldiers, even some heroes of renown, and so far as he could tell not a single one of them resented him the position he held. "Very well. Let us begin. There is much to do tonight. The emperor has shared a vision with me. We will start with that. Then, we must discuss the situation in Ori. Lastly, the heretic dragons; we must set a plan for them."

Rojo slammed his fist on the table and suddenly, all of them stood in the vision the dragon emperor had shown Rojo earlier. It played out... the small boy with the bundle, the high priestess, the attack, the titanic cloven hoof slamming into the valley of the city, the emperor's howls of grief that so many of his children had died. As the final image faded, Rojo spoke, "I command that this be added to the Book of Generations, in the appropriate timeframe of the first Dar Priestess. You shall all bear witness that this revelation came to me, freely given by the emperor and confirmed by inspiration to each of you."

They moved to the banks of the River, each of them taking on a younger-stronger aspect. The grizzled appearance and snow white hair so characteristic of General D'Rath became more colorful as red hair replaced white and his frame filled out with youthful vigor. The stone table remained, the River lapping up against it. Rojo, in this place, hurt to look at. His exhausted and grim demeanor became blindingly bright here like sunlight filtered through a prism. The somewhat lethargic anger of his voice here became a roaring cascade of confidence.

"My generals, we stand here to review Destiny." His hand swept open the maps and a single tome fell open. The markings on the map and the open pages bore the insignia of the Darkhold, a fell book of the Abyss that recorded the mighty magics of all realms, no matter where they lie. Rojo opened the Darkhold. The left facing page had a lifelike drawing of a human sorcerer touched with a priestly affect but twisted by chaos and undeath. The image moved from side to side as if impatiently waiting. Rojo covered the writing on the other page with a blank piece of paper. To read the Darkhold gave it claim to the reader's soul.

Each of them noted the familiar figure of the drawing on the page. "Bomoki," Rojo spoke. "Destiny brings us another chance. The boy in the vision, the one with skull and brown robes, and the hellhound we saw. That was Bomoki, the first of the hounds. His page in the Darkhold has updated. The reader noted, in usual Darkholden style, that Bomoki is undertaking a great quest to seize something called the "blood sceptre", that he would be confronted by the unseen dragons, that he would triumph except for the "sleepless king" and the "rageful knight".

"This prophecy notes certain conditions for Bomoki's success, or our success. We do not know what the "blood sceptre" is. The "sleepless king" could be myself, but could also be any king in a state of sleeplessness, for example, the daimo of Ori; his soul was taken by the lich. It might also be my successor as of yet unaware that he is to be the next king. That disturbance we all felt earlier, that was the lich attacking the royal family. We suspect the "unseen dragons" are either humanshifted dragons or Tanians able to dragonshift –"

Dar Kell stepped out of the shadows twisting around them on the River's banks and interrupted, "Or it could be the shadow dragons. I believe you planned to discuss them as well Rojo?"

Everyone startled and nodded to Dar Kell. The high priest walked up to the table and turned the Darkhold to a different page, "I have read this page. Cor'tanos. Patriarch of the Shadow Dragons." His finger trailed the text and tapped towards a new inscription at the end. "I will have to consider this. The shadow dragons are noted as "dark wyrms" rather than "unseen" but there is a new reference here to the "blood sceptre". I will study this more. Please forgive the intrusion and continue." Kell stepped back from the table and watched.

Dar Rojo bowed and gestured for the generals to give Kell room. "This other reference to the "rageful knight" can only mean my successor referred to by the same term in that revelation. If the shadow dragons are somehow involved with the blood sceptre?" He leaned back and stretched. "So, if we get this sceptre first, or if we place the sleepless king and rageful knight in Bloodstone near the gate to thwart him, we win. A tactical victory continues the war, but I'd rather be skirmishing with the Jade God than waging outright war, as we saw in the emperor's shared vision."

General Shak placed his hand on the table indicating a desire to speak. "This also places a king and knight in a position to destroy Bomoki." Heads nodded around the table. "If Bomoki," he continued, "is on a great quest, perhaps we should seek this sceptre first and bring it to a place we control and use it as bait to destroy the traitor once and for all."

Rojo questioned whether sufficient volunteers and others could be found for such a quest, "Bomoki is an unascended god. There are not many who could stand against him." After much debate, General Shak said, "My king, given we have unanimous desire to end Bomoki, it appears the exact manner by which we win is open. I will own this. I will prepare a plan and return."

Another general indicated that he would seek out the blood sceptre. "I will prepare a team. Until we learn otherwise, I will assume it is an actual sceptre important to necromancy. The team will be ready and its members kept ready. For now, shall we assume it is different than the Jade God's wand?"

Rojo looked them all over. "This sceptre, lets pretend it is as dangerous as the Jade God's wand. No one is to touch or look at it. I want a second team ready to intervene and end anyone showing unnatural influence."

The general nodded. "I will lead and assemble both teams myself. I ask for the Temple to take command of the second team."

"You are wise. I commend you all and thank you. Dar Kell will see that the Temple contacts you immediately so that you can begin preparations. Dar D'Rath, for the time being, assume the "rageful knight" is this newest member of the Order of Water. I will have his battle priest debrief you."

Dar Kell said, "We must discuss the shadow dragons. Their nature is one of betrayal. The Queen does not trust them, nor will She allow them back without price."

Rojo nodded. "Tell us Dar Kell, you know them better than any of us."

"I stopped dragon-shifting when I realized their truth. That truth is this: the shadow realms are killing them. They entered as eldar but are becoming inert. Being what they are, Cor'tanos has likely emerged as the strongest because he is robbing the others of their power. They can no doubt last for aeons in Shadow, but are desperate to re-enter this world, at any price. The easiest way for them to do this is to take possession of one of us. Myself, Malcor, others like us are the most likely targets."

A quiet pause around the table ended when Rojo observed, "If they took possession of you Dar Kell, it'd be very bad."

"Yes, but most especially for me. I have spent much time researching and studying this. When we dragonshift, we add to the dominion of the Queen and Her children. When a shadow dragon-shifter shifts, there is no dominion to add to. It pulls the dragons to us. Cor'tanos, I believe, wanted to take me as his own. I have resisted and redirected his attention to this treaty with the Queen, but I do not see the shadow dragons honoring it. Ever. At best, this is a temporary truce, a calm before the coming storm.

"Malcor's appearance both in prophecy and as my son has caught Cor'tanos' attention. I recommend that we allow Malcor to pursue his own path and keep Cor'tanos focused there. The prospect of finding a new host like Malcor young in life slotted for kingship - these will ensure Cor'tanos does not act too soon. He wants a strong host and an assurance that there will be others for the rest of the clan."

One of the generals signaled a question and asked, "And when the time comes that the boy is strong enough, or that Cor'tanos tries to take you?"

Kell looked back at the general. "The Queen will not let Her most hated of enemies take me. Should it happen, Daryx has contingencies ready. As for Malcor and the others, it will be years. They had a taste of Malcor during his first rite with no doubt more to come in the second. Interested enough that Cor'tanos saved him. Also, the prophecy about the blood of heroes, and that Malcor has fathered a child, will all keep Cor'tanos at bay until he has a surety. As you know, dragon-shifting – doctrinally at least – is a blessing of the Queen. For the shadow dragons, it's more like allowing the dragon to take possession and transform the person. It's quite powerful because it draws from the dragon, not the host.

238

"What this means is that the dragons will not try and take over the host until they are sure of their survival and capabilities in this world. They will test and drive the host to greater and greater powers, wealth, and capabilities. All the things dragons are known to care about. But, herein lies their weakness. Their will has diminished since the eldar times. Cor'tanos will not take me because I can take him at will." He chuckled, "You could say we have an agreement."

Rojo summarized, "So for the shadow dragons, I accept Kell's recommendation. We will provide opportunities for Malcor to prove himself but be ready for any treachery. Though, I do have a question for you Kell. What is the end game?"

"The end game? We take possession of them. We bring them into the Queen's dominion through sheer subjugation. I have been ready for Cor'tanos for many years. It is proof that there will be others that has made us wait this long. Our end game is an order of shadow dragon knights with absolute devotion to the Queen. Please my king, speak with the emperor about this. Dar Ana at Bloodstone has been seeking out bloodstones to use to facilitate the transfer of the dragon from a slain host to another knight. The Book of Shadows has already been started, if not canonized yet."

"Very well. I will speak with the emperor. It shall be as you recommend Dar Kell. This meeting is over." The generals bowed and turned to step away from the River. "And generals, Shak D'Rath, take note: this knight - Malcor lasted the Rite of Pain for nearly five days." Eyes around the room widened and then swirling waters pulled them back into the world's flow.

Chapter Thirty Four - Respite

Several days had passed on the high plain. When not resting, Malcor trained and adjusted to the military life encamped. He learned that every single person in their group shared a common and radically different view of being a paladin than he had ever imagined. The stuff of heroes and legend, Malcor saw that even the healers, would qualify as a hero based on their individual exploits. The difference, more than anything, was the overriding sense of team. When you considered that each knight had a battle priest and two healers, and that this core group also included a powerful mage, "Apprentice" nickname notwithstanding, as well as thieves, Malcor at last came to understand that the group represented what must be the mightiest and most legendary and epic "hero" he could ever imagine.

The Order of Water trained in blood and it was not until Malcor witnessed a battle between the mage and another knight, and saw the knight obliterated, that he realized how powerful such a team truly would be. The battle priest approached the scorched husk of the barely living knight and healed him. The next skirmish pitted two knights against the mage, and then more and more. The mage proved worth five of the knights. Tembri observed, "Our lich will be orders of magnitude more powerful than the apprentice."

Following that, while the mage and knights recovered, the two thieves and the ranger sparred with each other to warm up while three knights made ready. Similar to the mage, Malcor noted with interest how the different skills and training gave each fighter advantages and disadvantages. The knights, who at first seemed invulnerable, gradually acquired wounds. At the same time, when they landed a blow on the non-fighters, the severity of the wound always required immediate healing.

As the fighting continued, a light rain began to fall with darker clouds on the horizon. His eye followed it and caught the looming spike of mountains across the valley where the lich waited. Both thieves eventually fell to dire wounds and tapped out. The elven ranger though continued a twirling dance of agility and weapon skill that made it hard for the knights to score a deciding blow. The knights tried a variety of ploys to lure the ranger in for close and distance attacks. Nothing worked. They tried waiting for the ranger to grow tired, but he just attacked them at distance. While the three knights and the ranger each wounded each other, it appeared to be a complete draw. At last, Dar Kendra snarled and stomped into the fray to join the three. "It's been a long time since I sparred with one of you," she said.

The ranger saluted and acrobatically dodged the two paladins charging from either side. Kendra's attack twisted her sword into that coiled serpent of energy that struck the ranger's boot just before he landed. Malcor could not believe his eyes when the ranger let her sword tear his boot free and still landed nimbly on his feet. Two knives rang off Kendra's armor. Her coiled energy blade cracked like thunder and pulled apart into her other hand and another razor whip lashed out at the ranger. He stood and caught the blast seeming to control it along his short sword crossed with a bow. And then, he re-aimed it at one of the other knights. That knight caught the blast with a prayer but had to stop his own attack while its power washed over him.

"There's a reason all the rangers come through Daryx," the mage said as he sat down by Mal and Tembri. "They are equipped as well as this Order is, and their training is excellent."

Malcor had never spoken to a mage before, not even at the forge in Klenna. He noted the odd smell of spices and spell components that hung about the man. "I did not know that rangers were like this," he said.

Apprentice pointed, "Look, his short sword, like your holy avenger, has magic resistance and its own powers. His absorbs and holds attack energy. The bow, for rangers, is not just a weapon. It's a staff, a balance tool, a shield, whatever they want. This battle reminds me of when Lady Kendra went up against Daryx some years ago. Now that was a battle! I'm surprised he's doing so well."

"Daryx and Kendra fought?"

"Yes, it was in a tournament during a holy day. The emperor intended it for public audience but when word got out who the fighters would be, we had visitors from all over the world show up. Their fight only lasted a few minutes but it almost overwhelmed the Mage's Guild protecting the audience."

"Who won?" Mal asked.

"Who do you think won?" Tembri laughed. When Apprentice did not answer, he asked more tentatively, "Dar Kendra of course. Right?"

Apprentice shrugged. "The Queen does not require the Order of Water to fight based on rules. She requires them to win." As if to emphasize this point, Kendra faked a sword attack that allowed her to punch the ranger. Her left hook hurled the ranger up into the air and then in a heartbeat, Kendra jumped past him and flat-bladed the ranger down into the ground. Though the ranger tried to dodge, his own momentum and uncontrolled but predictable arc betrayed him. Kendra blinked and as his body rebounded from slamming into the ground, he found the tip of her blade resting at his throat, and yielded.

Apprentice chuckled and Malcor asked, "Have you always gone by Apprentice? I assume you have a real name right?"

The mage looked over the battle field to see who was going up next. "Names convey power. There's a reason we don't ever say the Jade God's name. Part of what makes the Goddess who She is, is the simple fact that She alone knows the names of all the dragons. I have a name, but part of the Mage's Guild – the equivalent to your paladin rites – is forsaking your real name and burying it in anonymity. You don't really think your real name is actually *Malcor* do you son of Kell?"

The mage's words left Malcor feeling off-balanced. His way of talking, it made him feel unsure of himself. Without another word, the Apprentice stood and walked into the arena. Several of the paladins rose up to challenge him, but he waved them aside and pointed to Kendra's battle priest. "We are overdue for our rematch!" he called out.

Kendra's battle priest, an unremarkable man but one covered in tattoos, stepped forward and smashed his chest. "Yes, it is! Name your weapon mage!"

Malcor fell asleep watching the clash of weapons and magic. The brilliance of a magical battle augmented by weapons was fascinating at first. Apprentice fought with daggers and a staff where the priest used a heavy mace set along a staff. They must have agreed to not use magic directly except to heighten their weapons.

After some time, Malcor awoke to Tembri's nudging that it was dinner time.

Chapter Thirty Five - The Forge at Klenna

Ishan looked around the forge. The blacksmiths, ore processors, porters, apprentices, and so many others looked back. He cleared his throat, "I'm not very good at reading so bear with me." The mayor stood next to him and beamed smiles out at the group. Ishan fumbled to open the ornate scroll.

"Let it be known that Sir Malcor, initiate paladin of the Temple, has seized control of House Tor and been granted dominion over it. Though Tor has formally challenged dominion..." he stumbled through the letter coming at last to the part where Sai R'Dar and the priestess Ora had agreed to act and hold Tor for Malcor. He wiped his head and took a deep breath. "So, hey, Malcor made it!"

The mayor stepped forward and interrupted. "He joined a high order of paladins, as has my son Calvin. Malcor has brought considerable honor to Klenna. This letter," he held up a different letter, "is from Sai R'Dar, a member of the Circle and a Lord of Tania. He pledges his estate to protect the Tor Armory and appoints that priestess R'Dar Ora act as an administrator with the ability to act with Sai's full authority. It further states," and he clapped Ishan on the shoulder, "that Ishan here be appointed as R'Dar Ishan. Ishan, it is my greatest pleasure to welcome you to the ranks of nobility and leadership! You have worked hard and always served the Tor Armory and Klenna well. I know you will do an excellent job! Three cheers for our new R'Dar!"

The meeting had started out with a sense of dread. Since R'Dar Tor had fallen to Malcor's blade at the Aging, things had been tense. At first everyone had been told to work as normal. Then, they had all been fired. Then, the Armory had been closed and put into bankruptcy. Now, this newest revelation came as welcome but hard to believe news. Slowly, applause and then cheering erupted. The mayor guided Ishan out into the throng where the other master smiths congratulated him and next level smiths had already begun eyeing each other to fill Ishan's newly vacated master smith position.

As he made the rounds and the cheering quieted, the mayor signaled and the Tor Armory re-opened. It had been filled with food, snacks, drinks, and even toys for the worker's children. A band began playing and the Klennan Shrine's priestess blessed the armory, the group, and the feast. When the prayer ended, a silver falcon swooped down and landed on the sign over the armory's entrance. It caught everyone's attention as sunlight reflected in sparkles off its body. Its magical nature caught the light spinning off mechanical disks and gears. The mayor pointed and said, "This is a golem falcon. These types of constructs are what Sai R'Dar is known for throughout the Isles. He sent it here to deliver a personal message."

The falcon's head twisted back and forth and then its ruby eyes flared brightly. "Start. Through Sir Malcor, the Tor Armory is now part of my estate. My priestess Ora will watch over as surely as a mother tends to her children. We are in the process of assimilating the House of Tor. They are banned from entering this facility. I have appointed my friend here, this falcon golem, to safeguard you all at work, in your homes, here on the streets of Klenna until the assimilation is complete.

"After you have had a chance to enjoy the feast provided by Sir Malcor, please, each of you will place your hand on the falcon's head and state your name so that I may welcome you to my estate. I consider your families part of the Armory as well. Your work cannot take place without them. I welcome you to a new era at this armory. Already known for good work, we will be augmenting it. I expect excellence, your best. Give me that and you will be rewarded very well. Sir Malcor has also procured a military contract for resupply that will keep you all quite busy for years to come. End."

The falcon lifted its head to the sun and let out a falcon screech and then dropped to pick a slice of meat from the feast tables. The mayor took Ishan to the falcon and had him place his hand on the falcon's head. The band started playing again. Shortly thereafter, others began arriving to see what the commotion was about. As fast as the food and drink disappeared, more seemed to arrive. After the Armory workers all touched the golem, the falcon's eyes flashed and its head tilted, as if listening. It flew to the rooftops surrounding the armory's courtyard and where it landed, bright streaming colors of magical light began drifting and pouring down like a waterfall of colored mist.

Ishan's wife eventually found her husband. "Well Mr. R'DAR Ishan... are you now too noble to dance with me?"

He bowed low and took her hand, "My lady. I will never be too noble to dance with you!"

To the cheerful band, they danced. Above, the falcon watched and then narrowed its focus to a small girl standing just to the edges of the merrymaking. Through the falcon's eyes, the silver lord Sai saw her. Back in the capitol, he asked Ora, "This young girl with the blue eyes, this is the one Armageddon touched and spoke with - Klara?"

"Yes my lord. Malcor considers her a little sister. He saved her from winter cold and starvation."

"Most interesting. Her eyes are quite rare amongst Tanians. When you are next at the Temple, please check the records for the Kell Conflict and see if any of the priestesses, on either side have elven heritage. Please check Kell's wife's family specifically."

Ora nodded. "Should I find anything – "

"Send word immediately. Also, make arrangements to test Klara when you are next in Klenna. It must be you."

Chapter Thirty Six - First Rites for the Initiates

Calvin and the other knight initiates in his group, stood shivering high on the Dragon's Mountain with their instructor. The march up had been brutal as they rose into the never-ending winter cold. Though almost fall, the high peak never melted. "Perhaps, the great ice patriarch Ynt'taris will visit you when he is good and ready. You will be visited by a white dragon though. Prepare for dragonfear on a level you have never experienced before. While there should be no shame in such fear, you must endure to continue as a knight. You have done well to make it this far. I am leaving you now to return the shelter we passed at timberline. If you cannot endure, join me though for the sake of your paladin dreams, I wish to see none of you until after."

The long climb up the Dragon's Mountain had required two overnight stays at hostels along the well-tended road. All around them, there had been emissaries, tributaries, soldiers, and all the denizens that made up Tania's population. As they climbed, Calvin had stared out across the city that fell further and further below. It had always seemed humongous but from this view, it looked tiny perhaps even confining. And then they had left the road behind. The dragon-sized tunnel entering the mountain to Alerius himself had made Calvin feel small. He did not realize how truly small he felt until he had reached this glacial plain on the northern side of the mountain.

A huge pile of clouds covered the southern horizon, and though the sun beat down on them, the cold wind here whipped ice up into their faces making it feel as if they stood in a sunny blizzard. Calvin shielded his eyes and looked around for the thousandth time. His fingers and toes had long gone numb with cold. It felt like… "We've been standing here for hours," a young lady nearby complained.

Someone else pointed and said they thought they saw movement. It had already happened so often that Calvin did not even look. Like the others, Calvin felt something about the mountain aware, watching, and full of malice. "White dragons are diametrically opposed to the fire dragons, but serve the Queen same as any other. Their breath weapons take the shape of cold… air, snow, frost, water or even air so cold it freezes on contact. But, they are also called cold dragons because, of all the dragons, they are the most emotionally-detached from this world. The things about mortals that intrigue our emperor, are of no interest at all to Whites. To most, we are food. To some, like Ynt'taris who allies with the Temple, we are at best tools." Their instructor had been most specific on this point: "Remember, at best you are a tool. Think about a tool, the kind you would want to use. That is how you want Ynt'taris to see you. Would a saw run away from nail? Would a drill flee from wood? Would a lever complain against a weight? Does a pen flinch from ink and paper? Does a sword challenge its wielder in the midst of combat?"

Calvin moved his arms and stuffed his hands back under his arms. "Damn, it is cold here," he whispered again.

Another student nearby agreed and stepped up closer to Calvin. In the cold breeze, Calvin noticed the person had a strange odor about them but forgot the thought when he saw the most beautiful girl he had ever seen. She had blonde, almost white hair, and blue eyes so blue they reminded him of a summer sky after a storm. She shifted back and forth trying to stay warm, "I don't remember the last time I could even feel my toes," she said. "I'm scared to stop moving for fear I won't be able to move again!"

Calvin tried to laugh but the cold made it hard. "I just keep thinking of all the prep we've had for this. There were five dread lords at my Aging. It seems overkill to make us climb a mountain to meet dragons."

The girl agreed with him. "There were dread lords at your Aging?! That's awesome. Who were they?"

"One of the emperor's sons – Blaze I think. Maybe it was the other one? I can't tell them apart. And then a huge giant called Armageddon with Dar Shara. I never caught the others or who they were with. They were amazing but still."

"I think I saw a red flying over my town once, but it was so far away I couldn't tell. It was amazing. What was it like?"

Maybe it was the cold, Calvin could not tell, but he detected an edge to

248

her question. It did not seem to matter and so he told her about the dance and the columns of flame. Through his chattering teeth, talking was an effort, but at some point, he must have mentioned Malcor.

"I've heard of Malcor," the girl said. "He was the one in the central Temple, the one who went up the tower right?"

"Yeah, he and I grew up together."

"Have you heard about him since? I wondered if he would be in our classes."

Calvin had thought the same thing but as the days had passed and Malcor did not show up, he had stopped looking. "He must have died, or is in some other training. I don't know. I'm sure I'll hear from him eventually."

A cloud drifted over the sun and the temperature plummeted. The girl shivered so hard she almost fell over and Calvin caught her. They stood held tight together for warmth. A minute later, when the sun reappeared, they remained close. Calvin noted the other knights looking at them and shrugged back. She must have too, and snarled at them, "What? It's warmer together."

Time passed and the sun began lowering in the sky. Even without the sporadic cloud cover and even colder temperatures, as shadows stretched, so too did nerves. Soon, like Calvin, pairs of boys and girls stood huddled together shivering and eventually the others stood into groups, and then everyone came together as one single group for warmth and protection from the icy wind. It felt like a death sentence when, amidst a beautiful and fiery sunset, the sun dipped below the western mountains and twilight fell.

The girl closest to Calvin and even those around had long since stopped shivering and a grim sense of freezing and death by cold have come across them. Several times people commented on how it must be a test to freeze to death, like the Rite of Pain, so that they could then be healed. Eventually, stars dotted the heaven and while the speculation never stopped, they all flinched when one of the boys on the outer part of the group fell over frozen to death. Though his collapse barely made a sound at all, and though a nearby friend called out to him and tried to pull him back up, the sound there on that plain was like a thunder bolt. The girl near Calvin cried out, "We're all going to die! Either by cold or dragon fear, I knew I should have become a priestess!"

Someone else said they should have married and become a merchant and just like that, a torrent of regret washed over the group. Calvin thought about his life as the son of the mayor of a respected village. Even an outpost had honor and meaning, right? The girl asked him during a moment of silence, "What about you Calvin?"

It felt like an important question but the import of it registered as if far away in someone else's mind. "I," he stammered through frostbitten lips, "I will regret not having met Ynt'taris."

No sooner had he said this than a cyclone of snow swept up around them. The force of the wind, or maybe it was something hard that struck him, knocked Calvin backwards where he landed amongst fellow students laying in the snow. The whirlwind howled just behind them but there, from the center, the girl standing by him, stretched and split apart as her hands became talons and plunged into the snow as her arms elongated and wings erupted from her back.

Moment by moment and change by change, the transformation pounded in his veins. An overwhelming feeling of awe and dread and terror chased the cold away. Each shift and the sound of bones and skin built fright upon frightful until several of the students tried to run away, and vanished into a shredding whirlwind of ice. A momentary red spray of color in the wind and then they were gone.

Ynt'taris looked down at them all and shrieked, its dire breath slamming around them and hurling a few more students into the lethal wall of icy razors. The white dragon looked down at them and time froze as each felt the dragon looking into their character, picking apart their fears, and sinking its fangs deep into their most private insecurities. Though Calvin later learned that each heard something different, Calvin distinctly heard a voice whisper to him, "Though knightly, you will never be a paladin."

His skin, already so painful from hours in the cold, prickled anew at the words and reminded him of what Dar Shara had said. Was that only a month ago? Ynt'taris raised his wings and hurled them forward. This time, those standing remained firm though all quaked and shuddered with fear. The dragon's gaze held each and every one of them, and then the wind stopped. Everything fell calm and quiet. Freed of the raging storm, Ynt'taris gleamed in the night. Though dim, the white dragon scales acted like light amplifiers filling the plain with a clear and clean radiance. The cold threatening to kill them tangibly pulled out of them into the dragon leaving each warmer.

Ynt'taris raised his head to the sky, to where the moon would have been if not hidden by clouds, and sounded a clear almost musical note. It rang up into the air and fell down around and through them. The note rose and hummed lightly and caused visions of more primal times to fill Calvin's head and heart. He saw Ynt'taris as an eldar flying through a void that would become this world. The gleaming pleasure of creation as ice and snow and weather bowed to his will... and then Ynt'taris bowing before the Queen and offering his allegiance. The Queen, in this vision, stood as a titanic dragon with multiple heads each the color of the dragons giving fealty. As Ynt'taris bowed, one of Her heads took on white scales and writhed out to touch noses with him. A single snow white tear fell from Ynt'taris' eye and the vision ended.

Calvin stood still, trembling, barely able to breathe. The emotions of boundless pleasure and infinite loyalty warred in him. "The White Dragons serve you eternally my Queen. Your test is complete. Go." Without another word, Ynt'taris jumped into the sky and vanished into the dark clouds overhead. Immediately, the cold came back.

Calvin turned to note how few of his class had survived. All around them, statues of those caught in the ice razor wind stood still and frozen. For some, the ice wind had stripped flesh from bone and skeletal hands and faces rimmed by frozen blood caught the horror, pain, and terror they had felt as they died. Something in him awakened at that moment and he said, "Come, lets take them back with us."

Chapter Thirty Seven - Seline Conquers Flame

Far beneath Calvin, in the Dragon Mountain's many rooms, Seline sat with her new mentor in the Order of Fire. The room had a fire pit in the middle in which a dragon statue glowed red hot. Stone tile on the floor and walls held a mosaic of dragons at war. Dar Niss pulled a poker off the wall and turned around to face Seline. "We will mediate and then test your strength against fire. We will start at the furthest edge of the room." She pointed to a sitting mat to Seline's left and walked to a similar mat opposite. Sitting down, Seline did as instructed and recited verse from the Book of Flames. After a few minutes, a bead of sweat ran down her neck and back.

Dar Niss urged her, "Continue your recital, but know that we will move closer and closer to the fire. To endure, you must focus on your truth. Your truth is that you are a daughter of dragons! Dragons do not fear fire, not even winter dragons fear normal fire like this. As a dragon child, why should you?"

The recital continued with Dar Niss interjecting various thoughts, doctrines, and challenges. It took on a sing song kind of quality as Seline moderated her recital to the same rise and fall of Dar Niss' instruction. Soon, Seline's conscious mind disengaged and took in the fire, her teacher, and the room's mosaics. The dragon wars showed two Reds entwined in combat in mid-air. Fire snaked out of their mouths as they fought creating snake-like tendrils of flame that traced a path through the sky. "When a dragon breathes flame, they don't think – I will breathe flame. No, the flame rises out of them with passion and fury. Does the flame burn their mouths? No. It is no different than you picking up a tool, or using a pen to write. Once you know, you know and it is then your nature to know. And knowing it, your nature to use that knowledge and make it happen. You are a daughter of dragons."

At some point, Seline removed her clothing and large beads of sweat poured out of her skin as she moved forward to the very edge of the fire pit. She had long moved past the point where her skin and face felt like they were melting. At first she had fought to resist touching her hair to confirm it had not burned away. Now, with the fire right there, she stared into the embers and the glowing red hot dragon statue in the center. Dar

Niss sat opposite her eyes meeting her own over the statue's head. "You are at the edge of the fire. You have conquered the heat, now you must conquer fire itself." She poured oil from a bowl at her side. So close to the fire, the oil had begun to boil but Dar Niss's hands held it steady and firm. As the oil oozed out and hit the fire, it ignited burning hotter and more fiercely than would seem possible. The embers hit by oil exploded creating ripples through the flame pit. Seline imagined she could smell hair burning but resisted the temptation to confirm.

Dar Niss looked at her and confirmed eye contact. Slowly she turned and brushed her hair aside. There on the back of her neck was a burn scar the approximate shape of the glowing red dragon figure's head. "The Order of Fire marks its members with the fire dragon. Some mark their wrists. Others their leg. It can be anywhere. I leave it to you Seline. When you are ready, enter the fire and take your mark."

The figurine, while not large, looked heavy. She could not say why the red hot metal seemed more terrible than the flame. To have marked her neck, the priestess must have picked up the statue and held it just so.

She stood and tried to stretch. The movement made her dizzy and drawing any breath at all caused a terrible desire to cough. She choked it back and tentatively put her foot into the flames. She felt the fire but did not feel it burning. She stepped down into the glowing embers and felt her foot's weight press down through the upper crust. Sparks swirled up from her foot and landed on her face. "Good, good," Dar Niss cooed. "You are doing well. You are a daughter of dragons Seline!"

At last, when her foot firmed in the embers, she lowered herself almost knee deep in the embers and walked forward. Her imagination tortured her with images of disfigurement but soon she stood at the feet of the figurine, looking slightly upwards at its eyes. They burned like gemmy blood alight with an inner fire. She caressed its chest with her fingertips, again feeling the heat, but having faith she would not burn.

Strengthened by her faith, she grabbed the statue and tested its weight. Though heavy, she thought she could lift it and brought it off the pedestal to her back. Finally, she positioned it correctly and pressed the head into the back of her right shoulder. For the first time, she felt searing pain and blisters. She almost cried out but bit her lip. And then Dar Niss jumped into the fire pit and began dancing around her! "You did it! Welcome sister, welcome! May the dragons ever guide you!"

Together they placed the dragon back on the pedestal. Dar Niss splashed liquid fire and burning coal at her. She deflected it and then, encouraged by her instructor, did the same. It felt amazing to play with fire. It stopped being hot and felt refreshing, almost cold. Somehow, at some point, and looking back she could not remember why, she tackled Dar Niss and they dropped below the embers into the fire. Surprised she could see, she laughed at the sparks of fire and red magic that danced through the fire and outlined their bodies. "This is..."

Dar Niss just nodded. "This is how the red dragons see the world, as flame and fire and magic. Well done Seline. Welcome to your baptism of fire!" So saying, Dar Niss clasped Seline to her and held her tightly as the red magic and fire rose up through her into her and the surrounding pit of burning and filled them with divine magic.

Niss' flame strike transformed the natural fire into hot chaos and Seline winced against its brightness. She could not look away though from the hypnotic dance of energy. So electric, so sensual, so alive. She stopped feeling the individual coals and embers and reveled in becoming a creature of fire. With each movement of her hands or the parts of her own body she could see, she sent waves of energy crashing out to the edge where it then rebounded back at her. The turbulence had its own chaos and rhythm that coiled in and around her like a serpent. She never wanted it to end.

Time passed but she lost track and stopped caring until a deep masculine voice interrupted her. She had forgotten Dar Niss, lost in the sensation, but both of them sat up from the fire and saw a dread lord clad in mages robes. "Dar Niss, is this our newest member?"

She stood, completely uncaring of her nudity, and helped Seline stand. "Lady Seline of Dutchy, this is Dread Lord Blade, second son of the dragon emperor Alerius and head of our Order." Seline dropped prostrate in the ritual bow of worship, which took her below the fire. She heard Blade laugh and call her to rise.

"Lady Seline, does fire bow to flame? In the Order of Fire, we do not bow to each other. Though I am my father's son, I am not the god emperor. My Mother's gifts are towards magical fire and, like my father, I seek to uplift and uphold this world for the Queen and Her Children. I see you branded yourself in a place of painful distinction. The others will be envious."

Seline stood taking it all in. The emperor's son, in human form, would never be mistaken for a human. His skin had a red scale quality to them and his eyes felt overly-large and slit like a dragon's. They glowed red with heat energy streaming forth and rising from their corners. Unlike other dread lords though, this one stood not as tall, still taller and broader than a human, but less muscled and more refined. As much as she regarded him, she became aware that he regarded her. Suddenly aware of his eyes trailing over her body, she felt exposed and vulnerable and very much aware of her nakedness.

And that was when it happened. Like a lance through her chest, she felt her heart stop and impale on sheer terror. Her breath, her breathing, her awareness condensed into that dreadful moment and she knew. Beyond a shadow of doubt, she knew that this dread lord held her life in his hands and could take her, own her, destroy her, obliviate her, possess her, and she could do nothing about it. The terror threatened to overwhelm her and, as if from a distance, she heard that dreadful voice say, "She sheds a single tear."

Dar Niss replied but she could not understand it. "Her terror is sublime," that voice said again. Her awareness focused on the pain in her breast. That pain suddenly exploded outwards to her youth, her infancy, and one by one that masculine awareness pulled and picked through her memories sifting them like sand blowing through fingers. Each memory touched with shame, like her first awkward kiss, burned with humiliation that swarmed into her fear. Each moment of pride and achievement tinged green with fear that it was inadequate and the inadequacy rolled into the frothing terror griping her soul. Then, the images shifted to her clad in glorious armor and striding like a god through a battlefield of corpses. As one after another she saw glimpses of her future, a small flame of hope kindled and pulse by pulse, heartbeat by heartbeat, it began to drive the terror back.

Suddenly, she took a deep gasping breath and collapsed against Blade's chest. Her senses alive and burning as the terror emptied out of her and she quaked, holding herself up by his robes. He took her hands and she knew, "You know everything my lord, everything…"

"Yes," he said. So close his voice sounded like metal ringing on metal like a bell in her bones. "I know and I choose you as the Order of Fire's newest member. Welcome Lady Seline." With perfect gentlemanly affectation, he kissed her hand, bowed and left. When her line of sight lost him, she collapsed to her knees and sobbed. His presence, terrible and omniscient like it was, also had radiated the fire of passion and love and might and glory. She found she craved it, needed it, and noticed its absence almost as painfully as if burned by fire. Her body ached with sexual tension as well and moving so quickly through all of these raw emotions, she chuckled, laughed, and then roared with laughter as tears poured from her eyes. Eventually, she collapsed to her side where her maniacal emotions finally settled into deep wracking sobs.

Dar Niss held her and stroked her hair. "Dragons, especially those like the emperor, are so close to the Queen, they are quite overwhelming. The first time. It is hard to take it all in and when they leave… shhhh, it's going to be all right. The terror, the dominance, just imagine how this affects their enemies. To be effective in the Order of Fire, you must understand these feelings for what they are. In combat, Blade and the others will unleash their terror, and WE must withstand it."

Seline choked out, "What are these feelings?!"

"Love. Submission. You are his. We are all his."

She recovered a bit. "I am his." Saying it felt good and lessened the emptiness wracking her. "I am his?"

Dar Niss kissed her forehead, "No, by the Queen's will, you are your own. But unless you can master the Red's dragonterror, we will have to remove you from the Order. If we didn't, you'd become addicted to that feeling of love and mastery and lose your free will entirely. The Queen has bigger plans for you than addicted servitude. Like resisting dragonfear, you must control their other effects."

"Is the emperor like this?"

"Shhhh, I have never been honored to see the emperor's dragonterror. I have heard it is as if your entire essence is as a smudge of ink on a scrap of garbage. Your hopes and dreams and desires become as if nothing. Blade is the youngest son and has his father's might. I have seen the eldest Blaze, who carries Alerius' magic... it was," she smiled and quivered in the memory, "exquisite. There, there, shhhhhh..."

Together, they held each other and rocked back and forth.

Chapter Thirty Eight - The First Party Embarks

Dar Kendra beamed at her order. The group of knights and their attendants looked up at her. The several weeks spent on the high plain had given them time to prepare, gather more information, and bring in supplies. Malcor, now fully recovered from his Rite of Pain, looked strong and alert. "The first party has left Ori. It is a group of seven. Typical adventurer types. They still do the tribute but have had to borrow on credit to maintain it. The lich has not been seen since taking the daimo's soul.

"This party is what we have been waiting for. It means that, at long last, the lich will have something to concentrate and focus on. The ranger is monitoring them and will send us reports. Initial guess though is that they will fail. Word is that there are many such groups trying to organize and that word has spread beyond Ori to the rest of the Isles. Daryx is preparing a a fallback should we need it. This first party should reach the lich's mountain in four days."

Having said this, they began to discuss options of having members of their group join the party, even organizing themselves into a party. To that Dar Kendra laughed, "My dear knights, the Order flows and bends to the Queen's will, but none of us will pass as a rag tag band of Ori heroes!"

Tembri slapped Malcor on the back hard enough that he stepped forward and called out, "What about our newest member?"

Kendra looked down at Malcor and pursed her lips. "Maybe," was all she said.

Tembri added, "He has barely come through his first two rites and still looks like a blacksmith… and if you get him mad," he slapped Malcor's shoulder again and chuckled, "…no knightly indignation there!"

The others laughed and soon others began noting differences for Malcor as a newcomer from the more veteran group. "He still calls you Dar Kendra!" "He asks permission to join a discussion!" "He swings his sword like a blacksmith!" "His hand signaling is so stiff!" "He doesn't have a beard yet!" Initially, Malcor felt that egging sense of shame, the one he felt before attacking R'Dar Tor, but it quickly faded to self-mockery and he joined in and bowed accepting each jibe as it came.

Kendra jumped down to stand eye to eye with Malcor. "You are not yet a paladin Malcor. You'd be a myrmidon at best, a cavalier at worst. Tembri, the others, we could not go with you. And, you'd be a Tanian. Ori is accepting but they view Tania as an evil and forsaken empire ruled by a cruel religion. You'd have to endure it and keep your calm. Can you?"

"I will Dar Kendra!" Malcor pledged. More laughter at his use of her title followed that but Malcor held his stance. "I am ready!"

"This group," she sighed talking about the hero party that had just left Ori, "will likely die before they even reach the mountain. If things go poorly, you are to escape..."

Malcor began to interrupt but she grabbed his shoulders and continued, "Escape. *You are not a paladin yet.* We do not escape except as a tactic to win. You must escape and go back to Ori, and join the next group. Tembri, make sure he has sufficient healing and training for how to use it. Apprentice, he will need a ring of regeneration. Malcor, while you will of course take your sword, the tokens for summoning it and your armor will betray you as a member of a Tanian high order. Tembri you will take care of these and other preparations. Apprentice, we will place Malcor tonight. You have until then to be ready Malcor."

Hours later Malcor regarded himself in a pool of water's reflection. He looked a lot more like a carefree youth from before his Aging Ceremony and a far cry from the Order of Water. It struck him how easily he had moved into his dream, of being a paladin, of being a mighty servant of the Queen. He looked at himself side to side admiring how, even when trying not to, Tanian apparel had a certain flair and quality to it. "Tembri, I don't think they'll accept me as a soldier of fortune. These clothes are too nice."

"Aye, but the Apprentice will take care of that. Magic will age your clothing to appear correctly travel worn." Tembri carefully placed a ring on Malcor's finger. "Pay attention. This is important. This is a special kind of healing magic. It is closely aligned with necromancy. It uses the lifeforce of, criminals in this case, to replenish your own. It has a fixed amount of wounds it can restore. So long as you keep your head, and the ring on your finger, it will restore your life. BUT, and this is most important, you don't want to waste it on things you can control, like slipping and scuffing your knee, or being hungry or cold. Put this on when combat draws nigh or the Queen prompts you to. It is a powerful tool and one I rarely ever see used. It is priceless Mal. Don't let your new friends have it. It'll be magicked to appear as household crest for your family. Nothing special at all."

The preparations went on and on, and then suddenly, they finished. Kendra and Apprentice walked up and she asked him a few questions about his new alias. His attire and gear, in pristine condition, aged under magic and then Kendra kissed his cheek and wished him luck. "This should be a nice vacation for you, and also a chance to apply some of your training. Do us proud Sir Malcor."

The Apprentice, without a word, put his arm around Malcor's shoulders and they walked into the night. Cheers and well-wishes called after them and then the high mountain plain and bubbling river vanished and they emerged into a heavily forested pine tree type area. Broken trees, uprooted shrubs, discarded equipment and filth lined the newly-broken path in which they stood. Several corpses showing the signs of chew and bite marks gleamed moistly in the night. "First time seeing something like this?" the Apprentice observed, not so much a question as a judgment.

"I helped drive some bandits off once, other than that, my only real view on combat and death was what I went through in the Rites. Do they eat each other?"

"Some of the goblinoids do, if they're hungry. These do not appear hungry though. They probably have scavengers, like unallied tribes, following the main host. So…" the Apprentice pointed towards the mountains, "that is where the lich is. The other way is where the group of adventurers are. We have full info on all of them, but decided to let you be genuinely surprised. Remember Malcor, this first group is probably driven by greed and fame. Such groups can be vicious. May the Queen watch over you Sir."

The Apprentice walked away and vanished within just a few steps. Malcor found himself alone. Since the Ceremony, his life had been filled with noise, activity, and more pain than he'd thought possible. In this moment, he ran his hands over his scalp and looked up at the sky. Feeling good, he decided to set up a small camp, one that would be just barely visible from the rough-hewn path. Within an hour, Malcor sat back against a rock, propped his feet up and whistled an old armorer's tune.

With the fire crackling and suddenly free from the torturous schedule of the Order, Malcor felt light and airy. It was almost a let down when he heard an angry roar and the sound of combat reach him from the north. The Order's plan to confront the adventurers with some foe that Malcor would intervene in, as an introduction, had started. He stood up, brushed his pants off, and drew his sword. Into the night he sprinted, surprised at how easy it felt to move when freed of the knight armor, and hunger, and exhaustion. It felt glorious to feel how fast he ran.

He came up a gentle rise and over the slope edge, saw seven humans – five men and two women – engaged in combat with a horned ogre. Unlike normal ogres, this one had a single eye and a single horn jutted from its forehead. Instead of radiating brute force this one conveyed a sense of malice. One of the humans had fallen back against a tree with burning points of fire pinning it, immobile. Two of the other humans appeared to have been frozen where they stood. For the remaining four, they looked up briefly in fear as Malcor screamed out his challenge and charged. The looks turned to relief when Mal slammed into the ogre just as it readied to unleash some dire spell against a battered warrior standing between it and the rest of the party.

Chapter Thirty Nine - Malcor Joins the Imperics

The ogre leapt back, dodging Mal's sword sweep and taunted him. "Oh looky here. One of those ugly dragon men. C'mere chicky, I'm going to roast you over a slow fire and peel the meat off your bones!" Somehow, the ogre had woven a spell into the taunt and a freezing crushing force smashed into Mal. For just a second it caught and held him, and then with the sound of shattering crystal, Malcor blew through the force and cut up through the ogre's arm.

The blow should have severed the monster's arm, but golden bracelets caught most of the force and instead gashed open the ogre's arm in a torrent of blood. Again, the ogre fell back and Malcor called out his own challenge, "Boast all you want, it'll be hard to taste meat when all you'll be drinking tonight is your own blood!"

The ogre roared back at him and a green mist poured out of the beast's mouth. Malcor called, "Poison, hold your breath!" and pressed his attack again. Back and forth they went until at last, the Imperics recovered enough to join him. Blow by blow, they battled against the ogre until only Malcor and another battered and smashed fighter rallied for one last final attack. Sensing its own increasing desperation, the ogre turned and fled. Malcor almost gave chase but noticed that, in its haste, the ogre had dropped a satchel from its belt. He walked back and picked it up finding a vial of green liquid, a similar shade to the mist it had breathed at them.

It took too long to regain his breath but he felt better when his sole standing comrade continued to huff and puff for minutes after. The fellow looked at him suspiciously and then smiled. "Thank you for your help warrior. Though we did not need it, your arrival was most timely. I am Jaga." He bowed formally and Malcor did his best to return it.

"I am Malcor, from Morbatten." He held up the vial. "I wonder if this isn't an antidote? Shall we see how your group is?"

Jaga nodded and they walked back to find the group in a bad way. The fighter pinned by fire to the tree had slumped down and appeared unconscious. The two immobilized had fallen over, now limp, and gasped for air as if they could not breathe. The other three appeared fine but whenever they tried to speak or move, fits of coughing wracked them. Malcor pointed to the vial but Jaga looked unsure. "I've seen this before in Tania. I'm pretty sure it is an antidote." He took a small sip of the green vial. "It tastes foul but I'm sure it's a cure."

Jaga took the vial, sniffed it, and then tasted it. "Nasty, but yes, lets try." They walked over to what turned out to be a female archer, the one pinned to the tree by fire. The wounds had cauterized channels through her torso.

"It's amazing she lives," Malcor whispered. "Bless the Queen."

Jaga smirked, "Your Queen has no place here Malcor, but we appreciate your queen lending you to us." He poured a few drops into the lady's mouth. Immediately, her breathing calmed and the wounds took on a more normal color.

"Does your god? With her wounds, she will need healing or she risks death." Malcor tried to say it conversationally but found it hard that such a question even needed to be asked. Could they have come all this way without a priest?

Jaga pointed over his shoulder still looking at the woman with concern. "Our priest was one of the first to fall. The ogre seemed to go straight for him. Lets go see to the others."

As Jaga stood, dizziness swept over him and Malcor caught him. Looking into Jaga's eyes and noting their sickly pallor, Mal chuckled and said, "Looks like you didn't quite hold your breath Jaga. Here." Malcor took the vial and poured several drops into Jaga's mouth.

"My thanks. I thought I would be okay." He coughed and together they walked over to one of the two had been frozen. "The ogre seemed to know... this is our priest," he said kicking the leg of a cloaked man. Chainmail clinked below the robes. "This other fool is our mage. Sort of. He's also a skilled lock pick. My brother."

Malcor poured a few drops into each of their mouths amazed at how quickly they recovered. Within a minute, both sat up and looked suspiciously at Malcor but trusted Jaga who stood by clearly unconcerned about Malcor. Soon, the entire group had assembled together. Though a lot of their gear had been damaged, "We owe you a debt of gratitude Malcor," Jaga proclaimed. "When we first set out to track this horde, we knew ambush would be likely. None of us imagined our first foe would be a magic-using ogre! By Imperius, what a fight! I haven't been tossed about like that since I was in the infantry. Step up Malcor and tell us how you happened to find us."

Malcor stood and noted that, while friendly, this was clearly some kind of trust test. "Hi, I'm Malcor. I'm a fighter from the south of Tania. I had just finished my first stint in the dog soldiers when I heard of a massive fortune and chance for fame and glory had occurred here in Ori. Though my family is poor, my father served with my unit commander. Before I knew it, I had been given a leave and found myself on a boat. I arrived here several days ago. No one in the city would talk to me so I decided to take my chances. My camp is just up a ways when I heard the fight break out. I suppose I owe you all a thank you as that ogre could have just as easily attacked me."

Jaga laughed and patted his shoulder. "Some of us have been to Tania, which part of the south?"

"There's a small frontier village south and east of Dutchy. We called it "Edgetown". Not very imaginative huh?"

"I've been through Dutchy." The other lady who turned out to be the mage/lock pick spoke up. She pointed at his sword. "I've never seen anything like that in the Dutchy."

Malcor grinned and with a flourish drew forth his sword. "Before I joined the infantry, my father sent me to work in Klenna. This was a gift from my master there, who helped me make it. He told me it'd bring me good luck. And it sure has!" He thrust his sword straight up into the air and then brought it down level to the mage's eyes. "Would you like to try it?"

"Sure," she stepped forward. "So you worked at a forge? That explains why you're so big." She took the blade, letting her fingers brush against Malcor's, and ran her fingers along it. Malcor noted she had cast a spell and tried to maintain a poker face. The metal glowed a faint purple and then the glow died. Holy Avengers only held magic when their paladin held it. "It has the potential of magic, and is a finely crafted blade." She handed it back to him and then stared into his eyes. He felt another sense and that inner core of wisdom told him the magic was meant to charm him. He smiled and looked back at her letting himself relax. "Did you make this blade?"

He tried to sound disconnected and dreamy, "Yes, with the help of my master and the other forge workers."

"Are you really from south Tania?"

"I don't remember for sure. I was orphaned like many Tanian children are. I was a war orphan and was eventually raised in Klenna at the forge. I'm not entirely sure who my father is and have no clue about my mother. So... yes? No? Not sure? It's what I have been told my whole life."

"Why are you here?"

"I heard that Ori had come under attack, that the attackers had taken the royal family hostage, and that a great reward is offered to any who can free the royals. I also heard that there is a lich leading the attackers. The prospect of fortune appeals to me. My family, I, can use gold. The prospect of fighting a lich, even if I lose – it is my mission. It would bring me fame far above and beyond my current status. Also..."

"That is enough," she said. "There were rumors that a group of Tanian knights had visited the royal family. Are you one of them?"

"Really?! I would love to be with them! Surely Tanian knights would have already figured out how to best do..."

"Thank you. That is enough. My name is Sako. You love me with all your heart. You would never lie to me. You will fight to protect me. You will answer my questions freely. We have been courting and in love since you came to Ori. You will not remember any of these questions. For the past five minutes, we have been talking about how worried you were about me during the ogre attack. Do you understand?"

Malcor looked at her and tried to feign the dopey-faced expression Calvin always had when flirting. "I understand." He noticed and had to suppress his eyes shifting, that one of the fighters – or is he thief? – seemed very unhappy about this turn of events.

"When I snap my fingers, it will be as I said." She snapped them.

Malcor grinned at her and looked around. "I'm glad you're okay. When the ogre breathed out that gas, I feared the worst." He put his arm around her and kissed her head, and pretended to not notice the others laughing when she made a face. "C'mon, I have a sheltered camp up ahead with a fire ready and waiting." He turned to the thief, "You're not still mad that she chose me, are you?"

The others had to grab that one and hold him back from attacking Malcor. He thought he heard them say, "It's just magic. Calm down."

The rest of the night was filled with Sako enduring Malcor's approximation of "being in love". While she did not seem to mind, the others cracked jokes about everything: age, race, size, and on and on it went. At one point, someone said something offensive about Tanians and Malcor punched the speaker so hard it cracked armor and knocked him back into a tree several feet behind. After that, the jokes stopped and the group more carefully monitored their speech. "You really care about Morbatten," Sako observed in the silence following that.

While the others helped their fallen comrade stand back up, Malcor flexed his fists and arms and glared at him. "Yes, Tania is a great empire. In Tania, an Imperic like you would walk free and unmolested regardless of their gender, faith, race, or even creed. Honor and keeping one's word is all that matters. I have been told that Ori is not much different, but maybe I was wrong." He looked at her and added, "I love you with all my heart but I can't remember, did we meet in Tania?"

"No, we met for this grand adventure and fell in love."

"Oh, okay." He walked away and punched another tree so hard its boughs shook. He heard Jaga whisper to the group to be more careful or they could risk breaking Sako's charm. "I'll take first watch," Malcor called

266

back to the group. Alone, he stood on a boulder overlooking the path and thought about the fight with the ogre.

The ogre had worn fine clothing with a similar appearance to Malcor's of being magically aged. Like him, the ogre also had fought with a certain reserve born from hard Temple training, and then it had used magic. For just a moment, Malcor slipped out of the River and saw hundreds of troops walking like ghosts along the trail. Across the way, he saw the ogre look up and regard him. In this ethereal place, the ogre appeared glorious and mighty. The symbol of the Queen gleamed brightly where the medallion hung from the ogre's neck by heavy golden chain. "You did me honor great one," Malcor said bowing.

"To help the son of Kell, to serve the empire, and to please Dar Kendra," the ogre said returning the bow. "I will ambush your group tomorrow at twilight with goblins. A single goblin bearing a golden earring will have information about the horde ahead and the main entry to the mountain. See that it survives to share that information."

Chapter Forty - The Next Day

Malcor stood guard all night. The group, battered and smashed and poisoned as they were, missed their watch changes. Malcor woke Sako with a hot stew and Tanian energy tea. The aroma woke the others who expressed frustration that Malcor had not allowed them to take watch.

"Turn by turn, I approached each of you. Given last night's events, and that I am not tired at all, when not a single one of you stirred, I retained the watch. The night was uneventful though I suspected at one point we were being watched. Also I found the blood trail of the ogre across the way there."

They broke camp and returned to the path. Very quickly, Malcor felt a rising sense of confidence. This group of adventurers could barely keep up with him. Even their supposed scout seemed slow and clumsy. Freed of his heavy armor, Malcor moved with grace and speed and without tiring, without even getting winded. At one point, Sako slipped almost turning her ankle and he took her gear. Within an hour, he also carried her weapons and several of the ration packs carried by other members. When they rested for lunch, Jaga asked him. "Are all Tanians like you? You're strong as an ox!"

"Our training, especially in the infantry, is intense. We are expected to keep pace with chargers and, if needed, fight alongside dragons. As you might imagine, a religion dedicated to dragons might expect torturous physical ability. That I worked in a forge, helps too." He shrugged.

"But you were only in the infantry a few months right?"

"Yes, but martial training starts early in Tania. I don't know how Ori does it, but the Temple begins screening children as young as three years and directing education for those with any level of natural talent. It focusses on things the empire considers important as well as combat."

Sako sat down next to him. "And what is important to the Temple? Memorizing prayers." She poked him in the arm.

"Sako my love, the Queen does not need memorized prayers. We are children of the dragons. They do not require that we repeat canned verse. They require loyalty and respect. But, you might be surprised. All Tanian youth go through basic education that includes reading in both Common and the Draconian, what you might call TempleVerse or templescript. Some are taught to write if they have a knack for calligraphy. Swimming. Orienteering. Knot tying. Map reading. Counting. And of course the empire and the Isles' history as recorded by the dragons and the Temple."

One of the others piped up, "So, in Tania, everyone learns how to swim?! That's crazy!"

Malcor just shrugged. "At the age of six, we are all required to pass a basic swimming test." He looked around. "You do know how to swim right?" Everyone shook their heads no with only Jaga indicating that he knew how to swim. "The dragon emperor observed in the Book of Fire that humans are too two-dimensional, and it makes us weak. He ordered swimming and other survival type skills taught to everyone. It's a requirement to even enter the coming of age ceremony."

One of the party spat on the ground, "Your doctrine is so twisted and warped. How can you take a religion seriously when it is full of "observations" about swimming? Haha."

Malcor tensed up but then countered, "Your god Imperius supposedly was one of you, here on Khasra. So, at what point does your doctrine begin to matter for the lives of your people? It's just a bunch of empty platitudes that pre-existed your god."

"Are you saying the holy lord Imperius is EMPTY?!"

"Yes, I am!" Malcor stood and cracked his knuckles. "Because of my goddess, I know how to swim. How about you?" He was enjoying himself.

The fighter stood and took a defensive posture. "Because of my lord Imperius, I know that I serve a god of Good."

"Your god allowed a lich to besiege your city and steal away your wealth and your royal family."

The fighter attacked. Malcor noted how rough and slow his movements seemed and saw in that moment that the man would spin and aim a kick at his head and then sweep around with his dagger. Malcor held his ground and then stepped into the kick. He grabbed the man's knife through the kick and slammed him down, the knife pressing into the man's crotch. Malcor spit on the ground next to his face, "Your god cannot teach you even simple martial combat." Malcor raised his fist and then slammed it down next to the fighter's head. "Do not challenge me again."

Sako and Jaga stepped forward. Jaga grabbed Malcor's shoulder and pulled him back. "Imperius is young compared to your goddess, true. But, the path of Imperius is one of quiet distinction, honor, and glory. Surely, we can share in these common beliefs and set our differences aside."

Sako added, "Malcor you promised me you would not do this." He felt that tingle of magic and almost attacked her.

At the last second, he relaxed his tension and turned to her with a smile. "Sako, you should have told me your friend," he kicked the fighter still lying stunned on the ground, "would be so brutish."

Sako could not hide the relief from her face and then renewed her magic and said again, "You promise you will not attack my friends?"

Malcor stared back at her, met her gaze, and pushed his will against her until he felt it almost snap. "I will not attack your friends, but I will also not allow my goddess to be mocked. Mock Tania all you want. Sako, Jaga, you would be welcomed there as new citizens. This one," he kicked the stunned man again, "would not be fit for even street cleaning. He is nothing." He met the gaze of those there. "I'm going to walk the camp perimeter."

They made fast progress throughout the rest of the day with Malcor enjoying how great he felt in spite of not sleeping the prior night. As the sun began to set, he looked around and saw a large cluster of boulders ahead around which the path wove. Though they would reach it before twilight, that location seemed ideal for an ambush. Jaga saw it too. They drew weapons and approached the boulder cautiously, reaching it just as the sun set. An hour of searching and they had found nothing amiss. Jaga ordered camp to be set and Malcor to take the last watch so he could catch up on his sleep after dinner.

As the sun set horizon faded and their camp fire lit the boulders around them, Malcor asked Sako to go for a walk with him. She refused looking very uncomfortable when he flirted with her and let her know they needed some time alone. Against the quiet chuckles of her party, she refused. "Your loss," Malcor said and sat down with his back against one of the boulders.

Across the fire, the fighter he had stunned glared hatred at him. Without even thinking, Malcor gave a hand sign targeting that one for a concentrated attack. He did it without thinking and the man furrowed his eyebrows and called out, "Hey Sako, your boyfriend is trying to cast a spell at me or something."

He had done so without thinking and being caught like that pulled him back into the moment. He laughed and did more hand signs imitating Sako when she cast spells. At last, the warrior stood up and walked away with a look of disgust.

Chapter Forty One - Ambush

Seconds later, his startled cry alerted everyone that had come under attack. Malcor stood and took his time rushing to the fighter's aid. When he reached the area, just as Jaga and the priest did, the fighter had his back to a large boulder and seven goblins held him there. An eighth goblin had climbed over the rock and held a boulder ready to drop on the warrior's head.

Jaga called out but it was too late. The large boulder slipped down and though he tried to dodge, it crushed his leg and rained debris down all over him, effectively blinding his eyes with dust. Malcor noted that the goblin up top wore a golden earring. "I'll circle around and make sure there aren't any others!"

Jaga and the priest attacked as the rest of the party closed on the ambush site. Malcor came around the back side and found two goblins who had probably helped the third get up top. They were trying to hand up another large rock and Malcor's sword cut them down, stranding the one up top. That goblin looked down and shrieked in fright, but seeing his more numerous friends cut down, it chose its chances of escape and leapt down in a hail of small stones and dirt at Malcor.

Malcor turned his sword flat and tried to club the goblin, but it slipped on the stone's edge and fell by Malcor's feet. Somewhat blinded still, Mal felt the goblin land and so dropped his sword and tackled the beast. He felt several cuts from a knife, but his armor took most of it and then his hands closed on its throat and he squeezed until the goblin fell slack. Keeping it pinned, he tied it up and assessed his own wounds. They were not bad. When Jaga came over, he found Malcor wiping dust from his eyes, two dead goblins, and a terrified and utterly bound third goblin.

"None of them had anything worth taking," Jaga complained. "Why did you spare that one?"

"I thought we might learn about the path ahead of us."

"Ah. Lets hope it speaks the common tongue."

At first the goblin was too terrified to do anything except shriek. But gradually, with some help from Sako's spellcraft, it relaxed and described the road ahead. "Everything is waiting for you. The master has set many traps. And the ogres, they are hungry for human flesh." It giggled and went on to describe how the cut path eventually enters a valley before climbing up into the mountain foothills. "Tall towers watch for groups like you, to tell the master. To see how far you can make it." When asked about the traps, the goblin only said that they were all created by walking dead ones and he only knew that the first part of the traps involved a large chamber full of water.

Jaga seemed to know something about the water area and said, "Yes yes, I think that sounds about right," but dodged any follow up questions by Malcor.

They dispatched the last goblin and moved their camp to a more secure location. From there, they continued on. It would be another day or so before they reached the valley.

When they at last reached the valley, the party gaped at the ring of towers guarding a yawning cave mouth about a fifth of the way up the mountainside. From their current watch, they would have to make their way down a gentle and coverless slope, across a raging river via a very rough looking bridge, and back up a gentle slope to that ring. The towers stood like needles with bright firelight and smoke drifting above them. No doubt there would be sharp-eyed creatures stationed there. "It's impossible," Sako declared. "We'll be seen and intercepted, even with magic."

Jaga nodded and they pulled back. "What about charging it at sunrise? Goblinoids have weakest eyesight then."

"Even if, we'd be exhausted before we reached the entrance," someone else chimed in.

It had been like this since that tense first day and the subsequent ambush. Growing negativity and being on edge did that to people. Malcor went along with it, but found it ironic that this first group seemed so green and untested. "I can do it," Malcor said. And again, all eyes turned to him. "I can run that far. If we charge and if we are intercepted, I can either fight or try to slow them down so the rest of you make it. I'm not scared of goblins. And..."

Sako stroked his hair, reminding him again that they were supposed to be in love. He had enjoyed testing that during these rough days and more difficult nights. He felt that tingle of magic but this time did not go along with it. "Malcor, you are very brave but you alone cannot take the mountain."

He sucked air through his teeth, a habit he had picked up from these Imperics. "Yes, I can. I was ready before I met you. Besides, think about it. The lich wants us to get there. What good is the lich's challenge if every group is intercepted before they even reach the mountain? I think this is for show. They will watch us. They will let us in. We don't need to run. We accept the challenge and walk," he pointed his hand like a spear, "right into the cave."

Jaga and several others sat back and looked at Sako with mixed alarm and dismay. He said something in their strange vowel-based language and she shrugged. "Jaga, our love is strong but Malcor really wants to get into the cave."

"Jaga," Mal added, "think about it. The lich could have taken the city that one day the walls and gate melted. The lich wants us to play this game. The worst that will happen is we get intercepted and retreat. We'll take stories back to Ori that will result in better prepared parties and plans. But, if we make it, we will be the first. And there is glory in that. If you won't go with me, I will go by myself. Watch."

"Sako," Jaga growled. "I think we need your boyfriend to calm down. He is impetuous."

Her fingers tentatively touched his arm and the singsong tingle of magic touched him again. He turned, grabbed her hand, and squeezed it to the point of almost breaking her fingers. "You know," Mal said, "I don't think we are lovers. You are all cowards."

Weapons jumped into the hands of those around them but Mal kept his focus on Sako. "Tell you friends to put their weapons away or your spell casting days end right now." He squeezed just enough for her to cry out with pain.

"Stop, stop! Mal, what do you want?"

"Why have you all been lying to me? I fought by your side against an enemy that almost destroyed you. I have endured your slow pace and only offered you my good will. You. Are. All. Liars. And Cowards."

Jaga put his weapon down and held his hands up, wanting for the others to do the same. "Malcor, you insult..."

"You sir are the worst. Do not talk to me about honor or insults. You do your own god a disservice by lecturing me about such when you have been taking advantage of my good intentions. Why are you lying to me? And, why do you care if I go alone? Fight me now and be done with it, or let me go to my own chosen death." He gave Sako's hand slightly more pressure and smiled as she screamed trying to twist out of his grip.

"We need you. Is that what you want to hear?" Jaga asked back. "You arrive in the dark and fight off an ogre and expect us to welcome you with open arms? Would we have fared so well in your land?" As he spoke, Mal noted a casual hand signal.

Mal twisted Sako's hand so that her arm locked rigid and spun. His other hand drew his sword and he slashed through the air behind him. Sako's scream as her arm dislocated caused birds to leap out of the trees around them. One of the group, a doughy faced Imperic who seemed to have a love interest in Sako had just barely avoided Malcor's wild slash. What would have been a backstab, instead turned into shattered metal as Malcor's sword connected with the blade and snapped it.

Malcor lifted Sako by her arm and threw her into the backstabber. The move caught everyone by surprise, and then Mal slammed into both Sako and the attacker. His sword poised to spear through both of them. "I swear to Takhissis, if any of you try this again, these two will be the first to die. You should know that our king Dar Rojo has shared his love of Ori with all in Tania. You would each be welcome there."

275

The others circled him warily, eyeing his sword. It did not move, even a little and Mal let the rage he had felt crawling along at their tiresome pace show clearly in his face. An archer with arrow knocked looked ready to take aim.

"Mal, you are not welcome in this group." someone else hissed.

Jaga told them to hush and turned back to Mal. "You have our mage and our thief. We could use a warrior like you. I had hoped you would enjoy Sako enough to stay but ok. No more lies Malcor. We want the gold and could care less about the daimo. Except for the priest, we are part of a group that seeks to enrich itself. We do not follow Imperius' ways of honor."

Mal twisted his blade so that it scraped along Sako's back. She shuddered. "That makes sense, I guess. None of you quite pulled off Imperic honor, at least not as it had been described to me during my journey here."

Jaga pulled his bracers back to reveal colorful tattoos encircling his arms. "These are the marks of my gang. What is your price to join this quest?"

"I have been completely open with you about my goals. Fame, fortune, and fighting the lich. They have not changed. But, if you want me to join you, I must have your trust. I excel at squad tactics. Always have. It is clear that none of you have adventured in the wilds like this. The ogre we fought that first night, wiped out all but 2 of you. Keeping up with me at even half pace is exhausting all of you. The question you should be asking yourselves, is why I would join with such an ill-mannered party of thieves?"

"We have an inside contact," Jaga answered.

"Excuse me? How is that possible?" Malcor countered.

Jaga ordered everyone to put their weapons down and he sat. "Malcor, it is a long story. Ori is open to orcs who forsake their ways. Some who have forsaken their ways run into problems. My gang, we help them with their problems. They owe us favors. One such orc now fights with the

276

lich. We received a note that if we can get into the cave, he has left us a map in a secret location that will lead us to where the treasure is."

Malcor twisted his sword again, and then released it. Sako drew a shaky breath as did her comrade beneath her. "I suppose you will not tell me where the map is? Or your friend's name?"

Jaga shook his head no, but added, "The treasure is vast. Not just the tribute but the lich has wealth from the eldar times! Think on it! Even if all you do is fill your pockets, you will have wealth beyond your dreams."

Malcor pointed to the two beneath them, "And their wealth, their share will be mine too. That is my price. Plus..."

"Agreed," Jaga pledged over the sudden objections.

"...I will lead this group from here on out. You Jaga remain leader of your gang, obviously. I do not want that. For this adventure though. I am the leader. Agreed?"

"I agree, but Malcor, this is a vote matter. Can you all agree to this?" One by one, the voters signaled by hand yes or no.

Malcor felt surprise that only one person did not vote for him. It was the thief who loved Sako. "I see the vote is," Malcor's sword cut through the man's arm and it fell wetly to the ground. "Unanimous."

The cleric rushed over to the armless thief screaming at his bloody stump and falling into shock. Malcor wiped his sword on Sako's cloak and resheathed it. "Don't ever try your magic on me again."

Jaga nodded. "Agreed! And Malcor, I would have taken his little finger for voting against me. Your plan is to walk to the cave?"

Chapter Forty Two - Enter the Lich's Mountain

They walked slowly at first with the priest trying to heal the thief's arm. They all held their breath, even Malcor did, but after a mile turned into two and they reached a rough wooden bridge over the river, they began to relax. The needle-like towers looked made from melted wax, smooth and glossy mud. Any number of the lich's soldiers stood at their top but no one challenged them.

When they reached the cave's mouth, they found a small war party guarding it. "These are a test," Mal said. "We attack without hesitation or mercy." He charged slamming into the group, his sword already wet as the hapless goblins screeched and scrambled for either cover or weapons. By the time the rest of the party caught up, Mal had dropped or stunned half the war party. Tiny creatures half his size, Mal turned and caught a sword thrust into his leg forgetting in his battle rage that he no longer wore his paladin armor. His counter cut through the attacker and left the war band's leader standing alone and cornered. The unmistakable look of fear and terror gave Malcor pause, "Have I become so formidable?" he wondered. He lost initiative and the leader turned and ran into the cave's mouth. An arrow chased after it but either missed or failed to kill.

Mal wiped his sword on a corpse's dirty cloak and resheathed it. The blood rage slowly chilling and bringing back clarity. Jaga laughed as he pulled a small coin pouch off a fallen enemy and then spat when it was full of garbage. Malcor gave them a moment and then led them into the cave. "Jaga," he growled. "Find your map. Send the thief ahead of us. I want our group's light to be seen and I want the thief to stay in advance of it. If he sees anything, he is to leave a chalk mark on the wall, either side... and continue if possible. From here on, everything is a trap or ambush."

The thief, still exhausted and sore from the march and simultaneous healing, grumbled but with Jaga staring him down, he quietly slipped ahead of the party. Sako augmented the two lanterns with faerie fire and they marched into the cave. After several minutes, they came to an intersection. The straight through passage had a chalk mark along it as did the left side. They turned right. The passage sloped downward and after several hundred feet became slick and wet. After meandering side to side, a small stream ran along the floor and on several occasions party members lost their footing. Not seeing any chalk marks, they came onto a ledge and found the thief crouched down.

The ledge overlooked a vast room. Like the passages, the chamber bore the lich's telltale work of melted and glossy walls. Water had long since pooled and began to fill the center. From this height, it was impossible to get a good read as to how far down or how big the chamber really was. Jaga knelt down by the thief and they exchanged words in their language. Malcor asked the archer to shoot an arrow across the chasm. "Lets see how far it might be to the other side. Can you light the arrow?"

Moments later, a flaming arrow arced out into the room. It seemed to burn forever and then turned down falling. Just as it did so, they got a brief glimpse of the far side of the room and a large passage that continued from where they stood. Meanwhile, the thief had rigged a climbing rope and secured it to Jaga. "The map is close," he said. "Wish me luck!"

Jaga lowered himself down over the ledge with the thief and others holding his line secure. After a few moments, he called back up, "I found it. Give me just a few moments."

"What is that?" Malcor asked.

Sako shrugged, "What is what?"

Malcor signaled for quiet and Jaga called up asking if everything was okay. "Look," Malcor pointed. "The water flow is increasing. Something has changed." The water puddled in a place on the side ledge before falling down into the pool below. The surface suddenly rippled, shaking. Even though they could not feel it tremble. "Something is coming," Malcor called to Jaga. "Hurry up!"

"Got it!" Jaga signaled and they began pulling him up. Just as he reached the edge of their position, another vibration hit and they felt it this time. The water stopped flowing.

"It's coming from behind us. To the sides!" Malcor ordered. As they scrambled, Jaga did not quite make it up and Malcor grabbed his security line and pulled with all his might. Jaga fell ingloriously over the ledge dragging through the muck just as a large tube full of teeth shot past them into space, and then plunged down into the pool. Malcor's arm strained to hold Jaga' weight and then the priest steadied Malcor as his feet began slipping in the muck.

"Now we know what made the tunnel, and why it is not guarded." Sako said wryly. "Was that a snake or worm?" A loud splashing and thrashing from below told them the beast had landed in the pool. "Jaga, did you get the map?"

"I have it," he said still dangling from Malcor's grip on the rope holding him over the pool.

"Do we have to cross this room?" Malcor asked.

"I haven't had time to look at it."

Sako sent her faerie fire down and called back, "The pool... is full of them! They are swarming up to us. Uh, two minutes before they get here?"

The worm had interrupted the water flow which returned finally with a vengeance. It slammed into Sako, who was caught by the fighter next to her. The shelf they stood on began to crumble.

"Cleric! Any inspiration from your god?" Malcor demanded. He pulled Jaga back up.

The priest closed his eyes and began praying, but with their footing fast disintegrating, Malcor had to choose. "Back up the tunnel!"

They turned and tried to scramble up. The worm had left a trail of slime not quite washed clean by the water. It made it impossible to get any traction. They had barely made it ten steps back when the ledge collapsed raining rock and debris down on the swarm. The priest indicated that with all the commotion, he had lost any inspiration that may have come.

Malcor sighed and noted all eyes on him. "You are all going to hate my plan." He grinned. "But, I do have a plan." A third vibration shook through the stone around them. The worms would soon reach them. "It's too bad you have not been able to trust me yet, this plan requires a lot of trust. For right now, we wait. When the time is right, you will all follow me. Or likely die. We cannot fight the worms like this in this place. I cannot guarantee this plan works, but it gives us a chance!"

Another vibration shuddered the ground making them almost lose their footing. "Hold it just another moment," Malcor screamed as the noise grew around them. "Follow me!"

Malcor turned and ran towards the chamber just as a huge worm's head slithered into view. Sensing food, it opened its mouth into which Malcor leapt. He caught a sword-sized tooth and spun to the side as the razor maw started to close in on him. His sword leapt up as he invoked "Coming undone... all that is made..."

The worm bit into his sword and then shrieked in agony as Coming Undone stabbed into its mouth roof. Someone else, others, slammed past Malcor's legs and then they began to fall back down. Malcor strained to keep the worm's mouth open but when the worm bumped into others as it fell backwards, he lost his footing and hung by his sword and the tooth. Even that grip vanished when they smashed into the water. Lost in the darkness, Malcor chose to slip into the ether. Seeing the worms from the River felt disjointed and odd. There bulks rippled the flow but seemed to move around his team mates in the eddies and currents swirling around their massive bodies.

At least three others had made it into the worm. The worm enwrapped them like a cocoon of grass when viewed from the River. "My Queen," Mal prayed. "Help me fulfill this quest and bring you glory!" The worm tried to swallow him and Mal cut even more deeply into its flesh. When he did so, the worm began thrashing about and opened its mouth to drink. Mal had never teetered between the two worlds like this and found new appreciation for Dar Shara's dance on the razor's edge of the River. He cut again and the worm choked stopping the water and began swimming. Mal hoped it was to the other side as its nearby fellows, perhaps sensing something wrong, tried to bite at it. Fearing he would drown, Mal counted to three and then cut with all his might. The worm coughed and then vomited them up and out. Mal cut again and again until it stopped moving.

With water quickly filling the void of the worm's mouth, Malcor called to the others to come towards his voice. Heaving with all his might, he forced the dead monster's mouth open. From his unique perspective, he saw at least three crawl past him. Their wounds leaving pink swirls in the River's flow. Then, he crawled out in the water. With relief, he found the water no deeper than his knees. He sat back, water lapping the stoney shore around him. "Anyone able to make light?" he asked the darkness.

A dim glow of a ring on Sako's hand answered his question. "Sako here," she said. "Miraculously. Anyone else?"

Several grunts and groans answered them and she brightened her ring. Jaga, the archer, the cleric, and, "You're a tough bastard," Malcor said as he helped the thief stand. Their party of eight had lost three members.

"We don't know that they are dead," Jaga noted. The sounds of worms shrieking and fighting echoed and reverberated all around them. "And that is an effective way to let the entire mountain know something happened here."

"Do you want to wait for them?" Malcor asked. "This is a dangerous place." Small worms no larger than his arm had latched onto the corpse and began chewing into it. He pointed, "No doubt others will come. I'd rather fight the big ones than a swarm of the babies."

Jaga looked at the corpse and at the survivors. The priest shook his head negative. "We'll leave and tie a rope down. If they make it, the rope will help them escape."

The water around them took a long time to remove the worm's blood and juices. When finally clean, they turned to the next task - climbing up to continue the passage. Step by step and only with great difficulty, they eventually reached it only with Malcor supporting and partially throwing the thief the last bit. Like the other tunnel, muck and a flow of water made it impossible to retain hold or find a climbing perch for longer than a few seconds. When they finally reached the top, Malcor's hands and arms ached. "Aren't thieves supposed to excel at climbing?" he said rubbing feeling back into his arms. The thief frowned back but said nothing.

They resumed their former march with the thief on point ahead of their light. Unlike the first tunnel, this one had multiple side branches obviously chewed by worms and they stuck with the main passage. Eventually, the water flow stopped and the overall tunnel became increasingly refined and dry.

When they came to a mostly level widening in the tunnel, Malcor called for a halt. All of them had suffered wounds. All of them felt a guilty mix of relief for having survived and dread wonderment at what may have happened to the lost three. Malcor found himself ravenously hungry and ate into his field rations. Sako obsessively scrubbed blood and mucus off her hands not realizing all of their clothes had turned purple from the worm blood.

"Check your gear and Jaga – that map, figure out where we go next."

Jaga pulled a wax-sealed tube out of his pack. It had been crushed but survived intact, if damp. It showed a circle with a water symbol. It showed a series of lines and an "x". Jaga explained, "Assuming this circle and water was the worm chamber, we are in the right place. It looks like we continue to a six way intersection. Then we have to be very careful. This mark here means that all six of these passages are guarded. And, then there is this smudge here." He held it up from different angles. "We had agreed that, if he could, he'd mark possible traps or dangers. This looks more like some kind of note to me. Hmmm." He stroked his facial scruff and thought about it. "Well, we should plan on there being something in each of the passages, past this intersection."

"And after the noise, we should plan on the intersection being guarded," Malcor instructed the group. "That was rough and we lost important members of the group. We cannot assume they survived, but we cannot rule them dead either. Hope for the best. Lets use the markings to show them where we go. We are still too close to that place for me to feel good about resting. Lets hope we find a place less exposed soon." So saying, he stood, stretched and made ready. When Jaga did so too, the others grumbled to their feet.

Their path took them past several branches that either appeared unused or unrealistic for moving large sums of treasure. One thing though quickly became apparent – the farther they progressed, the darker and grimmer their surroundings became. At first, it was just a rat skittering away from them but as they continued they started to see gnawed bone fragments and then overt signs of necromancy. At one side passage, they found a room full of rotting goblin and orc corpses stacked against the walls and propped up by wooden beams. Maggots chewed their way through the corpses and several bore the signs of bone and organ harvesting. The cleric shuddered and urged them to move on.

They walked through the flickering lantern lit corridors until Malcor finally called for a break. The others collapsed in cold sweats and dove into water and food rations. The thief came back looking haunted and exhausted. "I can't continue with this level of vigilance much longer, not without rest." Jaga nodded and asked Malcor if they could encamp.

"This is far from ideal, but I agree. I will take watch. You all rest." Several eyes raised at him but he reassured them, "My training and my constitution have already been tested. I can function for several days without rest. Unless I call for help, I want all of you to sleep and rest." He picked up a lantern and walked up so that they could see him but his lantern light left them in shadow. He drew his sword and relaxed his stance.

Jaga grinned at Sako, "You missed a chance to bed a fine warrior Sako." They chuckled.

"Have you ever fought with a Tanian like him?" she asked.

"No, not like him. As a rule, Tanians are fiercely proud, as you would expect from people who revere dragons. He is more so, both for ferocity and pride. I don't know about their infantry, but Tania quickly elevates and trains anyone with special skill or talent. Malcor probably is one that will rise quickly, if he survives this fool quest."

"I expected more evil and danger. But then Tanians in Ori were always all-business. I never spoke to one without it being about some kind of business deal."

Jaga nodded, "Even their merchants transact money as if war. But, this one," referring to Malcor. "There is something special about him. I once adventured with a Tanian from their thieves guild. Not like ours, they sanction their thieves to be more like spies. He brought the same attitude Malcor brings to combat, but to stealth and traps. He was amazing. Taught me how little I know."

Sako listened but so talking, they drifted asleep. At one point, Sako awoke and imagined she saw Malcor smashing a skeleton against the wall, but he did not call for help and the clamor quickly died. When Malcor woke the group, the never-ending darkness of the tunnel tugged at their spirits but Malcor's cheerfulness and disregard for a few slight wounds from guard duty, carried their morale back to the journey. Sako pointed to several smashed skeleton bones to Jaga. Apparently, it had not been a dream; Malcor had destroyed seven skeletons at least during his long watch.

Chapter Forty Three - The Antechamber

The passage opened wider and wider until the group could walk abreast. The ground changed from that melted gloss to tool-marked stone. From ahead and down side branches, the sounds of pick axes and drills echoed, turning the area into a noisy mess. A gradual bend turned to the left and eventually empty torch brackets gave way to dead torches in those brackets and finally bright flickering torchlight. Malcor signaled for them to stop and sent the thief ahead. The thief reported a group of ogre bosses supervising a mix of goblin and skeleton diggers working to either side of a giant metal door. "The door appears locked even to the ogres. It bears runes like I have never seen and two huge orcs in full armor stand guard there."

Jaga pulled out the map and turned it around. He pointed, "See this? Maybe the smudge indicated a door here. If so, the intersection is on the other side of the door."

Malcor ran his hand through his hair, "Five ogres, two orcs, and a mix of goblin and skeletons. Can we take them you think?" he asked the thief. "What about traps or an ambush?"

"It's a brightly lit area, perfect for their eyes. Okay for us. No advantage there really. If you give me time to sneak up on them and create a distraction, if Sako and the priest and the rest of you gain surprise. Yes. We could. I assume there are traps, but am not in a position to look for them."

Malcor signaled for Jaga and the thief to lead forward and take a closer look. The passage opened even larger with the ceiling arching far up into darkness not illuminated from all the light by the grand doorway. Seven large and high steps rose up from the floor to the doorway, easily large enough for a titan pass through. The digging crews appeared to be carving equally sized side passages from the door. Malcor noted immediately that the two orcs were probably not orcs. For one, the ogre bosses stayed far away from them. Secondly, the "orcs" stood at rigid attention. "I wonder if they are some form of eldar undead," Malcor speculated. As for the rest, the skeletons would be problematic but once the ogres fell, the goblins would likely flee. He also noted that the skeletons appeared to be made from goblins.

They retreated and Malcor shared his observations after Jaga and the thief failed to note anything not already reported. He decided to leave the orc question out of it. "Oh yeah, I wondered about that," Jaga said when Malcor noted the goblins likely worked to death and then were raised as skeletons to continue working.

"So, the challenge here is the ogres and possibly the orcs. The skeletons may continue digging away so long as we leave them alone. I doubt the goblins fight hard if at all. So, five ogres. Maybe a few goblins caught in the crossfire. I want to set a plan that allows a clear escape for the goblins, leaves the skeletons alone, and focuses on the ogres. We'll need to be wary of the orcs. They trouble me."

They set aside any items that would interfere with the ensuing combat and made ready. Sako cast an invisibility spell on the thief, who Malcor finally learned was named Hiroshi. She also cast a silence spell on the area just beyond visible range to give them some extra time to close distance. The archer and others moved into position while Hiroshi crept to what looked like the strongest ogre. If everything went as planned, Hiroshi would backstab the ogre at the same time several arrows and Sako's magic would hit it. Assuming it survived, Jaga would open a path for Malcor to finish the ogre.

They held their breath waiting, eyes straining for any telltale sign of where Hiroshi might be. They felt too close to the diggers. Sweat and tension began taking a toll until at last, the targeted ogre screamed out and Hiroshi darted like a shadow away from the mark. On cue, arrows and gleaming magical darts shot towards the ogre as Jaga and Malcor charged through the area of silence.

The closest ogre seeing a huge fighter bearing down on it, stepped aside to confront Jaga. Malcor slashed at the ogre and jumped past it as did Jaga. Malcor's afterthought attack ensured that Jaga dodged and just as Malcor thought he'd have to finish the largest ogre, another arrow struck through its throat and it collapsed. Without missing a beat, Malcor and Jaga turned on the next largest. Its shock and surprise at finding two enemies so close and its boss dead welcomed it to death as both Mal and Jaga scored critical initiative and hits. The slower cleric now joined the fray, his holy order of Imperius symbol raised towards the skeletons and his heavy war mace gleaming brightly. As Malcor had predicted, the goblins fled. In all the chaos, Malcor called out his thanks as Hiroshi scored another backstab against his next target. In just moments, the last ogre had fallen.

The skeletons cowered back away from the Imperius' symbol's bright light. The two orcs by the door did not move except for their heads to follow from one party member to another. The archer and Sako brought up their gear as Malcor and Jaga considered what to do next. The two orcs radiated a fell evil that made Malcor's skin crawl. Something most certainly different than an orc stood before them. He thought about shifting to the ether and seeing what they might be, but an inner voice cautioned him to avoid doing it. Instead, he prayed to the Queen asking for guidance.

Hiroshi walked around looking for any sign of traps, as did Sako and the cleric. Malcor continued praying. When they reported they had found nothing, Malcor picked up a piece of debris and tossed it at the steps. At about the third step, the object hit an invisible wall of energy and fell as if striking stone. He walked up to the first step and tentatively touched it with his foot. The orcs regarded him, their faces dark voids beneath their helmets. As he stepped onto it, he felt a tug at the back of his mind. He looked back at Sako to see if she had cast a spell, but she just nodded encouragement. He paused and prayed again asking for guidance. In answer, he heard a voice roil through his mind like a shadow in the sunshine. It called to him, "Show me your power, your true power. Show me your anger and rage. Bring me your fire. Glory, fame, and fortunes await on the other side of that door."

He steeled himself recognizing the voice as not being the Queen's. "Sako, priest, do you feel the voice?"

They shook their heads no. He stepped up again and reached out his hand to the force wall. When his hand touched it, the orcs both moved their hands to the pommels of the dread-looking swords at their belts. Malcor steeled his grip on his sword and began calling to it, *Coming*

Undone…

He pressed through the force wall, which caved before his will and barely managed to pull his sword through in time to deflect and parry a vicious overhead chopping attack from the closest orc. Like a machine, the second attacked as the first blocked Malcor's counter. The orc's blade cut through Malcor's armor drawing a wound that would have been far worse had he not twisted aside. He jumped forward, trying to gain the topmost platform and a hoped for tactical advantage. The dark green and gray metal sword began to frost white and crackle where Malcor's sword had caught it. Though he yearned to step out of the River, that cautionary feeling prevented him. He took another awful wound but not before his own blade slammed into the helmet and neck armor of the second orc. He noted the rest of the party moving up to help. They would not be there in time.

He still had not gained the top step and so turned to focus on the first orc. Another strike would shatter its sword but his fight would not be won by disarming his foe. He cut straight at the orc's armor hoping to blow and shatter it away. *Coming Undone…* A terrible cut ripped through his back as his armor tore apart. He steeled his will against the pain and cut backwards aiming for the same place he had struck the second orc's head. Whether by the Queen's will or luck, his sword hit close enough and the shattering cracked armor blew apart. Black and red dots danced before Malcor's eyes. The orc inside the armor, as he had thought, turned out to be a shadowy wraith-like creature full of chill and death. It seemed to enjoy Malcor's pain and realization. "Not an orc…." he imagined it jeered. "Wraiths!" he called back to the team. Exposed to the other one, it cut at him but its weakened blade broke on Mal's remaining armor and reminded him of his worsening circumstances. The rest of the party appeared stuck at the force wall.

The first orc-shadow dropped its ruined sword and the gauntlet holding it to reveal its dark hand. The other readied its sword to attack. Malcor realized that he could die, without Tembri, without a priest to bring him back. He thought he'd feel fear. Instead, he felt anger. Just like those other times he had felt pressure to perform, his blood boiled. He grabbed that edge of raw emotion and recited his favorite verse from the Book of

289

Fire in draconian. It gave him calm and he centered his anger there. He felt a blade cut into his side and his remaining armor tore free. A cold icy hand grabbed his throat and breathed hate at him. Though it turned his insides cold, it fanned his anger and he let it wash over him.

Berserk now, Malcor grabbed the wraith's hand and he drove his sword up into the wraith's center. At the same time, he spun holding the wraith in front of him like a shield. It caught the second orc-shadow's next attack. It cut into the wraith and Malcor drove his sword through into the other, where it bit deep into breastplate armor. He felt his vitality draining but the rage had him now. He swung the wraith back and off his sword ignoring the claws ripping against his throat. Without hesitation, Mal unleashed an onslaught against his new foe. Coming Undone ripped through the orc's armor, shattering it to pieces and bit several times into its blade as it tried to parry. Disgusted with its sword and realizing it was ruined, the orc threw it at Malcor and reached out to grapple him. The shadow hands tore into Mal's flesh but Mal screamed back, "You, not me, shadow!"

It hissed back as, like the other, Malcor grabbed onto the wraith against the burning chill, and drove Coming Undone through its torso. As its shadow form disintegrated, Malcor dropped to one of his knees and looked at the growing pool of blood spilling out from him. He saw the frustrated looks on the rest of Jaga's group stuck on the other side of the force barrier. He screamed back at them and threw his sword point first at the wall. The force of his throw spilled his body down the blood-wet steps and darkness took him for a time. He saw Sako scream at him in silence as his sword tip shattered apart the magical barrier. From that small shatter point, an explosion knocked Malcor back into the door and he fell unconscious.

His dreams felt strange. He heard a seductive female's voice speaking to a stilted Imperic and he remembered one of those voices saying, "Did you know he would be a shadow, or even a berserker?"

"No, the children of Kell are not known that way. They surprise us always, but mostly they die before we see their gifts."

Malcor awoke on Sako's lap. They were on the other side of the door. A dull thudding sound drew his attention to the door, which had been braced with scavenged gear from the slain ogres. Something on the other side was hitting the door with a battering ram. Jaga looked down and smiled at him. The cleric laboring over Malcor sat back, hot and sweaty and shaking. "Jaga, this is as good as I can get him. He was easily beyond death but the holy god lent me strength." He collapsed back.

Malcor's stomach growled and before he could say he was hungry, Jaga helped him sit up. Food waited for him. "How are you feeling Malcor?" Jaga asked.

"The fog of war takes me sometimes. It leaves me hungry. I see we made it past the door?"

"Yes, you defeated those demons and shattered the barrier. Surely, you are no mere infantryman."

"I want to be a knight," Malcor said in reply. "You never asked me what I wanted in life." He chuckled. "A poor armorer needs to draw attention somehow. So, after I blacked out, what happened?"

Jaga, Sako, Hiroshi, and the others explained that when the wall shattered, hidden doors all around the large room had burst open with orcs rushing in, as well as several likely wraiths and shadows. While the priest, who Malcor learned now had a name too – Noboyuki – took care of stabilizing Malcor... "Malcor, you were cut to pieces. To pieces! I have never seen a man so horribly wounded and yet you kept fighting. It was amazing!" the cleric Noboyuki said at one point.

Jaga continued, "We figured out how to unlock the door, Hiroshi and Sako did that, and then we secured it. We made it just in time. As we closed the door, something else came. A vampire maybe. He looked like one of us, an Imperic. We almost let him join us. Noboyuki almost lost you saving us from that thing."

The priest called Noboyuki added, "It was definitely a vampire. It still bore some of the tokens of Imperius. I'd guess it had been a monk."

The thuds continued and Malcor tried to stand up. He saw his ruined armor and sighed. Scar serpents ran along his body from varying angles where he had been cut by the wraiths. His throat and chest ached and he noted claw tears of dead flesh that had not healed, places where the wraiths had torn him. Sako touched his shoulder and said, "You have more on your back. It looks awful. Does it hurt?"

Noboyuki apologized, "I will not be able to totally heal you Malcor. Your life is no longer in danger, but as you know, natural healing will leave scars."

Malcor picked up his sword and tried a few practice swings. It hurt and he grimaced. He tried walking and going through some simple kata. It hurt and while doing it, he slipped the regeneration ring on. He immediately felt better and began dancing through the katas in spite of the pain. At one point, he felt the cut on his back tear open again and he stopped. When Noboyuki finished the healing spell, Malcor had practically healed all the way with the ring and spell's help. He slipped the ring off before the scars faded entirely and complimented the priest on his skill and power.

Chapter Forty Four - Calvin's Combat Test

The skirmish field had a fall wind blowing through it and Calvin noted the other side. He and two others had been assigned to guard a member of the Mage's Guild. The skirmish today would use illusion magic to simulate an actual attack. While Morbatten did not often play the role of defender, Tanian and Tanian-trained battle mages became instant targets in any combat. The Order of the Shield served to defend and protect these mages and other specialists like them. Across the field of combat, his classmates probably were reviewing things as well. Four mages, twelve paladins, and he had lost count of how many support personnel made up the skirmish. "So, this is a platoon," he noted to the knight on his left.

Their mage, an old veteran of many winter war engagements, ignored them. He had already made it clear to them that this whole thing wasted his time, "Unless you initiates pay attention, my whole day will be wasted. I have important work going on. I hate these pointless exercises."

Calvin's healer stood behind their position, shifting back and forth from foot to foot. Calvin noted a courier stop and give him a note. A moment later, the healer told Calvin that Seline and the Order of Fire would be leading the offense for the other side. As of yet, Calvin had no idea which order commanded their attack.

Without fanfare and still lacking clear direction and leadership, the skirmish began when a barrage of heavy missiles catapulted towards them from their left. Calvin called for defensive positions and their mage reached out with a titanic magical hand and batted the missiles across the field of combat towards the other side. No sooner had that passed than heavy cavalry burst out of the right flank. Heavy chargers with gleaming armor and lances sprinted out as the sky overhead darkened with arrows. The mage group closest summoned an air elemental to deflect the arrows and gusted winds into the faces of the cavalry to slow them.

"Lets move forward to our alpha point, and signal the start of the advance," the mage ordered.

Something felt odd about taking orders from a mage but Calvin shrugged it off and the moved forward to the alpha position. That and other points had been designated on the field as reference points. As they reached it, the mage ordered them to turn. From this position, they had a flanking advantage to the heavy cavalry and the mage scorched the attackers with chain lightning and fire. The light display called attention to them and they quickly came under attack as the other side summoned flying creatures to swarm them.

Calvin ordered them to create a shield wall around the mage. From this protected position, the mage could cast his spell rising up at the last second to unleash spells as needed. Besides commanding the mage's defense, Calvin needed to keep an eye on the heraldry banners signaling changing battlefield conditions and positions. He also noted a small group break off from the advancing rank of the enemy. It appeared to be Seline herself taking the lead. He smiled hoping she had fared well since they had last spoken.

When it became clear that Seline's group had been sent to intercept them, the mage ordered them to position beta, a point where two other squads would cover their sides. They reached it just as Seline signaled a crossbow attack from the infantry advancing with her. The bolts ricocheted off armor and shield. As the mage prepared a counter and just as he unleashed it, a wall of fire erupted between them. That wall burned towards them. Flaming crossbow bolts igniting through the wall of fire continued to smack into the earthen barricade at their defense spot.

The mage chuckled and ordered Calvin and the others to huddle with him. An earth elemental flowed over them, sealing them off from the advancing fire. A minute later, the magical mud warmed and began flaking down around them as Seline's group advanced over them. Everything sounded muffled and the mage conjured an image of their attackers focused on a replica of their position about ten yards from where they actually hid. Calvin readied to attack but the mage ordered him to hold. That chafed and Calvin choked back his protests.

At last, Seline's entire group had moved past them and the mage allowed the mud to uncover them slow enough for their vision to readjust. As they came out, ready to attack the vanguard, he heard a voice from behind order, "Fire." A barrage of crossbow bolts slammed into them and just like that, they were out. As Seline walked past him, she paused and said, "Good to see you again Calvin. Your mage has a reputation for tricks like this." And then she was gone.

Though still beautiful, she had a serene almost joyous look on her face. Normally Calvin would take offense at words like that, but coming from her, with so much confidence, he just nodded. The red glow of ember fire in her eyes also unsettled him more than it should have. She had moved past him to an entirely different level. A twinge of jealousy touched him and he remembered Malcor.

The skirmish wrapped up. Calvin's side lost. While they had successfully defended the initial attack, their enemy outmaneuvered and outclassed them at every other point. All four of their mages were "killed". They had managed to only "kill" one of the other side's.

In wrap up, they walked through the basics of the combat with each side explaining why and how they had lost or succeeded, what went well and what did not, and what they learned. At the end, Calvin and the others who had lost their mages were pulled into a review with the Mage's Guild. As he sat down for what would no doubt be hours of chastising, he wondered what Seline would be doing, celebrating most likely.

A senior member of the Mage's Guild entered the room. The five "killed" mages filed in behind and sat down. One by one, the mages described how they were killed and why it was not their fault. Calvin's squad mage practically insulted them. "I did everything in my power to protect them but when we pulled the earth elemental back and they all leapt forth, we were mowed down by bolts. The enemy seemed to know and we fell without taking even a single one of them with us."

Calvin seethed and stood to retort but was told to shut up and sit down. It went for several hours as the Guild representative grilled the mages. At last, he turned to the knights. "You have heard your failings. Now, before you have your own say, please think carefully. You will each have five minutes to speak specifically to the failings and what you need to improve."

Five minutes?! Calvin's seething became a knot of anger. When he stood to speak he had to fight to retain composure. "Honored members of the Mage's Guild, I am Calvin, Order of the Shield. My squad defended him," he said pointing at the mage. "After careful consideration," he swallowed and at the last minute adopted a more tactful approach, "my failing was to let my respect and regard - for a veteran of so many wars - cloud my tactical judgment. I let my respect for him cloud my judgment and I scarified leadership initiative because of it."

The guild representative looked down at Calvin from the stage and smiled. "Well said sir. While the battle mage has command of the magical battle, you have command of the mage's protection and in such matters, you own the leadership role. These battle mages train solely for one thing – to retain spell focus amidst the chaos of battle. That's it. They are not master tacticians. They are not knights. They cannot survive the wounds that you knights shrug off. But, they can cast spells while under duress. I agree with you Sir Calvin. Your failing occurred exactly at this moment. You allowed the mage to hide you and determine when you came out of protection. Had you come out when you felt you should, and remember, while we all serve the Goddess, we trust the knights to follow Her guidance and inspiration, you may have won, or at least taken many of them with you. Lets look now at Lady Seline's report."

Seline's mage entered the room. "The lady ordered us to intercept the squad here," pointing to the map's alpha then beta position. "The knights and infantry kept pressure with missile assault that I augmented with illusion. As we drew near, I created a rolling fire wall to advance and Seline sent a forward unit with illusions to cross the area of interest. She ordered the rest of us to reload and wait.

"As soon as the fire passed with no casualties, we knew that they had hidden. Lady Seline ordered me to hold though I wanted to blast the area with more than a firewall. When she ordered the crossbows ready, I thought she must be insane. But she is Order of Fire and so I prepared defensive magic. We didn't need it. They all fell to the crossbow volley. After that, we took heavy fire from the two units but with our unit at the center, we drew the entire line of attack and our cavalry outflanked and killed the others."

"Why did you not capture the mage?"

"The lady gave the kill order. I did not question it."

"Why did you not question?"

"I am a battle mage in the service of Tania. Lady Seline commands and I obey."

The mage turned back to Calvin. "Look at that man there," he said pointing to Calvin's battle mage. "You did not command him Sir Calvin. Yes, he is a three time veteran of Bloodstone and multiple winter wars. Yes, he is a spell caster. This was your first time. You are forgiven. Do not make this mistake again. Sir Calvin, you are dismissed!"

Several days later, Calvin caught up to Seline at the Temple. He grabbed her arm and she whirled around. When she saw Calvin she smiled. "I hope you survived...?"

"Yeah, it was rough but I learned how you beat me. I promise I'll win next time. How have you been?"

"Well enough, I'm heading to a seminar. Join me?" She offered her arm.

Together they walked across the main chamber to a side area and on into an amphitheater that looked out over the city below. Calvin found her reluctant to talk about the specifics of what had happened but lit up when asked about the dragonterror challenge. Again, without specifics, Calvin noted that, like her quality of gear, she had experienced a fundamentally different rite than he had with Ynt'taris. Sometime later, the lecturer arrived, a Dar priestess who lectured about the concept of Time.

The priestess finally said something that caught Calvin's attention. "When adept as a paladin, or any hero class, you will be able to step out of the flow of time. By doing this, your attacks, defenses, your senses in battle will be sharpened. You'll be immune to lower level magical effects. You'll see and understand things at an entirely different level. It is overwhelming though. Our minds are not created in this world to comprehend that one. That world, the River of Time, is the threshold of the gods and the many realms outside of this world.

"If you have witnessed someone wield the River like a weapon, raise your hand please." Seline, Calvin, and a few others did.

"Tell me about it, any one of you please."

They each briefly described it. Calvin told about how Malcor had fought off a challenger. Seline spoke about a time during her training, before her Aging Ceremony, where her instructor had tried to show her. Most were like that, demonstrations of speed and agility. The instructor picked that up, "It can almost seem prophetic. The River Wielder knows where to go and what to do. In reality, they are moving so much faster than us that it only seems that way. Everyone who can, does. It is easy to get addicted to it. But, and this is important, assuming that each of you someday masters this, it is exhausting. The longer you stay the more your focus in this world is distracted, drained, and ultimately leaves you at risk. If you stay too long, you will fall back to this world weak.

"There are dangers there too. Only physical beings bound by time are visible in both the River and the real world. Magical creatures, immortals, gods, demons, very powerful heroes, and the like are able to mask their presence, even fight from the River. Some are more powerful there, others less. However, for us, we are always less powerful there. The farther we get from this world, the weaker we are. So, for us, the advantage of the River is speed and perception."

The lecture continued but Calvin once again lost interest until towards the end, he tuned back in. "The more time, the mightier the magic, the greater the challenge, the more a human is drawn is out of this world. The side effect is that aging can stop. I'm sure you have all noticed that our Dar priestesses and many of the R'Dar ones hardly seem to age? They appear locked in their late twenties, or early thirties – forever powerful and beautiful. Part of that is the Queen's grace, but it is also a side effect of their being drawn out of this world. They still age. They will still die of old age, but it will come suddenly and without warning. As such, I caution you. When you meet a cleric, of any faith, and they are in that age range, be on guard. They might be far more powerful than you think, or they could just be a young adventurer. Better safe than sorry."

Though Seline paid close attention, the topic for the most part went over Calvin's head. When it ended and he escorted her back to her mentor, he asked her if had made sense.

"Yes," she answered. "You?"

"Oh, of course. Fascinating really. Time flowing like a river and at different rates for us. Sure. The applications to warfare and our service as knights is profound."

Seline nodded with enthusiasm. "It was good to see you Calvin. There is my teacher. Good-bye," she waved and ran over to a Dar priestess who nodded her head towards Calvin. For a second, he thought the priestess was nodding at him but then his own mentor called to him from just behind.

His mentor did not praise Calvin's performance in the skirmish. The tongue lashing turned into a slap across the face turned into a challenge to fight to the death. "I told you the mage would try and do this. The whole thing, all of this, everything is a test! How many times must that be pounded into you?? You want something that isn't a test? Look out over the city. Everyone there could be you right now except that you had this special something... and you are wasting it! You want a challenge that isn't a test? Fine!" His mentor pulled Calvin's sword and tossed it to him while aiming roundhouse kick at his chest. The kick connected just as Calvin caught the sword. A ring formed around them in the main Temple hall. "C'mon boy! Not a test!"

Calvin tried to parry his teacher's punch and instead caught the full force of the blow along his blade, which knocked his sword back into his face. He suddenly felt clumsy and self-conscious. He tried to apply his skills and training but, like the skirmish, his teacher outclassed him in everything. Blow by blow, Calvin apologized and asked for surrender. The more he apologized, the angrier his mentor became.

Blow by blow, he saw his master's growing intent to kill him. At last, Calvin dropped his sword and bowed in the formal fists on the ground salute. A brief pause gave him hope and then his master's boot crumpled up into his breastplate and threw Calvin up and back into the crowd. "You, are my student no more!"

He heard steel drawn and saw his death coming. As the sword cut downwards, he waited to die, and then nothing. He hesitated to open his eyes. When he did, everyone in the hall had dropped prostrate. Dar Shara stood her finger just barely touching his master's blade. His master had just realized who it was and dropped down prostrate on his face. "The young knight understands R'Dar. He is your student no longer. Remember, these are wards of the Queen. I free you of the boy's shame. You are dismissed."

Chapter Forty Five - Calvin Enters Officer Training

Shara touched Calvin's head and pulled him to his feet. Calvin noted that the dread lord Armageddon stood behind her. For the first time, the dread lord regarded Calvin and they made eye contact. In that moment, Calvin felt his life pull up before the dragon and he relived Shara's words at the ceremony, that his desire for knighthood was wrong. He felt the wrongness and remembering that moment, he looked up at Shara and said, "But I have come so far."

She reached out and touched his cheek, "You have Sir Calvin. You have. Farther than most, but you lack the core insight and faith required to go much farther. There is no dishonor in changing course when confronted with the correct path. There is however dishonor in continuing an incorrect one. I offer you what I offered in your Ceremony. Be tried now and I will show you your destiny."

As she spoke, the dread lord's eyes ignited with crimson fire and grew relative to the giant's head, consuming more and more of Calvin's vision. "Your destiny as a knight," Armageddon growled and suddenly, Calvin's chest burst open and the dread lord removed his heart starting at it from different angles. "This is your destiny, but behold!" and Calvin's heart wept blood falling across the hearts of other hearts beating and then they died. "Though you may be a shield, many will die because you lack heart."

The growling voice rumbled through Calvin's pain and then another vision appeared. This vision showed him serving as a cavalier under a paladin. The vision flowed between his master, Seline, even Malcor. "These are known to you. As a weapon, as a tool in the emperor's arsenal you are loved and precious. A hammer used as a saw is not loved. It is despised. You are a saw." The vision shifted and spun to Calvin commanding armies in what had to be Bloodstone. "The mantle of leadership is most certainly with you. It allows you the things your heart craves. Companionship. Love. Friendship, Women, and popularity. Trading on loyalty. Knights are bound to absolute love of for my Mother. It starves your heart Calvin. A child of Morbatten, lacking heart, is only food. You want to be a hammer, but you are a saw."

The vision passed and Shara let her touch drop. The circle around them had grown. His master had stopped by a raised doorway and watched. Shara stepped forward and kissed Calvin's cheek, "Choose the path of love Sir Calvin. You and your master are freed, but you can mend this by asking him for release." Though her whisper seemed overly loud to Calvin, it did not penetrate their circle.

Calvin met his master's gaze and stepped back, bowing deeply to Dar Shara and the dread lord. Though harder than anything he had ever done, he held his head high and walked to his master, and bowing prostrate, asked for release from the knighthood. His master nodded, helped Calvin stand, and together they walked to the Soldier's Fort.

From across the chamber, Dar Niss and Seline stood together watching. Seline had rushed to intervene when Calvin's master had nearly killed him. Dar Niss' command to stop had stopped her though and together they watched as Dar Shara intervened. "Very few initiates make it as far as Calvin and then leave. Most are too prideful to withdraw. He will have a fantastic career as captain in the Tanian war machine. An officer who understands what it means to have been a knight is often more valuable to the emperor than having a knight. Skills, attributes, and heart - Dar Shara saw it correctly. Your friend lacks heart. Do you know why my student?"

Seline nodded and said without hesitation, "He gets too distracted by a pretty face and a kind word. He lacks single devotion to the Queen."

"Indeed. That is correct. In Taysor, a knight like Calvin would become an outcast. All that training, talent, and skill would go to waste. As written in the Book of Generations, we must take a higher more divine view of a child's potential and see the dragon within. Calvin's heart is dragonliike but he requires more visible motivation than religion."

Dar Niss took Seline's hand and they returned to the Order of Fire compound.

Chapter Forty Six - The Lich Meets Daryx

The lich stood on the other side of the large golden door with his vampire general. He felt the humans on the other side. Absentmindedly, he tapped the door and shook it to its foundation. His other hand summoned the ogres into undeath service. The scattered bones of the skeletons and others that had fallen, he knit into a twisted beast of gigantic proportions and then breathed the vanquished wraiths into it. Those bones chittered and seized as the two wraiths and the many bones became one settling into a carriage-sized beetle made of bone and suffering.

He tapped on the door a few more times and ordered the next area made ready. "I did not think this group would make it this far," he mused with one last tap. He had watched the combat through the eyes of the wraiths. The dark-haired boy's ferocity and initiative had surprised him. Clearly not an Imperic, it had also surprised him that the Imperics had accepted the boy's leadership. Maybe he would add the boy to his menagerie. Still though, something bothered the lich about the wraith's report. A touch of the eldar lurked around the boy and something partially-obscured his view of the boy's true nature. As an eldar, he had never experienced that before except with the most powerful of the daimo's house, like that Imperius-obsessed priest.

Also, something had started to trouble the lich. Though he chose to not sleep, he felt like something watched him. Dark green eyes and a skeletal ram head always flittered on the edge of his thoughts. Looking at the beetle monster, he noted for the first time how flecks of bone dust appeared to blow off the creature. Granted, the miniscule amount made no difference to its overall structure but it reminded him that the beast would not last forever. It would decay. It would die. He looked at his own hands and saw a part of himself detach as if a leaf in the wind. He tried to catch at it but it twinkled unattainable. His vampire Shiniba slowly blew away next to him. Compared to the tendrils of skin and energy ripping away from the ogres, it was nothing. The transience of it though bothered him.

He stepped from that room back to the place he most commonly referred to as home these days. The ogres called it the "throne room" but the lich had dismissed that given he did not see himself as a king. "Would a god take a lesser title or dwell in a place suited for just a king?" he had challenged the ogres when he first heard them refer to his throne that way. The large chair of molten stone sat high over a pool of water and blood from which the lich could scry any area his troops had claimed with his symbol. One of his ogre commanders waited for him. As he sat down and the scrying pool stirred, he called to his revenants and sent them to watch the dark-haired boy. "Should he fall, bring his body to me."

The ogre reported that five more parties had left from Ori and that tall ships with grand white sails had arrived bearing Sorian marks. "Those ships, they bear the sun god's marks. Cursed Pha Rann and those people will seek you out as a mighty evil to be destroyed master."

"Pha Rann?" the lich restated. "Do you mean *Phaer Daroon* I wonder. A bright light of creation in the dawn sky?"

The ogre stared back with blank expression. "My master, I only know that the empire of Taysor worships Pha Rann as the sun god, destroyer of evil and lightbringer. They are allied with Ori and no doubt will bring many powerful heroes and magi against you."

Shiniba added, "The paladins combine combat skill with priest magic. I have seen it myself from, from my life. They will seek you out great one."

The scrying pool shifted to the docks. "Excellent, your friend has kept his word." The tall ships came into view as horses and humans of all kinds disembarked with their gleaming armor and shining weapons. What served as the noble house greeted them. "See commander? They bring us more tribute. Excellent. I grew worried that Ori would run out and we'd have to destroy them before any ran our trap."

The ogre commander chuckled wickedly and the others joined in. "Master, I will lead a war band to greet these Sorian heroes!"

The lich looked at him and then said, "Granted. We do not need the mountain troops. Take them. Shiniba, something troubles me. I have been sensing a ram skull, watching us."

"Great One, the ram skull is sacred to the demon god of necromancy – "

"No, there is no necromantic god."

"Apologies, but there is. My people and the people of this world have fought against it for, well, forever. The ram skull is its divine symbol. If you are seeing it, perhaps that god is seeking you?" Shiniba shuddered.

"Why do you tremble?"

"You have made me a vampire. Without you, I would be forced to serve that demon. It is a fate more horrible than I can consider."

While Shiniba told what he knew, the lich turned his attention to the pool and watched the waters swirl. He could see the area around Malcor but Malcor himself blurred. As he watched, one of his revenants moved into the shadows to watch. Malcor and the priest looked directly at it sensing something but then let it go. The boy had almost completely healed. The lich scarce believed the boy had defeated his two best wraiths. No human in his times could have done such a thing. Truly, things had changed. He tried to view the boy more closely but the pool blurred more and more as he got closer.

"Something is blocking my view of this one," he said considering the possibilities.

As if on cue, his pool rippled and a face appeared there. Non-descript and unremarkable, the face greeted the lich in the language of the elves from millennia ago. The lich smirked and waved to remove the image but the face just grinned... and remained.

"Greetings master from the ancient times," the visage spoke. "My true name, great one, is Malyx Do'Allariss, though the Imperics and my kinsmen know me as Daryx. A humble servant to a power that wishes to speak with you. I bring you information, a warning, and also an opportunity. Would you speak with me?" Daryx smiled.

Behind Daryx, the entire Mage's Guild had assembled to create this opportunity. The emperor's son Blaze, gifted in fire magic, and the emperor himself watched, ready to intervene if needed. Criminals sentenced to die lay chained to a pentagram from the center of which Daryx stood and spoke.

The lich looked with more interest at the pool and tried to switch view. Nothing happened and Daryx grinned more allowing his dark elven fangs to show. What the lich did not see was several members of the guild collapsed resisting the lich's attempt to change the scrying pool's focus. "Speak elf."

"Yes, lord. First, some twenty-seven thousands years have passed since the time of what we call the Eldar. Those, like you, who walked in the dawn of chaos and creation are fading. The world is different. You have expressed and seem to use a form of magic aligned with undeath. I wish to warn you that there is an awesome foe who claims that dominion. It will seek you out to enslave you. You will lose your free will should you be found. That is the information and the warning.

"The opportunity is join an empire that fights against this foe, and join with a few other survivors of the eldar. Learn about this world. Become a god if you wish; there is a path. Or stay with your free will intact. We want to help you. I'm sure we can find common ground."

The lich smiled back at Daryx. "There is no god of undeath. There is no claim to necromancy or ownership of magic." The lich reached out to take Daryx's soul. Back in the Mage's Guild, a series of runes inscribed on Daryx's body flared brightly. Matching runes marking a chained criminal simultaneously ignited and that criminal's soul flowed into the lich. Another member of the guild fell unconscious.

The lich expected Daryx to scream, not smile as his soul entered into him. It lacked potency and power. The mind had been destroyed and yielded no information. "Great one," Daryx said. "The world has changed. Even as an Eldar, new magics allow us to defeat your manifest desires. Tell me, you must have chosen the path of immortality in that peculiar form before the River began to flow. Why?"

The lich sneered, "Why? Because I could and it gave me greater power over the weak things of the world."

"You can take other forms. If you give up this one, the god of necromancy will never be able to take you. But, the longer you stay, the longer you continue to use necromancy, the more this world will pull at

306

you. You have seen it yes? The ebb and flow of your existence washing away. We can help you understand it. We can help you find a place should you wish to leave. You could even become a god, have your own kingdom, whatever you want. Your current path is one of enslavement to the Jade God."

"I suppose you want something from me?"

"No, not at all. Should our common foe claim you, besides losing your free will, my empire will gain a terrible enemy. We'd rather have you as a powerful friend first, a neutral relative second, or even as a distant separated "lets stay far away from each other" than see you become a servant of the Jade God. Don't get me wrong, your power will be many times what it is now, but you will be a mindless slave. We have seen other eldar succumb and become such. I am prepared to give you a book that describes these things. A gift from my emperor to you."

"A bribe?"

"A gift of respect."

The lich sneered again and bared his teeth at Daryx. "Dark elves in my time were mightier than humans. How is it you serve them now?"

"I serve myself. My empire second. Humans and elves have not always walked together, but I choose my own path. I invite you to walk it with us. Since Time began flowing, my peoples have fragmented and worship Lolth. Her religion has destroyed what they were."

The lich reached his hand out and pulled at Daryx to bring him through and physically place this annoying interruption in his presence. Behind Daryx, more than fifty criminals had been shackled and made ready. Souls began ripping free and then bodies vanished. As they appeared before the lich, he threw them to the side and pulled again. Daryx whispered, "We send the book as a gift. Watch, as you do this... your essence begins to die and flow in the River that ends with your enslavement and ultimately death."

The lich snarled as body after body that was not the dark elf shattered to ice glass before his rage. The mountain trembled and even the undead paused as they bore witness to the first time they ever saw their master lose self-control.

"Shiniba," the lich growled. "Return to me."

Minutes later, the vampire stood before the pool, "Yes great lord?"

"Let the Sorians come here to the mountain and engage the many traps you set for them. I have a different task for you." The lich removed his gauntlet and held it over the pool. He dropped it. Without a splash, it fell into the water and immediately the pool filled with spirit lights of those captured as they thrashed about seeking an escape. The lich waved his hand over the pool and re-attempted to scry Malcor.

The boy's image filled the pool at a distance, but like before his image remained blurred. "Bring me two ogre magi," the lich muttered.

Moments later, Shiniba had them standing before the pool. About to introduce them, he felt a compulsion to strike them dead, and did so. The lich held the magi in paralysis. Their large bodies fell draining blood into the pool. The purple swirls pulled into the scrying image of Malcor and it tightened enough for the lich to see the many scars criss-crossing the boy's torso and thighs as patchwork armor barely held together.
"Shiniba, bring me the prisoners, those heroes of Ori. Also, canvas the armies and find me ogres, orcs, and others of reknown. Bring them to me here that their blood may be added to the pool."

At his command, his gauntlet levitated out of the pool and returned to his wrist. "Remove all the water before filling it with blood, and Shiniba - when the pool is full of blood, let me know."

Chapter Forty Seven - Eldar Genesis

Daryx pulled back into Tania as the last apprentice fell and the last criminal died. Dar Reznor, head of the Guild and many others heaved for breath. Only the dread lords looked unaffected. They were not part of the chain. Daryx looked around and bowed to the emperor and his son. "I will need to visit again."

Alerius nodded. "Word will be sent for volunteers this time. My children are too law-abiding and well-behaved these days. The jails are emptied with this project."

Back in the mountain, as souls and bodies with broken minds came through instead of Daryx, the lich shrieked his frustration into the dark. One of the bodies had a book clutched to its torso. The lich pulled it to him and read the first page:

"The brightest of the eldar created the world. In answer, the darkest created the anti-world. So that the two would never meet, the eldar who loved the world separated them apart and ordered the chaos therein into all manner of life, each with its own path of birth, life, and death. These cycles repeating an infinite number of times channeled the life of the world into the anti-life and created a current that flowed over and through all. Takhissis the Dragon saw this flow and named it the River and demanded that it stop flowing.

"But, Creation refused and the River flowed for the first time defying the eldar. So, Her Consort Bahamut commanded it to vanish and it rebuked him by continuing to flow. Each in their own way, commanded the River to cease. And, it mocked them by killing their creations. Some said, "Here, lets us protect ours by creating a safe place away from this foul River of Ending. So came about the Gods of Good, the protectors of creation. Some said, "I will not be mocked and will fight" and so armies were raised and cast against the River and it ran red with the blood of creation. Seeing the torrent of death, they said, "We need stronger armies." and they removed their remaining creations to a safe place to strengthen their forces. So came about the Hells. Others said, "Behold how sweet the River runs red, lets us dance in the River and call it

chaos!" They stayed and danced and so came about the abyss and its hells.

"But one of those did not dance. Alone he stood and despised those who retreated for safety, fought for life, and those who danced in death. This one said, "The River changes forever but my creations shall never die. I will freeze them forever so that the River flows over them and they drown but remain my own." And this one became The Necromancer whose name must not be spoken, the jade god, the green sickness of death and infection that carries its contagion for power through the River and yet withstands the River. It listens. It waits for that time when it can freeze the entire River in undeath by baptizing the life and light of Tehra, this jewel amongst the stars of chaos, in death and freeze the flow of change.

"Children hear me and listen. The River still flows in undeath but more slowly. Obsessed with locking chaos in its place, The Necromancer would only reverse the cycle so that instead of life flowing along the River to death, death would flow to life. Twisted by the abyss and chaos, the beauty of the Eldar and their free ability to shape and work with chaos would twist, as it does for The Necromancer.

"Woe to the jewel that is Tehra, my home is empty and has no mother. My children weep in the dark and the beasts of the dark rend them even as the River slays them. For the aching in my bosom, I turned my head away from Tehra and prepare now a home for the children. I leave behind my sons and their Fires to hold back the dark and usher them to me, until at last I return to succor the mighty and enfold the fearful. This is my creed and so it shall stand for all time, for I am the Mother of Fire and chaos is my love just as each spark of life grows into a flame, and the flame is beautiful. I know you in the chaos and hear you calling for me."

A handwritten note had been inserted that said, "Give your soul gem to Malcor if you wish to join us. Whether you ally with us or not, we will help you and show you how to preserve your free will. Your soul gem is our security that you will leave our empire safe." It was signed by Malyx.

"How interesting," the lich muttered. He had not considered his soul gem in so long that it took a moment to remember it was the same gem he used to capture the souls of others. "I remember..."

The lich closed its mind and a detached part of him wished he might close his eyes. He went back to a different time in memory, when the world was new and creation still sparkled with the chaotic energies that rippled through it before settling into its this form. He remembered the dragons. They were the largest and most glorious of the Eldar, flying through the void effortlessly. In their wake, currents and eddies of magic had formed and into these, other Eldar had tapped to use and shape the chaos more easily. His hand squeezed the stone of his chair and yet it did not budge. In this world, he felt it crumble but the crumbling worsened the chair. It did not manifest into a golden sceptre infused with power the way he had imagined it.

The void granted wishes and the lich had once wished for every and anything he could imagine, except that he lacked imagination. The dragons did not. They filled the space around them with sparkling and shining things, and sometimes even life. For every marvel, there had also been disintegration. The demons that plagued the world, he had dodged them and stayed far away from them. Except for that, he had chased every extreme of emotion and had stumbled upon several he had never imagined could exist. Envy had been hard for him.

Not gifted with the innate ability to thoughtlessly control chaos like the dragons and some of the others, he had gravitated to following eddies and whirlwinds of power left by others. The grand entourage of those like him that swirled around and behind had slowly divided the chaos between those powerful entities that allowed it and those that did not. He had found himself following a dragon almost impossible to see in the void, but its wake rippled throughout like a tidal wave. So, even at a distance, the power intoxicated. A small group of others like him followed at safe distance, but close enough to avoid the demons when they had come under attack.

Drunk on chaos, the demons' forms twisted into disgust and sensing that disgust, he misshaped his form even more to create fear and shock in their prey. It should have been easy to fight them off, but one of the creatures grappled him and pulled him away from the power flowing all around. Fighting for his existence, he quickly began to lose power and then his fear-infused power, like a narcotic, began attracting more and more of the demons.

Soon, he exhausted the energy he had consumed and began tapping into his own nature. Until this fight, he did not understand that nature as he had never feared oblivion until this moment. The original demon, he cast off where lesser beasts rent it to pieces and slopped it up. It gave him a moment to see how bad his situation had become. He tried to remove himself back to the entourage, but to no avail. Each time he tried, the demons fed on his will, his lifeforce, his bright desire for safety, and his growing fear. "I should have died," he whispered.

Then it had happened. Some other eldar, so high above him that it probably did not even notice, glided through the space of his battle. It smashed him and destroyed the demons in his way. Its passage spun him off and away and he drifted without form, thought, or cohesion, barely alive. Eldar draw their power from creation and destruction. The will required to cause such things shaped and gave form to the void and became the instruments of that willful intent. The lich wanted to live, to survive. Unable to create himself and unwilling to end himself, he pulled the last of his energy and created a gleaming light and then set it alight with the force of his desire to live. The cold of the void so far from affected chaos made him grow cold and it warped and chill-burned his flesh. That gem and the light therein must be the soul gem this Malyx had asked for as a token of good will.

Chapter Forty Eight - The Pha Rannic Knights

In the throne room, he opened his eyes – rather made them work and looked at the blue gray cold leather that enwrapped his hands. He summoned an ogre and said simply, "I am going to Ori. Ensure the war bands attack but do not kill more than half the parties. If they appear formidable, use the undead and the goblins." The lich walked away into the dark and reappeared at the southern gate of Ori. The moon had just risen and its light sparkled down around him. Unlike the bright sun that burned, this moonlight felt wonderful. He removed his helmet and looked up at the soft disk, ignoring the commotion his appearance caused.

The moon renewed his mood and when he turned to look at the city, he found a monk bowing there, waiting for him. "I wish to speak and learn about someone named Malyx Do'Allaris." The monk bowed and signaled for the lich to follow. He led him to the palace and informed the lich that while Ori has much knowledge of that person, the group just arriving from Taysor would have more information.

Gates opened, doors opened, and their path cleared as they made their way to the royal house. Runners moved ahead and by the time they arrived, the lich expected there would be all kinds of readiness and preparations. Since he had taken the daimo, the people only ever sent lower level and less important people to act as emissaries with the lich. When the final door opened, the lich saw that things had changed. The room contained the expected functionaries, but also contained seven heavily armored and armed warriors and three priests each bearing golden symbols of the sun wrapped on a square motif. Like standing in sunlight, the brightness burned but the lich paid it no mind.

As he entered and the monk announced him as the grand commander of the southern armies, the three priests and the seven warriors held their symbols forward and concentrated at him. The searing burn intensified and the lich sat down before them. "I assume you're trying to do something to me. I do not appreciate it. I have not come here to fight you, but to learn. If you continue in this, I will take…" and he raised his gauntlet and spoke the word the Imperics had come to fear, "Yinta'ryx kor!"

The strongest looking priest in the room screamed a blood curdling cry as his head stretched and tore with his soul pulling free. The other two priests turned him and began praying to their Pha Rann. Interestingly, the soul tear slowed. The lich smiled as the warriors drew their swords and made ready to attack. "I can take every single one of you. Is this why you came here? Is this how you greet someone who came to talk?" The fighters paused but two of them, bearing slightly different insignia – their sun was white instead of golden and the square had spears radiating around it – screamed battle challenges and attacked.

The lich remained seated and just as one of the fighters struck, he moved the physical form of the priest whose soul he claimed into the path of the sword. It cut deep, slicing through enchanted armor. The look of shock on both the priest and the paladin's faces were worth the effort and then the priest's soul fell into the lich's gauntlet. The fighter stumbled back praying to his god for forgiveness. The other fighter stumbled suddenly unsure and the lich took his soul as well.

"Lets try this again. I want information about Malyx Do'Allariss. I know the Imperics have told you this. My price for not killing you is the two souls I have claimed. They will be added to the tribute that you came here for. Do you wish to continue?" he asked turning to glare at the other fighter who had dropped to his knees praying.

One of the fighters, with the golden symbol rather than white, resheathed his sword and gestured for the others to relax. He stepped forward and said, "I am Alan of the Holy Order of the Sun God and Creator Pha Rann. By the holy temple's decree, we do not tolerate evil and cannot abide in its presence unchallenged."

"Yes, and so you have challenged me. How long must this tedium continue?"

Alan looked to one of the priests, who nodded and then said, "We must consult Sir Alan. There is no precedent for this."

Alan bowed and then walked over to the knight praying and dragged him back to their line. "You should be stripped of your rank and title fool," he said but the man remained praying.

The lich sat, unmoving and let his gaze strike each of them. He felt a ripple in the invisible ether around him and allowed his focus to drift to that strange place that reminded him of the void but had that weird flow of energy that always went in only one direction. The two priests stood within the flow and watched him, and talked. The lich regarded them from out of the flow and for just a minute, the lich was not even sure why, he allowed his true Eldar form to show. It shocked the priests who fell back down into the flow.

In the world of the real, the two priests whispered to Alan, "The lich is not a lich, well not at least any we have ever encountered. As such, there is allowance, Pha Rann willing, to speak with evil."

The lich snorted, "Evil? Is that what you are here for? Pathetic."

Alan stepped forward and sat down in front of the lich and asked, "Why is resisting evil pathetic? The desire to destroy for destruction's sake must be resisted for the sake of the innocent, the weak, and the gentle. That is my role as the leader of this group. So, what of you?"

The lich held out his hands and allowed the paladin to see what he expected. Brown dessicated skin under which dry tendons and bone writhed showed his body's undead preservation and function. "I am the commander of the army besieging this city, and I hold the souls of your party members. I desire information. That is who I am. You are one some group that has come to save the royal family and the daimo, maybe even defeat me. The Imperics trusted that you could tell me about this Malyx..."

"Yes, we know of Malyx. He is a lord in the nation to our south. A drow elf who forsook Lolth..."

"Lolth is known to me. I take it then that her great creations thrive... so this drow elf forsake Lolth?"

"Umm, yes. Well, no. Actually, I don't know how this relates to Malyx. Morbatten is a strange country. They accept all kinds but regularly ally with us to fight against necromancy. Malyx, or Daryx as he is called there, is the head of that country's military most concerned with foreign affairs. I could tell you much, but must ask, is there something specific you want to know?"

"This Malyx appeared to me and spoke with me. He resisted my soul tear and my summons. I want to know more about a person able to do this."

Alan shrugged, "Very well. We know that Daryx joined Morbatten at the express summons of the dragon emperor Alerius, a red dragon who rules that land. Very long ago. In the span of just several years, Malyx joined the Inner Circle, a group of advisers to the emperor. That was three hundred years ago. In that time, Malyx has recruited far and wide and seems at the heart of every military action and epic quest undertaken there. While we do not have any information about his involvement with you, it is likely that Morbatten has already determined that Ori needs help. I would guess that Daryx is assessing whether you are a threat to Morbatten. Knowing them, they probably also offered you an alliance?"

"And what if I am? What if they did?"

Alan shrugged. "Tania does not look at things the way my people do. I would guess that they will do whatever is necessary by any means necessary to prevent you from falling into the Jade God's hands, the god of Necromancy has warred with them for millenia now." Alan looked at the lich and stepped forward to the seat next to the lich. "I have teamed up with Tania on several occasions to fight against the Necromancer."

"And this Malyx fights against the Jade God, or for Morbatten? I don't understand how one of Lolth's…"

"He has forsaken Lolth though we do not know if he serves the Dragon Queen. You may know her as Takhissis?"

"Ah, yes. That name is known to me. She was mighty long before I was. And this Jade God. Please tell me about him."

"It. Actually, we don't know if it identifies with a gender. In the light of Pha Rann, our doctrine teaches us that shadows grew in the void as the sun's brightness increased. The light illuminated both good and evil. The light gave hope to creation. It also enabled evil to covet creation and to seek to own and control it. Out of all the demons of the abyss, there is one who seeks to not just control but to freeze and hold things into eternal sameness. This is the Jade God. Like Morbatten, we fight against it as well as all other evils. Morbatten has fought multiple wars against the hellhounds, pardon me, the generals serving the Jade God. To be honest, I am shocked that a hellhound has yet to appear here."

"A hellhound? I'm familiar with them. They're nothing."

Alan shifted uncomfortably. "Actually, the term hellhound can refer to two things. There is the common hellhound... maybe you talk of those? They are easily defeated in this world by skilled warriors. Then, there are also The Hellhounds. They serve the Jade God. It is a term Tania, errr Morbatten, started applying to them some centuries ago. They are titanic hellhounds with some small measure of free will and infused with the Jade God's desire to baptize all of creation in undeath. The Jade God watches through their eyes and can use them as a vessel to enter this world. Any undead creature, such as yourself, falls instantly under the Jade God's control when confronted with a hellhound. You would be... a prize."

The lich's eyes flashed purple, "I am no prize."

Alan smiled and boldly stated, "You sir are a lich. One of the most powerful of the undead and you retain free will. Our doctrine, both Pha Rann and Takhissis', agree on one thing. The histories show the Jade God will stop at nothing to acquire you. You are a lich right?" Seeing the lich's anger still kindled, he added, "I only ask because you resisted the combined might of my group and we have vanquished liches before. You appeared affected but are clearly not vanquished."

The lich let his anger fade. "Before what you call time, I self-created. There was no trade where I gave up something for what I am. I feel your Phaer Roon but it does not affect me anymore than it did in the eldar times."

One of the priests came forward and Alan nodded to him. "Sir, you use an archaic term for Pha Rann. Phaer Roon only ever used that name in the writings about the world's creation. After the world, the sun god took the new name Pha Rann. In our language it designates a shift from the role of creator to the role of preserver. Do you have a name?"

"I do." He turned his attention back to Alan, "Your doctrine then agrees with Morbatten's, the Jade God would consider me a prize. Tell me then, if I were not a threat…"

"But you are a threat. Daryx would not speak with or tell you his name if you did not represent some threat to Morbatten. Though their goddess is evil, we have found and continue to find common ground when it comes to our fight with the Jade God."

The lich sat in silence and then said, "Tell me of my elder sister Lolth."

Alan blanched, "I am a paladin of the sun god. I'm sure there is nothing I could say that would be complimentary."

"She yet exists and has not come under the Jade God's control."

The priest who had spoken earlier responded. "Lolth is not and does not touch the dominion of The Necromancer. The Mother of Spiders and creator of the dark elves, she has attained her own dominion. Even if, and this is solely my opinion, she would not fall under the Jade God's sway. Her dominion is strong enough…"

"I do not understand this "dominion" you keep referring to."

Alan supported the priest to continue. "Consider sir, Pha Rann. I am uncomfortable speaking of Lolth but the example should carry. As the creator, this world, this universe, and everything in it that has, is, and will yet be created pass through Pha Rann's dominion. Just as the sun shines forever, so long as there is life, whether it acknowledges Pha Rann or not, they worship Pha Rann through the act of living, of surviving, of hoping. This is therefore Pha Rann's dominion. Those of us who actively choose to worship Pha Rann and follow his teachings, magnify our worship. As we align with his will, we are able to heal wounds, resist evil, and act as agents in this life to the benefit of the innocents."

"So, Lolth's dominion of spiders and drow…"

318

"Rather, the existence of spiders and drow"

"Is her dominion?"

"That is correct sir."

"The Jade God's dominion is death and undeath. As a lich, with free will, why am I a prize?"

Alan shifted uncomfortably. "You must free the souls of our friends or I will not be able to continue. The information is delicate. How you use it is everything. Will you free our friends' souls?"

The priest shook his head and said, "I would rather die than tell…"

"Your death is easy enough to arrange," the lich commented.

"You will be cast out," the priest pled.

"I can atone."

"You must not."

"I grow tired of this," the lich said. "Tell me what you know and I will decide its worth. If it is worth your two friends, I will return them. If it is worth more, I will return others I have claimed."

The priest grabbed Alan's arm, "We must not."

"I am at peace with this," Alan said. Turning to the lich, he asked "I have your word?"

He was interrupted by the other knight with the white god symbol. Hurling his sword and praying, it ignited with white fire and impaled the lich through his torso. The knight continued to pray and the white burning fire ignited the air around him. He leapt at the lich.

Alan tried to block the paladin, but missed. A barely visible purple aura flashed around the lich. Into this shell, the paladin smashed and stuck. Small tendrils of purple energy caught the paladin there. Though the white fire burned many away, as more and more tendrils caught the knight, the white fire dimmed and then flickered out. Within the shell, the lich pulled the sword out of his torso. The metal hissed and flared burning the lich's hand with black oily smoke. The hole in his chest popped and bubbled with ichor and smoke. Wincing with some degree of pain, the lich disintegrated the sword just as the paladin's life force ebbed and then imploded into the aura.

The others went on attack and another younger fighter bearing the same emblem leapt onto the shell to pull his friend away. A purple tendril brushed his hand and instantly, his arm withered to powder. He leapt back screaming in agony. Just as the other paladins went to attack, Alan commanded all of them to stop and stay still. "What Cuthbert wills and how they choose to die is no concern of ours. We were not sent here for this mission."

Within the shell, the lich looked at them and questioned, "Cuthbert?"

Alan sighed, "Cuthbert is the god of an order of paladins within the worship of Pha Rann. Like the sun casting a shadow, they view the world as their god does – through the absolute of good and evil. They are fanatics. Part of their doctrine is that evil must be destroyed. My speaking with you violates their doctrine."

"Alan, I came for information but this is getting tiresome. Do you accept or not?"

Alan ordered his knights to restrain the last knight of Cuthbert, who still struggled to fight one-armed. "I must have assurance that you will free my group. Should you deem this not worth, I will offer to take their place. Is this acceptable?"

The lich nodded. "In this world, no the eldar times, you are a lich. You are therefore part of the Jade God's dominion already. Your very presence empowers it. More so, as a free-willed eldar, there are several paths you could take. The first is to claim your own dominion and become a god in your own right." Looking at the lich, Alan probed. "I'm sure Daryx mentioned something like this?" The lich nodded.

"In this world, only in this world, there is a path to do this, to Ascend and claim a dominion of your own. Though you are mighty, I do not think you will survive the first part of that quest. At some point, you become known to the Jade God and he will marshal all of hell to seek you out. There have been a few rare attempts to claim part of the dominion of necromancy. All have failed. I'm not saying you may fail. I'm saying you will. You are too great a prize to the Jade God. Remember, any contact with undead exposes you to the Jade God. Any contact with a hellhound and you are his.

"The last is to protect you from the Jade God and you continue as you are now. The issue for Morbatten, even for us, is that as an eldar lich, should you become the Jade God's... you will become a new hellhound. Even the weakest of the hounds is mighty beyond belief. You would likely be among the mightiest, ever. Morbatten fought a twenty year war against the weakest and was nearly destroyed. I do not relish such a fate for my own people, or any people.

"There is a final path, which is your destruction. Given what we have seen here, it will take heroes equal to a hellhound to slay you. Like it not, heroes will seek you out, eventually, mighty heroes will come for you. Cuthbert has paladins more powerful than these who would welcome such a fateful quest. Your war here with Ori ensures that it is only a matter of time before you are forced into one of these paths. Right now, you can choose."

"Claiming my own dominion and becoming a god sounds nice," the lich whispered. "Tell me more about that."

"I cannot. I have only heard rumors of it though our doctrine contains the story of the knight Cuthbert who ascended and is now worshipped by such as these," he said pointing to the writhing knight straining to attack the lich. "The people of Ori have a similar doctrine with their god Imperius. It is not known to me how it is done. But, I believe in it and in my heart, Pha Rann whispers to me that this doctrine is true as surely as I feel that you are not entirely consumed by evil."

Chapter Forty Nine - The Role of the World Jewel Tehra

The lich eyed the struggling Cuthbert knight as the healers restored his arm, then turned his attention back to Alan. "This doctrine you believe in, it does not apply to Pha Rann?"

"Sir, I have not studied it enough to say for sure. Maybe the priest here can elaborate but Pha Rann was before these gods who ascended in this world. Where you are an eldar, I just don't know."

The priest nodded and added, "Yes, you have it correct. Pha Rann was one of the mighty in the eldar times. He was the first. He never ascended. He just is and always has been the sun god, our creator, now our protector."

The lich regarded the two and the others trying not to stare at the lich too obviously. "And were this Morbatten here, how different would – say – the doctrine and teaching of Takhissis be I wonder. For the eldar, for your Pha Rann, for their dragon queen, for ascending?"

The priest smiled and sat down asking for a parchment and quill. "It is true that they will have a different story, but the basics share a common base. Even they acknowledge Pha Rann as the first. You see, one of the key differences between how Pha Rann and Takhissis define good and evil is this."

As he spoke he sketched a diagram. "Here, in the center... this is our world, our universe. To the top is the creation force, what we call heaven. To the bottom is the destructive force, what we call hell. All around is chaos, but it is no longer the Chaos the eldar – you – once enjoyed. It has been partitioned and claimed. Benign space we call the ether, or the River; it's that flow of time you can see. Neutral space is the astral. Malignant space is the abyss, where demons lie." So saying, he drew a triangle around the world in the center. "While creation and destruction and all these are continually moving, one thing remains true."

"And that is?"

"This world, Tehra, is at the center. We are always equally between all.

Now, Pha Rann and what our religion calls the "good gods" reside here," pointing to heaven and creation. "The evil gods and hell and destruction reside here," he said sketching the area between the world and destruction, but somewhat to the side related to neutral astral space rather than the malignant. "You see, hell and the abyss are enemies just as surely we fight against both in the name of Good."

The lich asked a few questions and then the priest continued, "The powers of heaven share in all their heavenly dominions. And all dominions cross through Pha Rann as the creator and protector. Hell on the other hand is divided and claimed. Takhissis has claimed what we call the first plane of hell as her throne plane, but she has never called it home." He drew a circle and wrote "Dragon Heaven" in it.

"Morbatten however claims this whole world for Takhissis. Because we spoke of Lolth, lets now talk about the abyss. Truly mighty abyssal beings shape the malignant and destructive chaos around them to suit their tastes. Her realm is probably one of spiders and shadows but she is the absolute dominatrix of her throne plane. Lets say that she is in the middle of the abyss, well maybe not quite the middle," and drew a circle with her name in it off-center towards the malignant.

As the priest spoke, the others gathered around, many of them never having heard it explained like this. "Remembering that Tehra is at the center, any creature, any being, any human here may ascend – that is, to cross over into any of these other realms. Likewise, the shortest distance between any of these realms is Tehra. Here in this world, magic is infinite in its power as is the potential of the free-willed creations here. Any of us, even goblins, even dragons, even the innocent and meek may ascend to their respective place in "heaven" wherever that may be. Certain of the creations of Tehra, like you, like dragons, like elves, are so long lived that they are essentially immortal and they resonate and continually pull the dominions in which they move towards Tehra. You sir, as a lich, have in a sense already ascended."

He made two circles in the malignant and destructive space labelled the abyss. "This is the gate between Tehra and the abyss. It is claimed by a lord of chaos. As a creature of chaos, it can shape and mutate and reshape creation at will but cannot create. This circle next to it is where the Jade God claims its dominion. Necromancy is neither creation nor destruction. The Jade God is the anti-creative force that seeks to freeze all and lock it unchanging for as long as the creative potential remains. Now this is key…"

He pointed to each of the circles in turn and then said, "Our world is the closest gate between all of these places. That is why magic exists here. No doubt there are other worlds within, say dragon heaven or Lolth's demon spider nest, but the magic there will draw directly from the god. Only in Tehra does our using and crossing through dominions add to a god's power. As servants of Pha Rann, we seek to protect creation, that is our creed and we do it through a doctrine of staying within Pha Rann's domain as much as is possible. Now you had asked about where Morbatten might be different. Because they see this world as their goddess' rightful throne plane, they see any and everything in this world as her dominion and freely use it to achieve their ultimate doctrine of achieving this. Their dragon emperor may even be known to you as the mightiest of the eldar red dragons who survived the flow of Time. I do not know his true name but he goes by Alerius here."

When the lich said nothing, the priest drew a line and an arrow from the creative to destructive potentials through Tehra. "This flow is Time. It began flowing at some point in the eldar and destroyed most of you. They saw Time as a sickness, a disease. All of this," he waved his hands over the drawing, "came about because of Time. Surely you feel it."

The lich flexed his skeletal hands and nodded, "It is uncomfortable to me."

The priest nodded and then said, "Takhissis is a hell lord. Her throneplane is not this world. It is here in hell. The Tanians may mean well and certainly fight evil to great effect. They seek out the mightiest heroes for the most epic of quests, but against all that they do is a belief that this is where their Queen belongs, this world not hell. We therefore fight against them to prevent the world becoming dominion to a hell lord, and supplanting the pure worship of any god based on any creation's free will." The priest smiled genuinely at the lich and added, "So far they seem distracted in achieving this end and instead wage war against the Jade God."

He drew a line from the Jade God's abyssal circle to the one by it and then to the world. "There is a way for the Jade God to reach us…"

"The hellhounds are able to move through to Tehra unnoticed by the chaos lord. I see." He pointed beneath the destructive circle. "This is?"

"Shadow, anti-life. The fragments and cast offs of creation when so warped and twisted that it is unrecognizable, are dominionless. We call it simply "the shadow plane". Eventually, even the undead fall through this into shadow. There is no heaven, no paradise there. Just inert reactive oblivion."

The knight of Cuthbert blurted out, "That is not true! We fight the beasts of shadow!"

The priest looked at the knight annoyed and smirked, "And none of you return. You waste your destinies fighting imagined evil when this world and its gardens go untended. And the innocent die."

The knight looked like he would attack the priest but Alan ordered the fanatic to be quiet and still. He turned to the lich and said, "So that is what we know. Is it enough for you to return our party?"

The lich took the parchment and nodded. "Yes, and as a token of gratitude." The lich walked back into shadow and vanished. As the room regained its light, the priest and the knight and the daimo's bodies lay there unconscious. Though all recovered, it remained clear that the lich held onto the daimo's soul. Monotone and lacking verve, the daimo could understand and respond but had no initiative. Though an improvement, it remained clear to all that the lich still intended for the parties to come and run his gauntlet.

Chapter Fifty - Orcus' Throneplane

The executioner, mightiest of the hellhounds, basked in the green sunlight washing down on his vast estate. The entire world basked in that light where the sun rose and set for the world all at the same time, based on their god's mercy.

Humans, orcs, and other humanoids toiled in farm fields. They looked healthy and strong, as their creator-god would have them be. Executioner stretched and walked out to see how things fared. At the charnel house, the free-willed vampires waited in the green light of day for blood. Ghouls stood farther back from them. As workers finished in the fields and returned to their homes, they stopped and the vampires fed. Feeding was rapturous and ecstatic because that is how their creator rewarded their hard labor.

The hellhound laughed at the irony remembering vaguely his own life before he had begun feeding. As he watched a lithe femme vampire feed in a frantic coupling of blood lust, he heard a voice and looked up. The green disk of the sun now held the visage of their god, Orcus supreme lord of undeath. At the same time the Executioner looked up, all beings on the world fell to their knees. The femme tossed the drained corpse to the side and also fell to her knees. The ghouls that waited to feed looked anxiously at the discarded corpse and groveled before the sun. All bowed and the wind and weather and waves ceased their motion.

"Hellhound, it is your time. Proceed to Tehra. A prize awaits you. My sceptre awaits you." The god's voice amplified throughout the world whipped the undead into a near blood frenzy. For the humans and the living, for whom the voice meant eternal fear and darkness, they cried out for mercy but lacked the free will to choose resistance or hope.

All around the world in perfect unison, all creatures cried out "All hail Orcus!" and then returned to work, to feeding, to dying, to birthing, all exactly as decreed by their god. The hound sniffed the breeze and stood in prayerful reverence as the jade sun returned to normal. When the god had finally left, the hound turned his back on the ghouls tearing into the corpse and walked back to his manor. Already, the voices of other hounds whispered out to him their envy, jealousy, and their hopes that he would fail and die. He sent back to one such voice, "The great god commands you to join me. Come."

"No," the voice came back. "You lie."

"Take it up with Orcus then. I will be at the gate soon. Be there." He cut off the voices with a final challenge daring any of the others to do better. A small part of him nagged that in his life before the Jade God, he had been free to choose more than his preparations to carry out a command. A small choice granted, but one that reminded him of a time so long ago and lost ago that he barely remembered the sun on his face, the wind in his fur, and the leering ram skull sceptre he had seen lying in the shadows by a tree on his path.

Entering his house's shrine, he found a replica of that wand floating in a pool of blood, kept alive by the great god's will, the blood connected to all the creatures living on this world, and kept the wand potent and ready. The executioner picked it up and whispered his prayer to Orcus. As he prayed, blood began to stream out of the eyes, and of this blood, he drank until almost an hour later, the eyes stopped weeping.

All around the planet he ruled, the living and the dead withered and screamed in agony. The living seized in an agony of torment as they aged years, their hair grew and skin wrinkled. The old died. The young matured. For the dead, it started with a sizzling as those in the green sunlight whimpered and then ran for cover. All around the world, the hellhound fed on their suffering. When full, he entered the pool of blood.

The pool moved him from the Jade God's world to another. Blood became something akin to water and he sat up. A desert of insects writhed and crawled seeking food and somehow not dying, so they ate each other. The chaotic powers of this place swirled death into a mass and dissolved millions only to reconcile into millions of different ones. The desert dunes flexed and pulsed moving like waves. The abyss looked a bit self-fascinated today as many of the creatures sported eyeballs, more so than any other shape. All around the hound, flying bugs leapt into the air as they tried to bite and found they could not get near the hound. They fled. Atop a nearby dune, a similar cloud took to the air. The hound walked that way and found his challenger who bowed low and whispered, "I came as ordered Executioner."

"Well said Mauler. Orcus wishes us to find a great prize. His sceptre awaits us in Tehra." He stood and closed his eyes and drowned the sound of the thronging insects. A spider the size of his body leapt at him and fell back stabbing in vain at the magic sphere protecting him. Mauler swatted it aside and then also closed his eyes as roaches and ill crawling things ran away from his giant claws.

"The Tehran gate is that way," Executioner stated and keeping his eyes closed began to walk. Mauler followed.

Around them, the desert rose up in a great tidal wave of chattering mandibles, crunchy legs, and oozing pus. It rose up and punched down at their protective spheres. With their eyes closed, the wave washed over them unable to feed on anything. The hounds continued to walk. Eventually, they came to a stone stair rising up out of the dunes and waves and clouds. Only when they reached the top did they open their eyes. The gate shifted in all possible colors but, as Executioner touched it, the surface rippled grey and black full of lightning. At last, jade green flames flickered through it.

Behind them, two tiny spiders unlike the other tortured insects of this place, blinked and reappeared unseen in the shadows behind the hounds. The spider's dark grey and silky, almost liquid metal surface, reflected all around it and made it undetectable camouflage. The two spiders watched the hound called Executioner grab the gate with both hands and strain to bend the two dimensional slice. In a moment it bent, and then the hound spun the gate. The hole in reality burst into light and the hound jumped back rubbing its bloody hands on Mauler. The light scared the insect desert, which scurried back and away leaving the bleached and cracked bones of gods, eldar, monsters, and heroes protruding from the ground.

Without warning, the portal turned vibrant blue and revealed an ocean somewhere in Tehra. The two hounds leapt through. The spiders knew its master Sai watched through them. A command came to one of the two, "Follow the hounds that I may see where they arrive."

Chapter Fifty One - Malcor's Challenge

His sword hand broken, Malcor held his sword in his left hand and struggled to keep the ogre at bay. Behind the ogre, a teaming throng of goblins waited with poisoned and rusty weapons. Whenever a clear space opened, arrows snapped at him and he kept struggling to keep the ogre between him and the horde. Though the ogre bore any number of wounds, its bloodlust before a crippled opponent drove it on and on. Mal barely parried a smashing down strike by bouncing it aside. His kick, though it connected solidly, barely registered with the brute who laughed at him.

The regeneration ring on his broken hand buzzed and throbbed as it reknit Malcor's wounds but he was taking them so fast, it barely kept up. Then, just like that, his snapped bones mended and though still in excruciating agony, Malcor transferred his sword and masterfully parried and then countered. This time, his sword dug a trench across the monster's forehead gushing blood into its eyes and blinding it. The scream of frustration followed a series of random attacks hoping to take Malcor, but he dodged and then cried out a taunt at the beast. It whirled on him and then Malcor ran into the horde. Though goblins scattered and arrows raced to him, just as many struck his armor or the ogre. Even more enraged, the blinded and hated boss turned on its underlings killing and maiming far more than Malcor could have by himself.

For the horde, they saw Malcor coming at them followed by their gigantic boss, with both appearing bent on slaying them all. Morale, which had soared when the ogre looked like he might win, plummeted and many ran away. For the remaining, a magical fireball exploded as Sako and the others attacked. The remaining fighters turned tail and fled. Hiroshi felled the ogre with a deft slice across its throat. Jaga was about to compliment Malcor's fighting when he turned pale white. Malcor thought it might be from the many wounds and then felt a deathly cold rise up behind him. More instinct and luck than anything else saved him as he drove himself forward.

The creature facing them had once been a citizen of Ori. The Imperic growled in frustration and cried out its hunger. Finger nail claws, fangs and pale white skin in the torchlit cavern made the vampire's black eyes seem to glow with fire of their own. Noboyuki leapt forward presenting his symbol of Imperius and rebuked the creature as it readied to claw attack Malcor. The symbol gave the creature pause, who looked up at the priest's eyes with something like recognition. Its skin began to burn and the vampire shrieked. Lifeless goblins leapt from the ground at the priest and shielded the vampire from the symbol. As fast as they faced the holy symbol, they collapsed into ash but it gave the vampire time to grab and throw one at the priest. Mid-air, the zombie's body turned to ash that then blew into the priest's eyes. Sako barely pulled him away just before the vampire could rip Noboyuki's arm off.

Malcor had regained his footing and the group turned to face the vampire just as Hiroshi attempted a backstab. Something gave him away, maybe the sound of his pulse even, and the vampire struck Hiroshi to the side amidst the sounds of ribs breaking. The vampire's eyes danced back and forth between the priest and Malcor as if trying to determine who he should go after. In that moment of hesitation, the priest swung his mace at the vampire. Holy water blessed by Imperius for cleansing leaked out of the mace. Even though he missed, the water splashed the creature with more ear-splitting cries and howls of hunger. Malcor and the others charged. Jaga suffered the thief's fate and fell to the side. Malcor activated his sword curious to see how the undead would react to its magic-unravelling. His sword cut along the vampire's arm with a shattering sound but no visible reaction. Sako's magic struck it and jolted Malcor with electrical energy. They moved to place themselves between their fallen and the monster.

The next round started with the vampire summoning darkness that fell over them like a blanket. Only Noboyuki's glowing symbol remained alight creating dark shadows that made it hard to see the vampire. Fearing they would lose any advantage at all, Malcor unleashed a furious barrage of sword cuts looking for a mark. He found it, and grappled the monster crying out his location, "I have it! Here!"

The vampire bit into Malcor's breastplate seeking blood and found it, but not very much and Malcor ignored the chilling pain and the allure of its deathsong. Turning his sword for a moment, Malcor began punching into the beast's torso trying to drive his fists into and through the almost rock-like chest. The pommel of his sword bit slightly deeper but the vampire continued to tear through his armor. Already, a clawed hand ripped through his side plates and gashed him so terribly, a normal person would have died. But Malcor had trained for this and fought through the pain praying for a break. It arrived in the form of Sako who shot silvery darts into the vampire's face that somehow dodged around him to hit their target. At the same time, the priest struck down into the vampire's head where it fixated on tearing into Malcor's heart.

The vampire fell still, its hand buried in Malcor's sides as it had started pushing up to his heart. Malcor felt the regeneration ring fighting to keep him alive. He almost laughed when he tried to pull off the corpse but the hand pulled at him and he froze. Their faces bore equal looks of disgust and relief. He steeled his will and pulled the hand out. His life gushed out of the wound and he lost consciousness.

He heard voices talking about him. Slowly, Noboyuki's voice became clear. "Without Malcor, this vampire would have killed us all. I don't know how he absorbs so much damage and remains alive. He has truly amazing constitution. I have never exhausted myself healing like this, ever."

He felt Sako wiping his face and opened his eyes. He was not expecting her to be so close to him and she blushed. He tried to say a greeting but his lungs started to ache and he fell over coughing so hard he began vomiting. The priest caught him and held him trying to relax the still bleeding wounds. "Imperius has healed you Malcor, but you keep suffering wounds beyond my healing. You need good food and rest. Sadly things we will not find here."

Malcor nodded trying to repress a cough and noted that the regeneration ring had reached its limit. Just another pretty gemstone ring now, it still had an aura of wonder to it but no potency. Sako knelt down on his other side. Though the worst of his wounds had healed and he was no longer in danger of bleeding out, he still felt awful. The priest explained that he had suffered all kinds of injuries and, "We must rest. I am exhausted and need to replenish myself. Tomorrow, I can attempt more healing."

The battle had left gore and corpses everywhere, but they had no choice. Wounded as they were, they established a watch, except for Malcor, and made the best of it. Their gods watched over them that night and it passed uneventfully. Malcor awoke feeling a thousand times better to see Noboyuki looking like death warmed over. Jaga and Hiroshi had bound their wounds but clearly, Malcor had exhausted the priest's healing abilities again. He carefully stood and stretched. "Good as new," he said. "I feel the fatigue of healing, but have trained to fight through it. Many thanks to you Noboyuki."

"The holy god Imperius remains impressed by your fighting spirit and dauntless valor Malcor."

Sako had scouted a bit and reported that she had found an area, "It has to have a secret door or something. It strikes me as being off. I can't say why though. I need help." With Jaga and Hiroshi still suffering severe wounds, Sako and the priest went down to investigate the area.

Malcor smiled at Jaga and Hiroshi. "I've never fought a vampire before. I think somehow I might try a different tactic if there is a next time."

The two of them chuckled and then laughed. They had never fought one either. "The stories always make them seem so grand and seductive. This one seemed pathetic and frightful in its hunger, but that was all." Jaga picked up the skull and pried the eye teeth out. "Here," he tossed them to Malcor. "Without your sacrifice, we'd all be dead."

They heard stone moving and Sako called back to them to join. They walked several hundred feet farther in and found a section of the wall titled. "We can't get it to open all the way," they said looking at Malcor. "The wall is super heavy. We think it's intended for the ogres."

Malcor stepped forward and pushed against the wall looking for a handhold. He finally found one and then strained with all his might. Stars and red spots danced before his eyes and then the wall shifted, opening just enough for them to enter. "I think we found paradise," Malcor said looking around.

The secret door opened to a supply room containing all kinds of salted and preserved meats, sausage, and cheese. Kegs of ale and bottles of wine lined shelves to the far side of the room. At first they all approached the food tentatively wondering if the salted meats were human flesh. But, they turned out to be beef and lamb. While they still had some rations left, the food tasted wonderful. They closed the door and braced it and ate their fill. When food and drink had been sated, they found lantern oil and torches and resupplied. The time allowed Noboyuki meditation and time to heal the group some more. Watching made Malcor realize how he took Tembri's instant healing for granted.

Something changed in the party as well. The unexpected relief and resupply lightened their mood considerably. Malcor had come to expect their suspicious natures, but after so many days of combat, battle, danger, and peril, they began treating him as a member of their group. While Sako and the thief Hiroshi grew closer, it became apparent to all of them that Sako did have feelings for Malcor, just not amorous ones. She held him in a strange fascination, asking questions about Tania, about his upbringing, his sword, as if she could not get enough information about it. As Hiroshi saw that curiosity drove this rather than affection, he also began asking questions, and relaxed. Knowing they were all gangsters did not lessen the surprise that even Jaga had played the part of thief in his youth. Only Noboyuki, the priest of Imperius, had joined them outside the thieving world and even he was connected through his wife. She had grown up on the streets and carried some kind of obligation that Noboyuki sought to repay.

Though exhausted, he allowed himself to enjoy the conversation and even teased them back a bit as he mended his gear and re-sharpened his sword. He stood for first watch, resting against the secret door. Though a wonderful camp, the lack of retreat made their current location less than ideal. Mal steeled himself from drowsing and hummed a Tanian song from the days when the barbarians worshiped the emperor as a god, and their surprise to learn of the Queen. The others fell asleep to his whispered singing. With relief, he woke Hiroshi for the next shift and slumped down cradling his sword.

Malcor's sleep had strange dreams. Dar Shara danced in fire, and dragonshifting priestesses kissed him. Then R'Dar Ora came and seduced him while the dragons danced and spun around. The images suddenly shifted when darkness fell over them and while the others ran away terrified, Malcor stood and held his hands up high as if greeting the shadows. His dreamscape went pitch black and then resolved into grays as a darkly-robed figure stood before him. He felt his dream pulse, and in his sleep, he gripped his sword tightly. The robed figure held its hand out to Malcor and took a deep breath as if to scream. Instead a roar issued forth that pulsed the dreamscape and dropped Malcor to his knees.

He grabbed his ears but the insane noise began to blow him back and he grabbed at the shaded ground fearing he'd be blown into the sky. And still the noise and power increased in waves each threatening to hurl Malcor into darkness. He grabbed even tighter at the ground and noted that it crunched beneath his elongating black nails that twisted into claws. His right arm exploded as tendrils of his own blood arched out into the ground and reformed as an oversized dragon claw. His forearm lengthened to almost twice its size as black unreflecting dragon scales climbed up his arm from his claws. He stared at it with fascination and noted the sound had stopped.

The dark figure's hand also had transformed into a dragonclaw. From somewhere behind and to the side, a single bright light shone and that figure's claw now a shadow on the gray ground pricked Malcor's shadow. Stabbing pain lanced through his right arm. "Malcor, your name in this place is Kell'Tayris. You wage war with fury. I am pleased. Very soon, you will need this. Your time has come. Accept this mark as your father did."

Malcor woke choking for air and covered in sweat. His right hand, halfway between wrist and elbow held a tear drop wound the size of three fingers and it bled furiously and burned setting his arm afire with an agony beyond a normal wound. Though he tried to keep quiet, he could not. Hiroshi looked over when he heard Malcor groan, and started to move to help. Malcor shook him off and turned his back, cowering over his wound that quickly bled through his attempts at bandaging it. Hiroshi touched his shoulder expressing concern but Mal shook it off and began praying for help.

When Hiroshi woke Jaga for the guard change, Mal heard their exchange. "It happened out of nowhere. I felt something and then Malcor awoke with a terrible wound in his arm. He won't accept help."

Hiroshi lay down by Sako who cuddled up to him. Jaga went over and sat down by Malcor, offering him a drink. Malcor took it and drank. "Were you attacked?" Jaga whispered.

Mal shook his head "no" but then added, "In Tania, gifts often come with pain." He tried to smile but the wound pulsed again. Jaga removed the bandage and looked at it wondering how such a thing could be a gift. Mal just shrugged and rewrapped the wound. "Noboyuki will not be able to heal this. It will need to heal naturally. Don't worry about me."

When Jaga completed his shift and went to awaken Sako, Malcor interrupted him. "I'll take this shift. I can't sleep anyways. The pain has calmed, but is still too much to rest."

After what felt like only a few minutes from Jaga's return to sleep, Malcor heard a sound they had all dreaded. Outside the door, the corpses clicked and twitched to unliving motion. Something on the door's other side called to those corpses. Through the stone, they could not tell except the occasional sounds of metal scraping across the stone or a growl. One by one, Malcor held his hand over his friends' mouths as he quietly woke them one at a time. The sounds were either moving past their door or coming towards.

One by one, they drew their weapons. The priest had rested nicely and suggested they hide, rather than wait. Sako nodded and quickly flipped through her spellbook and indicated she'd be ready in about ten minutes. They moved back to the end of the storeroom. "I'm going to use an illusion to make us look like we're part of the dark "undesirable" part of the storeroom, at least I hope so, from an ogre's perspective." She began casting her spell. "It's important that none of you move. My illusions cannot adjust if you move. So get comfortable and stay very still."

Step by step, as she chanted, she moved to stand with them. When almost finished, the door shuddered and they heard an ogre spit profanity. Streams of dust rained down from the ceiling, and then they extinguished the lights and everyone stood still. A few moments later, the door pulled open as torch and lantern light burst into the room. "Hold very still," Sako whispered. "We are cast off junk..."

A scarred ogre looked into the room. It stepped aside and four orcs in fine Imperic-styled armor entered and began stuffing food, ale, and other supplies into satchels that they then handed back through the door. The orc closest to them sniffed and looked in their direction at one point as if sensing something, but at the ogre's questioned threat, went back to work grabbing things. Several minutes later, the same orc looked down at the pool of blood to pick up a link of sausage that had fallen off the table. As he picked it up into better light, it noted the fresh blood. The ogre misunderstanding the intent as hunger, chose that moment to lurch forward and slap the orc's head. "You! Pack! No more warning!"

The orc stood back up from where it had fallen and reached for his satchel, which had fallen in Malcor's blood pool. Its eyes narrowed and it looked around the room, peering into the dark back area intently. Being more careful to avoid the ogre's wrath, it continued to scan. Everyone held their breath but with the ogre ready to beat it to death, the orc did not have time to express its concerns. They finished gathering their materials together and then left.

Chapter Fifty Two - The Storeroom War

About an hour later, they heard the last sounds of the group's passage leaving the area. They all sighed with relief and relaxed tense muscles. Malcor slumped down cradling his arm, which had soaked through multiple layers of bandages and still freely bled, though more slowly now. Noboyuki insisted on trying against Mal's objections to heal the gaping wound. The warm flow of healing washed over Mal and eased his suffering but did nothing at all to the wound. Without Malcor at full strength, they would not be able to open the door so they settled down for another day. Malcor, soothed by the failed healing spell, fell into a fitful sleep.

At some point, Sako shook him awake indicating the need for quiet. Outside the heavy stone door, they heard sounds. Metal on stone, clicking, and occasional grinding sounds reached them. As the noises progressed, the anxiety of the party grew until Malcor said, "Noboyuki, will you use another healing on me? I will attempt the door. I do not think it wise to stay here much longer."

The others quickly agreed when Mal noted that the orc may have finally been able to talk to someone who listened. "We must be ready for the worst. We come out of here with everything we got. I will open the door as fast as I can, but use it as a shield as long as you can."

They made ready. Sako prepared a fire spell that would roll out from the doorway. Hiroshi would try to get past the door and secretly outflank and backstab whoever the leader turned out to be. Noboyuki readied a holy fire spell, similar to those Malcor had seen the priestesses use in Tania. Jaga would fight and give Mal time to clear the door.

They girded up their armor, readied their tactics, and Malcor moved to the door. Gripping it at ogre height made the wound in his arm tear open and though torrents of blood ran down his arm, he strained and pushed. At first, nothing happened and then the door ponderously sighed, lifting just enough for the counterweights to engage, and Malcor pushed with all his might. The uneven stone floor grated as it moved. Blood and rivers of sweat poured off Mal's body. On the other side, something snapped and the door flew off its track. They saw a brief glimpse of light as a hailstorm of arrows, darts, stones, and crossbow bolts launched at them. Caught off guard and off balance, Malcor fell forward with the door, which shattered into pieces when it smashed to the floor.

The dust and debris and door protected Malcor who prayed for his friends, and then his training and devotion carried him upright as Coming Undone leapt into his blood-slick hand. Not expecting a warrior of such dreadful countenance to be outside the room, the goblins and orcs nearest him cowered back as those behind rushed forward to attack the room. Malcor began singing in draconian to take his mind off the pain. As he did so, he felt energized and better.

"Oh Mother, where do the children fly? They left yesterday for a place to die. The River flows and fire burns but Mother she loves us forever. She loves us. She guards us. She watches over us till the fire burns and the children come home. Darkness waits for them, the children in the dark cannot see. They cannot breathe. They cannot stand the light. I will stand as their light. I will be their shining star. I will be their guide until the children come home."

Coming Undone tore through limbs and armor as Malcor charged into the center of the archer group. Though they scrambled to reload, he made sure that another volley did not occur. Behind him, a ball of fire rolled out into the horde. In its light, he saw the orc from the storeroom earlier. No ogres. The orcs commanded this time instead of the less cunning ogres. These orcs wore gleaming regalia marked by purple shaded swirls.

Malcor noted the orc commander and started cutting his way at it through the horde. Seeing him, the commander ordered orcs into line behind the more easily-scattered goblins. Malcor cut past an outthrust saber and smashed into the orcs' shield wall. They caught him and almost faltered and then pushed back trying to gain some distance. He reached up to the top of the shield with his left hand and stepped back while pulling down. The unfortunate orc, being pulled forward and trying to push that way at the same time fell at Malcor's feet as Malcor used its head like a stepping stone to slash left and right behind the gap. Though the orcs tried to close the gap, Coming Undone chipped and shattered armor adding the sound of broken glass to the combat. Several reinforcements jumped forward with pikes seeking to skewer him. One of the pikes cut through the bandages on Malcor's arm. As if time had frozen, Malcor felt himself slip out of the River pre-wincing in the surety of how much a pike attack against the teardrop wound was going to hurt. Instead, he stood up from the River and felt his arm quiver. Still holding his sword, his arm elongated and dragonshifted into an oversized black dragon claw... and then the River took him again.

The pike tip shattered on black dragon scales and the orc dropped the pike shaft as it frosted over with cold. That caught Malcor's attention briefly as black dragons typically used acid, not cold. His dragon arm, almost as long as his body, swiped out. He caught his sword in his left hand while the dragon arm smashed goblins back from his right side. The claws on this arm and its scales reflected no light. The orcs scrambled backwards from the transformation, fear and alarm darkening their combat fever.

Malcor pressed his advantage. His dragon arm raged stronger than many men and the orcs fell back trying to avoid his wide-ranging claw attacks. He moved forward and saw the orc commander grin as it dropped his steel helmet and raised its sword and shield to accept the challenge.

Behind him, a blade stabbed into his back and he swung full circle with both claw and sword as his sword decapitated and then his claw slapped the headless corpse into a group of fighters. The orc commander called out its challenge and Malcor tried to complete his spin, but off-balanced with his new arm and dropped to a knee just barely recovering. The orc cut down and though blocked by the dragon scales, it cut and gleamed with fell magic power. The wound hurt more than it should have and the orcs around it, cried out joyously seeing this man-beast able to be hurt.

Just like that, Malcor lost it. The waging emotions in him going from peril to triumph to unexpected dragon arm and victory and now to another twist in the tide of this battle – it was simply too much. His mind shut down and primal fury took over. His mouth went ice cold and darkness shrouded his vision. He tried to step out of it by leaving the River but instead got stuck there. A dim part of him registered his combat with the commander, but it felt weird watching him fight, taking damage, inflicting damage, and feeling absolutely nothing. Feeling nothing, but watching it… fascinating. He could not take his eyes off the dragon arm. A living weapon grafted to his body, it seemed to have a will and mind of its own. Just now, a weapon shattered on his hand scales and then the remnants of that weapon frosted back towards the bearer. Instinctively, the arm twisted to slash at the orc and as it did so, several finger talons shot out to clip nearby orcs. With fascination, Malcor watched those talons barely seem to touch but eviscerate those warriors.

The commander's sword gleamed in this darkvision but against the seething lightless claw of his right arm, it barely glimmered. Finally, Malcor caught that sword on Coming Undone and just like that, the battle was over. Disarmed within seconds, the orc resorted to hiding behind its shield. Several strikes by Coming Undone shattered the shield into freezing glass. A brutal claw attack speared the commander into a fountain of gore. With the commander's death, the others fled. Malcor noted how few were left. Without thinking, he used his dragon arm to catapult himself forward and rend another orc. Its death screams made the others run faster and Malcor felt his pulse quicken. He smelled their fear and it was delicious.

His darkvision caught movement and he whirled noting intense golden radiance and the darker barely-there forms of the others – not orcs. Someone was missing and the many wounds oozed red. Feeling nothing at all, Malcor watched his body leap forward to attack the brightness, which came from Noboyuki's holy symbol. He tried to call out, to warn Noboyuki, but his body did not respond. Noboyuki though stood equal to the task and struck a ringing blow that blew Malcor over backwards…

…and his head smacked to the blood wet floor.

"This is becoming too common," Malcor grumbled as light, sound, and pain wracked him awake. He found himself tied and bound. "Why am I tied up?"

Jaga leaned forward, "Do you remember attacking Noboyuki?"

"I saw him, he was bright and shining and everything was so dark…"

"Do you remember your arm turning into a black claw?" Sako asked.

He nodded. Noboyuki spoke then, "You changed Malcor. You became enraged and began tearing through our enemies as if they were paper instead of flesh. And it grew so cold. You kept fighting, as you do, even with wounds that would kill the rest of us. I tried to approach and calm and heal you but you turned on me. Lucky for me, you were so weak, I hit your head and you went down."

"The orcs, there were so many, and I did not know what the rest of you, if you would live. All I thought was to take out their leader and hope the rest would run away. One of their weapons struck my arm and the rest is hazy. I saw it, but it did not feel like me."

"Your arm still will not heal. It bleeds Malcor." Noboyuki checked the bandages again soaked with blood. "The wound appears to have snake scales growing around it. Are you a dragon?"

Malcor chucked, "No, I am not a dragon, but my father. Well, my religion calls us the children of the dragons. There are legends of some of Tania's heroes being able to become dragons. Certainly, the dragons walk with us as humans. Why not the other way around? If I am, I do not know it."

"Are you a berserk warrior?" the priest asked.

"I think so. Though in Tania, that is a discipline and I was not selected for training in that path."

Sako spoke now, "You always talk about your life and future there as if it is determined by others. *I was not selected... I was not chosen...* what do you want Malcor? Do you ever get a say in selecting and choosing your own path?"

He looked at her, "I feel calm, you can untie me. Sako, I want to be a paladin. Berserkers cannot serve as knights. They become a tool of the war machine and are owned by it. You cannot trust a berserker in combat. When the fury takes over, they fight until they die or are..."

Jaga finished, "Knocked unconscious. Like you Malcor."

"I am not a berserker. I choose to not be one. If I get to choose, I choose to be a paladin."

Sako pulled his hair back from his face. "Malcor, if all Tanian knights start out like you, then they must be the most powerful fighters ever. But, you went berserk. How is what happened to you different than the others?"

She untied his bounds against the group's discomfort and helped him up. He sat up and rubbed his wrists and stretched. Hiroshi brought him some food and drink. Same as his Rite of Pain, he felt ravenously hungry, and they scavenged the destroyed storeroom for remnants of food. "I was aware. I remember seeing Nobo. I remember fighting. Berserkers do not. I feel no sorrow, only regret that I could not stop any aggression towards you. There is a difference between the fog of war and the fury of a berserker. My apologies to you Noboyuki. I was not myself and clearly have some work to do with self-control. Especially in combat."

Sako touched his right shoulder as if scared it would attack her. "And this is you? Or is it something else, like a curse?"

"It is a blessing," Malcor whispered, wincing with pain as he flexed his arm. "I had a vision, of dragons. And then this was here after."

He stood up and took stock of their situation. He could easily tell the enemies he had dropped before and during his transformation. Elegant sword attacks changed to gaping and terrible wounds and scattered gore. He guessed that he had taken out more than half the fallen by himself. Sako's rolling ball of flame had done lots of damage as well. "We can't stay here any longer," he said to no one in particular.

With that, he began gathering his gear together and made ready. Without comment, the others did as well. The dark passage loomed before them.

Chapter Fifty Three - Calvin as an Officer

Calvin sat in a class in the Soldier's Fort. The transition had been hard. He felt utterly exposed and self-conscious and though several weeks had passed, he still felt like the knights knew as they looked at him, that he had once been a knight, and had fallen out of the knighthood. Though no one said anything, quite the contrary, all of his comrades had either fallen out of the knighthood too or had chosen the officer path rather than paladin. Truth to tell, he had never been more afraid than when he walked up to the Fort's massive gates that day Dar Shara had saved his life and ended his ambitions as a knight. "Morbatten recognizes multiple ranks of soldiers. However, they are all variants off the core ranks. Sir Calvin, what are the core ranks?" the instructor barked.

"Sir, Sargent is the first officer rank. This is followed by Lieutenant, then Captain. After that, R'Dar and Dar become the main designators with military insignia showing specifics."

"Excellent Sir Calvin. You," the instructor said pointing to a woman in the front row. Calvin had noticed her earlier because she had lithe and feminine body but when he saw her face, the diagonal scars made her downright ugly. "What insignia designates an officer in command of 100 captains?"

The lady stood and Calvin noted for the hundredth time how horribly her face and probably her upper body had been sliced up. She may have once been pretty, but now, she appeared only pitiful. "A 100 captains are commanded by a Dar, any Dar. The exception would be a dread lord, who takes command by being present."

The instructor smiled. "Perfect answer Lady Ayden. Impress me further. Can a paladin command 100 captains?"

She titled her head and without missing a beat responded, "Paladins are like dread lords. By being present, at any level, a paladin may take control of any group of soldiers. However, unlike the dread lords, they must ask and be granted command when the commander outranks them, militarily-speaking."

"I am impressed. So, class, under what circumstances would you tell a paladin "no"?"

The class fell silent and Calvin remembered how his lack of initiative had contributed to his being cast out of the knighthood. He answered, "We should never tell a paladin "no". However, the correct thing to do would be to understand the knight's desired outcome and ensure it is achieved. If the knight insists on taking command, we should make use of our own lines of communication to ensure strategy is not compromised by a mid-battle shift in priorities. The paladins are motivated by the Temple towards religious not necessarily tactical outcomes."

The instructor looked at Calvin and then nodded. "Very good. Let me share a story from our history with you. A great myrmidon, one of you, a professional soldier of the empire named Dar Glaz, commanded an army of Tanians, Sorians, elves, and Imperics. This was in Bloodstone. The Dar priestess of Bloodstone, from the Temple at Bloodstone, had joined with her retinue to push the undead back from the valley floor where a party of knights had been trapped underground in a new tunnel. Dar Glaz had been given explicit instructions to rescue the knights. The Dar priestess and even her dread lord entrusted Dar Glaz with this single outcome. How many of you know this story? All of you, yes?" Many heads nodded. "So, one of you, tell me – what happened?"

A fellow student answered, telling the story of how Dar Glaz led the army into a pincer attack with one group timed to attack and then retreat so as to draw the main horde of undead away from the tunnel. The second group would then race to and hold the tunnel while a group of heroes went in and reinforced the paladins, who had come under attack by a hellhound. "Dar Glaz's strategy worked flawlessly."

"Wrong," the instructor said. "All of you take a deep breath. This story is widely known as you told it, but the truth is far different. The truth is this: Dar Glaz was a captain, just like each of you will likely be. He was one captain of many. A paladin ordered a full frontal attack assuming the Queen's might would save them, even though they were vastly outnumbered. The hellhound killed the knight and left our forces leaderless. Dar Glaz ordered a retreat using the knight's banner, and set out this strategy. Some of the knights labelled him a coward and the second pincer, in Glaz's strategy, refused to wait. They pre-emptively attacked, which then pitted a divided Tanian army against the entire horde. Things were going poorly until Glaz convinced the Dar priestess and the dread lord to follow his plan. Even with their support, the knights refused to follow him and Glaz abandoned them. The dread lord glassed the valley floor and they had to later open a separate rescue tunnel. Only three knights of the twenty trapped survived. The Bloodstone protocol failed the slain seventeen who all raised up as servants of the Jade God and continue their fight against us even now."

When the instructor stopped talking, the room's silence ached. Into that silence, the instructor whispered, "What do we learn from this story?"

Another student said what Calvin thought, "That Tania's stories are maybe different than what happened?"

The instructor smirked, "Don't be coy with me. You all know the emperor closely follows our culture, society, and stories. While it is true – there are legends and then there is what really happened, there is something else to learn here."

Ayden spoke, "The knights are not always right. They can focus too much on a tactic and place the strategy at risk. In this case, the glory of fighting a mighty foe compromised the knight's orders to rescue their fellows."

"What happened to Glaz?" Calvin asked.

"Sir Ayden, you are correct again. Sir Calvin, what do you think happened?" When Calvin shrugged, the instructor told him that, "Glaz and the fellow captains had the objective to rescue the knights. Seventeen of them died, never mind their entourages and others with them. This was their order – all of them. They were all disciplined. Unlike the others though, Glaz came back from his discipline with the Queen's grace. Within a year, he took command of the military in Bloodstone. Some years later, the emperor recognized him with R'Dar title and his legend never stopped growing. When he retired, he changed his name through marriage with a priestess. His new name should be recognizable to you all… Debruce Tel'Cori." Seeing the eyes of the class grow wide,

"Yes, the founder of the Adventurer's Guild here in Morbatten."

They had many classes like this. When not in class, Calvin trained with all manner of weapons and all manner of armor. When not training, he went out with already established officers on patrol. When winter arrived, he and his class would be sent into the Winter Wars. Small squad tactics meant everything and through small squad tactics, the myrmidons would achieve rank and eventually command.

One day, during maneuvers in the highland plain behind the Fort, Calvin saw a stream of heavy chargers come over the road's rise and noted Seline at the column's head. Her armor gleamed in the autumn sunlight and a pinion from her lance lashed the air over the column behind her. Seeing her pained him but he swallowed his pride when he saw her course would bring her by him. Continuing his training, he stopped and bowed low as she rode by. She immediately recognized him and pulled aside to allow the column to continue. Dismounting, she gave him a hug and asked how he had been doing.

"It's been difficult, but I feel better here. It is certainly less painful!" he joked. "I see you have made it in the Order of Fire?"

She nodded and a moment of remembered pain passed through her face. "Yes. The Order of Fire. It's funny. Until it happened, I did not know there are different groups of paladins. Oh, your friend Malcor – the one you often spoke about. He is in the Order of Water though I haven't seen him or even that Order, anywhere. They are absent all of the training and skirmishes." She looked around noting the less polished but far more practical gear of the officers.

Calvin hefted his blunted training sword. "Yeah, as a knight, the tools are pretty specific – armor, sword, faith. Officer stuff is nowhere near as glorious as you Lady Seline. Of course, no one here is nearly as beautiful as you either," he spoke with a flourish and bow, "but perhaps the Order of Fire will need troops capable of marching in straight lines and fighting with other weapons." He pointed at her glorious sword, "Speaking of Mal, did he make that one for you?"

She shook her head and drew the sword for Calvin to see. "No, I've never seen him, just heard some stories about him. Does he make swords like these? This is a holy avenger you know, though I have yet to claim it."

Calvin ran his finger along its blood groove. "An amazing weapon Lady. My friend Malcor, he made a sword similar to this. In Klenna, the knights were always bringing him swords like this for special treatment. He has a gift."

"Calvin, about the training, I…"

Calvin looked up at the sky and interrupted her, "No need. You listened to the Goddess. I listened to a grouchy old mage. Dar Shara was right about me. I am not cut out to be a knight. Close enough to be, but not actually able. I like this. We train hard, play war games, and eat well. But still, I miss the regimen, the sense of purpose and belonging, of being part of the Temple. My family will no doubt be disappointed." He shrugged but Seline could see how hard it was for him.

She smiled wistfully and agreed. "I've missed you Calvin. I'm glad to see you doing well. I need to get back to my unit."

Calvin bowed low and watched her turn to mount her horse and leave. His training counterpart observed, "She sure is something."

"Yes, she is special."

"What is this Order of Fire and Water thing? Water seems a bit out of place for one of our orders."

Calvin shrugged, "Go figure. It's an elemental thing perhaps. It probably kills my friend that he didn't make it into the Order of Fire. He always wanted to be the best."

They went back to sparring, practicing switching hands with their weapons, and using the hand signs common to the soldiery. As they sparred, Ayden came over and watched during a break and then asked if she could work her way in. "I saw you talking to that lady." They continued sparring, "I knew her back in the Dutchy."

347

"Oh? I was in her class in the Temple, before." Calvin answered during a parry. "She's very good."

Ayden smirked and began a series of kick attacks where the sword's movements would create opportunities for kicks. "She's okay I suppose."

They continued talking and sparring and Calvin sensed she wanted to say something. "You have more you want to say?" he asked.

"No, it's nothing. Just something I thought about when I saw the two of you."

They continued sparring until break was called.

Chapter Fifty Four - Seline and Blaze

Seline stood beside an ornamental tree, in its shade watching. Calvin did seem a lot more relaxed than he had been at the Temple. Even when she had caught him during the skirmish, she had struggled to tell if his reaction had been disappointment or relief. She felt a warm tingle along the back of her neck, and her skin prickled with excited arousal. "My lord Blaze, I did not realize you were at the Fort today," she said, watching Calvin and that disfigured girl go back and forth in their duel.

A deep rumbling behind her confirmed that dread lord Blaze had indeed walked up behind her. "You like that boy."

"Am I so transparent Dar Blaze?"

"All humans are. He is beneath you. Put him out of your mind and heart." He put his hand on her shoulder and turned her around. "You Lady, are transparent. In the River, you are beautiful. That boy down there, in the River, is dying. Someday you will see how unworthy he is of your regard."

Seline blushed and felt a growing anxiety. Blaze had this effect on her, and the others. Dar Niss had explained it to her as fire being a reference to more than actual burning flames. "Fire can also be passion, anger, rage. You never hear of red dragons playing games that require patience. They want what they want and take it. For us, interacting with them, this aura will call up all kinds of desires. I tell you now Seline, there are not many lady paladins in this empire. They all fall under the spell of the dragons and succumb. If you can last, if you can endure it in chastity as the Goddess requires, you will be rewarded beyond your dreams."

"And if I do not?" she asked. At that time, so soon after her Rite, her body, soul, and desires had wracked her between desire and terror. Her voice had shaken.

"There is always the priesthood. You would make a grand priestess," Niss said cradling her tightly.

Standing now with Blaze, she tried to focus on this. His hand on her shoulder turned her stomach to butterflies, and his scent so close in this intimate place, she could almost taste his lips...

"I will show you." Blaze's voice so strong and serene uplifted her and she would do anything for him. She nodded.

He turned her back towards Calvin and leaned forward so that his mouth was next to her ear. His face just barely touching her own and those butterflies made her clench her legs and stomach to avoid falling over. Her passion must be apparent to him and part of her cared and another part did not. "See the River," he whispered and her passion spiked dropping her to her knees in the path.

The world before her eyes charred to ash and blew out before her eyes. When the transformed view reached Calvin, the ash blew into a current of flowing embers and then liquid flame. He fought his match in exquisite detail and color and sound and smell. It all assaulted her in this place and she remembered her teachings. Trying to focus on Calvin and tune the rest out was difficult. To her surprise, the disfigured woman fighting Calvin looked radiant and glorious and awesomely beautiful. It took her breath away. To her side, a god of fire and desire held her still and pointed. "See how he drowns, but his partner – she aches for life. He dies. She will live forever."

She looked at her own hand and saw how it scattered tiny burning sparks and occasionally pieces of her scalded and burned away. She gasped and Blaze took her hand. In his pure being of red energy, her hand looked like pale garbage and she trembled seeing how insignificant...

"You are not insignificant to me, to my father, or to the Goddess. Your worship is seductive and amazing. Like that woman's," he pointed to Ayden. "Your friend though, Calvin? I see only relief that he is no longer held to the knight's standard. He lacks faith. Lacking faith, there is nothing to hold the River at bay, and he is murdered each second. For his lack of faith."

Did this god say my worship is seductive?, but even as she thought it, Blaze turned her face and kissed her farewell.

350

Air rushed into her lungs making them ache and she caught herself holding her breath. She knelt alone, shaking with longing. Her lips tingled with heat. Down below, Calvin and Ayden walked away for a break. She touched her shoulder feeling the warmth of the dragon's touch. Her lips reached for the sensation of Blaze's kiss. She remained alone but felt alive, her heart pounding.

She floated away from the sparring arena and rejoined her troupe later that night high on the mountain looking down on the Fort. To her, it seemed as if she had teleported from the field to the bonfire. Dar Niss came forward and greeted her, and then caught her hand and pulled her away from the fire.

"What's going on?" Seline asked. Her voice sounded drunk and slightly hoarse.

"You are in no state to rejoin the group. I see our lord has spent some time with you? Yes, come with me." She led Seline around the camp's perimeter to her personal tent. Her guard held open the entry and the two of them walked in, Seline stumbling and giggling a bit.

Dar Niss led her to her sleeping area. When Seline began giggling even more, Niss sighed and pulled her down. "Here, lay down, relax. I want you to open yourself up to me and trust me."

"Ooo," Seline cooed. "That sounds nice and perfect." She stretched back arcing her back seductively.

Niss prayed to the Goddess and with a soft touch, pushed Seline into a deep sleep. The young paladin dropped backwards, a soft smile on her lips. Niss pulled a lamp over and noted that the girl's lips had changed color; they glowed with soft red fire. She mumbled gently in her sleep. When Niss blew out the lamp, in the darkness, she could still see the ember fire dancing on her mouth.

"The girl is asleep. No one is to enter. If she awakens, call for me no matter what. Do not let her leave my tent," Niss explained in whispers to the guard.

Seline suffered exquisitely in her dreams. When she finally opened her eyes, she could not remember where or why or how she had come to this place. A pitcher of water by her side almost proved too difficult for her to drink from and she fell back. The blankets around smelled of arousal and felt soaking wet from her fevered dreams. She wiped hair stuck to her face from her eyes and tried to sit up. Her lips still burned. She tried to stand up but fell over and knocked the small tray of water and snacks to the hard ground.

Minutes later her mentor entered the tent. "Why am I like this?" Seline mumbled.

"Our lord Blaze had some fun with you. He does this to test the resolve of all new members, often at a time when you're distracted or not expecting it." Niss helped Seline stand and sit down on a chair. "Men experience this differently. Think of it as the opposite of dragonterror. Men experience a type of combat euphoria and invulnerability. Women, well," Niss smiled remembering it, "we experience a level of passionate abandon." She took a wet towel and wiped Seline's face. "The test is to endure. I apologize for tricking you into sleep. You've been asleep for almost three days."

"Three days! That's…"

"Exactly what happens when you step out of the River the first time. Or are tested by Dar Blaze. Actually, any of the red dragons. Why I have heard rumors about the high priestesses when they were tested by the emperor. It's scandalous."

"I saw a torrent of energy and fire… I saw myself disintegrating. Calvin, he was."

"Pale and empty. Yes Seline. When he entered the Temple, he bore a token identifying him to the Shields. Even his mentor saw that he lacked a certain level of conviction. But because of the token, he was given a chance. The girl he sparred with, she has hope to enter the Temple. Her officer training will determine whether she has the required understanding and insight to serve as a battle priest, healer, maybe even a proctor."

"Mistress, may I ask – why is he so dim? I thought all of us are consecrated to the Goddess."

"Consecration is different than having active faith. Even though that one has walked with the king, spoken with Dar Shara, danced with dread lords, and been friends to a child of destiny, he takes it for granted. There are worshipful acts but when done with no regard for the doctrines of the Queen? Even if he has ability, there is no desire to elevate the Queen, only to serve. And he expects to be rewarded. Though the Queen rewards us many times over, She finds the expectation insulting. It makes him less desirable to the Queen, but the dragon emperor saw and noted this millenia ago. Even the weakest tool is still a tool for the building of the Queen's throne. Your friend Calvin, unless something in him changes, will live and die. Sure, he may find glory after a measure but it will be pale by comparison to if he held firmly to faith and fire."

Seline started to feel better and asked, "Is the River, was it the red energy I saw washing over him, over us? Is it here in this room? I remember studying and reading about it but nothing prepared me for it. I saw the river once in the Dutchy, but it felt like a dream. My parents told me it was a dream."

Niss pulled over a chair and poured herself a drink. "The River is central to the Queen's teachings. She exists, and we exist because of the River. Simply put, the River is Time. While we are in this world, in this place, it washes over us. Some it drowns and they die of illness, old age, or accidents. Others see glimpses of it and learn how to shape it, becoming magic users. We in the Temple are given divine insight into how the River can flow at the Queen's command and similar to but different from magic users."

"Lord Blaze is different though. All of the dragons are."

"Yes Seline. They are. The eldar, those like the dragon emperor and the gods who existed before the River, are different. Their children are different. So are the undead, elves, and those not as strongly touched by time. You have much to learn but eventually you'll start to see these things for yourself."

"Blaze is, amazing. Dar Niss, I wanted to give myself to him. To be his. Forever. If I think about it too much." She shuddered. "Tell me more. I can't think about it or I feel I will explode."

Niss smiled and squeezed her hand. "Very well, lets go for a walk." They exited the tent and her guard fell in behind her. "The Queen is an order of god just below what we call the Prime Aspect. The Prime Aspect is the creative and destructive powers that existed in the time of eldar and used to be one and the same thing. Their separation created the space in which the eldar formed. It is prophesied that someday, these forces will recombine and destroy everything. Though not a god, we recognize it as a power beyond anything we can understand. From this power, magic, the divine, and the inexplicable things of the universe come.

"Into that the eldar formed themselves from the pure stuff of chaos. Each gravitating to its interests. Each a magical and wonderful creature that lived and breathed chaos. The Queen is one of these, timeless and perfect. She saw the River begin flowing and took steps to protect Her children. There are other gods like Her, each within their area of interest – we call it a dominion. The Queen's dominion comes from an enjoyment of chaos in all its forms that then led to the colored dragons pledging themselves to Her. You have a question?"

"Two actually. Why are the guards with us and what does dominion have to do with the River?"

Niss put her arm around her shoulders and said, "The guards are here so that the men do not take advantage of your current condition. I don't know if you have noticed but you are having quite an effect on those around you." Seline blushed and looked down when she saw that any male with line of sight to her was staring at her like she was the most desirable woman they had ever seen. "To the other question, the River and dominion are closely linked. The River flows always from creation to destruction. Its course washes through and over and within everything in all of creation. As it flows through a dominion, the god of that dominion becomes stronger. Yes child?"

"What happens? I mean, I feel this excitement this urge to…."

"Lady Seline, you are sworn to the Temple. Unless released from that oath, if you did, you would be removed from the Order of Fire. Unless you atoned, and that is very hard to do as a novice, you'd never be allowed re-entry to any Order. Put it out of your mind."

"So, I can never," she started to ask but Niss cut her off.

"No, never. Not unless you want to leave the Order." She stopped and signaled her guards to back off. "Look Seline, Dar Kell and the king Dar Rojo have done much to change the Queen's religion to be more fair. But, one thing that never changes is that this is the worship of the Goddess. The Goddess chooses the time, the when, the who, and the dragons obey. So too do her worshippers. The priestesses choose the time, the when and the who and the worshippers obey. Even Dar Kell obeys this, now and after extensive atonement. You, as a paladin, as a woman, are in a difficult position. But, you knew this joining. Put it out of your head. Find something else."

Seline laughed, but it sounded lonely and cruel even to her as she attempted to make light of it. "So the male paladins, they can be chosen by a priestess. Can a male priest choose me?"

They resumed walking and Niss said, "The male priests do not choose, they are chosen as well child. Like I said, find something else."

"Like what? What do the others do?"

"Seline, there are not many female paladins. In an empire ruled by dragons, the talented, the beautiful, the skilled females, we are treasures. It is rare to find a gem like you applying for the knighthood. I'd suggest running, martial training, and weapon mastery. Anything physically intense and exhausting. The urge will fade and you suffer more now because of Dar Blaze. Remember, the thing that makes you most beautiful to them is your commitment to not becoming their slaves. They want our worship, not our subservience."

"Not many females you said. How many are we?" Niss started to explain and answer but in a moment of clarity, Seline blurted out, "You used to be a knight! Oh no, I'm so sorry, I didn't mean to say that out loud!"

Niss began laughing, for real this time. "Indeed Seline, I was. And Blaze overpowered me. I had a good mentor. A man. He passed away years ago. He tried to help me and how it tormented us both. I still love him. I loved him every day. Resisting me, helping me, he fell in love with me too. He sought distraction in Bloodstone and after several tours there, he retired. I left the Order for the priesthood, to be with him. So, you see, it isn't all bad."

"But you have regrets. I can see it. So that is why you helped me, put me to sleep?"

"Yes, I regret that I never stood as a holy knight in Bloodstone. Though I have stood there as a priestess, and though my children have fought there as paladins, I regret missing that experience. And since he passed away, I wonder if my weakness did not somehow pull both of us out of the Order."

"Back in the Dutchy, there was a boy. We fell in love. Well, I think it was love. He had a perfect face and made me laugh. He told me he would search the whole world over to find me a perfect gift, and when my sixteenth birthday arrived and it was made known I would try for the knighthood, he brought me his perfect gift. It was a flower, potted in soil, from a field where we used to play as children. My head was so full of dreams of glory that I mocked him for his perfect gift. I can still see his hurt in his eyes. But he bowed and gave it to me. I never saw him again. He avoided the farewell and send off parties my father threw." Seline sighed. "I regret how I treated him."

Niss nodded. "A gift of wealth or a purchased gift, even if sincere, is still a token expression of that wealth no matter how well-intentioned it might have been. You could always leave the Order, become a priestess, or join your friend Calvin as an officer, and return to your perfect boy," she suggested.

"I will write him a letter Niss. When he gave me the flower all I could see was a pathetic attempt to squash my dreams of becoming a knight. Now, I see what he saw. The flowers I used to play with and say that he loved me, he loved me not. When I was with Blaze, it felt similar but more glorious. In the fire, all I wondered was whether the dread lord could ever

356

love me. In my armor, surrounded by my father's retainers, dressed like a knight, I must have seemed dreadful to him and I regret leaving him unanswered. Yes, I will write a letter."

They walked in silence for some time, the clanking armor of the guards and the sound of the high valley wind pacing along with them. Finally, they came to the top of a hill and Niss pointed, "Look, from here we have a clear view of the dragon emperor's throne. Look there. I want you to remember this feeling you have, this razor edge of self-control on one hand, and an utter surrender to meaningless passion on the other. Remember that this is the true nature of dragons, especially fire breathers. Someday, you'll meet the dragon emperor. What you experienced with Blaze will be a thousand times more powerful with the father. Unlike Blaze, the emperor is an eldar. He swore fealty to the Goddess and accepts the title of "son" but he is so close to being a god that you may as well consider him one. If the Goddess is a step below the Prime Aspect, then consider that the dragon emperor is too, except but for one thing. For the Goddess' glory, he CHOSE to be part of *HER* dominion. As strong as he is now, he gave up a lot for Her. I like to think he did it for love. Can you imagine even asking him this?"

From their vantage point, they could see a long winding train of business heading to and from the mountain's intricately carved and sculpted entrance. It seemed alive and Seline imagined she could feel it breathing. They watched until the chill wind at this altitude eventually made Niss shudder and she suggested they return to camp.

"Do the dragons, do they ever, you know *choose* to be with a human?" Seline wondered aloud.

Niss did not answer for a while and then said, "It's hard to say. There are no scriptures that suggest the dragons have, but given the nature of the eldar, who knows. You should study it Seline and let me know. They certainly don't seem to mind taking human form and interacting with us, though most dragons do not."

"Oh really? I thought they all could."

"No. Following the hierarchy, there are dragons separated from the eldar

357

or created by the eldar. The ones who did not pledge themselves to the Goddess or to Her Consort on the other side, fell into the River and have become weak and disconnected over the ages. Those are what most people think of dragons. They are a lesser order, though they can be brought back through conversion. But, that is not a task for the Order of Fire. And, truth to tell, there are many other creatures similar to these lesser order beings that miss their true potential. They have intelligence, or at least a spark of it, and sometimes even free will. The River does not claim them entirely but it does carry them along. More powerful undead, and divine servants would be like this.

"Continuing the earlier discussion, you then have very long-lived creatures like elves and lesser undead. Past that and you have us. We can extend our lives with magic, healthy practices, and divine blessings, but eventually the River takes us as well. Our only hope is to find paradise after death with the Goddess, or to ascend into immortality on our own terms. As they separate from the River, they grow more powerful and comfortable with their power. The dragon emperor for example, I believe is comfortable in his power in any form. A wild red dragon though, even if it could, would never shift into a human or anything other than a red. Their egos will not allow it. Now, blue dragons and other colored dragons, well, it just depends. Ynt'taris, the white who guards the upper glaciers of the mountain can and does shift into all manner of forms. I have been told he does that to experience places he cannot go as a white because of the climate."

Back at camp, Niss made sure that Seline had eaten dinner and felt strong enough to be alone and then called several other members of the Order over. Older men, they stood rigid and at attention but at the same time pulled off a relaxed look, even with full plate armor and weaponry. They agreed to look after her. Left alone, sort of, Seline reflected on the day's conversation and found the burning urge growing again. No matter what, her thoughts kept drifting back to Blaze. "So, tell me if you would, when you met dread lord Blaze, you both wanted to conquer the world?" She smiled and tried to pass the question off as casual conversation.

Both of them grinned back at her and the older one replied first. "When Blaze showed me the River, I came out of it wanting to rule the world.

Conquering it would be easy enough. I was lucky though. The Kell Conflict had just started and my family had already sided with Kell. Instead of ruling the world, I threw myself into the fighting with all my heart and soul. I had a fever for blood and it never ended. There was always someone else I needed to attack, to defeat. After several weeks, it gradually faded away."

The other paladin had a similar story except his experience had happened after the Kell Conflict. "I was mediating at the Temple when the dread lord came and sat by me in the Great Hall. I had visions. I was told we meditated for almost two days. When I stood up, I knew that I was destined to be King. So, I set off to challenge Dar Rojo to a duel for control of the empire." Seeing the look on her face, he quickly added, "I'm not joking!"

"So, what happened? With the king I mean."

"I caught up to him during a public assembly. I called him out. While he did not appreciate it, he enjoys a good fight. I fought him with every ounce of training and skill I had. I think he sparred with me. At one point, I grew so enraged with my inability to kill him, I went berserk. When I came to, Dar Niss was tending to me. She told me that Rojo had allowed me to put on a good show for the sake of public morale and that if I wanted to fight again, to meet him here at the Fort in two days' time at dawn. I did. He had a line of challengers and sparring partners. I watched him beat knights and officers far exceeding my own skill and still went at him with everything I had. Unlike the others, he beat me within an inch of my life and left the healers instructions to let me heal naturally until the madness had passed." Both of them laughed heartily. "We have a good king."

"I would have thought the king would kill you for embarrassing him in public," Seline wondered.

"No, not our king. You'll probably meet him soon. Beneath his dark mood, he is just another citizen of the empire who wants the Queen's glory for everyone. He always takes challenges and even loses some of them. He always makes it a point that the king does not have to be the best or the strongest. We aren't some pagan empire that way. As Dar

Rojo would say, "I am king because the emperor required it. It could have been any of you. When I am gone, it will be one of you." Lady Seline, I believe Dar Rojo would say that even you could be King."

Seeing her beginning to sweat, the older paladin asked her, "What now my lady?"

"I think I'm going to try running."

They set off on a jog. Their valley encampment sat in the center of a roadway that made a half circle to the trails leading the mountain's summit. Seline asked what the Order's best time for summiting was. "Four hours? We got this!" and she took off at a sprint.

Chapter Fifty Five - Hellhounds in Khasra

Executioner and Mauler walked out of the ocean onto a beach. The beach lay several hundred miles east of Ori on the island of Khasra. They sniffed the air looking for the scent of undeath, or necromancy, or living flesh. Any would work and the blood of a Tehran, of any Tehran, would feed them deliciously. Unlike their master's throneplane where everything that happened did so by the master's command, Tehran life had a wildness to it. That sweet taste infused with free will and different powers flavored Tehran life and enhanced the hounds' powers. "This place is blank. It is clear. Only random death lurks here. There is nothing for us," Mauler whimpered. He knew what would come next.

Executioner nodded and turned to him with an evil grin. "I see what you are thinking younger brother but worry not. This time we will hunt together. I do not need food. Perhaps Orcus will bless us before then. Remember, he did say his wand had been placed here in readiness. Lets hunt."

Both of them leapt forward headfirst. Their human, if somewhat alien forms, stretched and then grew into the limbs of giant dire wolves. Both put their heads back and howled enjoying the startled flight of coastal birds as they fled in primal terror. Somewhere, their now keen ears picked up the sound of something large running away. The hellhounds leapt after it and soon scented the cloying smell of fear.

They tore through the jungle after their prey. Their hunger driving them forward and the sweet terror teasing them. Jungle trees blurred past the hounds and they burst out into a clear space bordered by a torrential river and littered with rocks. A herd of elephants stood in a ring, the bulls with their white tusks facing the hounds. The bleating cries of their innocent young sounded from the center of the ring. The hounds split in opposite directions and circled the group. They relished the fear almost as much as they would enjoy the coming bloodbath.

As they circled, the elephants backed towards the river. More importantly, the hounds failed to notice the boulders scattered around the field moving behind them. At last, the hounds had reached the end of their patience and they attacked the elephants. Their attack would tear into the strongest and leave the weak and most fearful for last. From the carcasses, they would construct an undead abomination as their first of many more to come.

That is what should have happened. Instead, the herd of elephants burst apart as dragonfire speared through into Mauler's face mid-pounce. The fire tore the illusion apart and Mauler, through burning and charred eye sockets fell into the ether where he realized his dire mistake. The herd of elephants was one of those cursed Tanian dragons. From the taste of the flames killing his mortal body, Mauler recognized it as the one commonly-called Blade. True to his name, the fire flowed like a cutting and slashing waterfall of sword-like talons that shredded Mauler to bloody froth.

Executioner fared better. At the last second before he jumped, he sensed something wrong and veered to the side. The bull elephant he almost jumped on unleashed a series of magical and divine attacks and that also shredded its illusion. More importantly, he noted the tiny paladins hurtling through the air at him. As they came close, their holy avengers ignited with dragon flames and columns of the Dragon Queen's fury and fire ignited around them. They smashed into the area where Executioner would have been had he not changed direction. Three paladins, and he noted each wore the emblem of that accursed Bloodstone valley, wheeled to face him, and then tortured agony tore through his side as their dragon priests – how did he always forget that Tanians never fought alone? – approached him with the many dragon-headed symbols of their Goddess calling for his banishment.

His head twisted into two heads with one confronting and snapping at the priests while the other turned baleful eyes on the three paladins. He noted Mauler's death as the dragon burnt away flesh and then even the skeleton cindered away. The dragon continued to breathe flame on Mauler as its talons tore into the corpse's bones. Mauler's death cry sounded exactly as bad as Executioner's would if he failed. Orcus did not appreciate failure on this level. He screamed out, "How?! How did you find us?"

The three paladins charged and Executioner tried to jump back and keep space. The damned priests continued their advance calling for his banishment. He bumped into something though and only his Master's blessings saved him from a wall of earth elementals rearing up behind him. Completely cut off and trapped, Executioner did the only thing he could do, he called for his brothers. Each hellhound's instinctive ability to summon the others had saved them time and again. He felt the gate between Tehra and his own realm tear open. Instead of his fellow hounds appearing though, seven humanoids came through the gate. He howled in frustration. Normally his howl would drive any humans insane but he had fought all of these before. Still, howling made him feel better. They must have been waiting at the abyssal gate. Somehow, his brothers had been delayed. How? *HOW*? He raged and fed his rage into strengthening his attack and defenses.

Daryx led the charge through the gate as the other six paladins ignited their holy avengers. The three paladins augmented their speed with magic and closed the gap. The dragon leapt into the sky to ensure there would be no escape. The cries for banishment grew louder. To be slain here, by these, would banish him from this place for a hundred Tehran years. He looked at the gate longingly, if only he could jump through it. The dread lord Blade, as if to mock him, breathed fire at the gate and kept it drenched in killing flames that would do to him what had been done to Mauler.

Daryx hit his back and though the cut did not feel deep, he felt something pressed into his back. It worried him and he spun trying to dislodge one of their greatest enemies. Daryx was known and sat almost at the top of the Master's death list. And then the other paladins landed on him, cutting and chopping. A serpentine cord wrapped around one of his heads and another top of the death listed person held the other end, Dar Kendra. She twisted the whip of her sword along the bladed coils wrapping his second head, and it decapitated. But at last, he had recovered from his surprise. The priests would be the easier foe and he charged at them, spraying hellfire from his remaining head as he screamed Orcus' name for aid. No doubt his master watched and may come to his aid.

His attack smashed into a force wall and there behind the priests, at last visible stood the one called Apprentice. *Had they brought all of the death listers here to stop him? How?* The dragon pushed his mouth of fire into the gate continuing to expel fire while the gate closed. Executioner was cut off. The earth elementals enclosed his only path of retreat and freed of the gate, the dragon circled overhead with a smug air. Daryx and the other paladins jumped off Executioner's back and they encircled him. He tried to claw at one and while he succeeded in scoring a bloody wound, that snake-like sword found its way around his remaining head. Dar Kendra commanded, "Stop."

His body quivered aching to attack but fear of failure and his Master's wrath made him listen. Daryx stood next to Dar Kendra and ever so slowly, Executioner felt razor spikes extrude along the coil around his neck. Daryx bowed with a flourish. "Hellhound, it has been a while since we have seen one of you outside of the Valley. I am Dar Malyx, of Morbatten. I believe you know us, my comrades, and what will happen to you should you die here. What name do you go by?"

"I," his voice seethed with rage and hatred. "I am Executioner. Humble servant of Orcus the all-powerful."

Kendra twisted her wrist and the spikes dug into his throat. "Speak that name again and you die permanently."

"What do you want of me drow?" Venomous spit drooled from his mouth as his other head began regenerating.

Daryx replied, "The same thing you do. To accomplish our mission. Of course, right now our missions are at odds with each other. You are here to first recover your master's wand yes? We will make a trade. In exchange for telling us where it is, we will let you return alive to your master."

The hound looked at the dark elf and saw the gleam in his eyes. "You enjoy this drow. Too much."

Daryx shrugged, "You know, I really do. The pleasure of well-laid plans and to bring one such as you down, fills me with delight. I live for your humiliations." He laughed. "If I still served Lolth, no doubt she would

364

enjoy this as much as do I. Tell us where the wand is, or die. Takhissis will be just as pleased with the death of you and your brother as She will be with the wand."

Executioner seethed. He looked around noting that, even if he could escape death by Kendra's sword, there were at least ten paladins, thirty priests, and that mage. Clearly, the mage would be key as he controlled the several hundred earth elementals cutting him off. And then he would have to deal with the dragon. That one, Blade, would make a mighty dracolich someday. Even if he cut down the mage, he would still die. Even if he destroyed the dragon, he would still die. Even if he, and herein he knew he had lost, while he might slay one, the others would end him.

"Orc-, my master, said the wand waited for us here. You interrupted our feeding. From there we would seek out the wand. It is here somewhere." His second head had started to recover. He sniffed the wind, "It is over there," he looked out towards where the lich's mountain lay. Besides his head, which could see now, the wounds on his back and flanks had healed and he felt itchy bumps there.

Daryx demanded, "Has the wand been activated? Is it possessed?"

Executioner sniffed the wind, "No, not yet. But it has identified its prey and lays plans for possession."

Daryx made a hand sign and the group backed away. The dragon pulled back from where the gate had been. "We honor our agreement. You may return to your master."

Executioner growled snapping at the paladins as they backed up. He re-opened the gate. For a just a moment, he considered calling his brothers through. As if reading his thoughts, the dragon's maw began dripping fire. Kendra, who had yet to release her sword's razor grip, whispered, "Permanent death hound. Go home."

He released his tension and her sword uncoiled leaving a necklace of bloody gashes. Executioner snapped at Kendra, who did not flinch, and then jumped up to the gate. It opened just in time and closed behind him. Blade landed on the ground, shaking it with his dragon form. Daryx signaled the Apprentice who nodded and began casting a spell.

Executioner landed in the abyss by the gate and wheeled looking for his brothers. The entire area around the gate had been scorched by Blade's breath weapon. On the portal's stand, the charred skeletons of three of his brothers slowly reknit, mending from the terrible damage they had suffered. His back grew even more itchy and he lengthened his second head to look back. Seven bloody gashes along his back from Daryx's charge slowly mended but the wounds looked wrong, bumpy. Across the wispy plain of chaos and soul worms, a distant figure walked towards them. Their Master came. This would be bad. He could feel Orcus' wrath and curious anger from even this distance.

His brothers had regenerated enough that they began moving, testing out their claws and legs. Their master drew near and his terrible voice demanded report. "Master, the dragon humans, they ambushed us before we even had started. They..."

"Filth. Worm. You are my greatest general and you were ambushed by food? Your brother Mauler is slain and I have cast him back into the muck. Your fate will be..."

"Lord, hear me. The dragon humans they do not know, they asked where your sceptre lay and I lied to them. All is not lost."

Orcus grabbed Execution by one of his heads and slammed him down on the steps, breaking bones and shattering his body. The dread god's power held the hound alive and those healing began howling with pleasure as their most powerful brother suffered. One stood up on reforming legs and demanded to know how failure felt, when the bumps on Executioner's back exploded. Each exploded in perfect sequence igniting and feeding the growing ball of fire. Executioner's life burned away and Orcus fell back from the blast. Even the god had to shield himself from the might of Tanian magic exploding in this place. Worse, the power of its destruction caught the attention of the sometimes master of this place.

His hounds dead and burnt to ashes, Orcus took one last glance at the portal closed to him and longed for his own portal to the Tehran world.

366

He noted his enemy would soon arrive and howled fury and hate at the Tehran gate. "Bomoki, my gate! I want it now!" he screamed over and again as he punched the pulped mess of the hellhounds barely alive by Orcus' will. He wanted them dead but he wanted them to suffer and so they lived and they suffered. Another punch and they fell through the ground to Orcus' throneplane.

In the realm of the abyss controlled by Orcus, Executioner and Mauler writhed and twisted in the grip of their brothers. Orcus squatted before them his titanic ram's head leering at them as he studied their agony. "Mauler, you were my fifth. You are now last. That you died at the hands of a stupid dragon, you're pathetic. A worm. And you are of no use to me until you can return to Tehra. Yes, you shall start anew. Bury him in stone and let the ghouls feast on him until his time has passed."

Vampires grabbed Mauler who seized in divine terror and a rapture of agony. Because it is what his creator decreed. He could already feel the ghouls tearing through the stone. At first, only dirty fingernails would scratch him and then the holes would widen and fists would tear into his starving flesh. No food. Hunger. He would be eaten and would heal and would feel everything. Because his master punished him so.

"Master, I'm sorry! Forgive me! It was Executioner's fault!"

Orcus watched the vampires pull Mauler away and then turned his omnipotent gaze on Executioner. The universe of universes that made up Orcus' domain turned to watch as one of the mighty went calm and fell silent. "Executioner, you failed. Your hunger for Tehran blood and ambition betrayed you. To have fallen so easily to the dragon people." Orcus looked up at himself in the sun washing over this world with his pale green rays and roared. "You had one job, one task. Retrieve my wand and open my door. Though you have failed me before, you have never failed in such an easy job." He roared again, its roar echoing out into space and everywhere his creations fell to the ground and covered their ears, or hid from the suns shining the light and fury of their god. "Yet, you did not die and instead brought dragon fire back with you and killed your brothers here. They hunger for your flesh, for your blessings. You who are my mightiest creation, tell me. How is it that you failed and yet did not die at Tehra?"

Executioner drew a careful breath and groveled at his master's gaze. "Divine Father, the dragon humans KNEW, somehow. Daryx and those damned fighters tricked us! I know how to defeat them, allow me to go back. They seek your mighty wand. Forgive me, allow atonement. I am still worthy and will not..."

"Enough!" Orcus roared. "You dare counsel me on strategy?!" He huffed and roared and commanded Executioner, "Down and beg!"

At the command, every bone in Executioner's body burst and shattered and yet the master's power held him alive. "Failure does not advise a god!" Spittle rained down around the broken hound and even the hounds holding Executioner fell back from the master's bellow. He waved his hand over his hound and pulled the dust of his bones and blood into the air, and still he lived. Orcus, master of all unlife, flexed his power and the hellhound that was Executioner reshaped into a wand capped by the hound's skull. Sick green fire and intelligence moved into the wand and Orcus smashed its end into the ground. "Hear me my worshippers! This wand will go to the mightiest of you. Let any who claim it, receive the power to finish what my mightiest hound failed."

The wand began to bleed into the ground and Executioner screamed. Orcus stood and all creation bowed before his glory. "My blessings on you all, and freedom to the victor!"

The god faded into the sun watching down on the world. The bowed creatures, the undead, the living, all held their breaths, and after one heartbeat, two heartbeats, the hellhounds attacked each other. And, across all creation, creation turned on itself and fought for the prize of the wand, and the freedom to have free will. It was their master's will that drove them to so fight. In fighting, each combatant received a measure of free will to choose their tools of war and decide for itself. The undead forgot the living and a great alliance of humans, elves, and dwarves rose up to war for the prize.

Chapter Fifty Six - The Aftermath of Hellhounds

Blade humanshifted to stand and speak with Dar Kendra and Daryx.

Daryx had a particularly pleased look on his face as he heard that their one casualty would recover to full health within the day. He held a small silvery spider in his hand, which jumped to an amethyst circlet on his brow. "The cost of watching the portal, immense as it was, was worth it! The golem spiders Sai made are exquisite! And one yet remains. Having the Order of Water already here, priceless. The dragon emperor will be pleased. Lord Blade, you were masterful! May I ask, how many of the hounds did you catch offguard through the gate?" He sounded giddy. "We have never so thoroughly defeated them. I do believe this is a new record!"

Blade factually stated, "Four. But just in case, I razed the plains around the gate hoping to awaken the chaos lord."

Daryx laughed out loud and even Dar Kendra cracked a smile. "Come Apprentice, come!" Daryx called to the mage. "This could not have been done without the support of the Mage's Guild! We will be sure to let Dar Reznor know the role you played here." The Apprentice bowed low. "Come all of you!" Daryx called out to the group. "Though this is hardly the time or place to celebrate, I want to congratulate you. The emperor wishes to congratulate you! I do believe that this is a new record for how quickly a hellhound has been defeated! In point of fact, as Dread Blade just informed us, there were four on the other side. If all went well, the Mage's Guild's firebombs should have detonated when Executioner met his master." His voice trailed to a low whisper as he spoke and licked his fanged teeth after finishing this thought. "Oh to be there and see it."

General Shak D'Rath spoke. "All our preparations resulted in this flawless victory. I regret only that your newest member, Malcor, could not join us. I do believe he would have enjoyed this. I do believe the Jade God will remember this day." He looked around and counted. "I see all of us have already earned the enmity and spite of the Jade God. Good, so nothing new there." He laughed.

Fists raised and cheers of "hoo rah!" filled the group. When they calmed down, Dar Kendra signaled her desire to speak. "Order of Water, my brothers and sisters! Again, we have defeated a mighty foe. Let the names of those here be recorded in our lore." She bowed deeply to Daryx, and then all present bowed except for Dread Lord Blade. "And let our lore, as always exclude the heroism of Dar Malyx, our benefactor who must not be written. His involvement here shall remain secret."

Daryx nodded and said, "My thanks. I am honored to serve with the Order of Water and advance the Queen's great purpose. We will take a break and then we must speak of the real reason the Order of Water is here. Let us return to your base and make ready to discuss Malcor."

Later that night, with several bonfires burning brightly, the Order of Water, the dread lord Blaze, and Daryx sat in counsel. Daryx relayed their interaction with the lich and noted that Malcor had exhausted his regenerative ring, but is "so very close to his objective." He also shared that Sorian knights had finally arrived and had almost fallen to the lich in the royal house. He laughed describing how the Cuthbert zealots had practically ensured their destruction. "The only real good thing to come of it is the Sorian commander, a Sir Allen who is known to us, has been brought much closer to outright alliance if not friendship with Tania."

"So, the real question is this: knowing that the hellhounds came for our lich, knowing that our lich is not yet necromantic, and knowing that," and he was interrupted.

One of the battle priests, a veteran of many seasons of campaigns, rose to ask a question and Daryx conceded to him. "You say not yet necromantic. Do you imply that the lich is still more eldar than of this world? How is that possible?"

Daryx shrugged. "The Circle has discussed this with the emperor. Our best guess is that the lich was cast off into the ether so far from the River that when he resurfaced, this much time had passed. Whether by his choice or by some other eldar event, he became a lich before the Jade God had claimed undeath and sealed that part of the Immortality Quest away to the abyss."

The Apprentice rose and added, "In this world, becoming a lich is only appealing to mages of a certain sort. Cut off from advancement by the ravages of time, the Jade God offers lichdom at the first immortality shrine. In that moment, the mage must decide. The veil between Tehra and the principle dominion is very thin at that shrine and virtually all mages fall to the Jade God there. This lich here, from reports shared by my master Reznor, he is capable of necromancy but executes it through chaos magic, exactly as an eldar does, like the emperor. The more he does it, the more his chaos energy will pull at the necromantic dominion."

Tembri rose. "Is Sir Malcor safe?"

The abrupt shift in topic drew them into silence and Daryx looked up at the night sky carefully choosing his answer. Before he could speak, dread lord Blade stepped forward. Not as proficient at humanshifting as his father and brother, Blade retained a distinctly non-human appearance and his words lisped against his scaled and toothy mouth. "He is not. Our ability to scry him was cut at the same time Daryx spoke with the lich. The high priest Kell visited him in a vision and found him suffering. Kell reports that Malcor pushes himself too hard and his faith has already started to pull away from the Queen towards shadow."

A pregnant silence followed as the faithful members of the Order each reflected back on their early times when their faith had been so sorely tested that they had waivered. Tembri restated, "He is in danger of losing his faith then."

"More to the point," Daryx continued, "is that the lich is aware Tania is watching and has closed his fortress to scrying and no doubt seeks out to know what else we know. This puts more than Malcor's faith in danger. It makes him a magnet for an increasingly desperate lich. Desperation is the heartstone of the Jade God's sceptre. Either the lich or Malcor will find it. Fortunately, the lich is a far more appealing target to the sceptre than Malcor, for now. The Temple has foreseen a contest between the two."

Dar Kendra signaled for silence and turned to Daryx and Blade. "Malcor's last orders, from me, were to seek out the lich and we – the Order - would prepare his victory. You are telling us, telling me, that the

Order will not know when this contest or WHERE this contest will occur. You have left Malcor alone and turned me into a liar. Malcor is not ready for a contest involving the sceptre!"

As she spoke, her eyes flashed and rage burned in her countenance. Daryx did not flinch, but he softened his tone even as Blade's aura ignited the air around him. "My lady, we are doing everything we can to locate him. And…"

"What?" she practically growled at the dark elf as she stepped right into his face.

Daryx stepped back and his eyes narrowed glinting with purple faerie fire. "Dar Kendra, as you yourself know better than most, combat plans -"

"Never survive combat. Yes, you dare to lecture me with catch phrases?"

"You need to hear me out. I understand you are frustrated. So am I. So is Dar Rojo and Dar Kell, and I must tell you the emperor is also not particularly pleased with how this is turning out. Faith Kendra, we must have faith."

"Faith! You dare to speak to me of that?!" Dar Kendra exploded and in an instant her cry that Daryx had betrayed her turned into a dragon-like aura that rose up around her towering in its glory and radiant with silver fire. As she drew her sword, Daryx pulled back, keeping his hand on his sword, but the tension in his body crackled with energy. Blade looked at the two and growled something in draconian. For all present, their leader's anger and frustration sounded a clarion call to action but, like her, they recognized that Daryx was not the real target.

"Faith in Malcor! You need to hear me out," he stated again. "The Circle, the emperor, the Queen – they did not send me here for an execution. When Dar Kell visited Malcor by vision, he found the boy shadow-touched. No prophecies, no portents, no plan for that either Kendra. He most certainly is a member of this Order, but as a shadow-touched, he belongs to Kell." She stepped forward and to Daryx's credit he stepped into her sword tip as if daring her to skewer his neck. "You've seen what happens in Bloodstone with the cascades. You know our history. If the

Sceptre becomes aware that Malcor is bound to Cor'tanos AND you all go piling on AND Tania sends all of its resources to assist, a Cascade will happen. Here. On Khasra. Think about it Kendra. We lose Malcor, 100% sure. Not only do we lose most of the Order, but we lose the shadow dragons to the Jade God. I guarantee you, as much as the Queen hates Cor'tanos, the shadow dragons enslaved as dracoliches to the Jade God? That would be a nightmare we might never undo."

Her gleaming fire raged around her as she fought for self-control. Finally, she turned and smashed her fire towards the river. In its passing, molten soil and glassed stone hissed and lit the darkness stretching to the river. Blade roared into the heavens and then it fell silent. Kendra glowered at Daryx. "One of these days elf," she swore.

"Drow, or dark elf, please. And the pleasure will be mine *human*."

Blade looked at Daryx and then began laughing. His dragonvoice rumbled deep and then spilled out hoarsely. "You are so amusing." His eyes darted back and forth between the two several times, "Alone, either of you might triumph but I cannot foresee who would win."

Kendra started to reply that it would be her but Daryx beat her to the point. "Only Tania's enemies would lose in such a fight. Please, think this through. You out of all people understand best what shadow-touched means. Malcor does not have much time."

"Did my brother name him?"

"Yes, he named the boy after his own surname – Kell'Tayris. Cor'tanos will come for him the same as he came for Kell. To our benefit, the boy is young and surrounded by allies who know what to look for. Unlike Kell though, Malcor's youth and berserker rage edge him towards Cor'tanos. The emperor does not think the truce will provide any protection."

General D'Rath interrupted, "Lord Malyx, I doubt most here know of the truce." The General turned to them all, "As you know, the Queen cast the shadow dragons out. They took home in the plane of shadows past the gates of destruction. Because it is anti-life and inert, the shadow dragons are losing their potency, their power, and have lost their ability to procreate. They are slowly dying as a race. They were looking for a way out when Kell first uncovered the doctrine of dragonshifting. There has been a truce ever since. The truce allows the shadow dragons to interact with dragonshifters choosing or becoming shadow dragons, like Kell and now Malcor. It prevents them from fully re-entering the world until the Queen or a dragonshifter allows it. Kell does not. Malcor is far away from where we can guide him in how to handle this."

The general closed his eyes and said, "The emperor related it to us like this. He said, *My children are many and multiply. Should your shadow touch any of them, they will become a bridge between our doctrines. Brother, the shadow is no place for a dragon. You must come back into the light.*"

Dar Kell, a rage-filled former paladin and then priest was the first to be shadow-touched by Cor'tanos. The Kell Conflict that consumed the empire left many scars, but the Circle knew the truth. It took Kell years to master and eventually tame the darkness that filled him. Though Malcor did not have the same sorrow and suffering, Daryx said, "Malcor is young, Kendra, and feels great pressure as a son of Kell to bring glory to the Order of Water. His desire to succeed and his youth both make him prey to Cor'tanos," Daryx said. "So, the question isn't IF. And it isn't WHO TO BLAME. It is what we do about it. At least we know and at least Malcor will be far less formidable than your brother was. Plus, we have the lich to deal with."

"Truly? He is shadow-touched like Kell?" Kendra whispered.

Tembri chose that time to stand as did many others in the Order. Soon all stood with an attitude of anticipation and fire. Kendra and Daryx broke their warring gaze and looked at them. "You all have questions…"

"No," Kendra interrupted the dark elf. "They stand with their brother. We will attack the fortress head on, even if Tania will not aid us. I accept the risk of a Cascade and put my faith in Malcor's fighting heart. Now. Begin your preparations, all of you."

The camp erupted into action. Kendra turned to Blade and bowed, "Dread Lord, would you like to ally with us?"

Blade licked his lips spilling fire like drool. "Aye, I will."

Daryx smiled and before Kendra could ask he said, "My place is not here, however, I will prepare contingencies in your favor. Remember, my task and goal is the wand." He looked at Blade and almost reminded him that it was the dragon's task as well. He decided against it. "The hounds confirmed it is in this direction. I would use your attack and Malcor's rescue as a distraction to find and secure it."

Kendra frowned and he said, "So I will be with your cause, but consider, should I fail and Malcor shadowshifts in the presence of the wand, or the lich is taken by it. I must obey the emperor." He bowed and withdrew from the belligerent conversation.

"Fool," Kendra spat at the ground where Daryx had stood.

Blade returned to his human form and clapped her shoulder. "You are all fools to play games with my father, but tonight Kendra, you are my fool. It has been too long since I have seen you unleashed."

Chapter Fifty Seven - Tembri

From the shadows, Malyx watched Blade and Kendra walk away from the camp together. He smirked. *These humans*. He turned and went to look for Malcor's battle priest. He had to consult a note to remember the fellow's name. "Tembri, may we have a word?"

Tembri rose from where he had set out his armor, potions, and weapons, in addition to his basic underground gear. When he saw the elf, he bowed and said, "Of course Dar Malyx. Of course." General D'Rath walked up to them as well.

"Your ward Malcor, it is likely that either Kendra's attack or Malcor reaching the prize draws out the lich or the wand. The emperor made it very clear that Tania cannot afford to have the wand take possession of an eldar or Malcor. If either happens, we must withdraw and set defensive plans." Seeing the priest's coming objections, he continued, "But, that won't happen because you will reach Malcor first. That is, if you can refrain from doing anything overtly battle priesty."

D'Rath nodded. "The boy is precious to the empire. Alerius counts him already as a jewel of Tania. But, should the sceptre become aware of him, should the sceptre take him, we will have to slay him."

Tembri looked at both of them. "You have seen this?" They nodded. "If it means saving Malcor, yes, I can do anything."

"Even if it means passing up a golden combat opportunity, full of glory? Even if the Queen's voice directs you to engage?"

Tembri looked at them both with distaste. "I am a priest, disobeying the Queen is not an option."

"Sure it is! I'm not talking about heresy or apostasy. I'm only saying that this whole quest is the Queen's will for Malcor. If he falls to either the lich, the shadows, or the sceptre, well then we have all disobeyed the Queen!" D'Rath rumbled this out his voice rasping a bit and Tembri had to remember that, though he looked like it, the general was not a paladin - a great officer and hero but not a paladin.

Tembri reflected back on his long career. "I see you twisting different objectives to suit your needs, but one thing is crystal clear to me. Malcor was entrusted to me and he is important. I will do whatever it takes to respect that trust. I will not let him down nor will I fail in my duty to safeguard him."

Daryx smiled, "Excellent. I am going to clear this with Kendra so that, well you know how she is." He turned and walked off.

D'Rath remained. "Tembri, had things gone differently, we would have brought the boy with us to face the hellhounds. But with Kell finding him shadowtouched, it is too risky to have him known to the Jade God just yet. We cannot control when, but Bloodstone would be the ideal place and time. I felt you should know."

Tembri smiled, "That makes sense and is more in keeping with normal paladin training. I worry that Malcor will be so far alienated from the rest of the knights that he will be more pariah than prodigy."

"He serves, as do we all. His way though is more... complex. He is lucky to have you as his priest Tembri."

"He is lucky to have so many aware of and thinking about him," Tembri countered.

"Tell me," the General said, "do you remember our last campaign at Bloodstone? The one with the mine and that dwarven overseer – Bostic?"

Tembri, feeling the shift in conversation, flowed with it. "Yes, I will never forget it. I can still see Bostic guarding the beer against the horde of zombies. I don't remember ever having laughed so hard in all my time there."

They started swapping other stories and a healer brought them food and refreshment while Tembri finished packing. Several hours later, the Apprentice found Tembri and they bowed to each other.

The Apprentice held out a ring and scroll. "The ring will make you into an invisible gas. The scroll will summon an elemental of air to transport you to where Malcor lies. The elemental has been instructed to take you where you want to go "with all due haste". That means very quickly. The world will pass by as a blur and only your willpower and focus will take you to Malcor. Since we and the air elemental do not know exactly where he is, the elemental can only use your desire as a guide.

"So, that being said, if you pass through the actual treasure room where the soul gem is, or you pass by the lich and you feel you could take him by surprise, or you encounter the Jade God's wand… any of these things, if you even notice them, will cause the air elemental to drop you. As a priest, I expect you have an ability to stay focused. The issue will not be that so much as if you see these golden opportunities and the Queen's voice begins speaking and you listen, you will be dropped where you are. Do you understand?"

Tembri nodded. "Yes, I must remain focused on Malcor, no matter what. I can do that. Tell me, what will I find when I reach the boy?"

"It depends," the Apprentice shrugged. "We have excellent records of Lord Kell's challenges. It is very early and so he should seem normal enough. The issue will be when he rages, or despairs, or sees some goal he cares about slipping away. In those moments, if he asks the shadows for help or overly-relies on them, he will begin feeding the shadows' dominion. Cor'tanos is after all, an eldar. He has felt the power of worship from Kell and hungers for more no doubt.

"Malcor is travelling with the original group of Imperics, though we do not know how many remain. I suspect that you'll find him looking tired, haggard, and travel worn. The regenerative ring is not the same as the Queen's healing. He will have scars that will never go away. Kell said he looked 'ravaged' was the word I think he used."

"Will I need to kill the Imperics?"

"I doubt it. They seem fascinated by Malcor. Tell them you were captured by the lich from the Tanian group in Ori, and managed to escape. It's not the best story, but it'll explain how a powerful battle priest is in the Fortress. My opinion Tembri is that they will be so grateful to have another member of the group that it will not be an issue."

They discussed the general tactical situation and then Tembri asked, "I have one last question. You said that the loss of a desired goal could trigger Mal. He has a strong desire to be a knight. Though not yet fully a knight, I'm curious. How did Dar Kell handle the loss of consecration?"

"Well said. The shadow dragons never joined the Queen and She cut them off. In spite of the emperor's attempts to win them back, they are not back yet. As such, you should look at shadowshifting as a desecration of the soul. Malcor is not yet powerful enough to feel the consequences, but Kell? He was a mighty and high-ranking paladin and then became a priest capable of defeating the most powerful priestess of our generation. His desecration pushed his insanity to levels you'd expect from a demon. With the boy, until he understands what is happening, he may not even notice it at all. The exception will be the River, which he moves freely in. That will change for him and I'm sure he will notice that. Hopefully, he confuses it as part of his progression rather than an obstacle. But, Tembri, Kell stopped shifting years ago when he understood the consequences. Only the shadows coming back to the Queen will fully restore what he has lost."

"Will his father help him I wonder." Both men looked at each other, neither knowing. Tembri let the silence hang and then speculated, "Kell visited him though when scrying failed. So, I would guess yes. The shadow dragons, they are not a doctrine I have studied very much. There is a story of Kell when he attacked one of the provinces and their armies. He dragon shifted and destroyed the entire army. Is that possible? To do so without being wounded?"

"It is for a shadow dragon. Their realm is far past the River's ending. As such, they exist at the end of Time and the end of life. They are anti-life. Darkness is their cloak but light, especially in this realm, gives them power. While it exposes them, they do not have bodies the way we do here. Here, if I cut you with a knife, you bleed. The shadow dragons do not as there is nothing to cut. To hurt them, you must have weapons that reach into the shadow realms where they actually are. That being said, their time and function in this realm is limited. Their powers change with the light, almost at random. When possessed fully, Dar Kell described it as if he watched the dragon and it felt like reading a book about the events he did. He had no control and did not care."

"If he did not care, how did he create so much death?"

"They cannot seem to help it. This world is the opposite of everything they understand and believe in. Consider this, the fire dragons they see us as creatures of emotion. That emotion can be beautiful by virtue of faith, commitment, and devotion. It can also be beautiful by how quickly it flares and then drowns in the River. The shadow wyrms, they do not see it or even care for it. Uncaring, they do not restrain themselves. They are terrifying all the time. They are dragons all the time. They do not shackle their powers the way the emperor and his children do. As Kell once told us, "I could speak, but why would it matter what you might hear or say back to me? If you heard my words, why would it matter at all?" So, you see, if Malcor does this, your only real options are to remove him to a safe place, knock him out, or remove yourself to a safe place away from him."

Chapter Fifty Eight - The Attack Begins

Back at camp, the group had assembled, ready for war. Tembri and the Apprentice joined them as Kenda and General D'Rath led their briefing. "Order of Water, your earrings are updated with the most current maps prepared by our thieves and scouts. We will enter the southern side of the mountain and take a short cut to a main tunnel. We also have word that the Sorian knights have reached the main entrance. We will be breaching the fortress just before they do. This creates a two flank approach. Once inside, we will divide into two groups and sweep the fortress slaying anything in your path, dividing in half at each branch to unit size. Thereafter, the units will determine their own approach. There are three exceptions: the lich, the sceptre, and Malcor. Dar Blade, the Apprentice, and I will circle the mountain and be ready. Contact me when any of these are found. Come now, we pray and say farewell to R'Dar Tembri who is tasked with the objective of finding and securing Malcor."

All present clasped their hands on their weapons and bowed their heads. The prayer, a hymn comparing human desire for glory to a dragon's lust for treasure rose and ebbed through the night. As they sang, Tembri slipped on the ring and vanished followed by a stiff breeze that tore through the trees around them and darted towards the lich's fortress.

The Apprentice then began casting a teleport spell. When the hymn ended, the entire group of warriors stood at the base of a granite cliff. A small crack opened into dark wall in front of him. Blade dragonshifted behind them and took Dar Kendra onto his neck. The Apprentice walked to the small crack and began another enchantment and then pushed his hand forward against the rock wall. His hand pulsed and when it touched the wall, the wall disintegrated in a straight line opening a circular tube almost thirty feet in diameter that stretched into the mountain.

He slumped back on his staff and a nearby paladin caught him. "The tunnel," he choked, "should remain open for the next quarter hour." The paladin helped him walk back to Lord Blade, where a giant dragon claw scooped the Apprentice up and placed him in Dar Kendra's care. Battle priests prayed and silenced the entire group, which came alive with Tanian hand signing. As one, row by row, the Tanians ran into the magical tunnel.

Blade flexed his titanic wings and the heat generated by his body set the ground astir with clashing wind currents. He jumped and spread his wings and soared into the night sky. Down below, the left side of the Tanian knights peeled off to the left tunnel as the right did the same. As they ran, the battle priests behind the knights readied themselves for combat even as the healers readied themselves to heal, and if needed to fight. The Queen's Prayer lent speed to their movements and each column fell on scattered patrols and wandering monsters with swift and sudden execution. Their surprise attack would be total. Their victory, as always, would be flawless. Girded in their faith, they knew this.

At almost the same time, Blade came around the front of the mountain and they saw the Sorian knights break the war band at the mountain's entrance. Unlike Malcor's group, they fought with battle-hardened determination and slew the entire band before entering. Down in the plain by the river bridge, another small band of so-called heroes crossed the bridge and tried to ignore the taunts of the towers' armies.

Unseen, Tembri had blown past the Sorians just before their fight and proceeded at a dizzying pace through chambers and side tunnels that left torches sputtering behind them and knocked patrols and undead to the ground. Just now, they dove down a humid tunnel and through a water sodden chamber full of some kind of worm creatures. Through it, they blew passing up into better maintained chambers. They hurtled around a bend and saw a group of Imperics fighting an army of goblins in front of oversized golden doors. Some type of undead, mighty, stood in disguise watching the combat and for just a second seemed to stare right at Tembri. He steeled his resolve to Malcor, and they gusted through a crack in the door to the other side.

The signs of combat showed in this next space with fragmented walls and fire-scorched ground. Moldering corpse fragments waited for something and then they spiraled to the side around some other mighty undead that also seemed to sense them. Up ahead another group of adventurers fought a horde of undead seeking to overwhelm them by numbers.

Tembri turned to watch wondering if it was the lich and then caught his focus almost too late. The air elemental wavered and then continued in its spiral down into a hole that lasted forever. When they came back into light, gold coins, dust, and fragments of treasure littered the floor but grew more frequent till at last they came to a round seal imprinted with purple-glowing eldar runes. The air pressed against the seal, reaching for cracks and then smashed again and again into any likely candidates. When none presented themselves, the elemental began swirling around the edges of the seal and the surrounding walls, floor, and ceiling.

Eventually, some openings were found that entered into unformed caverns of crystal and ore, or into hidden storerooms, and some into ambushes set to entrap those looking for riches. Malcor was not here though and so the elemental blew out the way they had entered rising up through the pit and back into the tunnel where it came to a large open room full of stone rooms carved into the side of the cavern and lit by quartz crystals near which lanterns had been hung. In the center of the room, a small band of heroes stood against a rising tide of skeletal warriors and even as Tembri recognized Malcor, the air elemental stopped moving and then vanished as a light wind. Tembri deactivated the gaseous ring took note of his position several hundred paces from the main fighting.

Chapter Fifty Nine - Tembri Joins Malcor's Party

Malcor stood between the horde and the three Imperics at his back who launched attacks and tried to protect Malcor's sides. More and more skeletons pulled out of the walls and rose up from the ground and moved forward. Though Malcor hewed them as if with a scythe, Tembri saw the exhausted fatigue of a knight stretched too thin. He had the same spastic movements he had witnessed during that five day long Rite of Pain.

Watching his ward, Tembri felt the Queen's Voice rise up in his heart as if it would burst him asunder with sorrow; no paladin should be so abandoned. He choked it back saving the power for the coming battle. His mace dropped to his hand and a shield to his strong left arm. The shield and mace emblazoned with the Queen's insignia started to rage fire against the undead, but Tembri held that back as he charged.

He rolled into the back of the horde like a boulder and when his momentum slowed, he unleashed the Queen's Voice. A column of fire leapt up from his feet incinerating the enemies around him and then the flame strike pulsed outwards in its width dropping every skeleton within ten paces of him. As the flame column died, Tembri cried out to Malcor and in the Queen's Divine Name commanded the skeletons between him and the boy to "Die!" Against the Bloodstone veteran's command and faith, hundreds of skeletons puffed into white powdery dust.

In the space, Malcor looked up with a measure of hope and saw Tembri. Unconsciously and as per his training, he hand signed for healing and Tembri pointed his mace at the boy and poured his soulful prayer to the boy. Like a dragon awakening from a long sleep, Malcor felt the Queen's power and as it swelled his muscles with health and vigor, he charged to meet Tembri. At the distance though, he saw Tembri continuing to pour his healing energy even as the horde finally recovered and turned on the priest. With perfect execution, Malcor saw Tembri neither flinch nor deviate from his master's command for healing even as swords, spears, and razor claws began tearing through Tembri's armor and unprotected flesh.

Malcor signaled for a defensive position and like a machine, Tembri unleashed another flame strike. The skeleton biting through his helmet scorched away to dust and in the space, the two met clasping hands. "Tembri," Malcor said his voice choking with emotion. "I had almost forgotten what this is like." He called back to the Imperics that help had arrived.

Tembri whirled and swept the oncoming wave of undead back with shield and mace. "Sir Malcor, we can catch up later. Kendra sent me and I know where we must go. What is your situation?"

Back to back, they fought working their way towards the others. Hiroshi's training and skills mattered for nothing against an enemy like this and they saw him pulled down under that relentless tide of clutching white bone stabbing down and rising red. Jaga and the others saw them and began working towards them. Malcor called out to Tembri, "We need to get out of this. Lead on Tembri."

Tembri nodded and stepped back behind Malcor, his voice already rising in prayer. In moments, both he and Malcor grew to the size of hill giants. Fortified by strength and size, they swatted the skeletons aside and ground them to dust. Malcor picked up Sako and Noboyuki while Tembri grabbed Jaga and then they sprinted, scattering their foes as they ran. Both placed the Imperics in the passage leading towards the pit and then grabbed shattered stone tiles and hurled them at the overhead ceiling. A deadly rain of debris and boulders would not stop the skeleton tide, but it would buy them time. They then turned, grabbed up the Imperics and sprinted to the pit.

In giant form, they dropped down into the pit bracing their hands and legs against opposite walls and began climbing down. "We have to hurry," Tembri said. "Soon the horde will sense us. Priest of Imperius, are you able to mask us?" he called to Noboyuki.

Noboyuki looked at the newcomer with suspicion and then nodded. "I can, if that is what Jaga or Malcor desires." Jaga nodded and he began praying to Imperius as the giants shimmied their way down.

Sako touched Malcor's face and whispered to him, "Malcor, who is this?"

385

Malcor shrugged. "He's Tanian, I recognize him as a hero of the realm. Beyond that, he is someone who is helping us." She nodded and Malcor said, "I'm sorry about Hiroshi. He was an excellent thief." Holding his face, she began crying her tears leaving clean streaks down her face.

It took almost an hour to climb to the bottom of the pit. When they at last reached the bottom and returned to normal size, Malcor was relieved to hear Tembri formally introduce himself to the others and Malcor. "I am Tembri, a battle priest of the dragon queen Takhissis and a citizen of Morbatten. I was part of the group sent by the emperor at Ori's request for aid, but were driven out by the lich and I was captured. The lich has been holding me as a hostage, but I managed to escape. It seems you aren't the only ones in the mountain these days." He hefted his mace. "Are any of you in need of healing? The Queen urges me to secure the group."

Noboyuki had exhausted his power during the horde attack and everyone had suffered terrible wounds in addition to fatigue. Tembri healed them all as if they had never been hurt. Malcor saw their amazement and said, "I knew you are a hero of Tania. I recognize you from one of my reviews. You are stationed with a group of paladins?"

Tembri nodded. "Yes, I joined with Dar Kendra and a few others to come and help Ori. It will not surprise the priest here that my leadership had a falling out with the royal family over what approach to take. I went out to the southern wall before we left and was ambushed by vampires. Next thing I knew, I was here and the lich was asking me all kinds of questions about Morbatten, Ori, the Isles, everything."

They began walking and when Malcor moved in front of Tembri, Tembri gasped. "Boy, your back, what happened?"

Malcor looked over his shoulder, "We had a fight with some pretty powerful undead." Before he could say anymore, Sako began telling Tembri the entire story of how Malcor had defeated multiple ogres and then dropped the two wraiths and the vampire.

Tembri stopped and demanded to see Malcor. He noted the dragon tear, now scaled over with lightless void black scales. Malcor had puncture, burn, acid, amputation, and several other scars but the worst by far was the jagged cut from his hip over his spine to the back of his head. "Your name is Malcor right? If you want, I have some of my Tanian gear that might fit you. Armor, things of that nature."

Tembri took out Malcor's armor and standard paladin gear. Being his, it fit perfectly and Malcor flexed feeling its might and remembering how well it protected him. "My thanks."

At that moment, the ground shook and dull exploding "thud" caused dust to rain down from the ceiling. A few stones along the pit walls fell filling the cavern with thunderous noise. "What is that?" Jaga asked nervously.

"As I said, you are not the only ones in the mountain." Following his words, another rumble shook the ground. "I think the ogres said there were at least five groups here now." Tembri touched the dragon insignia on Malcor's armor. "I will pray for you Malcor." Both bowed their heads and Malcor found himself standing with Tembri on the banks of the River. The River looked different though, dimmer. Black gray tendrils floated around him. He dismissed it.

"It's good to see you Tembri. I take it that Dar Kendra ordered a full out assault?"

Tembri nodded and smiled, "It is good to see you too Sir Malcor, but damn if you did not get cut up worse than we imagined. We don't have much time so let me be brief. We are about an hour or so away from a giant golden seal. On the other side is either the lich, the soul gem, the wand of the Jade God, or any mix of those. The Order will not be here when we breach the seal. Your second rite, the plans, it was never intended you would face the lich alone."

"I am not alone R'Dar Tembri. I have you. I have my new Imperic friends. They know of my desire to fight the lich."

Tembri choked suddenly overcome with emotion. "Sir Malcor, you do me great honor. I must however counsel you – "

"Stop, the plan was always for me to face the lich. The Order would help, and it has. If the Queen's will is that I succeed, I will. I know it."

Tembri looked at Malcor awash in the ether and saw the boy's glorious faith and determination. He also saw a black splinter like poison radiating from the tear drop scale on his arm. In this place, it hurt to even look at it. He reached out, his own hand radiant like a star and cut through by red and blue bands of light to the wound. Malcor held it forward and described the vision and the circumstances of the wound. "It still bleeds sometimes, though I feel myself changing rather than the wound healing."

"You must be careful Malcor. Being a knight requires an iron will and undeviating faith in the Queen. Berserkers do not last long in the ranks of the paladin. This can be a gift, but it can also be a curse. We'll figure it out. There is not a single hero or legendary character in all the world that did not overcome some terrible obstacle or impossible sacrifice in their journey. Even the Queen lost Her Consort when Heaven and Hell rose up from the River."

Malcor took it all in and said, "We should get back. Try to avoid berserking. You're a hero. The door with the golden seal opens to something bad. I got it. Tembri, I trust you. We got this."

The prayer ended and both of them sank back into the River. Malcor felt the blessing like a warm blanket drape over him, and they continued on through the passageway lit by torch and lantern. Trails of dust drifted down in streaming tendrils. Their footfalls and hushed conversation chased them to where the giant seal finally appeared. From a distance it looked normal-sized, illuminated by torches burning to either side. They walked on through the interminable darkness not realizing how large the seal was until suddenly, the darkness ended and they stepped in the light shining around it. A dragon could easily fly through the seal. An inscription at shoulder height wrapped around a hand-sized hole reaching into the seal.

Sako cast a spell and the inscription resolved itself to her view. "It says that treasure beyond our imagination lies behind the seal, and congratulations on having made it this far. That is all."

Chapter Sixty - The Lich's Treasure

The lich sat on what he had come to think of as his throne. At that thought, the chair shifted and became ever more like a throne worthy of a king. The pool of water he used for scrying had been dark since he had ceased any and all scrying magic in his mountain. "My mountain," he voiced rolling the words around in his jaw. "My throne," he whispered, gripping the arm rests and shaking it.

One of the ogres down by the entryway looked up with a mix of dread and interest and then looked away quickly when the lich met his gaze. "You wish to speak?" the lich rasped.

The ogre flinched and then flexed its strong arms and turned to bow to the lich. "It's nothing my lord. All this time I have served you, never have I heard you speak so." The lich looked at the ogre and on a whim blinked to stand right next to it. The ogre flinched but quickly recovered and dropped to his enormous knee. "How may I serve you lord?"

"I want to show you something, and while we walk, tell me what you know of Ori, Morbatten, and this new place Taysor." The lich walked through the entryway into a grand hall. After several hundred steps, stairs roughly cut led down.

The ogre stammered as they walked, "Ori is the city of humans we fight. Well, fought before you ordered us to stop. Every season, we rally war bands to raid their settlements. Sometimes we win, most of the time we are paid by orcs to help. For the other places, I have heard of them but do not know if I ever fought them. Morbatten is the dragon people. Crazy people who think only of dragons. They fight good. Taysor is better. They have bright shiny and valuable gear we can take for treasure. They look nice but not all of them are good fights. I once heard that smart ogres could join Morbatten, but why would that be done? I don't know. Taysor kills us."

The lich listened and then asked, "If you were smarter would you, join Morbatten I mean?"

The ogre's voice rose. "I smart enough. I don't know. I like fights. If Morbatten had lots of fights, I could."

The stairs ended at a magically sealed door, a smaller version of the giant seal Malcor had encountered. They stopped there and the lich stared at the ogre making it uncomfortable. Finally, the ogre could not stand it anymore and dropped to his knees, "Master if I offended with jabber, forgive."

"No, it's not that. I have a job. A special task that I cannot do for myself. It is very dangerous for you, but if you do well, you will be rewarded with power and wealth you cannot imagine now. I will also increase your intelligence so that you can outwit and outthink any of your fellows, even the clever orcs. Interested?" The lich touched the seal and it rolled sideways into the wall.

The room beyond illuminated with magical lights reflected off a mountain of treasure. The walls themselves, carved through a large vein of gold ore gleamed and sparkled. The ogre sputtered and forgot to breathe. "Master, this is more than we took from Ori – "

"Yes, I know. That is beside the point." The ogre started to walk in but the lich stopped him from crossing the threshold. "I cannot enter right now. See there?" The lich pointed along the ogre's sight to a stone dais drowning in metal coins and golden treasure. Only part of its leading edge remained visible and on it rested a green-glowing wand the color of mucus. As long as a man, the grip appeared to be made of a twisting spine and its top lay crowned by a skeletal ram's head. The ram horns curled down and around the ram's face framing its empty eye sockets.

Under the ogre's scrutiny, those voided eyes began to glow and suddenly the ogre felt a need to seize it. The lich touched him, for real this time, and freezing cold shocked the ogre into awareness and he looked to his master. "You feel it too then. This is my problem. That thing appeared here some days ago. It calls to me and offers me things I have never cared about, but over time, I am beginning to care and I should not. I do not know what it is. Do NOT look at it again for now."

The lich pointed to the massive golden seal door along the side wall to their right. "On the other side of that is the first group that might make it. When they come through, I want to be right here and I want you to go and pick up that green wand so that you grabbing it is the first thing they see."

Something about the lich's voice made the ogre feel like that would be the most incredible thing ever. He could already see all his dreams and desires coming true. The wand also seemed to offer him power; what could go wrong? The ogre nodded, "Yes, yes! I will do this for you!"

To ensure the ogre did not compromise his plans, the lich paralyzed the ogre where he stood. "I'm going to block your eyes so that you don't find yourself obsessing over the marvelous wand that will make you powerful." The lich leaned back against the wall and thought about what this Daryx and the Sir Allen had said. It had been so long, too long since he had really thought of anything being his own. "So much changed while I was lost... If I give my soul gem to this Malcor, what then? Can I abide lesser beings? Do I want to be a god?" After a time of being lost in his own musings, he summoned one of his wraiths and sent it wheeling to the other side of the great seal. "Give them incentive to come through or break them," he ordered. The wraith lingered a bit though and the lich commanded it to speak.

"You ordered us to watch and report to you on the events. The lower group, no one knows where they came from or how they entered the lower fortress. They have split into twelve groups and are destroying any and everything they encounter. Even the vampires, even the orcs and their shamans, even the sorcerous ogres are cut to pieces. They decapitate the fallen so the fallen die. They appear to be searching for something. One of the ogres said they are dragon people from Morbatten. The other group, the ones you met - Sir Allen - have entered the upper chambers. They just finished slaying all of the pool worms. There are some other groups at varying points but they are either trapped or dying or will be soon. Your orders remain?"

"Have the outer armies enter the fortress and attack Sir Allen's group. Awaken all that sleep and have them attack the dragons. Send word to the orc host that the time has come to destroy Ori."

The wraith fled to carry out the lich's orders. The lich noted how the motes of energy had accelerated their pull along its body. His decay horrified him. Always so sure, he struggled with uncertainty of decision. Before, none of this mattered. Things happened because an eldar made it happen. The more powerful, the longer the change endured. The lich knew, a crucial moment had arrived. This next group of moments would flow in a straight line... like an epiphany, the lich slammed his fist into the wall. Time flowed. The consequences would be real. In his mind, that ram skull smiled and whispered to him about a new eternity as god.

Daryx and Allen's words though conflicted with this Jade God's promise and the lich suddenly wished he had conversed with Daryx longer. He felt a tidal pull of magic in the next room and knew he did not have much time left. Just in case, walked back to the scrying pool now filled with blood. A spectral green light filled it now making the blood look coagulated and purple-black. That voice whispered, "Come and see! Look on me and reign supreme as my right hand. None shall ever mock or make you afraid again."

The lich's hand wavered and he almost scried the treasure room where the ram's skull wand sat. Instead, he steeled his will and removed his gauntlet. Whispering in the eldar tongue, he touched the stone one last time, maybe and then said reverently, "Malcor, I give this to you. I hope to meet you one day in the body." The gauntlet bearing the soul gem pulled under the blood and vanished.

Malcor ate some of Tembri's rations, remembering how much he hated military food back when he was not starving and fighting for his life every moment. It tasted delicious and he wolfed it down. Jaga noted, "This whole thing is a trap. I'm not going to stick my hand in that hole. Too bad Hiroshi didn't... oh sorry Sako. We'll figure it out. It'll be okay. I promise."

Sako nodded trying not to choke up again. She sat back against the wall and looked around, "Maybe there are hidden doors, bypasses?"

Though Tembri knew there were not bypasses, he shrugged. "We could look but come what may, we must get to the other side of this door. I'm sure we will not be left alone for long."

Noboyuki studied the scene from more of a distance. "Such a large door. For such a small treasure. The wealth of Ori does not require a door like this. Neither do the few souls taken in Ori. I have consulted the great god Imperius and though no answer came, I know in my heart that great danger lies behind this seal."

Tembri walked over to Noboyuki and they both studied the door. "I feel it too. Destiny and valor are on the other side, and I feel great evil. Anxious waiting on this side. I was too long a prisoner to sit here idle. What do you recommend?"

Noboyuki, dwarfed by Tembri's large frame, was caught off guard by Tembri's request. "Surely, your own Queen has provided you with –"

"She has not. There is an enchantment over this place that blocks our connection to the divine. At least for communication."

"Oh. Well, there's the obvious hole into which a hand or something is supposed to be placed. Jaga, did your map refer to a key perhaps? No," he saw Jaga shake his head. "We could test it by inserting something."

Malcor interjected, "If the lich is expecting a hand, I'm sure there is something that would detect that and, assuming it is trapped, would fall to the person inserting the object."

Sako said, "I could fire a magical bolt into the hole from a distance."

They all agreed that they should do that. They removed themselves to the maximum distance from which she could cast her magical missile. The four glowing darts Malcor had seen her use in virtually all of their combats shot out from her chest and struck one after another into the hole. Immediately, as if a gong strike, the seal and then the chamber made a loud metallic booming sound. It rose in volume until they had to cover their ears. Eventually, it faded by degrees and they returned to see the inscription had changed.

Sako read it, "My armies come for you. Why so scared? Lend me your hand."

"I'll do it," Malcor stated rolling up his sleeve to the scaled over teardrop.

An argument promptly erupted. If Malcor lost the use of his arm, or were immobilized, they would lose their most powerful fighter. Each would be rendered useless in a fight. So it came to the contributions to a fight. Without meaning to, all eyes turned to Jaga and his look of annoyance spoke volumes about how he felt. "Sako, Noboyuki, you both owe me big time. As leader I will not."

Tembri smirked and said, "Do it and my Queen will heal you should anything happen, if you're bold like a dragon."

"We don't know anything will actually happen Jaga san," Noboyuki said reassuringly. "I will help heal you as well should, you know. Malcor has suffered far worse wounds in the past few days than losing a limb. Without him, you, or I, or any of us would have taken those wounds and perhaps died long before reaching this point."

Sako added, "Think of the treasure and fame Jaga! It will be all you as the fearless and brave leader and his adventurers who saved Ori!"

Jaga seemed caught in indecision and his eyes darted from their eyes to the hole in the door. "I…"

"Jaga," Malcor said. "I will come back to Ori with you and tell everyone of your heroic exploits."

"I, uh, okay, but give me a second." Jaga flexed his left hand and paced. He rubbed his fingers together and stared at his hand compulsively. "You guys better get ready because once I do this, I'm either going to die or the door will open. Give me some space and be ready." He started hyperventilating and his pacing became a bit more frantic. He uncorked a small potion flask, "Sake," he said and swallowed the small mouthful. "I was saving it for something special. Kanpai!"

The others made ready. Jaga appeared to work himself into a frenzy and then screamed at the top of his lungs as he ran at the door. He hesitated and slowed as he went to shove his hand in the door. The others cried out their encouragement, and at the last moment, Noboyuki shoved Jaga's hand into the space. Jaga's scream became a shriek and his entire body froze. Everyone waited while beads of sweat rolled down

Jaga's body for something to happen. But when moments turned into enough time that Jaga exhaled and then took a shakey breath, everyone relaxed.

"I feel a gear wheel of some kind," Jaga said. "I really want to take my hand out now. I think I should turn the wheel?" Everyone nodded and he flinched anticipating the worst as he strained to move the gear. Somewhere in the door, a counterweight creaked and then thudded. At the creak and noise, Jaga ripped his hand out of the space and fell back behind Noboyuki's armor. Pale and sweating, he downed the rest of his sake.

Another groaning noise and then chains began clattering. Then they stopped. After a tense moment, a massive counterweight dropped and they felt the thud in the ground. Slowly, ponderously, the golden seal began rotating open. "The trap was to make us think there was a trap?" Malcor speculated. He walked up to the edge as an outline of light appeared.

It took several minutes for the door to move enough for Malcor to see. What he saw confused him. "I see a room full of treasure, more wealth than I have ever seen before. Enough to fill the Fountain of Dragons! There is also an ogre? He is stumbling across the floor with gold ore and coins slowing him down. He seems hypnotized. There is a mound of treasure blocking what he is walking towards, but whatever it is, it is shining with a weird green light."

As Malcor said that, Tembri pulled him back. "That's the wand. I know it. I can feel it. That's the evil I felt. We must be on guard. This entire thing just became a thousand times more dangerous."

The Imperics looked at them both and Malcor said, "Wand? Why would a wand matter? You talk like I know, but I don't."

Tembri sighed remembering that Malcor had a character to play here. "Malcor, every Tanian knows about the Jade God right? Tania came here, I came here in case the Jade God tries to capture the lich. When things like this happen, somehow the Jade God's wand, a physical token of his necromantic power always, always seems to appear. If you look at it, it will take possession of you forever. If you touch it, you are dead. If it touches you, you are dead. If the wand feels threatened, it can attack and by itself is as strong as one of that God's hellhounds."

The door continued its slow opening and they all saw gold coins and small gems begin spilling through the seal. A bright flash of intense green suddenly cut through the door's edges. "The wand has found a host. Apparently, the ogre reached it. This is both good and bad. Bad because the wand is more powerful when it has a wielder. Good because an ogre is not a very good host for it. If the ogre dies, the wand will look for a new host. In this group, I am the most likely target. Then Noboyuki. It prefers clerics and sorcerers. Lets hope the lich is not around. The Jade God enjoys the irony of seizing its Master's enemies first."

"I have heard of this but never imagined I would see it," Noboyuki said. "The stories from Tania and Bloodstone are told here in Ori, but to have it so close. It feels sick."

"Malcor's friends, we must enter that room. We will support you from a distance but will only get directly involved if we absolutely have to. Remember, do not touch the wand, even accidentally. And while not touching it, do not make eye contact with the ogre or the wand's ram head!"

Malcor shoved his way in and then helped pull Sako and Jaga through. They were at the bottom of a large round room, bowl-shaped towards the center it appeared. A smaller door higher up with stairs drowning in treasure lied to their left. Movement was hard as the treasure underfoot continually shifted and their feet rolled on fist-sized gems hidden by bullion. Malcor thought he saw movement in the other doorway and they peeked around the heap of tapestries and ornately decorated items to see the green light.

The ogre stood on a table just above the level of the treasure. In its right hand it held a wand carved or made from vertebrae. Its back faced them but as Malcor looked, a ram's head atop the wand twisted and rotated as if on a neck and something shot at him. He pulled back just as the pile of treasure in front of him burst asunder and then began to turn molten. He pointed to another mound and ran as best he could.

He imagined he could hear laughter, insane demonic laughter. From the side, he saw the ogre turn but the wand never took its eyes off him. In fact, he noted that the wand's head seemed to take on two other aspects all imposed on top of the original to stare at and track Sako and Jaga's sprint. He skidded to a stop noticing that three other heads had appeared on the wand. Two looked at where Tembri and Noboyuki waited outside the room, but the other looked up at the doorway. He helped pull the other two out of the green light cast by the wand.

Suddenly, a compulsion struck them. Malcor felt it like a siren call offering an amazing dream. He wanted that dream no matter what – all he had to do was touch that sceptre. If he could just touch it, everything would be his. It called to each of them. Malcor calmed his mind and felt the teardrop scale on his arm burn. The burning there helped him focus on what was real: the treasure beneath his feet, the small portrait of some long forgotten man standing on a beach over there across the way, his friends. Sako, next to him muttered her mouth twitching. Jaga though, Malcor saw a problem. "Yes, yes," the older man mumbled as he began to stand up.

"No!" Malcor cried as he jumped and tackled Jaga back down.

"Let me go! My wife, my wife, she is there. I can be with her again. She has my little boy! Oh how I missed them… he died so young, so young… let me go!" Jaga collapsed beneath Malcor in a fetal position sobbing. "They took you from me, I'm so sorry! I'll come for you, yes, I'm coming."

Fearing Jaga would become violent, Malcor drew back and punched him as hard as he could. The blow rocked Jaga back. He barely noticed a blast of green energy lance through the air where he had become visible to the ogre during his tackle. To make sure, Malcor punched him again and then quickly bound Jaga. It seemed like a good idea so Malcor also placed a blind fold over Jaga's eyes. "Stay here old man," Malcor whispered.

Sako did barely better than Jaga but at least responded to Malcor when he asked her how she fared. "I'm, um, here Malcor." Her body shook and trembled. "I hear voices…"

Malcor put his hand on her shoulder reassuringly. "Stay here, support as you can. Remember what Tembri said, do not look at the ram's head."

Malcor glanced back at the door and saw Tembri watching. Silently, he hand signed and Tembri nodded. Moments later, Malcor's shield magically adjusted with a narrow eye slit opening along its length to help Malcor see. Then, his body filled with strength and the Queen's blessings rained into him. He took a deep breath of faith. From that breath, he hummed a hymn to the Queen. The battle hymn started low and quiet but as his strength and energy increased, he let it grow louder and louder until Sako looked up at him and her eyes widened. "Your Goddess?" she asked. He nodded and flexed his fingers as his sword, shield, armor, and every aspect of his being increased from his large human frame to that of a giant.

The green light focused on him as his back and legs became exposed. He ignored the malevolent feeling and then Noboyuki's prayer for strength filled him. Though less potent than the Queen's, he felt Imperius' power as a brightness in his morale and courage. He grinned and winked at Sako and then crouched. "Good-bye," he said to her.

His jump scattered treasure at his feet and he landed some thirty steps from the ogre and the wand. Using his shield, he saw the ogre's mid-section and the bottom portion of the wand's spine. Without looking, he knew the wand sought for him. He needed to close the distance and signaled to Tembri for a jump. A second later, he felt it and he leapt at the ogre moments before a green lightning bolt cut into the treasure where he had been. He felt the shockwave and heat boil the metal coins where he had stood and then his shield slammed into the ogre. His battle hymn changed to "*Let that which is created, come unmade. Coming Undone - Rage!*"

He thrust into the space behind his shield and felt his sword connect with something. Either the ogre or the sceptre, he could not tell so he slashed twisting back and forth. He saw the ogre try to jump away but with unsteady footing, it slipped. He felt, in that moment, how much the sceptre hated the stupid and clumsy ogre. The ogre pointed its other hand at Malcor and magical bolts like the ones Sako used shot in rapid succession cutting through his armor and burning into chest. Already wounded and now this as one after another they smashed into him. He signaled for healing and felt Tembri respond even as the bolts continued to burn into wounded and healing flesh. After what felt like minutes of those fiery darts, they ended and Malcor resumed his assault.

Behind him, the lich watched his ogre lieutenant transform into something not quite undead and not quite ogre. With that bone ram's head, the lich suddenly doubted if even he had enough power to defeat the stupid monster. When it activated, the lich had turned aside to watch what happened next with a simple viewing spell. When the wand looked at him through the spell, he had barely managed to close it down as he felt his existence's thread condense into one temptingly seductive promise of power and life eternal. "You will be the greatest...!" He still felt that promise. Envy, and aching, and yearning for a wish was a new sensation. To covet power at this level rocked the lich to its core.

He had been following Malcor from that first group and noted the fighter's peculiar talents. Seeing him leap towards the ogre though had impressed even the lich. When the wand screamed, it tore at the lich the way a mother's child's cry of pain would. The lich, for the first time in eons, ached with emotion, with desire to run to his brother and help. The sceptre of Orcus called to him. The sound reminded him all at once of the eldar times, of the bounty of creation, of how matter and life changed at his whimsy. The pain and anguish and that promise overwhelmed the lich who had not felt real mortal emotion in far too long. The lich turned the corner and walked into the trove, his hand reaching for the ram.

Chapter Sixty One - The Sceptre of the Jade God

Sako saw the lich and shot her magical bolts at it. Though they hit, the lich failed to even notice. A crackling sphere of energy became visible around the lich. Full of purple and blue fires, it had started to crack as that sick green light bathed the lich. She thought she saw the lich wipe a tear from its eye. Its hand uplifted, reaching out for the sceptre, begging for it.

Just moments behind the lich's entrance, one of the Order's units scythed through a battalion of orcs fortified with a variety of undead. The commander of this unit, R'Dar Verit and his battle priest disintegrated the undead in the Queen's purifying fires while his healers defended their sides. When they turned their fury on the orcs, and with great initiative, the orcs nearest Verit fell before his holy avenger. A flame strike by the priest pushed them back and when Verit cut through to the next passage, the surviving orcs fled. They heard the sceptre's scream and felt the Queen's Voice urge them forward with all due haste.

Outside the fortress, Kendra and Blade both felt the Queen's warning. When they heard the wand's scream, it hurt their ears and Blade roared his defiance back down at the mountain. At that sound, the armies encamped around the mountain seemed to lose their focus. Held in impatient waiting for weeks against the rumors they helped spread and the tribute they had helped take from Ori, the armies raced back towards the mountain, or scattered to the wilderness. Blade noted the fortress' entrance where a wraith commander had suddenly appeared. Kendra knew what Blade would do and so echoed her dread lord's action. "Glass it," she whispered and patted the dragon's neck and began signing her favorite battle hymn in draconian.

Behind her, the Apprentice leapt off the dragon and stood mid-air. "I will monitor and ensure none escape." Already a gate had begun to open behind him from which he would call forth any creature required to guarantee victory.

Blade, with a paladin on his back, no longer had to worry about the less hearty mage, and so at last he stepped out of the River and let go of the self-control that enabled him to exist side by side with these frail mortal things. So far above the mountain, his shadow of terror and might fell on the monsters below. Many of them collapsed to the ground shaking in fright. Those closest to any cover, ran like possessed for it. Those already escaping into the wilderness began to sprint, casting aside gear and weapons in their haste. Blade drank their fear from the River into his belly and felt it kindle and ignite. At a distance, he dove for the mountain's entrance as fire drooled from his jaws.

Kendra cut herself from the world of the real and joined Blade on the River's banks relishing in the ecstasy of her lord in his glory. Like a burning god, Blade's flames rained down over the mountain like a meteor storm. In contrast to the vivid red swords of fire, the mountain looked gray and sickly with cracks of green and purple running throughout it. The fire tapped the River and part of the River turned and smashed into the mountain. The pale sick gray of chaos-drunken stone burst into the molten red and orange of the dread lord's particular aura. Within the River, the fire consumed and drowned all it touched with death. Even the mountain stone writhed and liquefied into glass that dripped down to trap the burnt bones in an eternal coffin.

Blade opened wings just before smashing into the mountainside. Molten glass splashed up from his landing and the mountain quivered as his massive claws tore at the tiniest cracks to spear and smash those still surviving. He turned his fire on the upper parts of the mountain as the River's fury glassed it to slag. Perhaps in terror or mindless survival instinct, a few orcs turned their bows on the dragon but the missiles deflected against the updrafts heat raging around Blade. Kendra noted them and flicked her sword their way, where it snaked across incredible distance to spear them. The destruction, as befitted a dragon, was total but left just a few survivors running into the wilderness to tell the tale.

From the gates above, the Apprentice pulled in elementals from the realm of Earth, who fell to the ground and then melted into the glass. Moments later, an Order of Water paladin found the hot steam and lava-riddled passages that would speed their way to the golden seal.

Within the vault, Malcor slashed into the ogre and again the wand's spine caught his sword. Unlike other times, Coming Undone had no effect on the sceptre; it mocked his faith. And again, Malcor felt his sword shriek as the unclean sceptre tried to bend its will away from its wielder. Again and again, he stabbed and slashed at the ogre's lower extremities using his shield to block any accidental viewing of the wand at the ogre's head. Each time, he saw the ogre try to move towards the lich, he slashed and battered it into the slippery treasure floor. His shield became a hammer. Only the Queen's power held it and him together. His shield arm had broken but he hardly felt it.

The Queen's Voice overpowered the dissonance of their combat and he obeyed. "Feint right, tumble left, jump, counterthrust, kick…" and so it continued. Though he did not know it, his heart leapt with joy when Blade's landing rocked the mountain with an earthquake. Around them, support piers and pylons shattered as Blade raged on the mountain. Suddenly, the voice in his heart screamed a warning and Malcor fell back only to bump into something soft.

The lich's sphere shield caught Malcor and then let him through. Malcor stumbled to his knees looking for better footing, and then the cold death of the lich brushed him. He tried to roll away but the lich, like a child trailing its fingers in water, just barely brushed Mal's arm. From just that moment, his vitality raced away from Malcor, and then the lich broke contact.

Though he had felt undead attacks during his Rite of Pain, the lich had in that single moment taken more from him than hours of the Rite had. He looked down at his arm holding his shield and saw how his skin had turned into leather and how his bones and tendons could almost be seen. His shoulder aged and withered and then skin worms began crawling along his fingers, which turned gangrenous. Air rushed into his lungs to scream in agony but he felt asthmatic, choking for breath and not getting as much as he wished. He signaled for help, praying for Tembri to notice, for the Queen for anyone to respond and help.

Tembri saw Malcor wither against the lich and fall back but the lich's sphere still held Malcor even as the lich reached out to take the sceptre. The ogre seeing it pulled the sceptre back but the sceptre had other ideas. The ogre's flesh collapsed when the wand declared, "Anorex." Dying in that instant, the ogre fell through death into unlife and knelt to present the Jade God's sceptre to the lich. The ram smiled wide as the vertebrae snaked along the lich's arm and interlocked into and along the lich's back to place the ram's head like a helmet over the lich's head. Though Tembri's flame strike consumed everything around it, it did not penetrate the lich's sphere.

In desperation, Tembri enacted an atonement for a desperate battle priest spell, and sent his own vitality to Malcor. For just a moment, their arms superimposed on each other and then averaged out their relative health. Tembri grunted in shock and pain at the level of sickness the withering had inflicted. Though muscle and connective tissue mended, the bones did not. With the spell still struggling against the continued decay of Malcor's fingers, Tembri slammed his arm against a treasure chest, and pulled so the bones would correctly align, and prayed Malcor would remain conscious.

R'Dar Verit charged into the chamber just in time to see the dreaded wand interlink with the lich's spine. "No!" he screamed signaling for power. His battle priest's flame strike, strengthening, healing, and blessing rose up around him as his jump carried him to the lich. At the last second, he saw the sphere of power surrounding the lich. Like Malcor, the sphere let him through and though he landed on the lich's back, the lich did not move. The sphere shifted colors then to expel both Verit and Malcor. An invisible force kicked them flying through the air to smash into the walls surrounding the vault. Verit landed nimbly, while Malcor hit with a damning crack of bone too far away for Tembri, Sako, or anyone to help. He landed broken and limp bleeding on priceless piles of treasure.

Still connected, Tembri sent what he had left to Malcor and prayed for the strength to retain consciousness and free will. When Malcor breathed, Tembri ended the spell and felt deep abiding pain in his hip, spinal sections, jaw, and several ribs. If Malcor died now, they would not be able to revive him. Tembri began re-enacting the atonement but the Queen cautioned him, "Have faith precious Tembri. Trust the son of Kell."

Verit signaled the need for reinforcements and a mage even as tunnels opened into the vault around them. The paladins of the Order of Water stood in each looking down at the possessed lich. Verit ignited his holy sword and began voicing a prayer of faith to the Queen, one that would protect him from all manner of magic. His sword burning in Takhissis' multicolored flames, the knight walked towards the lich with only his faith to protect him. The other paladins did the same and began advancing on the lich.

Malcor looked up and saw Verit, exactly as he imagined a knight should be when confronted with a mighty foe. His shield arm broken. His hip, multiple ribs, lower back maybe, he could not quite tell through the pain, all had shattered. Though miraculously, Tembri had done something that preserved his life. Any movement felt like agony and he knew, "I should be where Verit is." Again, that fading dream and hope began to crash in on him and his teardrop scar ached and itched. "I must be with Verit…" and Malcor reached his right arm out and pulled his body forward. Black pain threatened him with unconsciousness and his vision swam. "I must…"

He saw Tembri running towards him, but looked very far away. Sako also appeared to be scrambling to his aid. She also appeared far away. His teardrop ached and he watched helpless and crawling as Verit smashed into the lich's shield with blue lightning crackling along his sword only to be thrown back against a wall hundreds of feet behind him. The lich laughed and its richly evil cackling filled the huge room. The ram's skull split apart into many to keep its eyes on Verit's comrades and those watching from the tunnels high above.

With a familiarity born by the Jade God, the lich stretched out a pointed finger and said, "Morbatten, how I spite thee! I will take your lands and your peoples and your Queen as my pet whore. Despair and die!" Underneath the vast floor of treasure, the lich had interred thousands of long dead soldiers from the Ori fighting and endless tribal struggles. The mountain had also held several orc tribes that had buried their strongest in this room. Necromantic power called them to life even as the lich cancelled the scrying block so the sceptre could open a gate for his hellhound brothers to come through. "No dragons here to help you," the ram's head jeered at them.

"Arise! Come! Feed!" the lich shrieked at the rising undead as the treasure trove's floor shifted and swayed as if a stormy ocean.

A passwall tunnel suddenly opened with Dar Kendra and the Apprentice standing there. Seconds after it opened, molten glass began trickling down from the fortress' main gate. Verit alight with black ash that sizzled and popped walked purposefully towards the lich again. "We have fought and defeated and captured the likes of you before Ram. You have no hope here." He raised his sword to cut down into the shield, the floor erupted as bony hands broke the surface of the treasure. Verit fell backwards into clutching hands with dagger sharp finger spikes. Beneath that seething mass, things much larger began snapping together knit by leather tendons and animated by spite.

Malcor saw Kendra point at him and then she and Apprentice stood by him. Though skeletal hands clawed up all around them, none reached for him. Kendra removed her gauntlet and touched Malcor's pain-creased brow. "You have done well squire. Here, let me help you up."

He tried to say thank you but found he had almost no energy left. The lich's touch had ruined him. "You'll need more than my touch Malcor, but remember, the Order would create the opportunity to fight the lich, not the wand. This is different. Let it go. Your second rite has changed and you passed! Do you hear me? You passed! Now, together, as one of us, you will stand with the Order and we will either capture the wand or destroy it."

Tembri struggled to fight his way to them. "There is another way!" he called. Over the din of combat, no one heard. "Malcor! Kendra!"

She helped him stand and signaled all the others to make ready. The lich spun to look at them all as they dropped down to the floor. Though the summoned undead were mighty, as soon as they appeared, they disintegrated away under the focus of the battle priests and their healers. Their awakening though made the combat floor a chaotic place and the Order struggled to advance.

Chapter Sixty Two - Tania Raises the Stakes

Far to the north, in Morbatten, Daryx sat with the king and the dragon emperor. The emperor's scrying ball had suddenly reactivated. Already other members of the Circle began to teleport in. They saw the lich taken by the sceptre. They saw Verit and Malcor try and fail to attack the lich. Dar Kell, Shara, and Reznor all studied the ball in silence. It centered on Malcor. Another one near it watched the emperor's son Blaze where he continued to slag the mountain and pound it to boiling mud. A third watched Dar Kendra. At Daryx's touch, a fourth one lit to life. That one centered on a small spider, so small it would barely catch notice. "Hello my beauty," the dark elf whispered. The spider wiggled its legs. Just out of the spider's view sat the slowly spinning abyssal gate.

Each of the scrying balls focused on a different member of Morbatten. Their surroundings could be seen, and Daryx touched the sphere and whispered to the spider in the harsh-sounding language of the drow. The spider shifted and reappeared closer to the portal, but in the background of the portal's reflection, the empty plain and a small black speck could be seen. Then another black spec appeared.

Reznor touched the Kendra view and shifted it to his apprentice and then to each of the members of the Order until at last Verit came into view just about to strike down on the colored shield glowing around the lich. They noted the wand had interlocked with the lich and appeared to totally dominate. Verit brought his sword down and black dragon energy splashed against the magical shield hissing and popping, and then the color changed from gray-green to black green and the sword and its wielder where thrown back by a powerful explosion.

"At least two hellhounds have answered the wand's summons," Daryx said observing his golem spider.

"Do it," the emperor ordered.

Daryx whispered to the spider and in a blink of an eye, thousands of phase spiders appeared around the gate, and then on the plain, and then in unison, they bit poison fangs into the ground. They all vanished just as the scrying ball went completely black. "It is done Alerius," Daryx reported. Thousands of poisonous fangs awoke the beast of the abyss, Demos-Gorgos. And, the beast fell on the hellhounds.

The emperor nodded and asked Kell, "How fares our next king?"

Watching Malcor, Dar Kell reported, "He struggles with letting go of his original mission. He, not Verit, was to face the lich. The boy does not understand the changed mission nor how dangerous the wand is. But, he understands Dar Kendra's orders. His heart wonders what it all means, and the shadow dragons call for him to act. He aches to face the lich and prove himself to us. He knows that his human body is broken, but Cor'tanos whispers that if he dragonshifts, even his arm, he can rejoin the battle."

"Reznor, send word to Kendra. If Malcor chooses poorly, he is to be slain." The emperor's command reached Dar Kendra and suddenly, all four of the scrying balls came alight with her face as she took control of the scrying. She looked very angry.

Reznor touched one and refocused it on Verit to have a view of the combat, and then another burst afire as Blade spoke through it. "Father, the woman desires that Malcor must live."

"Silence," Alerius breathed in draconian at his son. He turned back to Dar Kendra. "Kendra, I see your rage and love you for it. Aid the boy in choosing wisely. Or he dies. We cannot afford a shadow dracolich. We cannot risk a shadowtouched hound that would then draw Cor'tanos' clan to the Necromancer. My enemy must not become aware of the shadow realms. You know it will trigger a Cascade Kendra. This is NOT Bloodstone."

Her face went poker flat but the anger still burned in her eyes as she returned to combat. Alerius turned his head slightly to one of the priestesses always watching, "Bring R'Dar Ora. Now."

The other paladins surrounded the lich and with holy avengers burning with the Queen's zeal, they advanced one step at a time. The lich had exhausted his normal magical attacks and grew increasingly frustrated

407

as the knight's immunity protected them from things that should have slain them. Worst, the knights taunted him observing that the Jade God had ruined his powers. The lich felt his free will slipping away, exactly as Daryx had said it would.

Behind the knights, the battle priests and clerics advanced calling for his banishment. While any single one of them could not touch the lich, faced with so many and some very powerful, even the sceptre questioned what would happen. It poured information into the lich's mind identifying the known fighters of Tania that had thwarted Orcus too many times already. And of course, there stood the Apprentice by the leader of this group – Kendra. At least the one called Reznor was not here. Oddly, it noted that Kendra stood by what looked like the youngest and weakest of the bunch. Though he had nearly defeated the Wand's prior host, the boy hardly warranted the attention of the Order's leader. Seeing the Wand looking at them, Kendra blew it a kiss and ignited her holy sword.

Malcor felt Kendra's heat next to him and blinked through vision growing dim. Though the room burned with fire, molten treasure, and the knights themselves, a dark veil had fallen across his sight and his teardrop ached. Kendra strode purposefully towards the lich and Malcor struggled to follow. He knew that if he could get close enough, he could score a dragon claw attack. It had turned the tide of his previous battles - he found Tembri taking his right arm and helping him walk. "Be strong Malcor. Remember, you are a knight. This is a knight's task. You are a knight in the Order of Water. This is what you have trained and lived for and dreamed of since you were small. You do not need the shadows. You need to continue your faith in the Queen."

He nodded and choked. Wiping his mouth, he felt something weird and looked at his right hand. Dark grey non-reflective scales covered it and his finger nails had shredded through his gauntlet. Tembri grabbed the dragon hand, "Malcor, you must resist this. It will sever your connection to the Queen. Listen to Her voice. Just listen."

Malcor looked at the claw and barely-remembered visions of his storeroom fight flashed through his memory. "Can barely see," he mumbled. "So dark."

"Join me by the River," Tembri urged him.

Malcor tried to fall back into the River, to feel the familiar sensation of changed time. It happened and then stopped and then something caught him and pulled him through. So bright here that it made him wince, he registered that half his head rose out of the River, held by Tembri. The brightness felt terrifying and behind it, something dark and awful watched. He felt madness claw at his mind and Tembri grabbed his face and turned his eyes from the darkness to his own. "Malcor, you're a good man. You have dreams. Your dreams are not shadow! It can be a blessing, but it is mostly a curse. It is a curse Mal! It takes you away from your dreams. Right now, here is your destiny as a paladin. Let it be glory to the Mother. Look," he heaved and turned Malcor to look at the lich. The lich looked like black crystal, fragmenting and crackling apart as it moved to fend off the gloriously bright paladins and their entourages ringing it. The Wand, like a fractured green wound had infected the lich. "You want to be a glorious paladin! What do you see Malcor?"

Malcor tried to answer, tried to say about the infection, how it made him ill to look at it. His mouth though drowned in the River and he felt despair. Things grew dimmer. Against the despair, Malcor fought with all his might to remember something, anything, about those dreams but they felt so far away. Something else touched him and he felt Sako's hand in the real world cradle his head. Then he heard it, the Queen's Voice. No, not Her voice but R'Dar Ora's voice reading the draconian scripture to him from that sunrise just two months behind him. Her voice, sweet and crystal clear hurt but he could not deny the scripture. He felt a spark of hope and seizing it, he lifted himself up from the River.

Tembri whispered, "Dear Goddess, you are awesome Malcor. It can be a blessing, but your faith must equal the darkness. It must."

Malcor nodded and looked back at the lich. "Look Tembri, I see it now. The lich's soul gem – it is not with the lich. We can still win!"

Tembri nodded, "The other way. We can do this. I will help you Mal."

Air rushed back into his lungs and he lost his footing, falling backwards into a pile of treasure. As he exited the River, he heard a divine female voice say, "My children, so clumsy…"

Sako caught him. Above them, the circle of paladins closed and simultaneously their avenger swords struck the barrier. Half of them exploded backwards, were caught by their battle priests, enlarged, and thrown back at it. Safe in the barrier, the lich could do nothing and the gate opened by it to summon hellhounds remained barren. The wand shrieked and attacked one of the paladins, but its own barrier caught the blast. The paladin laughed and taunted the ram head.

Malcor stood up on his near shattered legs and dropped his armor. "Tembri, I miss my rings." Tembri shrugged keeping an eye on the lich. "We need to find it, fast. Sako, the lich's soul gem… get Noboyuki; use your magic ask his god Imperius. Anything. We need to get it."

Though his arm still ached, Malcor closed his eyes and with more focus fell back out of the River. Though not as smooth as it had always been before, he rose up by himself and looked at the treasure. Beneath the floor, the undead seethed upward only to be destroyed by the divine might raging against the lich. The frightening darkness around the edges of his perception still waiting, watchful, but no longer consumed him with terror. Some of the treasure, as he focused on it, glinted with sparks of energy. Then, Tembri rose up from the River. There on the banks, Tembri called to Takhissis for divination and cried out, "Our Queen, our mother, Takhissis god of the world, Malcor your son seeks answers!"

From the River, from somewhere all around them, a female's voice closer and more sensuous than Malcor had ever heard it before replied, "Let him ask."

Tembri pointed to Malcor who said, "Great Goddess, I seek the soul gem of the lich. Where will I find it?"

The female exhaled perfume and exotic smells and yawned as if stretching, "You will find it in the pool of blood before the lich's throne." Malcor had the sense of a titanic form leaving and then that voice pierced him through again, "You will suffer my son, and my heart aches for your pain. Remain true to your dreams and they will not fail you. I love you."

The voice, so beautiful it made his heart weep, left. Tembri's tears ran down his face and he whispered, "Great Queen Takhissis, we thank you for your grace."

They returned to the real world. Sako spoke urgently with Noboyuki and he nodded back at her and gave them a thumbs up. Tembri made a hand gesture Malcor had never seen and suddenly he became acutely aware that they were being watched. Speaking up into the air, Tembri hissed in draconian so quickly Malcor could barely follow, something about the lich's throne and could [some lord] move them to [water]...? Tembri seemed satisfied and called Sako and Noboyuki over. "Clasp hands, quickly," Tembri said grabbing Malcor's still partially transformed claw.

A second later, Dar Reznor appeared in their center. His sudden appearance caused the wand to lose focus and attack him again, only to be restricted by its own force wall again. At the same time, the paladins and battle priests increased their hammering of the barrier and Apprentice joined in. With it distracted, they almost broke through.

The five of them blinked and found themselves standing in a torchilt room. Reznor vanished saying, "I cannot linger. The risk of a cascade is too great right now."

Rock and debris had rained down but for the most part, it was intact. A large throne of melted waxen stone slightly angled forward to look down into the pool. Ripples skipped across the pool's surface as Blade assaulted the mountain. Malcor walked out into the blood anticipating some kind of trap or safeguard. It arose up in the form of spectrally-armored wraiths. Unlike last time, Malcor had Tembri and Tembri dismissed them. Though not powerful enough to disintegrate them outright, the wraiths fell back into the shadows and watched and waited. One tried to leave and Tembri ordered it to stop. Pushing his luck, he asked it, "We are looking for a large gem that burns with magic. We think it is in this pool. Is it?"

The wraith nodded. When Tembri asked it to show them, the wraith moved forward and pointed. When it drew close to Malcor, it tried to break free and attack, but Tembri asserted his control and it fell back.

Malcor moved to the area and found, laying at the bottom of the pool's exact center, a bracer in which rested a purple gem the size of an egg. Though it appeared just under the surface of the pool, Malcor realized the depth had increased to his hips.

Malcor tore part of his cloak and dropped it over the bracer to pick it up. Just as he bent over to grab it, struggling as his various broken bones and other wounds made it difficult, the wraiths all around surged forward to attack. Tembri felt their malign intent and called out warning, and then struggled to control so many. To his horror and dismay, a wraith rose up from behind Malcor in the pool. Formed of the blood holding so many souls, this wraith had a nearly demonic appearance and its face split along its mouth to its ears full of rows of fanged razor teeth. As it lifted its arm up, its taloned claws split and superimposed into many arms bearing many talons. Surrounded by the other wraiths resisting Tembri, Malcor felt nothing amiss and picked up the bracer.

Sako and Noboyuki screamed for Malcor and both dove into the pool. Sako caught the many talons in her chest as Noboyuki tackled and dragged Malcor under the surface. The Tanian felt so frail but feeling his bones shift and crack as Malcor screamed in agony, seemed surreal immersed in blood. Noboyuki struggled to regain his footing and lift Malcor up to breath.

Right next to them, Sako struggled against the blood wraith. Tembri had dropped his warding of the other wraiths to send his last healing spell to her, and he caught her on the brink of death. The wraith screamed into her face opening its maw to bite her head off. To her credit, and never having had Tanian combat training, she held on to her focus and hit the blood wraiths eyes with magic missiles. The others slammed into its mouth. Its scream changed tenor and it threw her back.

Noboyuki began praying for her health even as the other wraiths moved into the pool to attack. Just four peeled off to intercept Tembri with one of them scoring a hit as the battle priest raised his holy symbol to control them again. For Malcor, it all seemed to happen in slow motion. When he had fallen into the blood and submerged, he had felt it like when he moved in and out of the River. It felt easy this time, seamless and effortless. The Queen's Voice there welcomed him, "Though not the

412

heroes I would have chosen, this baptism works. Take their knowledge, their experience; I caretake it all to you Malcor Kell'Tayris."

With the Queen's words echoing around him, the River froze still. Mal pulled his legs out noticing how it crackled and flowed for a mere moment before those parts stilled. He felt all kinds of knowledge suffusing his mind and realized, *I understand ogre, goblin, orc, and hobgoblin languages now?* His vitality surged and though still broken beyond magical healing, he felt renewed in a way that healing never did. He saw the layout of the pool, the room, and how his friends all struggled in the most dire of combats. Ten wraiths and this blood wraith all froze in their attacks against the dim candles of his friends' auras. *They would die; I will die.* Thinking this, Malcor's arm seethed with power and the ever present shadow watching from the River smiled. It seemed about to say something but the Queen hissed at it and the shadow left.

The Goddess's voice came more his way and She commanded, "Recover your breath Malcor my son. You know what you must do when you re-enter the throne room. Your breath weapon." So speaking, the Queen left. All across the River, Malcor saw the battle against the lich with its stunned sceptre. He felt great enmity radiating at him and the others from the wand but some tremendous pressure and force from very far away made the wand and its master impotent. Looking at his hands, he noted how they trembled frightfully, but it was nice to catch his breath. Through the River's frozen pane, he saw himself rising up with Noboyuki's grip on what remained of his armor. Blood colored his skin and the whites of his eyes alone made him recognizable. The temptation to close his eyes and sleep beckoned seductively. That was when Ora appeared on the far banks of the River. Her otherworldly beauty and the kiss she blew him reminded him that he had not yet finished. He waved and reached out for her hand, and fell back into the River.

Just like the Rite when he faced the paladins on the brink of death and exhausted beyond belief, Malcor reached out with all his frustrated dreams, humiliations, hopes, and memories of his friends now that supported him. He unlocked his berserker fury and let it explode out of him in a torrent. Tembri now caught Sako and Noboyuki shielding them with his body and plunging them underwater as a flame strike of dark grey and red energy tornadoed out from Malcor's opening arms. The pool of blood boiled and then evaporated as the force of that battle hymn tore the wraiths to shreds and then shredded the blood wraith to ash. Though Tembri and the pool shielded the Imperics from the worst of it, scald and scorch marks riddled their bodies. Tembri's back blistered and cratered from the shadow dragon bled and Tembri screamed in agony. Malcor still held the tattered fragments of his cloak containing the lich's gauntlet.

Reznor reappeared. "Well done," he said. "You'll survive. Battle Priest, I apologize but since I am not a healer, I'll do the best I can." He blew at them and frost from his breath cooled and chilled and then numbed Tembri's back. A second spell, interrupted, "Priest, you must allow this spell –" continued and Tembri's mind stopped registering the pain and shock. "These will last till you can be attended by a proper healer."

Reznor took his bearings and then re-enacted the passwall spell. A tunnel of blackness two people wide opened and then shot out from his hand. Sunlight glowed at the end. "Your work here is done. I will see you back in Tania. Malcor, well done sir." A spectral hand appeared, scooped them up, and carried them floating out of the mountain.

As they rose up the magical tunnel, they saw several places where the tunnel had cut through other tunnels and in a few cases, appeared to have cut undead in pieces. When they got closer, they found the sunlight filtered through burning fires and smoke. They exited to the side of Blade's rampage. Wildfires burned everywhere giving the scene of the once large and wild mountain an apocalyptic slant. Seeing them, Blade swerved and dove to them, scorching and burning the mountain all around them as he landed. With his terror fully unleashed, Sako and Noboyuki fell unconscious. It was odd watching such otherwise brave people succumb to something Malcor had taken for granted though even he felt disconnected, like he watched this all happening to someone else. He bowed to the dread lord. In a flash, Blade scooped the four of them into his massive claw and leapt back into the air.

The world looked so small from the dragon's rapid ascent, but all around the mountain raged fires. Still glowing and molten rock dripped down the main face of the fortress. Blade circled the mountain letting his terror drive any survivors into madness. Whenever larger groups presented themselves, he raged down upon them. Tembri noted the intent to allow a few to live and explained it to Malcor. "The stories of the few who survive, repeated over centuries, enhance the terror."

Blade landed near the southern gate of Ori. Even at this distance, the burning ruin of the mountain rose from the horizon. Blade let his terror smash into the Imperics, most of whom fled the wall. Blade carefully opened his claw and let the two Tanians retrieve Sako and Noboyuki. Turning his head to the sky, he roared out a challenge heard and felt by all of Ori as a nightmare. After the chaos ended, a band of samurai stoically approached. Blade waited until they were almost in range and then humanshifted. The samurai drew a deep breath as the crushing dragonterror retracted like cat claws. Still tense, they walked up and bowed to Blade and then to Tembri. "Are you, are they," pointing to Sako and Noboyuki, "okay?"

Tembri nodded and clapped Malcor's shoulder. "This is a paladin from Morbatten. With the dread lord's assistance, we rescued these two Imperics. We also bring very good news." Malcor almost offered the soul gem gauntlet, but Tembri hand signed him to not and continued. "Dar Kendra, who visited your lord last month, has found a way to return the captured souls of your people. Even now, her troops assault the mountain and fight against the lich. Dark necromancy aside, we request a place to rest and recover from our wounds. When Dar Kendra arrives, she will be able to return the souls. I bring you this message as an offering of peace."

Sako and the priest started to stir and suddenly gasped awake, straining against the combat they last knew. Seeing concerned faces of samurai and the crest of Imperius, in the sunshine, they blinked in confusion. The samurai helped them stand.

"Did we get the soul gem?" Noboyuki asked.

Malcor shook his head. "Yes and also no, Dar Kendra needs it as part of defeating the lich. We sent it back with Lord Reznor."

Noboyuki bowed to Tembri formally and then with more warmth to

Malcor. "That adventure was, intense. I have fulfilled my obligations and regret our friend Jaga did not make it. That I made it, I thank you." Sako joined in thanking them.

The samurai in charge of the group nodded and said, "You are welcome to stay and await the return of your Tanian friends. Turning to Sako and Noboyuki, he added, "The high priest will want to speak with you both." Though the captain's face went pale looking at Blade, he swallowed and said, "Ori is in no condition to receive royalty from Tania Dread Lord Blade. May I – "

"Save it. I must return to ensure the lich's fall. An orc army also advances on your southern wall. I will dispose of them with fire." So saying, Blade leapt into the air and dragonshifted. The wind of his departure swirled about them for minutes and they watched him reach altitude and then faster than seemed possible, Blade tore off to the south. A warm wind blew back that whispered, "Though Tania would not hesitate to accommodate your royal family."

The samurai turned pale, choked, and asked Noboyuki and Tembri, "Lord priests, I did not offend I hope?" and swallowed again.

Tembri shrugged and said, "Well, look at it from his perspective. He's helping defeat the lich that almost destroyed Ori. He just brought you two survivors and news that Tania has found how to restore your royal family and their souls. But, you were about to turn him away? What would your daimo do if the dragon emperor greeted such good news and heroic sacrifice with that? And, of course Blade is the son of the emperor and a dragon."

The captain broke out into a sweat. "I'll see how we can make it right! Tell me, Tembri, did you hear from Sir Allen, he led a group of Pha Rannnic knights?"

"Only that there is such a group. I did not see them."

"Very well, we will find you accommodations near the castle. Please, all of you come with me."

Chapter Sixty Three - The Order versus the Lich

Far under the lich's mountain, back in the room of the golden seal, the lich's barrier had at last crackled into shards of magical light. The interlocking vertebrae clicked down the lich's arm and mace version of the wand appeared there. The lich, through the explosion of its falling barrier, pointed the mace at the closest enemy and commanded the female healer to "Die!"

A ray of green light speared the healer and she screamed, her life force draining but it did not take enough to slay her. The lich and the wand looked confused for just a moment and then Kendra's sword slammed into the lich's lower back as Verit and others pressed in from all sides. A battle priest nearby called upon the Queen to banish the lich, while others did the same for either the Wand or the lich. Though they failed, resisting a barrage of spells capable of ending them distracted the lich. In that distraction, a battle priest leapt forward and scored a critical hit. Though he just barely touched the lich's leg, the nullification magic he carried with both the Queen's might and the Apprentice's magic put the sceptre to sleep. Alone but still possessed, the lich raged against them.

Finger spikes grew out from the lich's nails and it swept down at the hapless priest, utterly exposed. The bloody gashes that eviscerated the poor man gave the others a chance to attack. Freed of the Wand's influence, the lich altered the gates to call something besides a hellhound. It flashed as something on the other side answered. Two of the paladins moved to intercept whatever would come through, their battle priests summoning shield and mace to cover them from anything the lich might do.

Kendra signaled a series of attacks to press the lich back while the Apprentice readied a new spell. The lich intuiting their defense of the mage, turned its fury on the mage. It summoned a force wall and sent it flying towards the Apprentice. At the last instant, the Apprentice finished his spell and blocked the wall with giant glowing hands that pressed back against it. The wall effectively cut the mage and the two paladins off from the main combat. However, the lich's attention on them opened him to Verit who drove his sword threw the lich's back, its fiery point bursting through the lich's chest plate. The lich used its strength to whirl but Verit jumped letting the movement carry him.

Spinning, the lich found three battle priests and two paladins attacking his face with holy might and razor weapons. Behind him, Verit wrapped his gauntlet around the interlocked Wand's spine and pulled. A bloodstone earing along his ear ignited with magic and lent Verit strength as he pulled.

Another battle priest seeing that called on Takhissis to bless him with dragon's strength, and then Kendra's sword wove into the slowly opening and bleeding gap to spiral up towards the ram's head. Like spider mandibles, first one then another of the device's connections to the lich's spine pulled free drenching Verit in ichor and stank blood.

The ram began to awaken as the first, then second, and then faster as all the other pincers began pulling free. The pain to the lich expressed itself as a foul mist of black ash and carrion insects the lich blew out at the fighters to his front. One of the healers failed to catch his breath and his body filled with vapor and then burst in an explosion of new ash. The wand, fully awake now, twisted and swept the area behind the lich with that green ray and then focused it directly on Verit.

The screams of agony that filled the cavern as insects crawled into noses, ears, and eyes biting and chewing into any tissue as well as Verit's agony galvanized the Apprentice who completed his spell. On the other side of the force wall, a wall of fire formed and then swept the entire chamber. The Order of Water clad in dragon armor and immune by the Queen's blessing ignored the flames, as did the lich, but it ended the black vapor and insects. Wiping blood from their eyes and faces, the Order regrouped while the lich suddenly blinked away and Verit fell to the ground convulsing as his body writhed in unholy light.

Reappearing by the gate, the lich triggered his soul sucking spell. It tore at the paladins there and they fought to resist it. Suddenly the soul tearing force vanished and the lich smashed his gauntlet as if it had broken. Behind the lich, the gate flashed a final time and large scaled balls floated through covered with eyes. The eye stalks immediately began waiving about and everyone present dove behind cover. The lich began laughing evilly as the wand twisted and placed its skull atop the lich's head. Connected again, the ram's head turned its focus on the undead rising up from the treasure floor, augmenting them and smashing them together into larger and more powerful undead. Every so often, that deathly green light would lance out and sear armor. Reconnected to the wand, the lich lost its fury and took on a more serene expression. The pincers began rethreading into the lich's spine.

Twenty floating eye-covered balls armored in waving eye stalks drifted into the room. The paladins and their support groups eyed them from positions of cover and then a thin gray line of light arced out from one of the balls buzzing and hissing through the air where it struck the ankle of a healer, who petrified into stone. A split second later, another ray of light but much wider opened on the treasure pile Kendra and the Apprentice had taken cover behind. The wide circle narrowed and then the treasure began to levitate, vaporizing into powder. From the midst of the floating balls, a cruel alien chuckle sounded and then the treasure pile vaporized leaving Kendra on guard in front of the Apprentice.

"Beholder!" Kendra cried. "Everyone, on guard and attack the lich – he is the prize!" At her command, multiple rays of magical energy cut out through the floating balls. Where they struck a few, the balls exploded in a foul mist that forced everyone to hold their breaths. "Mage, help." She leapt at the lich. Her fingers danced along her shield and Verit to her left acknowledged with a loud cry of "yes".

Strength, energy, healing, and the Goddess' blessing flew into them and the others as they charged. Kendra called on her sword and sent it snaking at the lich. The ram's head saw it and the small wand in the lich's hand parried. However, Kendra twisted her sword and the blade grabbed onto the wand. Furious, the lich pulled and Kendra used the creature's evil strength to speed her own mighty jump to clear the distance. Behind her, Verit leapt and vanished only to reappear behind the lich. His leap landed him on the lich's back, again. The lich started to turn, but Kendra caught him and lifted him off the ground as the other paladins and priests closed in around it.

From above, the deadly cloud of exploding gas balls drenched them in a fine brown powder that sparkled as if filled with gold. And from above now, those deadly rays of light cut through their ranks with petrification, disintegration, near death-like wounds, and lightning. One such ray washed over Kendra who swore, and then petrified.

Unbalanced by Kendra crushing him, and his right arm held by her sword the lich tried to leverage its other arm to pry her off, but another paladin grappled the lich's left side ineffectively, but still entangling it. The lich howled as the wand suddenly fell quiescent and Verit once again man-handled the spiny mandibles off the lich's spine. With a triumphant cry, Verit tore the wand free, the ram's head again detaching from the lich's head.

The wand immediately came alive like a boney eel trying to take possession of Verit. Freed again from the Wand, the lich remembered his soul tear had failed and he tried to walk forward, to cast a spell, to free himself, but the Order tackled him to the ground and punched, clubbed, stabbed, and then those deadly arcs of energy rained down and the paladin pinning his left arm went rigid and unmoving with paralysis. Kendra still bear hugging him to the point bones had started to crack, petrified. "My soul – " the lich howled and then a mace of dragonflames wielded by one of the battle priests smashed into his face.

Still holding their breaths, the Order once again ignored the beholder and sweeping off his cloak, one of the paladins dove at Verit and covered the wand. Verit and the ram's head were eye-locked in a battle of wills. Verit was on the brink of losing when the cloak enwrapped the ram's head and Verit fell unconscious. The others looked towards the beholder. Only a few of the barely different gas balls remained and they orbited the creature while eye stalks tracked the remaining members of the Order. Behind them, the Apprentice frantically danced through a spell and when the weakest healer was about to take a breath, the Apprentice finished and pointed at the beholder. A single word said simultaneously in the multiple languages boomed in the room, "Blind!"

Bright suns of light and fire sprang into life all around the beholder burning radiant and clean. The beholder screamed and all its eyes closed even as its large face singed and began to smolder. The Apprentice looked for guidance from Kendra, but finding none called out again, "Retreat now and you live!" The sun burning directly behind the beholder and between it and the gate moved aside. "Three," the mage demanded. "Two."

The beholder tried to open its massive central eye but the sun there exploded growing in diameter many times. "Flee or die. You will make an excellent trophy for Takhissis!" the mage said as boldly as he could. Stark shadows erupted throughout the huge vault as rays of sunshine gleamed in the smoke and dust of their combat. In the shadow behind the dais, a battle priest dragged the lich further from the wand and away from the beholder. There he finished the job by smashing through the lich's neck armor with his sharp-bladed mace. When the gorget finally shattered, the mace brutally severed the lich's head. Sprinkling it with water from Morbatten's great temple, the priest carefully wrapped it in scripture-written cloths and sealed it into his gear pack.

The beholder's evil smile cracked open and that alien voice replied, "You bluff. You were many but are now few. You cannot defeat me. I am a GOD!"

"Last chance, ONE!"

The beholders wavered and then pulled back through the gate, which closed behind them. The remaining gas spores exploded. When a magical wind blew the spores away, the Order breathed deeply and then took stock of their wounded and fallen. They bore the scars and damage and wounds of the vicious battles that had brought them here. They had arrived drenched in the blood of their enemies. They had fought. Of the forty-seven arriving, only eight remained functional. All were exhausted or so close to death, that they just stared in stunned silence at each other.

Though not wounded, the Apprentice looked haggard and worn. He coughed and blood dribbled from his mouth and then he fell forward vomiting blood as the exertion and toll of his magic wracked his frail body. Wrapped in a cloak, the wand screamed for aid and sought to tempt and seduce a new host, but it could not see. Its random attempts to exert control seemed pathetic. One of the battle priests found an Imperic silk tapestry and unrolled it. They carefully placed the wand in it and rolled it back up.

One of the healers went to the Apprentice and used his last healing spell to fortify the mage. He stood and called out in magic. From across the room, Kendra's sword rose up from where it had fallen and took on a human shape. "The wand, it must be guarded. It is what she would want." The mage then spoke another word of magic and the sword nodded and dissolved into a tendril of metal that coiled and wrapped around the tapestry roll.

Another fit of coughing and vomiting pulled the Apprentice over. The survivors gathered up the fallen and ordered them into rows. They found Jaga, the Imperic who had fought with Malcor lying in a congealed pool of cooling but still liquid gold. He was dead and his corpse had answered the call of the wand to rise up and fight. They removed his head.

Chapter Sixty Four - Clean Up

A moment later, they heard footsteps from the outer seal of the golden door. Sir Allen and the knights of Pha Rann burst into the room and then quickly sheathed their weapons. "I see we are too late Tanians."

Their arrival spurred the Apprentice to choke back his suffering and stand. "You missed a glorious fight against the lich, many beholders, a horde of undead." The Apprentice choked back another coughing fit and whispered, "The sceptre of the Jade God. But we have recovered the Imperic souls and the city's wealth lies here."

Sir Allen looked around taking stock of the survivors and noted that only two paladins, one battle priest, and healers remained. He smiled magnanimously and was about to say something when a knight behind him suddenly charged forward. "You have stolen what is rightfully ours! Cuthbert will – "

The Apprentice, frail as he looked, rose up with power and stood firm. A barrier flashed out from his hand and shield wall appeared in front of the aggressor. "If you take another step, you all die."

"You dare to threaten Pha Rann?! Cuthbert?!"

His voice raw and strained, but amplified by magic they could hear the pain but also the pride when the Apprentice said, "Your gods were not here fool. Takhissis has done your work for you. Evil is vanquished. Will you not rejoice with us?"

Sir Allen walked up and touched the young knight, pulling him back. "Shut up and be still," Allen hissed at him. He bowed low and said, "I recognize your tokens but do not know your name. I am Sir Allen of Taysor, commander of the Ninth Pha Rannnic Legion. We witness your victory. Though less the fight we had hoped for, we – all of us – will help. What is needed?"

The Apprentice relaxed. "You are wise Sir Allen of the Ninth. We are recovering our wounded and fallen for treatment. There is also a wealth of treasure that rightfully belongs to Ori. Tania has no claim on what is

Ori's. There is a mass of other treasure here though I claim for Morbatten. Do you acknowledge my claim?"

Sir Allen pursed his lips. "It seems that we are in an opportunity to SIGNFICANTLY help you. That opportunity should be duly recognized." His voice smooth and steady but full of the implication that the opportunity could become a risk, was not lost on those present.

A rod of pure gold swirled up from the treasure floor and the Apprentice caught it and then leaned on it. "I'm sure we can work out something fair Sir Allen. Come, join me. As you know, Tania is less interested in gold. Let us discuss what is fair." Their voices trailed off as they walked away from the group.

The rest spread out to recover fallen equipment. The Tanian gear made quite a pile. No one could tell what belonged to who and some of the armor pieces had suffered so badly, they were not even sure it was Tanian. As the Tanian cleanup came to an end, Sir Allen's knights shared their food and drink with the Tanians. Though their priests offered to heal and attend to the wounded, one of the paladins said, "We are grateful for the offer, but unless we are attacked, we will await the Queen's grace."

Sir Allen and the Apprentice had reached a general agreement but for a few sticking points. "I do not like that Tania has already claimed recovery of the souls. If I remember, your Order was expelled by Ori weeks ago."

"That is true, and we left at their request. However, we did not know you were here. You did not exactly go out of your way to inform or even attempt to coordinate with Dar Kendra."

"Still, the task of defending and aiding Ori was explicitly requested and agreed to between Ori and Taysor. It is not enough for me to return with Ori's tribute."

The Apprentice looked back at Sir Allen's small handful of knights. "Tania committed the entire Order of Water to this. Let's pretend Sir Allen that you had beaten us here. Given our casualties, do you think you would have survived to recover anything?"

"With Pha Rann's blessings and might, of course we would have. Our god is far more powerful against the undead."

The Apprentice stared at him in poker-faced silence. "I am not a theologian here to debate which god is most powerful. You obfuscate the truth. What do you want?"

"The lich's body."

"Unacceptable. We slew the lich. We have already claimed the body."

"Something else then."

"Such as what Sir Allen? You will return Ori's lost wealth. You will take them their treasure."

"The lich's soul gem."

"Also both unacceptable and impossible. It was destroyed during the fight."

"I grow weary of this mage."

"As do I. I can offer you more treasure, but I cannot let you take what is not yours nor can I offer you what is destroyed."

"Pha Rann will restore the royal family, not Tania then."

"It will require some doing Sir Allen, but we can accommodate that. There was a brief moment after we freed the lich from the wand and then destroyed the lich, where I was able to capture the souls into a different place. It will take seven days. I will give you a soul gem prepared for their release."

"Two days. We must march back to Ori and free their souls."

"With great sacrifice, I can do this in three days Sir Allen, but any faster and we place them at risk."

"Then we have no deal," he said coldly.

"And you lose all we have agreed to, and your time is running out."

"Is that a threat?" he demanded his hand dropping to his sword.

"No, it is truth. This entire fortress is ready to implode. And, well there is this."

"What?"

From behind Sir Allen, a flickering light grew in brightness until even Allen noticed it. Turning, he frowned as Blade walked into the room from the other side. "You would not even have made it here as fast as you did had Blade not destroyed the outer armies and sealed off the mountain's entries. Do you wish to argue claims with a dragon?" The Apprentice whispered, "Three days or all bets are off Sir Allen. No guarantees."

"Curse you mage. I agree."

Blade walked up to them as the Apprentice said, "We are agreed then." More loudly, "Dread Lord Blade, we are grateful for your presence. That you returned to us is cause for celebration. I trust you returned the Imperics to Ori. Was the news that the captured souls would be returned within the week well received?"

Blade locked his gaze on Sir Allen. "I know you. We met, no that was your father."

"My grandfather actually. He used to tell us stories of the dragons he met in Tania."

"Very good. That would have been when my father signed the cease fire and trade agreement with Taysor." Without hesitation but relaxing the intensity of his glare, Blade continued, "Yes, it was well-received. Tembri and the wounded Tanian will be resting. I imagine you humans will have some kind of a party when this is over. Status?"

"We won Lord Blaze. I will prepare a full report when we have secured the Order. Though we have wounded, slain, and in some cases worse, we will recover with time, healing, and the Goddess' blessing. Sir Allen and these knights from Taysor arrived to help. We have agreed that they

426

will return Ori's tribute and the souls of the royals. They will also take the bullion you see here. My lord, I did not know when you might return and with Kendra's fall – "

"Those terms are too rich for Sorians." Blade whirled back to Allen and just a hint of his dragon terror whiplashed out. To Allen's credit, he barely flinched. "Without my help, without Tania's Mages Guild, without too many to list, this is pointless. More so, we came with forty-seven and a dragon. You came with fewer than twelve." He blew on his hand and a spark of fire formed there. He threw it across the room and it left a sparking line of fire hanging in the air. "For those groups, I take the left side. Based on numbers alone, you would be lucky to get even a third. Based on the involvement of dragons, you are lucky I am being so generous." Blade's eyes came alight with flame and he looked at Allen daring him to say anything.

The young knight of Cuthbert saw the exchange and sauntered over, his hand near his sword. Blade's back was turned to the boy but he said, "I would so enjoy eating a foolish knight. The thousands of enemies I destroyed on the mountain were too charred to eat." Blade turned his head towards the boy. "I'm unused to challenges like this. Fight me or no. I am done. Apprentice, make the arrangements."

"Yes lord, we will drain this fortress of its wealth."

Sir Allen retained his stare on Blade as Blade turned and walked into the point of the Cuthbert knight's sword. Without flinching, Blade licked his lips and continued walking. The knight pressed and said, "Wait, stop, I'll kill you!"

"You can try," Blade said and the tip of the sword ran molten against his skin as the next stop brought Blade to the crossguard. The thicker metal hissed and melted as the pommel became too hot for the knight to hold. He dropped his sword as his gauntlets caught on fire. "Begone foolish child."

But the knight, either too focused on removing his gauntlets or too foolish to move, did not. Blade seem to flicker and then was walking away on the other side of the knight to inspect the Order's fallen. "I challenge you

– " the young knight cried out but blood erupted from his mouth as his head tore apart into five slices held in place by neck tissue. He dropped to his knees and then gurgled forward. Blade licked his dragonshifted hand of blood and locked his gaze with Sir Allen.

Sir Allen, to his credit, did not move but ordered one of his healers to save the boy. "And ensure he stays unconscious. He will be punished as per the treaty dread lord Blade."

Chapter Sixty Five - The Falcon Forge

Ishan looked out over the workshop. It hummed. The marvelous metal falcon remained perched on the shop's sign and in its honor, he had renamed the forge from "House Tor's Foundry" to "The Falcon, an industry of Sai R'Dar". Sai had tested them at first with normal work. As they proved industrious and some capable with the magical heat stones, Sai had sent incrementally more difficult projects to them. Even at what R'Dar Ora had described as easy it had taken weeks for them to adjust. Their first mending of a magical blade though had resulted in a flood of repair and maintenance orders.

Ishan had ordered an unused storehouse converted to a new forge and moved the normal metal craft there. Besides bringing in amazing business, the magical forge became somewhat of an attraction with Klennan townsfolks and travelers often stopping to watch the work. Gone were the days of forced shifts. In their place, a profit-sharing announcement had arrived by messenger. At first, when Ishan had read the message it had struck him as too good to be true. "Why would Sai offer any of us a profit share?" After a few days though, when he did not share the message with the others workers, the metal bird had called out to them.

"Come, workers of The Falcon. Come and hear my master's words. Assemble in an hour and bring all those not present." An hour later, the falcon spoke again and said, "I am Sai R'Dar, the master golem smith. I am alive and yet do not live as I was made by the dragon emperor to serve and am blessed by the Goddess with free will.

"Hear me. You have come to me through Malcor, one of you, who now serves as a paladin. And, his emissary to my house, R'Dar Ora and Ishan, master forger. Hear me, I desire that this forge become known for excellence. This requires proper motivation and drive to excellence. Many of you are talented, but you still work at the most basic level of metalcraft. As such, I have decided to offer you a profit share. You will work for my house for half your shift. Continuing my work thereafter will result in double pay. Alternatively, you may study and enhance your skills and in the other half or your own time, you may take jobs and use my forge as you see fit. You will keep half profits and pay me half of any side jobs.

"Ishan bring forward the first sword. This sword is beautiful. It contains simple magic held in quality metal. It can be enhanced at least two more steps. But this repair netted ten gold coins. In this profit share, had one of you done this work, you would now have five of those ten gold coins. This program is effective tomorrow and shall stand so long as the House of Sai operates this forge. Direct any questions to Ishan."

After a moment of silence, a rider pulled up that turned out to be R'Dar Ora. Still stunned, the group parted for her and she walked over to the falcon and stood by Ishan. "Hi everyone," she flashed her bright smile at them. "Welcome to Sai's new hopes for this forge. We operate another one in another province that is buried with work. As such, I have brought work from there. The details will be listed on scrolls like these." She held up a small roll of parchment. "Lets see," she unrolled it. "Magical amulet. Clasp broken must be repaired with 90% gold, 10% mithril. Thirty gold," she read. "So, if one of you wanted to do this, you'd sign your name here. That will trigger magic that will bring the amulet to you. When the work is done, you will keep half of that amount. Any questions?"

Questions erupted but most fell into whether it was really real or not. Tor had often offered incentives but rarely made good on them always finding some minor flaw or using schedule of delivery or cost of materials to dodge having to follow through. One after another, Ora answered and then began directing them to Ishan. Her beauty and easy-going grace helped somehow make it all seem more believable and easy to take in. After an hour, she interrupted the group and said, "I must return to the Capitol tonight. Between now and then, I will be at Ishan's house if any of you need healing or blessings."

It had become habit that these types of gatherings attracted the family members of the forge workers. As R'Dar Ora left, many trailed after. By the time she reached Ishan's home, a line had formed with children bringing gifts and presents. Ora had become a beloved member of their community and she attended to them. Klara was first in line, beaming and holding flowers. Ora made a mental note to test her later that evening.

Ishan looked at the scroll and reread it to the group. After a moment, he rubbed his head and said, "So much has and is changing. This will change everything. However, I want to make something clear to all of you. We all have special talents. For better or worse, we lived with those talents under House Tor and did the work we had to do. This makes it so we still have to do that. Though not stated, the expectation is that we are looking at half shifts, if and only if, you are able to take on this higher order work. You all saw the sword and statue our boy Malcor made in his spare time, such as it was. What you don't know is that Malcor – when he did that work – was hardly himself. Its magic work and it changed him. This work, will no doubt, change those who do it. But, above all else, the work we do for House Sai takes priority. All this other stuff, it only matters if you are still employed here.

"Furthermore, I would imagine that if you took something like this amulet and ruined it, there would be consequences. As such, before you all get too excited, we need to ask some questions and figure out who is going to be able to do this. Moreover, once any of us begin doing this work, we'll earn more money than we ever made in years working for House Tor. I want this to be fair to those talented enough to do the work, but – in short, we need to put some thought into this. Let's spend some time thinking about how this might work and beginning tomorrow and for the next two days, bring me any questions. We will send them to Sai R'Dar and see what he says.

"I imagine this other forge that needs help can tell us some things about how this works as well."

The rest of the day passed with excited and whispered conversations amongst the workers. Ora tended to newborn infants, blessing them and healing any wounds. One small boy who had been burned when he tripped and fell near a forge presented particularly gruesome wounds and she asked, "Why did you not go the shrine?"

"We cannot afford the requested tithe and thought that this would heal. Many of the workers bear similar burn scars."

Ora sighed and made a mental note to investigate the province. "Our forge operating like this, is not going to work for Lord Sai. While I am

431

happy to help when I am here, it is not Sai's intent that I am solely involved in this one venture."

"Tell us Lady, will the lordship ever come and visit us?"

Ora smiled and brushed hair back from a chubby baby's face. The girl cooed at her and she said, "Lord Sai does not often leave his estate in the Capitol. His appearance startles normal people and over the years, he has come to accept that he is not really welcome in Tania. Though everyone knows his name, he prefers to act through liaisons like me, and his golem like the Cystoran Falcon."

So saying, she opened herself up to questions from all directions about the magical bird. What is it? Did Sai make it? How does it work?... and so on and on. Finally, Ora quieted them and said, "Look, simply put a golem is a magical construct that can look like anything, like the falcon appears to be a falcon. The magic of its existence is its ability to fly, to look, and act like a real falcon. It is so much more though. Sai can see through it. If needed, I can see through it. We can also speak to you through it. The voice earlier was my master's voice. These golems, they exist, they can act. But, unlike my master, they act within certain boundaries. This falcon for instance, will not fly off and seek food, but if ordered it can kill prey. Sai recognizes twenty additional levels of magical smith work. Weapons and armor are at the most basic levels, slightly above tools. The falcon is the twenty-first level. Except for Sai, none of his apprentices have mastered it. Many have tried."

A woman back from the initial crowd, "My husband has worked here for almost twenty years! Will he go back to being an apprentice?"

Ora stood to look at her, "It takes a certain type of person to master working with magic. If your husband has that talent, he will need to apprentice and learn new things."

Someone else shouted out, "Are you a golem?"

Ora smiled, "No, I am human. A daughter of the empire and Takhissis. But remember, there are many forms of life in this world. Even a golem can have life." She whistled a peculiar sound and seconds later, the falcon flashed in the afternoon sun and landed on her wrist. Unlike a bird with the flutter of feathers, this one had a metallic sound to it and barely audible whirring sound. After it landed, it preened at its wing feathers and Ora stroked its head. It pressed up to her touch and seemed pleased.

She called a small boy up to her and placed the bird on his wrist. "It, it's light!" the boy cried moving his arm up and down. "I thought it'd be super heavy!"

Other kids came forward to touch the falcon, who seemed pleased by the attention and let its wings and legs be yanked on. As afternoon stretched into sunset, Ora eventually said, "I'd love to stay and play but it is time for me to call it a night. I suspect that I will not see you all again for at least several months."

As the crowd dispersed, Ishan's wife came up to her side and asked her, "You don't show yet, how are you feeling?"

Ora grinned. "That obvious?"

"No, but I know when I see that look. Plus, Malcor is like our son. Does he know?"

"He will. I told him to look for me at Tania's eastern gate when the snow first falls. But, I haven't heard anything from him at all."

"Nothing?" Ishan's wife gasped with deep concern. "We are so worried about him. All these things happening, it makes us wonder what kind of folk have taken him in. And, yet, he is just a boy."

"Not a boy so much as a dreamer. The things I have seen him go through. The last I saw him, he had completed the first rite – a combat ritual that is part of becoming a paladin. He set a new record in an Order that is famous for breaking records." She chuckled but it was hard to make it seem like nothing when she still so vividly remembered how Malcor had fought through the Rite of Pain, for days. "Do you think he will be pleased?" and patted her stomach.

"I don't know R'Dar. In all his years with us, we watched him struggle with girls, with courtship, and he felt inferior to his friend Calvin. Calvin always had his way with any young thing that caught his eye. Malcor, not so much. And, maybe this is me as a mother, but Malcor's size and intensity seemed to keep the girls at arm's length. Why, I remember this one time, there had been a festival at the shrine and Malcor, oh he wanted to dance with this beautiful lass. He wanted to ask her to dance and he just stared at her. Eventually, she came over and asked him if he wanted to and Calvin interrupted them."

"That sounds like him, though my interactions with him have been more on the intense side. I first saw him lying wounded and healed him. He had slain his attacker. Each time after that, his destiny chases him more than most."

"Ah, yes. That I have seen. I can't tell you how many nights we'd wake up to the sound of the forge and find Malcor there, unresponsive, working on that sword or his dragon. I assume it has meaning?"

Ora nodded, "Most certainly. It was a vision from the Queen. The dragon especially. Though it has a name, we simply call that one the Heretic, a dragon who chose a different path than the Queen's." Seeing the mother's look of concern, she hurried to add, "Oh, don't worry. That Malcor made such a thing does not by itself mean anything. In fact, it is remarkable due to the fact that the doctrine about the Heretic are almost never discussed. And Malcor's statue is an exact likeness. Even the dragon emperor was most impressed and the High Priest Dar Kell commented on how perfect Malcor's work was."

"And how about Calvin then? His father has come by occasionally to see if we had heard from Malcor and by extension Calvin."

"Yes, Calvin was with Malcor when I first met them. He was accepted into the Order of the Shield. Though after that, my duties with Sai only allowed me time for Malcor. I haven't heard a thing since. The first rites are brutal though and it's not like they give new knights a lot of free time. I'm sure you'll hear soon enough."

A small boy came over and marveled at all the gifts. "What are you going to do with these Ora?" While most of it was knick knacks with little value, all of it had been painstakingly made by wives and children. The falcon was a common theme.

Ora smiled. "Master Sai enjoys it when his work is appreciated. At a certain level, wealth and more glorious gifts become somewhat trite." She looked at the boy who frowned. "Trite means he does not care about those things. I have found in the few years as his estate's priestess that he seeks for new ways of viewing his creations. Remember, he is not human. He was never a child. He never sees his own work through the eyes of children. I will show him these and I expect that he will enjoy them greatly."

"To not care about wealth, he must be a very powerful man."

Ora looked out the window at the setting sun. "You could say he is less of a man and more of a god. Consider this, we are all children of the dragons. But, the dragon emperor made Sai personally."

"It must be marvelous to have such magic and talent for it. As a priestess, may I ask, how did you become one?"

Chapter Sixty Six - Ora's Genesis

"I grew up in a kingship just outside of Morbatten. Usual story. Some feud here prompted a lord to take his retinue and leave. They established a fort on the wilderness' western edge. The plan was to make it part of the route to the elven lands of Morilon. Things were good for a time, or so my parents told me. Then the fighting started. Another lord built a dam up river from us. It destroyed the lake and streams from which we drew water. War followed. My father died in it. My mother, well she considered fighting too, but at the last second fled and took me with her. I was barely nine when this happened. We were lucky. We almost starved to death when winter came.

"Looking at maps, you don't appreciate how far things are when you're cold and starving and constantly under threat of attack or capture as a slave or worse. A war party found us and to protect me, my mother agreed to enslavement at the price of her freedom – "

"But, no, slavery? Here?"

"Remember, slavery is illegal and criminal, yes. But, there are those who can choose to become such. That then makes it legal. I promised my mother I would find and free her. The slavers brought me back to Tania where they auctioned my mother off and I was set free on the streets of the capitol. Unlike Malcor and so many others who seem to have found a home, I had no one. Knew nothing. I was nine. It was still winter and I was alone.

"During the festival of the winter solstice, I remember laying down on the stone edge of the Dragon Fountain. I looked up at the sky. I remember everything about that moment because I was so alone and terrified and lonely. I knew I was going to die. And then I saw it."

"What did you see R'Dar?"

"I saw the dragons. The emperor's sons flew over the city and then, as the emperor does, he leapt from his throne and joined them. They circled the city. I realized how gigantic a dragon and glorious he is. He dwarfs his sons. For the first time in my cold weeks, I forgot about death and loneliness. Well, you've seen them first hand at Malcor's ceremony here right? Everyone around me bowed and honored them, but I could not move. A group of guardsmen came through to enforce respect and found me there, lying on my back, staring at the dragons. They ordered me to do them honor.

"I was nine, and starving, near death. I didn't know what any of this meant. They were about to beat me, when one of the dread lords came. The winter dragon Ynt'taris. Even though he rules over winter in Tania, he does not fly with them in the solstice festival. He walks among the people. "Leave the child for she is mine," I remember him saying. He touched my fingers and all the cold left me and for the first time, I felt warm. Ynt'taris is rumored to be cruel and vicious, but I have never seen that side of the winter dragon. He picked me up and took me to the Temple. On his orders, I was enrolled as a priestess and never looked back. He saved me."

"The dread lord must have seen something special in you then. Your destiny."

"I asked him why he saved me when I passed my first rite and saw him again. You meet him you know. That is the first rite. He came to me on the emperor's mountain and hugged me like we had always been family. I have never felt more a sense of belonging as I did then. Do you know what he said?"

By now, a new group of neighbors had formed and Ora looked out over their faces. Women, children, Ishan, and even a few of the other smiths. "He said, "Great things await in your destiny little jewel of the empire. Great things. I can hardly wait to soar the winter skies with a friend. And, you are a treasure far greater than a mountain of diamonds. I see Mother choosing you and in time the great Northern Temple will stand renewed in Tehra. By your hand." It was my eleventh birthday and I had yet to learn of the role that temples play for the Goddess. Have you heard of the Northern Temple?"

No one had. Someone listening said, "Only the Temple at Morbatten and the other at Bloodstone. There are many shrines though."

"In the old empire, there was a great temple called the Temple of Glass. Like a prism in the sunlight, the Glass served all dragons. Though it was desecrated and destroyed during the Kinslayer Wars, there is a priestess here who serves as High Priestess of that one and holds it in her heart. There are other temples too, lost in time and legend. The Northern Temple is one of these, a place of short sunlight and never-ending winter where the white dragons and those who love cold worship the Goddess.

"Anyways, this is neither here nor there. The winter dragon. He told me these things. Taught me these things. He was my mentor. By the time most priests are just entering the temple, I had completed my first and second rite. Because I was so young, Ynt'taris helped me and I faced and defeated my mighty foe."

Ishan's wife looked at her sidelong and said, "A mighty foe is the second rite. So, that is what Malcor and Calvin are doing? Hmmmm. I'm not sure that I like that. Very much. Let me guess… your mighty foe – you sought out your mother?"

Ora chuckled and said, "You are wise and savvy and surprisingly intuitive. Yes, that was my mighty foe. The dread lord was worried that, being as young as I was, I would let the victimization root in my heart and it would forever unnerve me. He may have been right. Facing the slavers as an eleven year old probably seemed comical to them. Fortunately, the requirement is to face a mighty foe, not defeat that foe. I challenged the head slaver to a fight and after beating me, he told me that my mother had passed away shortly after they had sold her to House Sai. Though beaten, I kept trying to fight and in trying I felt something awaken in me." She touched her heart. "I felt a coldness here, so cold it became like fire, and at my crying and desperation, the coldness moved from my heart to my hands and suddenly, I fought with the Goddess' power and authority. Oh, I could feel Ynt'taris' exultation and he roared when the last slaver fell at my command.

"Ynt'taris took me from that rite and victory to House Sai. I saw for the first time how beautiful Sai's golems are. And I met him. The rest is history. I officially became a priestess."

Chapter Sixty Seven - The Truce of Dragons

Alerius watched Malcor in the scrying ball by his golden throne. His fingers drummed one after another on the armrest and he said, "Be sure my ambassador uses this to reinforce our trade agreement with Ori. This Pha Rannnic knight, he angers me. For zealots obsessed with transparency and light, they have a knack for bending their own doctrine to suit their needs. Tell me, is the sceptre secure?"

Daryx, Dar Reznor, and Sai R'Dar knelt before the emperor. Sai spoke in answer, his clear voice saying, "Yes father, the golem sword of Kendra has enwrapped the device. I feed it extra power to hold the sceptre quiet."

"Emperor," Reznor spoke now. "My apprentice indicates the wand is of the greater order. It contains a hellhound, rather is a hellhound. As such, we must transport it back in the real world."

Alerius nodded. "Have you uncovered its name?"

"No my lord, before attempting such we wished to have your permission and the wand safely held here in your or the guild's laboratories."

"Daryx, make all needful preparations for the sceptre to be brought back here by ship. Guarded, and safe."

The three nodded and all left except for Sai. "Sai, you please me. Kendra's sword is more than even I had hoped for. You surpass my own skill. Do you know how treasured you are?"

Sai bowed low, "Thank you father. How may I continue to serve?"

Alerius pointed to Malcor and said, "A day shall come where the boy will be challenged, same as his father. But, as a paladin, he must have a special sword. An avenger of radiant sun so bright it casts the shadows of doubt and chaos from his mind, and yet empowers his shadow-touched soul."

Alerius walked off his throne and at a hand sign, the attending priests and priestesses cleared the room and great passageway. Horns blew as the entire area emptied. With each step, Alerius' human self pulled off as talons, claws, scales, and titanic mass clad about him like armor. His voice changed from his human purr to rumbling baritone, "The radiant sword must burn with the sun and with anti-sun. It must serve him as an avenger but, yes. He must have two swords. One for the sun and one for the shadows. And you shall craft it with him to protect his faith. My son, begin research into the applications of a shadow sword. The mace used by Kell should serve as a model, but it must channel and serve the Goddess. When Malcor brings you a bloodstone, that shall be the time of crafting."

The emperor opened his hand and caught Sai onto his palm. The speed of their passage through the great tunnel increased and then Alerius burst out of his mountain and spread his wings to catch the thermal currents rising up from the city below. He roared and then turned north. Sai moved to sit beside the many horns that curved around his face. "You are going to Oranstakar father?"

"Yes, I must speak of the shadow clan and safeguard the Forsaken Isles. Those knights also concern me. We are overdue to speak with Oranstakar."

They sped through the Barrier Mountains, a shield wall that separated the two countries and then the snowcapped mountains dropped to brown valleys and farmlands harvested and fallow waiting for spring. Cattle and sheep scattered as Alerius dipped down to take advantage of faster air currents. Soon, they crossed over a broken series of hills topped with towers and in the distance, the smokey haze of Commerce, Taysor's capitol, came into view. Alerius sped straight at it and then veered west towards a lonely mountain on Commerce's flank that watched over the city.

Warriors manning the city's walls and towers pointed but most hid their faces or cowered in fear. Alerius landed at the base of the mountain and roared. Moments later, a golden scaled dragon delicate and serpentine, looked out from a cavern above and hissed down at Alerius, and then roared. Alerius roared back and then rapidly ascended the mountain claw over claw until he was eye to eye with the gold. The two eyed each other and then simultaneously, they humanshifted. Sai bowed before each.

The golden dragon retained his golden skin and all gold eyes. Where Alerius towered as a mighty warrior clad in armor and weaponry, Oranstakar the gold dragon wore the robes of a scholar. Tattoos wove around his arms in silver and copper white platinum jewelry adorned his ears, neck, and fingers. "A simple letter by courier would work just fine," he said to Alerius.

"I need – "

"Yes, you always need."

"My children have captured the Jade God's sceptre. It bears a hellhound. We must remove it to Bloodstone."

"Oh, I see."

"A ship shall bring the artifact from Ori to Morbatten. It must reach Tania safely. For that – "

"What are your plans for the device?"

"We will take it to Bloodstone, and destroy it. Same as the others."

"Ah, but brother, you have not destroyed the others. I hear things. You have several? A few? Why keep them at all? They are vile and pose a risk you understand far better than most. Why not destroy it where it is? My people tell me it would not be hard."

"Your people lie to you on multiple fronts. Do not insult me with what your petty humans say. Your idiot knights of Cuthbert almost drove the lich to the Necromancer. The damage to Ori is incalculable and they are not even allied with my nation. You are dead wrong in that destroying these is easy. You and I may as well go to the Abyss and knock on the jade one's throneplane."

"So, you plan to bring it through your home and then on to Bloodstone?"

"Yes. During a cascade, when the gates are already open, only then can

441

they be destroyed. And yes, I have several because cascades do not occur often enough to do this." Alerius hissed and stepped right into the gold's face as he said this. "Perhaps if you put your research aside and noted the real world, you would already know this."

The gold dragon shrugged, his voice impassive and without care, "My people have a busy beauty to them but fail to understand that I am anything other than a good luck fetish, to counter the mighty and dreadful Alerius. You shackle your people with chains of religion."

Alerius put his hand on the gold dragon's chest, "Yet you see and covet their worship, still. What you fail to understand is that treasure is treasure not because of its respect but because it is treasured." Alerius pushed and Oranstakar fell back. "Stay out of my face gold one. The treaties with this isle require you and I to agree on any dragon involvement outside of our fixed numbers. But there is another thing we must discuss."

Oranstakar muttered, "My emissaries to Ori tell me that your people were most uncooperative and unhelpful. They had to restore the taken souls."

"Your people arrived after all the hard work was done. For it, they were richly rewarded. It would have been nothing to destroy them outright for presuming to take their claimed half of the treasure. I allowed the restoration of souls by your morons but if they get in my way again."

Oranstakar bristled and turned away. After a few moments of calming down, he turned to face Alerius, "I had forgotten how difficult these discussions can be. Given that we want the same thing, how about this – I want to view and access any pieces of your part of the treasure, maybe even borrow some for study."

"We could fight for it, victor takes all." Alerius flexed his gauntlets and smiled razor teeth at the gold.

Oranstakar looked at the fire dragon patriarch and then began laughing. "Oh my brother, your sense of humor comes through at the oddest times! And here I had thought you must have lost it in your obsession with the humans. Why did you bring Sai?"

Alerius scowled at the gold dragon, "Too scared to even try? How long has it been since we last fought?"

"In these forms? I wonder." Oranstakar materialized a golden long sword in his hand and stared down its blade at Alerius.

"Any form, anywhere. Say it. The treasure taken in Ori should suffice. Victor takes all."

"True, true though I do not trust your accounting methods. And your son Blade hurt my knight's feelings. I wonder if the truce would even allow a simple duel..."

"The god of these lands would make an exception, I'm sure. With the right persuasion." A red sword surrounded by black lightning appeared in Alerius' hand and he looked down its blade at the gold dragon. "I brought Sai as a witness. Also because, unlike me, he is not distracted from the reason we came here."

The golden sword vanished and Oranstakar smiled. "Alerius, you tempt me. But we must alas fight another day. And you are right. Sai is here!"

Alerius pointed to Sai who stepped forward. "I would like to offer my services to you, for the creation of a golem, your choice." Sai bowed low.

"At what cost I wonder," Oranstakar said as he ran his fingers along Sai's form.

"No cost, just an agreement regarding more dragons."

The gold let go of Sai and stepped back with concern showing in his demeanor. "More dragons? Perhaps the cost is too high for my liking." A scroll appeared in Oranstakar's hand and he opened it. It held a detailed map of the Bloodstone Valley. "It would help if you tell me where the sceptre will be. Taysor shall increase its units at that location." His finger moved over the map to Haven, "And we shall deploy a battalion here and here."

Alerius growled low and violently. "That location, is near a new mine shaft. You may as well ask for a bloodstone."

"May I then? My concerns will cost a bloodstone. Either delivered to me or my battalion will find one here," and he tapped his finger on the map.

Alerius thought for a moment then replied, "Very well Oranstakar. I will instruct the Bloodstone Campaign to expect your battalion at the Seventh Fortress by spring? For however long it takes you to build this golem, the Seventh shall be presided over by Taysor."

Oranstakar bowed and turned to Sai. "Tell me about these other dragons Sai."

Sai spoke just one word: *Cor'tanos*. "You wish to bring the heretics back? Even the Father refused them. Why and why now?"

"They seek to come back before their extinction. The shadow realms are killing them, diminishing them. They will come back, with or without us brother. With us, we can shape and help them. Without us, I have no doubt, the Jade God or some other abyssal or hell power takes that opportunity. Besides Sai, and a bloodstone, I offer you a registry of the shadow dragons so that you shall always know where and who and what they are."

Oranstakar summoned another book and flipped through some pages. "Bahamut cast the shadow dragons out. Unlike your Queen who chose to hold them in hate, they are not welcome in heaven or this world. I'm not sure I can abide their presence without challenge."

Alerius held out his hand and a transcribed page from the Darkhold appeared. "This is a copied page of the Darkhold regarding the shadow patriarch. Read it."

Taking the page in at a glance, Oranstakar nodded. "I see. You wish for your paladins to become hosts to possess the shadow wyrms. It will create a new order of knights, powerful beyond human imagination."

"Yes, I'm surprised I am so transparent to you."

The gold dragon chuckled and observed, "With you reds, it's always a straight line to war applications. The treaty requires parity brother. What do you propose?"

"A beginning and a foundation. My children are torn and tested by war and prophecy. There is no quiet space to forge them into this. There are perhaps two who can make this happen and they shall be the beginning. Our truce requires parity in this matter. I await your proposed parity however you propose." Seeing the gold look at Sai, the emperor added, "But you may not lay claim to my children."

"Very well. For parity, I will require access to your research for ten human years –"

"No," Alerius growled.

" – and assistance from Sai to work three bloodstones of my personal choosing into mighty artefacts against the shadow dragons."

"To the second term, no as well. You may have one. The one you have laid claim to. You will never have access to my research. While your people hold the Seventh, I will grant any bloodstone mines found to Taysor for ten years, exclusive."

"Two additional bloodstones then brother, and Sai's assistance in creation. That is my final offer. If the evil of the shadow clan cannot be contained, I will never compromise with you." Oranstakar summoned another book and while flipping pages, he absently commented, "and you'd be a fool to not create such weapons as well." When Alerius said nothing, the gold looked up and smiled. "I see, you already have. Very well. One bloodstone, Sai's assistance in creation, and my selection from the shadow weapons already created."

Alerius turned and while dragonshifting to leave said, "These terms are acceptable to me but you must agree, your people at the Seventh are still part of Dar Ana's command structure. We cannot risk a war between our people in that place." Without looking for agreement, Alerius' shoulders shrugged as his wings unfurled and he dragonshifted high into the sky. He immediately turned south and returned home.

Looking over the city of Commerce, Alerius allowed his focus to shift out of the River and enjoyed the twinkling chaos of humanity as it pursued its passions. He noted the devout, the passionate, and the lackluster all intermingling in the River. It would be good to return back to Morbatten where all of his children beamed like bright stars in the night sky. He let loose a terrible roar at the sun and watched as those lacking fervor suddenly came to life with fear. He chuckled knowing that Oranstakar would exact a price for that. "Let him try!" and he roared again as he crossed the city's southern wall.

Chapter Sixty Eight - Calvin's Foe

Calvin stretched back and idly took notes. It was hard to pay attention because the priestess who had entered to observe was seductively gorgeous. Below him on the stage of the amphitheater, an old man droned on and on about battle tactics and their evolution from the days of the barbarian tribes up to the current age. The other students seemed so engaged, but all Calvin could think about was how he would be visiting a local tavern where worked a very beautiful waitress. Not as beautiful as the priestess, but still. He found it hard to focus, to concentrate these days. His time as a knight had shown he could do it. He should be a knight. It was his right, his destiny. He sighed and rubbed his face trying to tune back into the lecture.

"The Ancients," the term he and Morbatten used for the northeastern barbarian tribes, "would set ambushes and then swarm their prey. Their earliest prey consisted of plains animals and larger wild game, but as they wandered more and more in the Barrier Mountains, they encountered prey they could not eat. Ogres, gnolls, and orcs. These enemies served as a honing wheel for the Ancients. They had to evolve. How did they?"

Ayden, the girl with the terribly scarred face, answered, "They sent out scouts to spy and then began modeling their own units to resemble them. Fast and ferocious fighters were modeled after the gnolls. Large and strong ones after ogres. And so on, but the real change was the discovery of iron."

"Very good Ayden. Tell me class, between the two – tactics versus tools – which is most important and why?"

A short and wiry Halfling girl behind Calvin answered and said, "Tactics. If you can't outthink or outsmart your enemy, the quality or type of tools becomes almost irrelevant."

Calvin raised his hand and when it was his turn he said, "I think there has to be a balance. A small child can outthink an ogre, but will still lose. At best the child can only hide and hope the ogre moves on. More so than

447

iron, wouldn't magic and divine spells from the Goddess matter more than anything? Who needs an iron spear when you have the dragon emperor mentoring you?"

The discussion became quite heated as the class divided into various opinions. As they spoke, doors to the back of the stage opened and soldiers dragged a gnoll onto the stage. The nine foot tall creature full of muscle, sinew, and topped by a jackal's head spit and howled at the soldiers. Its disheveled appearance and wounds seemed mostly self-inflicted as the beast pulled at the metal chains.

From the other side of the stage, an Ancient stepped. It was a girl probably no more than nine years old. She walked to the center of the stage and bowed. Behind her, another child walked onto the stage. This one, a normal Tanian, also bowed. Neither wore armor. Neither carried weapons. The instructor said, "We're going to have a demonstration of a place where neither tactics nor tools really apply. Both of these children are gifted with different kinds of magic."

The Ancient stepped forward and composed herself. As she did so, the gnoll looked up at her fearfully and then with increasing anger. At a signal from her, the gnoll's irons snapped loose and the creature leapt at the girl child. Everyone held their breaths as the girl, without flinching, looked on at the gnoll's onslaught. Its hand tipped with dirty claws raked down at her head and then at the last second, it stopped. Calm soothed its snarled and toothy face and its hand relaxed to instead the pat the girl on the head.

The girl took the monster's hand and turned to the audience and both of them bowed. The gnoll picked her up and spun her around the stage playfully. She laughed and giggled when the gnoll threw her some thirty feet into the air and then caught her. He put her down and bowed again. The girl pointed to the young boy and the gnoll nodded his head. Straightening his curled back, the gnoll carefully walked over to the boy and amidst much drooling and spitting said, "My friend says you're scaring her. Go away."

The boy replied, "And what if I don't? You going to stop me?"

The gnoll's face twisted into an evil grin and he howled, "Your blood!" The clawed hands went straight for the boy's neck but scant inches from the boy's body, lighting suddenly coursed through the monster electrocuting it. The boy caught the energy as if ropes and focused it down to the gnoll's convulsing body wrapping it in ever more lightning. After several seconds of noise and searing energy, the boy let go of the energy. The gnoll looked at the girl and winced. Though wounded, it was still very much alive.

The girl walked over to the gnoll and said, "Thank you for delivering my message. You're a great warrior and a mighty protector." At her touch, the gnoll healed and then fell asleep. The girl turned to the class, "My father is a member of the dire wolf tribe. To be a full member of the tribe, the member must possess a special something here." She tapped her head. "My mother and her mother and so on back to the emperor's coming have had an empathic ability to sense things. We just knew. Like I knew the gnoll wanted to live, to escape, to eat, to survive. I offered him that and he leapt at it because that's what he most wanted. I'll take questions later."

The boy stepped up to her side. "I'm not like her. My father retired from the dog soldiers and married my mom. Early on in testing, I scored quite well in certain magical abilities. I was placed with the Mage's Guild when I was six years old. While many people can use magic through study, the guild says I use magic without thinking, like a berserker. Things happen and when I respond, sometimes it is lightning, fire, ice, whatever. I can't really control how the magic responds. Also, I don't know that I will ever develop a defensive ability. Like you saw, the magic tries to eliminate the threat rather than protect me. I'll take questions later too."

The instructor came up and they gave the children a round of applause. "The power exhibited by both is remarkable. The Dire Wolf Tribe is one of those tribes that, should you ever do your genealogy, if it is available to you, you'll find most of us have some. The emperor wanted all of us to have either gifts like this or some resistance to such gifts. Like this girl here, the gifts can be extraordinary." He pointed to the boy, "And the Mage's Guild finds boys like this and raises them up to be fighters, but unlike a battle mage, they fight with the fighters in front line combat.

Their magic is too uncontrollable for most applications but the empire values their contributions as cavalry and battle mages. Questions?"

Ayden asked, "What are the limits of your abilities?"

The girl spoke first, "I can only work with creatures that can understand me. For example, if this gnoll did not understand our language, or stupid creatures like a forest animal. And when I press into the mind of another human, sometimes they can resist me. Go ahead, try it. I'm going to try and make you sneeze. Resist it." Ayden's face immediately scrunched up and her eyes began watering. She kept beginning to sneeze and would then choke it back. "You want to sneeze but in reality, your body knows you don't. It'll drive you crazy though, later today, when you do sneeze. You'll wonder, was it because of that little girl or because you actually had to sneeze?"

The class chuckled. "Now, lets see if I can make you feel really different. Emotional control is much much harder. Maybe there is a boy here you like? The problem is that I don't really know what love is and so that becomes a limit for me until I'm older. Don't worry Ayden, I won't tell anyone who you like. But also, you shouldn't worry about the scars. He doesn't care. He actually likes them. I'm going to stop now but keep up your resistance. You did a good job." A man next to Ayden sneezed and then one after another in a straight line, each person in turn sneezed.

The boy said, "My biggest limit is that I don't really have control over how this works. One night I woke up and my room was on fire. Another time, I wanted to go swimming and when I jumped in the water, it froze solid. Moreover, I'll never be able to do something delicate like making people sneeze. With my luck and the way this works, I'd end up drowning all of you in poison gas. The group I am with, we are very accident prone. I think that is the greatest limitation. Things happen and even amongst ourselves, we're never quite sure if it's because one of us did it or it's something that just randomly happened."

Calvin asked, "When you used lightning on the gnoll, how does your lightning compare with a trained mage?"

"It's raw. I'm always at full power. A normal mage can fine tune the lightning. They never expect the lightning to do anything other than what they summoned it for. In my case, with all of you watching, I just felt grateful that the lightning stayed focused on the gnoll. But, there are older wild mages like us who are more able to direct it. They say it's instinctive so, while they can't summon lightning, if the task is best suited for lightning, more often than not, lightning is what happens."

The class ended after a few more questions and then the guards removed the gnoll. They had a short break and then the last session of the day started, "Knightly Orders and Heraldry". A different instructor walked into the room. Unlike the last one, this next instructor wore full plate armor and walked with purpose. Even though he appeared to be older than Calvin's father, the man's carriage was strong and his eyes bright. He snapped to attention and his presence pulled the class to silent attention.

"Welcome!" he boomed. "You are here because either this is where you wanted to be or the knighthood determined you would be better as an officer. As such, we are going to talk about the knights. One of you impress me. I need a volunteer."

A few hands went up and Calvin was unsurprised to see Ayden volunteering. The man chose someone else though. Once on the stage, the instructor demanded, "By looking at me, I want you to tell me who I am, starting now."

"Um, okay. Lets see. You served two tours in Bloodstone. You have the Winter Warrior star. You have three commendations for honor in combat and another for service to the Temple – "

"Am I a knight?" He drew his sword and stabbed it down into the wooden stage. The blade ignited with fire that did not burn him.

"Um, I don't see anything, any sign of a paladin order – "

"Correct! I am not a knight. What am I?"

The sword's flame made it hard for the student to see. "I'm sorry my lord, but I cannot tell. Is there a medal I can't see perhaps?"

The instructor extinguished the sword's flame. "I am a captain. An officer in the ranks of the dog soldiers, same as you will be someday. My ensign of rank is my sword. Same as the paladins but without a sign of any paladin order." He tapped his sword's pommel. "This sword is different than the normal officer swords. Once you pass, you will all be sergeants. Sergeants carry the swords you all think of as officer swords. At the next rank, of captain, you receive a special sword, called an officer's blade. The sword, not you, is promoted. I am a captain because my sword's rank is that of a captain. Any questions? No, good. Lets talk about paladins. There are orders. What are some of the Orders you have met?"

Shield, Fire, The Wall, The Tower, and then someone asked if there is a dragon order. "No, there is not. The orders are elemental first, and then by function next. There are no dragon orders. Our friends to the north do that. The Order of the Gold Dragon or whatever nonsense. Their names get pretentious. They bore me. Order of Fire though, impressive. Who said that and how do you know?"

Calvin raised his hand. "A student and friend of mine was promoted to that order some weeks ago."

The captain thought for a moment, "A girl right? Seline, from the Dutchy?"

Calvin nodded. "Excellent!" the captain said. "Excellent, so tell me what you know!"

"Well, I don't know much. Seline was promoted mid-class. She had volunteered and a Dar priestess promoted her during the class. I never really saw her again. We fought in a sparring match and she beat me. I saw her the other day. Her eyes and lips glow red though and she has a feeling about her, of heat. I don't know how to describe it. Her armor too. Actually all of her gear, it seems – um, it makes the nicest stuff we have here look drab by comparison. I feel like she has moved to a completely different level."

The instructor nodded and agreed enthusiastically. "The Order of Fire is sponsored by the emperor's son Blaze. Think of them as the assault team. The front line fighters. The do or die spitfires you can count on to

452

fight like dragons and demoralize our enemies by smashing their strongest to ash. What's your name?"

"Calvin, of Klenna."

He paused in thought and looked around and asked, "So, you had a friend taken into another order too right? Do you know which one?" Calvin shook his head.

"Fair enough. Lets talk about the elemental orders. I've told you about Fire. There are three other elements. Of the three, which is the strongest? Form into four groups." He pointed and assigned an element to each.

While they talked about the relative merits of each element, the major would briefly listen and ask probing questions like, "Earth isn't just mud, volcanoes, landslides, mines, and construction. It's our home. What we stand on. It supports our crops, carries our water. Without earth what are we?" Calvin ended up in a group with Ayden and they talked about Water.

"What a stupid order. Water," Calvin said. "Water is weak. This must be the group that makes everything more difficult than it should be or cleans up afterwards."

About half their group disagreed and half agreed. When the captain came to them, he corrected them, "Without water, there is no life. Nothing. Not us, not anything. Even the most ferocious monster needs water. As such, change your perceptions of weakness to water as either the ultimate foundation of life or the greatest weakness of any living thing. By the way, Water is the strongest order. I can tell by your expressions that you don't believe me. *But teacher*," he imitated a whiny child, "*we've never heard of the Order of Water! There are no legends of the Order! They're all wet!*"

"Water is the strongest. Think about it."

Chapter Sixty Nine - Respite

It took many days but eventually, the healers restored the fallen and they recovered in Ori. Kendra quickly returned to command though was careful to not exert herself beyond the wounds she had suffered before petrification. Dar Kell tended to her personally as only he had the clout to enforce her healing time. For the most part, the Imperics left them alone except for when Sir Allen's group restored the souls of the taken. The vitality, as it returned to the daimo and his family, triggered citywide celebrations that lasted for days. It would be many more days before the caravans returned with the captured treasure of the mountain. Sir Allen's group and then only the top-ranking members of Morbatten were invited to the parties, which sat just fine with the Order of Water.

Malcor heard voices and tried to open his eyes. His face felt heavy and impossible to control. He fell back asleep. "How long has he been like this Tembri?" Kendra asked with concern.

"Dar Kendra, after we returned, I tended to him properly but he is exhausted worse than his Rite of Pain. I have had to use combat interventions to restore his heart many times." Malcor felt Tembri's rough hands touch his forehead. "I have had to ward his dreams as well. They are dark and I often have had to restrain him."

Kendra stroked his face. "This is bad. I feel responsible."

Then Malcor heard Kell's voice approaching. Part of him, from the darkness, rose up feeling welcome and happy. The darkness within the dark watched and was aware of Kell. Kell touched her arm and said, "You know better than most how things change with the hounds, shadows, and the sceptre involved. By itself, that Malcor confronted and fought the Wand satisfies the second rite. Retrieving the soul gem even more so. It is the stuff of legends. That he fought for almost a month to get there and the foes he encountered along the way, surely this must be a new record even for your Order dear sister. He is listening to us."

Malcor tried to say something but Kell cut him off, "Don't. Save your strength record-setter. Let me summarize. The regeneration ring you emptied, it heals you as an accelerated form of natural healing. It leaves scars. Normally, we would heal over those after inflicting far greater surgical wounds. You are too weak for that and will be for too long. You will bear these scars forever sir. We also had to restore you from the encounter that withered you, when the lich touched you. A lesser man would have been soul-sucked.

"On top of that is the dragon mark. You have been through a lot Malcor. Your goal to face a mighty enemy… you faced a god, in the form of that ogre possessed by the Jade God's sceptre. You then tried to attack the sceptre-possessed lich, which is like attacking a hellhound or even the dragon emperor.

"The worms. The lich. You did it. You also channeled Tembri's divination prayer to find the soul gem. Because of you, the empire has won a great victory where normally we would have won just a new member to our Order. The soul gem kicks it up a notch. So, rest. Relax. Remember your second rite and how long it took to feel normal again."

Kendra said, "Kell, this is my fault. The plans to help him encounter the lich…"

"Changed. Forever. The River has moved past it."

"No, not for me. Daryx made me a liar."

"I do not think the emperor will allow a challenge amongst members of the Circle."

"Then I will leave the Circle."

"Daryx would have had no way of knowing the Jade God would get involved. That he found out at all and effectively countered it, is miraculous. If anything the Jade God made you a liar."

"Daryx's job is contingencies against the Jade God. When the lich's eldar nature was confirmed – "

"You were immediately counselled. You could have pulled the mission. Let it go. Many others have sought to take Daryx down, and have failed.

The Queen favors him even though he is an infidel. She may not allow you."

"The Queen will allow a righteous challenge. I see it. I will resign from the Circle."

"And what of him?"

"Tembri will watch over him. You will too." Tembri grunted in agreement.

"I will Kendra, but I will not allow my sister to stand against Daryx alone. I will stand with you sister. Plus, the Circle must learn that the Temple and the Order of Water stand united, always. Cor'tanos must see it so."

Malcor only heard bits and pieces of this talk but later, when he finally opened his eyes, he found his room dark. Light edged in around a door and slatted window frame. He heard the sounds of a celebration and tried to stand up but fell back to the bed. Unconsciousness took him again.

Time passed and again Malcor opened his eyes. Tembri sat by his bed. Back behind him, Sako and Noboyuki both looked up and smiled. Sako rushed to his bed, "Malcor! You're finally awake! Guess what? You're going to be tested to join the paladins! Isn't that more than what you wanted?"

Her intensity hurt his ears and his head began to throb. Tembri pulled her back. "Malcor, you have made some friends it seems. Here," he helped Malcor drink some tea. It tasted good and he gulped it down. It hit him, how profoundly hungry he felt.

"More," he gasped. Sako and Noboyuki began laughing saying they had seen that look several times before during their adventures.

"Malcor, you are so very lucky to have a mighty priest like this help you!" Sako laughed.

Malcor listened to them talk and at some point, the two Imperics took their leave saying they'd be back. Tembri helped him eat until he felt like he would burst. He signed to ask if they were alone and when Tembri nodded, he asked, "Tell me Tembri, what happened to the party, the Order, I want to know everything."

"You are very tired and recovering from very serious wounds Malcor. There is much to tell. I'll share a very high level overview of the high points. We won. You accomplished your rite with golden ribbons and bonuses for overachieving. While the lich was the initial goal, your confronting and standing against the Wand of the Jade God transcends "a mighty foe". The Wand is considered a minor deity. You also broke the record for youngest/greenest paladin to successfully commune with the Goddess; that you did so and recovered the lich's soul gem made this overall adventure a rousing success for Morbatten. It was also, might I add, very profitable for everyone involved."

Malcor smiled, "So I did my second rite?" He tried to sound happy but it came out as a whispered yawn as he fell back into a deep sleep. By the third day, he was back to where he had felt he was after the Rite of Pain. Sako came and visited often. There was a huge ceremony where the Imperic Royal family thanked Sir Allen and the people of Morbatten for aid in both restoring the taken souls and the nation's treasury. Sir Allen made a speech that just when it started to upset the Tanians, the dread lord Blade stepped forward and removed him from speaking.

Blade's speech, full of victory, glory, passion of combat, great deeds, and self-sacrifice for the greater cause of Ori's national identity struck a chord with the people and roused by dragon-incensed emotions became a raucous din. While Sir Allen fumed in the background, the crowd chanted "Ori! Ori! Ori!" and when the daimo rose to speak it was minutes before things quieted enough for the old man to speak. He held up a written speech and then smiled broadly. "After that rousing speech, I throw this away! The truth is that Ori came under attack. Thanks to the mettle of you my people, the blessings of Imperius and the servants of the gods we call our allies, we have won! Ori shall never fall!"

Sako and Noboyuki were brought forward and then Tembri smacked Malcor on the back and propelled him to the podium. "You're not formally a knight until you take your oaths sir, enjoy yourself!" he said. Looking out over the see of spectators, Malcor felt every eye stare at him. He followed Sako and the priest in bowing to the people and then to the daimo. A medallion graced with the Imperic letter for Commitment was placed around his neck.

When the cheering stopped, the daimo rose and congratulated them. He then eulogized the fallen members of both their party and other parties who did not return. "A monument shall be built at the southern gate so that all who pass through to the wilds may remember the brave heroes who fought for our freedom! Malcor, step forward." The daimo bowed very low and very formally and then the entire plaza did. "You came to us from far away seeking fame, glory, and wealth. In doing so, you saved my people. You recovered my soul and my wife and my good friends. I understand from honored cleric Noboyuki that you fought with the courage of samurai, the mastery of kensai, the fury of sumo, and the honor of Imperius. You shall forever be a friend to the people of Ori!"

Similar speeches followed for Sako and Noboyuki though it was very confusing when Sir Allen stepped forward and was congratulated for liberating Ori's wealth and returning the stolen souls. Malcor tried to keep his face impassively stern like Sako's, but when the Queen of Ori approached him later on and asked about it he knew he had betrayed his true feelings. "I have no issue with Sir Allen's claim. It's only that we fought so hard and I don't remember hearing or seeing them, ever."

She empathized with him and said, "When evil and magic combine, it is sometimes hard to know the truth. Sir Allen is a friend of Ori's and his honor is beyond question. May I suggest you bring it up with your own people? Here, let me help you." She waved a gorgeous dancing girl over and put her hand in Malcor's hand. The old lady winked at him. "She will teach you our dances and ensure you have a partner. When it is my turn to dance with you young man, I will have high expectations!"

Just a few seconds of dancing and Malcor grew dizzy to the point that Tembri intervened. The girl bowed graciously and offered instead of dancing, "Would a massage help?"

They walked off to a side room and by the time that Tembri laid Malcor down, Mal had fallen asleep. The girl gasped looking at the many wounds, scars, burn marks, welts, and eroded damage to Malcor's skin. Tembri pointed to a few and told what had happened. "I'm sure he'll sleep for hours, but as a healer, I know a massage is always welcome."

Chapter Seventy - From Ori to Tania

Malcor continued to recover, gaining in strength and recovering his mental awareness. One day, Tembri grabbed him and said they had to go to a meeting of the Order. It was the first time he had seen them all. The mood was jubilant. The group smiled and more than a few broke into big smiles when they met Malcor's eyes. Kendra stood forward and said, "C'mon everyone, you're acting like I'm a statue or something!" referring to her petrification. "We won! We knew we would. We did not know the path our victory would take. Like a river, our path meandered, even changed several times. We have business to attend to and then happier things for all of us. First the business.

"The Wand remains secured by my sword and under our watch. A ship docked here today that will take it back to Tania. Lord Blade and two other ships will escort. Besides Malcor, I have asked Verit to attend to the Wand's security on the ship. I will be with dread lord Blade in the air. The rest of you will either be on the escort ships or will gate back to Tania with the Apprentice. Malcor and Verit, you will attend us after this meeting for more instruction.

"Malcor, Sir Malcor, please stand and come join me here." As Malcor walked up to her and bowed, Kendra spoke to the group. "The original parameters of our mission were to help Malcor fight the lich. The Order would weaken the lich and create a fair fight for our newest member to actually kill the lich. That did not happen, and while we all share some blame in that, I am most to blame and will take it up with the Circle and the emperor and Daryx specifically. The odds quickly became impossible when Malcor found himself alone, cut off from us, cut off from the motherland. But, like a knight, like a dragon, he fought on and on and on, past the breaking point, past the point where even paladins despair and angels cry out for release.

"He fought on and when, alone, he found a far greater foe than the lich. He found the Jade God's sceptre. He did us proud. He called on his battle priest for assistance and fearlessly challenged the great evil of the Wand of the Jade God. And when the wand called to the lich and got so close to becoming a hellhound, Malcor continued to fight, and was stricken, withered; his very life withered.

"In that moment, no amount of training, no dream, no destiny could have prepared Malcor to face the Goddess. Stripped of everything even his very life force, he succeeded in asking and understanding how to obtain the soul gem. And, because of this, we won!" She held the bracer with the soul gem out. "Here! This is the foe Malcor vanquished. We, the Order of Water, we proud and mighty few, we may have destroyed the lich's body and captured the Wand, but Malcor faced the Wand first and delivered to us the key to winning this battle! All hail Malcor!"

The Order, amidst much armor smashing, cheering, and congratulations, cried out their approval. When it faded down, Kendra said, "We will hold this soul gem, but Malcor, when you get back to Morbatten, you have one last task before you. You must ascend the emperor's mountain. You will take him the soul gem as your trophy. The emperor has asked that you take your oaths with him, witnessed by our Order. Having completed your second rite, you will then prepare for your Bloodstone Campaign. You ride at first snowfall, with the king Dar Rojo, to Bloodstone!"

Cheering erupted again and amidst it all, Malcor felt a dizzy sense of elation that had been completely absent when he had fought against the Wand. He turned and looked around at the Order, his band of brothers and sisters. Smiles, no envy, only glorious anticipation met him on all sides. Suddenly, Tembri embraced him and he realized the battle priest had tears in his eyes. "We're going to Bloodstone SIR Malcor! You are exactly what I have prayed to the Goddess for – a worthy knight to fight with! Thank you Goddess!"

The trip back to Morbatten passed uneventfully. With dragons escorting and the Mage's Guild assisting weather and travel, they made record time with no issues. Most surprising of all to Malcor was, when leaving, both Sako and Noboyuki sought him out and met him at the docks. Both gave him gifts. Sako gave him a delicate and gorgeous silk folding fan on which the character language of the Imperics she had written the word for "valor". Noboyuki gave Malcor a bottle of their famous rice wine *sake*. After presenting him these gifts, Noboyuki bowed very low and said, "Your priest friend Tembri, he says you are to fight in Bloodstone. If true, will you accept us in your squad? We wish to see and fight in this place!"

Sako added, "Ori feels so small now that I have fought outside of it. Though not as mighty as you, I have no doubt that our skills will serve your cause!"

Taken aback, Malcor looked at Tembri. "I have heard of Bloodstone but do not yet know what rules there are – "

"As a paladin-to-be Malcor, you will be a squad commander for your first tour. A squad may be as small as seven and as large as twenty. Having fought with your Imperic friends, I see they will be assets to you. The only thing to bear in mind is that Bloodstone is deadly, and also very profitable. Even a single bloodstone ruby is priceless. Squad members share what the squad finds."

"I see, then, yes. You may join. My orders are to leave for Bloodstone at first snowfall, but will probably not head there directly. There is a township called Klenna that we will pass through. Join me at Morbatten at first snowfall, or Klenna thereafter."

Both bowed low and expressed their gratitude and commitment to Malcor and the Bloodstone quest. "One other thing," Malcor added. "Do not bring anyone else. Please? I do not want to be responsible for any others I cannot vouch for. It's not that I don't trust you, but as my first tour, I want some flexibility in case Tania needs to add others to the group."

"Understood!" they both echoed. Sako indicated she wished to speak in private. Tembri and Nobo left and Sako fell to the ground prostrate before Malcor. "Malcor, I want to apologize formally and in person. You have been gracious and brave. When you first saved us from the ogre, Jaga ordered and it made sense to me to charm you. I did not know the man you are, that I know you to be. I regret and apologize."

"That time feels like it happened years ago Sako." He bent down and lifted her up. "Let's just not do it again. Though, once you're with me in Bloodstone, we may need that type of thinking, so let's just not do it to me all right?" They hugged and said farewell.

Outside, the ships awaited and Malcor found a high place near the bow to sit and watch the waves. The tranquility and ever-changing sea scape lulled him to sleep with only Tembri bringing him food. The crew and other passengers left him alone except during a few rare moments when Malcor felt good enough to engage with them though anything physical at all made him light-headed and dizzy.

Once they arrived in Morbatten, an honor guard of Dar rank heroes escorted the Wand from the eastern docks to Dragon Mountain. There, at the base of the mountain, Malcor saw R'Dar Ora from a distance. She smiled and waved at him. He was so pressed in by guards and the nobility though that he barely managed to wave back. At the long winding trail that ascended the emperor's throne, Dar Kendra met him and placed the lich's soul gem in his hand. A leather satchel along her shoulder contained the black dragon statuette he had made what seemed like lifetimes ago.

"Malcor," she said. "Remember. You are not the boy who challenged me in the Temple. You faced down Ynt'taris. You exceeded records held in the Rite of Pain. You have also set new records for the Second rite. As large as the emperor and the Circle may seem, never doubt that YOU are impressive to them. Do the Order proud. Stand without hesitation. Answer bold, loud, and clear. Give your statue, at last, to the black dragon. I bless you, Sir Malcor, newest member of the Order of Water."

She signaled and the draft horses pulling the wagon on which rested the sword bound and tapestry tied Wand began rolling up the path. Malcor fell in behind the wagon. As he walked, he reflected on his adventures. During the ship voyage, the fatigue and lethargy had finally passed. He still felt bouts of exhaustion but for the most part could compensate. His armor, his sword, his boots, all the gear he had trained in and then forsaken during his adventure felt so good to have back.

To his right, the sun finally rose over the Temple Mount and its light felt warm against the autumn wind. Leaves swirled along the path and the horses snorted. It felt good to be in the light although it did make that dragon scale mark on his right arm itch.

Up they wound until the leaves vanished and the treeline disappeared. The wind increased in intensity and patches of ice lurked in the path's shadows. The horses trudged on having been trained specially for this.

Along with Malcor and the Wand's escorts, Verit walked in silence. Other supplicants from all walks of life walked with them. Malcor did not doubt for a second that some of them were masquerading as such to provide extra security for the Wand.

That Wand. He never would have guessed that such a thing would have shaped the empire's history. It seemed fantastical that a dread demon god universes away would create such a thing. Tembri had told him everything he knew about the Wand. He thought on it as he walked to pass the time. "The Jade God whose name we never say, tricked a human mage into opening a gate from here to the Abyss through which that god could come. The mage's name was Bomoki. He became the first hellhound. Heroes from Morbatten, guided by the Queen, found and closed the gate. They could not destroy it. The gate taints the lands around it and that became the Bloodstone Valley. Because of that gate, because of the abyss and chaos and the Jade God's desire to re-enter this world, every once in a while, a hellhound will come through. There is a connection between the gate, the hounds, and the Wand. It almost destroyed Morbatten long ago.

"All of the guilds in Tania have a priority mission to recognize hellhounds and the Wand and fight it. The emperor takes it very seriously because the Wand is able to possess anyone, as you saw with the ogre and the lich. It transforms them into a hellhound. It can summon other hounds. With either enough power, like through the lich, or with enough hellhounds, they can open a temporary gate through which the Jade God himself can enter. The Wand is sentient. It is very magical and its allure is too much for most to resist. The closer a person is to the Jade God's dominion, the more seductive the Wand's power is."

At last, they reached a large promenade of large cut stones bound together with magical runes. Braziers alight with columns of flame illuminated the tunnel entering the emperor's throne. A priest or priestess stood by the braziers and bowed as they passed them by.

To their left, far in the west, the sun had begun to dip below the horizon setting the Soldier's Fort and the western mountain alight with fire. To the east, the Temple came alight with fire and a bell tolled. "So, this is the emperor's home." Malcor said.

Chapter Seventy One - The Dragon Emperor

Near him, Verit nodded. "Make no mistake, we are entering the lair of a very real and very powerful dragon. The Emperor and the Father. He is an eldar dragon and the patriarch of the fire breathers. After this, any other dragon you encounter will seem less. I met the emperor after my second rite almost a decade ago. It was amazing." Verit smiled and nudged Malcor forward.

The other supplicants were sent in while they waited. A priestess guiding them said, "The emperor wishes to have more time with you honored heroes."

After several hours, the other supplicants exited and began the long walk back down. Braziers alight with elemental fire lit the path and provided warmth. The view of the city from here resembled a floor of sparkling gems and Malcor realized that this must be how the dread lords see them and their society.

When the priestess walked off a distance, Verit guessed Malcor's thoughts and said, "We are their treasures. You've seen the River right? One day, one of them will show you how we look to them."

The priestess interrupted them. "You may enter now. Proceed straight to the doors. The guards will admit you. Do not stop. Do not deviate from the straight path."

They entered and Malcor realized that this tunnel was actually a launch ramp for a dragon that must be even larger than Armageddon. Their path sloped gently downwards. Heavily warded doors branched off the main tunnel on either side. A radiant heat grew as they proceeded and the gradually, the very stone itself began to glow as if molten. Doors so large a titan would feel small became visible and gradually increased in size. To either side of the doors, statues of shiny metal stood guard to the height of ten men. One styled after an Ancient warrior and the other a more modern paladin replete with armor and weapons Malcor recognized. The entire door, large as it was, bore tiny calligraphic script in draconian. Within one of the door's halves, a smaller but still very large door had been cut into the lower section. Separate braziers glowed there and smaller statues guarded it.

They passed near and then through the smaller door. Malcor felt the statues gazing at him. Verit whispered, "This is the fate of paladins who fall so hard they are refused entry into the Queen's realm and denied exit from this one. They are death knights, forever watching over the empire."

The huge door proved to be thick enough that it was many steps before they came through into the emperor's throne chamber. Gold and precious ore ingots made up the floor of the massive chamber. A relief of the Goddess decorated with precious and magical objects covered the entire walls and ceiling. The chamber would easily hold many dragons.

In the center of the chamber, rested a throne. As they drew near, a giant human adorned in armor and robes lounged on it. Seven steps rose, each step made of precious gemstones colored to match the chromatic dragons. The topmost platform dripped red and appeared to move like liquid. In fact, as he drew nearer, he saw it moving and sparkling with some form of fire burning within it.

The emperor looked flawlessly, perfectly human. Dreadful, immortal, and strong the emperor watched their approach. Malcor could not take his eyes from him. Beautiful and godlike yet human and dragon at the same time, when Alerius stood and walked down the steps to greet them, Malcor felt something in his heart leap and then emotions raged there faster than he could identify them. He would later remember it as a feeling of sheer and total awe.

Looking sideways, he saw Verit swallow and could tell he felt it too. Then, the emperor stood before them and Malcor's knees buckled. Trying to seem graceful, Malcor dropped to the floor and bowed on his hands and knees. Desire to serve, to be loved by, to fight for, to die for, to conquer, to acquire, to possess, to be possessed, and more warred in his heart. The emperor touched Malcor's head and said, "Malcor, son of Kell, child of Morbatten and now my son, rise." At those words, the fury of feeling urged him to stand and Malcor felt like nothing would stop him from doing it. And he stood, with all his energy and soul.

"Verit, son of Bellryn, good to see you again. Rise." Hearing the emperor speak to another and touch another was almost too much for him. A sudden torrent of jealousy and envy rose up in him, but he realized Verit must have felt it too.

"I am told that you both played legendary roles in bringing low an eldar lich, a hellhound, and you have brought me gifts. Well done, both of you. Come, let us see what you have brought."

Malcor retrieved the soul gem and the dragon statue and placed them on the floor, returning to his bowed position. The urge to worship this god-like being made his body tremble and shake. Verit walked back to the wagon and at his touch, Kendra's sword uncurled. Verit picked up the tapestry and brought it to place on the floor before Alerius.

Verit spoke first. "Dreadful lord and father, the Order of Water has captured the Jade God's Wand. It is bound in this tapestry." He elbowed Malcor.

With a shaky voice, Malcor started. "Great emperor, the Order of Water has captured the eldar lich's soul gem. I also bring to you a creation of my own hand's making, a gift for the black dragon." His voice recovered halfway through and remembering Kendra's advice, he finished boldly.

Alerius went to the tapestry and unrolled it. There lay the Wand. When it first unrolled, it bore an exultant look and Malcor felt it lash out seeking a host. Alerius picked it up and the Wand's exultation rose to a fever of excitement until the ram's head twisted around and beheld Alerius. The Wand's cry of despair filled the room with echoes of agonized pain. Alerius laughed. "What's wrong?" he asked mockingly. "Do you not know how precious you are? Submit to me."

At those words, Malcor saw Alerius as a dragon superimposed over and above the glorified human holding the wand. The Wand became instantly fearful and struggled to twist and writhe out of Alerius' hand. "You are here, in my house. Orcus will not help you here. Submit to me and be done with this. Or die. I care not." Alerius squeezed the wand's spine and concentrated heat flashed out from his hand. The wand screamed seeking a host but seemed unable to touch Malcor or Verit. "Your time grows short hellhound. Orcus will no doubt welcome you in his predictable way. Stay here and serve, or return to pain." Another flash of heat and another and another and then the wand fell quiet.

"I submit. I have a price – "

"You are in no position to ask for anything. You are mine. Never forget that I am not Orcus. I can do things to you here that Orcus cannot. Someday, should I choose to free you, never forget what Orcus will do to you in that place!" Alerius laughed cruelly into the ram's skull's bone face. "Your new role on Tehra is to work with my children to identify your brothers as they come through. That is all. If you do it well, with enthusiasm, you will be rewarded, even treasured. I offer you an end to pain and fear. More importantly, I offer you a chance for revenge against your brothers and creator who abandoned you here, in the world of dragons. Prove yourself first and when I am impressed, we can discuss your price."

The wand tried to say something and Alerius just stared at it, daring it to speak. It went quiet. "Excuse me a moment," Alerius said. He ascended to his throne and placed it on the ground next to it. The wand sank beneath the surface of the liquid red platform and then its presence vanished.

Alerius turned back to Verit and Malcor. "One of the great secrets of our empire is that we capture these. Orcus imbues them with his power and by our capture and locking them away, it lessens his power. However, this is not common knowledge and must never be discussed. Having captured it, I give you each these earrings. They are tokens designating you as Hound Slayers. There are fewer than fifty today with this emblem. You may discuss these matters with them and only them." The earring, made of bone and sprinkled with powdered bloodstone glistened in the chamber. "Accept these," and the rings crawled into and pierced through their ears. "Any attempt to discuss with any other and the rings will silence you. Whether they are worn or not. You may find them near impossible to take off, so do not try it my sons. We have captured thirty-six hellhounds. That is the thirty-seventh."

Malcor then presented the soul gem still wrapped in his blood-stained and travelworn cloak. When Malcor unwrapped it, they heard a voice whispering around the gemstone. It repeated the words the lich had said when the lich had placed it in the pool of blood. Alerius looked at Malcor with a question who replied, "This is the first time I'm hearing these words, great emperor. I do not know their meaning."

Like the sceptre, Alerius picked it up and regarded it, listening to the strange words. "This will require some research. But it is a prize beyond all the wealth you saw in Ori my precious sons. Being from an eldar, from before the Necromancer, this is unique. It is special. A normal lich would neither have been as powerful, nor would it have lasted so long. The River erodes even the undead, into powder and dust. I accept this gift. However, since the lich gave it to you, I only take it in safe keeping. Once we understand it, I shall send for you again."

Malcor lifted up the black dragon statue. "My emperor, as a child I had visions and crafted this statue as a gift for my Coming of Age ceremony. At the ceremony, I heard the Goddess tell me to give it to the black dragon. I have not yet done this, but believe it is my father."

"Very good Malcor, and tell me, declare it. Who is your father?"

"My father is Dar K - " but the words stuck in his throat. Suddenly, they felt wrong and he felt the tear drop scale scar on his arm burn. "My human father is Dar Kell, but somehow it feels wrong now."

"That is because you are claimed by another father, Malcor. Cor'tanos step forward and show yourself," the emperor commanded.

The orange glow of red and plasma remained as bright as always, but suddenly against the gemstone-crusted ceiling a titanic shadow superimposed itself, alive and moving. The shadow reared up as if walking towards them but not until it was about twenty steps away did Malcor and Verit see a blur of darkness in the likeness of a human, but giant like Alerius and the other dread lords. In spite of the cavern's warmth, the dark blur that seemed to suck light into it also drained warmth from them. The shadow of a dragon reared up behind the blur. When it stood next to Alerius, they saw hints of a similarly glorious personage but the darkness shifted and moved making it hard to see.

The figure had black eyes and its skin was dark grey. Long black hair cascaded down around its shoulders and like a snake, coils of black vapor wound and twisted around it like fire would and then arc out to the two dimensional shadow haunting the cavern.

"Malcor, Verit. May I introduce to you the great shadow patriarch Cor'tanos, dark lord of the shadow dragons. You might know him better as the Heretic, who took his followers away from Takhissis and Her Consort to find their own place when the River began its murder."

Cor'tanos nodded his head, "I see their beauty Alerius. This one," a shadowy finger pointed at Malcor and the dragon's shadow arced down to touch Malcor's shadow, "is precious to me. His soul wars between faith, fury, and the shadows. It is everything you described, simply breath-taking. I have touched him but it was Kell who marked him."

From the other side, Dar Kell walked forward out of the dragon's shadow. "Greetings Malcor. Hail Verit." He came up to Malcor and took his shoulders. "Malcor, part of the Conflict, part of the doctrinal shift was to open the priesthood to men. That you know. What you don't know is that it also enabled us to dragonshift. Cor'tanos taught me. I was the first. The shadows, the differences between the shadow dragon clan and those we know and serve, drove me insane. There are many prophecies but in you converge two. The first is about the king's successor. The second is about the homecoming of the shadow clan."

Alerius said, "You humans are treasure beyond imagination. When I first saw you, before the River flowed, I marveled at this new creation. Pha Rann outdid himself by creating a being with such passion with such curiosity flamed by the shortness of your life's flame. No elf or dwarf or goblin would sacrifice themselves to know what Kell came to know. None exist that would give up immortality to serve the Queen as Rojo does. Verit, you are here for a reason too. No other creation would risk themselves for their band of fellow knights and stand alone against a demigod. The prophecy touches on a guardian, a teacher.

"You are here to confront your destiny and choose. Malcor, before you lies a path of sacrifice, pain, perhaps insanity. You know what the Kell Conflict was. Strong as he was, as he is, Kell went insane for years before recovering with Cor'tanos' help. Cor'tanos is here. He will help from the beginning, where Kell had to find and convince him to care. Dar Rojo nears the end of his reign as king. Will you Malcor become Rojo the Second? Will you join Cor'tanos shadow clan and help gather the shadows back to the Queen of All Dragons? Will you write your name in the Book of Kings and begin the Book of Shadows?"

"Yes, yes," Cor'tanos whispered moving forward. "You shall. You can. You will be mighty and you shall be my son."

Kell looked at Verit, "And you, I name you Dar Verit, will be the guardian, protector, and lord marshal to fight in Malcor's name when the shadows take him. Will you?"

Without hesitation, Verit clasped his fist to his chest and cried out, "As the Queen wills. My life. My soul. I serve!"

Malcor presented the dragon statue to Cor'tanos. It was an exact likeness. The blurred and darkened human took it from him leaving his hand numb with ice from the brief contact. In that moment, and on a whim, Malcor stepped out of the River. There on the banks, the beings before him were stupefying massive. He could barely comprehend his own smallness next to them.

Verit clad in glory and burning with religious fervor gleamed brightly. Dar Kell and Cor'tanos clad in shadow looked beautiful and dark. He recognized Cor'tanos as the shadow lurking in his past experiences. Over and above it all, he felt, then saw from far away, and closer as a dragon and then a human female walked forward from the mists. Immediately, he recognized Takhissis and he fell to the River's banks. She stepped over the River and Alerius, Cor'tanos, Kell, and Verit all paid obeisance to Her Majesty.

Where Alerius' presence had made Malcor and Verit tremble, the Queen shook them to the core as every possible emotion and passion hit them at once. The shock of it threw them both back into the River and they collapsed barely aware on the floor in Alerius' throne room. The last thing they heard was a purring voice so beautiful so terribly feminine that they would die for it call out, "Alerius, you have our trust regarding the

Heretics. Bring them back to me." There was a pause and then Her voice faded into the distance. "Make them pay dearly for their betrayal so that they remember this trust is earned."

When the awe of Her Presence faded, Alerius pulled them back into the real world. "R'Dar Malcor, I would name you Paladin of the Order of Water. Will you pledge your soul, your faith, your fury, your heart and life to the great Goddess Takhissis, to me as your emperor, to Morbatten?"

Malcor pledged he would. "Do you swear on your paladinhood that you be my sword against the enemies of Morbatten's innocents?"

"I do," Malcor said boldly.

Cor'tanos and Alerius placed their hands on the other's shoulder and then touched Malcor's shoulders to bid him stand. "Arise," they said in unison. "Stand forth Knight of Water, blessed child of dragons!"

Amidst the noise of that command, Malcor felt a woman's lips kiss his and bring with it the mantle of a paladin's duty. When they let him go, he drew his sword, which ignited in dark grey flame. He turned to the throne audience and raised it. "I am Malcor Kell'Tayris, paladin of Morbatten!"

In the sudden and still silence, Alerius spoke a repeat of the questions from earlier. "You accept the mantle of paladin, but we would have your answer about the kingship and the shadow dragons."

Malcor swallowed sensing all eyes on him. He dropped even lower in his bow almost prostrate on the River's surface. "Dread lords and great Goddess, I will serve in any way you require, with all my heart."

Alerius quietly replied, "But you question your worth, when you sparkle and shine like a world star?"

Malcor shook his head, praying in his heart for strength and to not offend, "I ache in battle. I question my ability to be a king when I am still not even a year out of Klenna's forge. I do not question the prophecy, but surely I am not the only one that sees I am not well-matched for kingship, or even as a shadow dragon."

Cor'tanos began laughing and through that laughing dragon roar, Alerius and the Queen spoke together, "Even a sword must be melted, hewn, and tempered. You are not king yet Malcor Kell'tayris. Not yet. We accept your heart's best efforts in being what is required R'Dar Malcor."

Chapter Seventy Two - A Shadow through My Heart

Malcor, Tembri, and Dar Verit stood alone in an empty and barren valley. The sun obscured by clouds barely held back the bitter chill. Around them, the high mountain peaks covered in winter snow teased the still green valleys and plains below them. Their escorts, Ancients from the Griffin Tribe, stood behind them. Except for the wind, everything lay silent.

"It's going to start soon, I can feel it," Malcor said. His arm scar had begun to itch, a feeling he recognized near the terrifying, or creatures from the Shadow Realms.

Tembri pointed south and they saw a red dragon, dark and silhouetted against the sky crest a mountain peak. The clouds above swirled gold and red from the heat of his passing. Then another dragon, hardly visible for its pale grey skin followed. A faint trail of frozen vapor and cloud trail helped them see it. Ynt'taris no doubt.

The Ancients bowed and signed them good fortune. They turned and loped off, running naturally and quickly. The three figures waited.

Alerius struck first. Fire trailed the dragon and dragonterror swept over them even at a distance where they could not yet make out clear details. A moment later, Alerius vanished as a column of fire burst from his mouth. From so far it looked slow, but then it struck the ground a hundred paces in front of them. The shockwave and molten splash of vaporized ground washed over them and then the flames were upon them. When it cleared, Ynt'taris breathed ice vapor down in a sighing fan of mist. It hit freezing the molten ground and crystallizing the air around them. When it passed, they stood – unscathed.

Malcor's arm spasmed and agony wracked his arm. From far above the dragons circling back on them, a shadow twisted through the clouds darkening them with its passage and then from all around them, the shadows cast by burning and molten rock cast against the columns of ice, the shadows crackled twilight grey energy like black snaking lightning from all directions. It was like nothing they had ever seen or felt before. Their vision went blurry and then their skin went numb as a vitality-draining cold edged into them. Eternity seemed to pass and then the dark cold withdrew.

The three dragons stood in a triangle around them. Cor'tanos roared and his terror dropped the three of them to the ground. When they regained their footing and stood, the shadow dragon teased them saying, "You did better than last time, but WHEN Malcor dragonshifts you need to shrug it off the way you did the fire and ice. Shadow dragons attack from the shadows. As such, our breath weapon manifests from ANY shadows near our prey. The shadows to me, to Malcor, are real." So saying, he lifted a claw and flicked Malcor's shadow. It knocked him just hard enough that fell back to his knees. "If you feel my breath, my presence at all, Malcor when enraged will tear into that weakness and then you are his. You must do better. All of you. Malcor, you will never retain self-control if you have any weakness for the shadows in you. I am annoyed that you dismiss the fire and ice but are affected by shadow. I would expect better from the three of you."

Ynt'taris hissed, "It took Kell YEARS to master what you seek to teach in days."

Cor'tanos bit back and roared, "Kell is a human! He was alone. My presence is enough. Again!" He leapt into the sky and bereft of shadows in the air, lost his form entirely. Alerius and Ynt'taris shrugged their mighty wings and flung themselves into the air.

Suddenly, without warning, the shadows around them struck. It caught them completely by surprise and the three dropped to their hands and knees as their lifeforce collapsed through their bodies' shadows. "No," Malcor screamed. "To the River!"

The River around them boiled black as a whirlwind of dark energy seethed into it. Malcor stood against the pain and reached up with his right arm. Where he touched the darkness, his arm shredded into shadow and for the first time, he felt his skin first, then muscle and bone, slice apart into razors of darkness. He leapt into the sky and attacked Cor'tanos.

Somewhere, in the real world, the shadow patriarch chuckled and as Malcor attempted to blast the clouds with shadow, a giant claw materialized above Malcor and grabbed him. It seized his wings and then dropped him to the ground. In a fit of rage, Malcor thrashed about trying to escape to kill to find freedom.

Tembri and Verit recovered to see Cor'tanos materialize above Malcor. By size, Malcor was like a kitten next to a war horse. "I am the shadow at the end of light and you are my son! Behave!"

Malcor went still and limp the way a dog does when submitting to an alpha. Gingerly, Cor'tanos let go of Malcor. He flexed his wings and tried to step back but his non-human legs tripped and he stumbled in a pool of half frozen half molten lava. He began to fall back and flailed. He then completely lost it. Tembri and Verit made note that frustration triggered the berserk. Again, that massive claw pulled Malcor to a better footing and commanded good behavior. "You are a paladin of Takhissis. But, you serve me in this form. I am your god. Obey me and control yourself!"

Malcor calmed and his eyes, which refused to make contact with Cor'tanos, alighted on Tembri and Verit. "Good, good. Take the fury in your belly and expel it at them, unleash your breath weapon!"

Trapped inside the dragon, Malcor watched his body writhe and twist trying to break free of Cor'tanos without doing anything that would challenge the patriarch. He saw Tembri and Verit steel themselves for the inevitable breath attack. At Cor'tanos' words, he tried to feel the fury but instead of fury, he felt a singular apathy that pulled at him. These were his friends. He thought about it as Cor'tanos urged him to attack. A voice came to him in that moment of thought, it was Dar Kell's. "Malcor, as humans, we do not feel the fury Cor'tanos feels just by virtue of being here in the real world. I felt the same way. Your breath weapon is your most powerful attack. It is devastating. Find a different reason for it. The Queen. Your dreams. Some frustration. Surely there is something you can hold onto to channel. For me, it was and always shall be the memory of my wife and children's deaths."

Malcor thought and then it struck him. In his memory, he had been kicked to the ground at the king's feet. The king, the high priestess, and how many dread lords along with the entire village of Klenna? He felt the humiliation and his sword cutting through R'Dar Tor's side. Malcor's breath weapon exploded from his mouth in a stream of grey dust from which clawed hands pulled the stream forward and mouths open and screaming shrieked. In a instant, the ray of twilight claws and gnashing mouths slammed into his two friends. It seemed to last forever. The release pulled Malcor out of his apathy and for the first time, he became the dragon. He felt claws instead of talons and his mouth filled with lethal fangs and the smell of the world crashed in on his senses. Gone was the dullness of seeing things through twilight and in came the bright lights, the exquisite detail of viewing the world in reverse. Shadows appeared bright as day and suggested the form of the real world. Smell and taste and touch almost burned with their overwhelming detail.

Cor'tanos let go of him and he flexed his wings and jumped back, but his jump carried him hundreds of paces away. Tembri and Verit had risen up from the breath attack and he saw their shadows tinged with the cracked and fragmented blasts of three shadow breath weapons. Other things lurked in the shadows and then he saw Alerius and Ynt'taris. The two dragons gave off trails of red and silvery light as they circled overhead. The shadows along their bodies as they turned in the faint sunlight gave him a sense of their size and power. Both appeared full of power, where Cor'tanos and his own self felt empty. *No, not empty. Full of void.*

A shadow rose up behind Tembri and took the shape of Dar Kell. Like Cor'tanos, Kell's void appeared full and potent but within its center curled the devotion and worship of the Queen. Malcor put his head back and blasted his voice at the sun. Doing so made him feel stronger, more present. He turned his gaze back to the humans. They seemed so small but like Kell, the heart of their devotion and worship glowed, twirled and danced in their hearts. The magical armor and weapons and gear they bore gleamed duly compared to the normal things that hardly passed his gaze. The magic glowed softly in his gaze creating multi-colored shadows, but its beauty did not hypnotize the way Tembri's faith or Verit's sense of purpose did.

Malcor walked forward wanting to look more closely. As he did so, he heard Cor'tanos speak to him in a serpentine hiss. He had heard the patriarch make these sounds before, but now he understood them. "The treasure of the Tehran world Malcor. Look at them. Revel in being a dragon and work to control this. Let us return to human form now. Claw at the scar on your arm and try to remember the feeling of being human."

It took a while but Malcor finally pulled back to himself. His first breath after the transformation felt as if he had been suffocating. He rose to his feet and found the dread lords and the other humans looking at him with curiosity and concern.

"You did it," Kell said. "You'll learn the rest on your way to Bloodstone. Make ready and be prepared to leave when snow falls on the city."

Epilogue: Court of Dragons

The Temple, at Alerius' command, had been cleared. This rarely happened but the priestesses considered it their sacred duty to let the Temple dedicated to dragons to be used by the dragons at a moment's notice. Inside the great central chamber and before the massive statue of the Queen, Alerius folded his wings and leaned back against the obelisk he had raised in the time of Dar Tania, his first priestess. Sometime later, Ynt'taris entered and took his place by his column. Looking around, the white hissed, "Will he be joining us?"

Alerius nodded, "Patience brother. Spark brings us a gift."

Ynt'taris sharpened his claws and waited. To pass time, he asked Alerius, "How many sceptres do we actually hold brother?"

"We have secured the thirty-seven sceptres mentioned before Ynt'taris, yet we have another one hundred and seven lesser hellhound wands."

"Worlds removed from the Jade God's dominion. But this last one was different."

"Yes, not just a copy but an original. We only have ever seen one other like it. Bomoki wields that one still."

A gate opened by the unoccupied column and Spark stepped through it. "Apologies brothers, but I have taken great pains to ensure my involvement remains hidden from the Jade God. We came too close to a cascade in Khasra."

The form of the Apprentice washed away as Spark humanshifted. On the ground in front of him, the lich's soul gem pulsed. "I have returned the souls of our people to their hosts in prison. We did lose two and that was when the lich tried to pull Daryx's physical form through. The lich's name is Talai. Do you know it?"

When both Alerius and Ynt'taris said nothing, Spark continued, "I checked the Darkhold and it confirms our guess. Talai went adrift and froze so far from the River that he never experienced Time the way we did. He appeared here out of Time. Such things, they are not coincidence."

Ynt'taris questioned, "You suspect Orcus or perhaps Set?"

Spark shrugged, "One of the plagues of Time's flow is that we may never know until this has played out, but only the Jade God would benefit from Talai appearing when he did. Tell me Alerius, did you know that from Bloodstone, Dar Ana's reports describe several ancient mineshafts re-opening in the same timeframe as Talia's arrival in Khasra?"

Alerius answered, "No, but I will ask for more detail. To make this happen, it does not feel like the Jade God. Though that one thinks itself crafty and patient, all hellhound incursions are marked by tactical shortsightedness, impatience, and a drive to a clear objective. No, the Jade God would have simply taken the lich or pulled it to Bloodstone."

"Bomoki," Ynt'taris hissed. "How I yearn to devour that one."

The others agreed biting at the air. "We must be careful. The Order of Water will command the Nineteenth Legion. Dar Verit shall lead. We will make preparations for readiness, including the other nations," Alerius stated.

Ynt'taris spoke after a period of silence. "It has been too long since I found one of your humans that I liked. Malcor, he reminds me of Alaura so many ages ago. Have you found the mother?"

"No, not yet. She defies scrying and divination as well." Alerius dug his claw into the stone floor.

"We will know soon enough," Spark said. "In the meantime, we must consider all of these pieces together. Talai, Bomoki, ancient mines recovered, Cor'tanos, an original sceptre, and Rojo's impending Ascension. Taken together, it means we are on the verge of another great Cascade."

Alerius and Ynt'taris both nodded their agreement. The first "great" cascade nearly sixteen hundred years ago had slain his beloved Dar Tania and forced Alerius to push the cascade from Tania to Bloodstone. It changed the empire, and in unpredictable ways. "I cannot lose most of my treasured peoples again," Alerius said after a long pause. "The first was too painful to endure."

"She was our treasured friend and sister too," both said near in unison. Ynt'taris continued, "She affected us all that way. Unlike that time, we are ever more ready, and you - brother Alerius, will not face Orcus alone. The other patriarchs are ready."

"Green, black, purple, all the other colors, they've all agreed to join us at last?"

"Yes. When they heard Cor'tanos had come crawling back from shadow, they all pledged." Ynt'taris crooned. "If they only knew the truth about that one!"

Spark cautioned, "Careful Ynt'taris, soon that one will be joining our counsels."

"I have watched over your children a long time Alerius," the white continued, "and I grow weary of it. Perhaps, after this great cascade, I will return to Merakor."

"Surely," Alerius shot back, "there is beauty here exceeding the blight of that place?"

"Just two remain – Ora and Klara. My favorite jewel Ora is watching the girl now." Ynt'taris created a white ghostly image of the two females.

Alerius nodded at the image and asked, "I have not seen Ora's test report. I assume the child is a prodigy?"

"No, she is nothing. She is everything." Ynt'taris' illusion shifted to show Ora sitting in meditation holding Klara's hands. "They pray to Mother, but Klara is equally in this world and outside of Time. Ora could not determine if she has a created soul."

Silence reined for a moment before Spark added, "And yet, our debriefing with Armageddon noted that he and Malcor saw Klara's aura. She must have a soul."

The white dragon shifted the illusion to Klara and described the test. "Because my Ora could not see, she stood with Klara and only when talking about Malcor did her aura alight. She is a *reactive* soul."

Alerius commanded, "Say what you mean brother."

"She lacks a soul and so borrows from those she has bonded with. She will bond with Ora, very probable. If so, she will be an ice priestess. However, she has a strong bond with Malcor and were she to -"

Spark slapped the floor and said, "She would become a paladin!"

Ynt'taris told Spark to bite his tongue. "You would never understand the appeal of a gifted child, a girl child even. They have such potential. Klara, not Malcor, is the one to be king. Rojo's haste nearly killed Kell's son Malcor, and because of that haste, Klara had to present herself to Armageddon. The idiot brute did not see her lordly destiny, but I see it. We are lucky she did not bond with that brute."

Ynt'taris suddenly struck like a cobra at Alerius stopping just shy of contact, and whispered, "I would see Klara seated on the Dragon Throne and safe before I leave this place. I see great pain coming and Alaura still haunts me. Klara, not Malcor, shall tame the heretics and allow Morbatten to survive what is coming."

"Tell me brother ice," Alerius hissed. "What do you see coming?"

"Cor'tanos will rebel; this we already know. Malcor may or may not endure the role chosen for him by Fate. Against this, Orcus grows weary of these one-at-a-time incursions against us. Bomoki's return means this is an end game. We are either the spearhead or not, and yet the Pha Rannic messenger who spoke to Dar said Taysor would be the shield.

"We all know Taysor is not ready or willing. Instead, they have withered and lost their way in zealotry and self-righteous arrogance. Their rhetoric against us becomes increasingly hostile... a pattern we have seen before. You once asked where Bomoki has been all this time. I'll tell you – he has been in Taysor creating this end game. So tied up with your treasures, you miss the signs brothers. That the others pledge to us, even Cor'tanos, means they all sense the growing threat."

Alerius head butted Ynt'taris away from him. "Let them come. Even if you are right and Taysor fails as a shield, my children will win. I am unsure that Klara is the sister mentioned in the prophecy. That sister could be king. Klara may or may not. It feels wrong."

It caught Ynt'taris off guard and with renewed suspicion asked, "What do you know brother fire?"

Alerius' giant head swiveled to match Ynt'taris' movements. "Rarely do our prophecies become literal. By this age, we knew Malcor met the prophecy. That Klara has remained elusive this long, no. If true, she would have revealed herself to the King as well, at his call. She is something altogether different."

Ynt'taris humanshifted to his little girl form and walked out. At the grand doors exiting the front steps, she turned and looked back, "I concede and agree – we shall watch Klara though I believe she will be a better king's successor. To the spearhead, my brothers, victory at what price? Do we get what we want from this victory? I question the *price*."

She vanished into the evening fog with her last statement reverberating back into the great chamber.

Excerpt from *Bomoki's Gate*, to be published February 2017 as 300+ page book…

The hound screamed at the rising sun as its quarry dropped onto the fortress battlements. The damned sunlight already made him feel lethargic. He longed for the green sun of his homeworld and snapped at the two dragons fading into the distance. Feeling a mass of necromancy somewhere underground, the hound turned and found a small opening just as the first ray of light beamed to the valley's floor. The sun, even on cloudy days, allowed normal life to happen here as birds and other creatures hiding and struggling to survive awoke.

The hound crawled through the dark as its body reknit itself. How many it had absorbed to stay alive during the fight with that cursed warrior and dragon, he had forgotten. He stopped and rubbed his healing but still tender shoulder alongside a rock face. At some point, another hound greeted him. It bowed low in welcome. "Oh great one, we heard your call but could not come through."

"Then you were too slow coming!" Bomoki's Gate snapped back. "Everything was there for what you needed except MORE effort on your part!" He snapped at the lesser hound who jumped ahead of Bomoki careful to avoid any kind of a challenge.

They eventually entered a cavern with a pool of clear shallow water. Bomoki ran into this bite-drinking water and washing the gore and filth away before at last letting go of his hound form. From the pool, walked a slender man with olive skin tattooed and scarred many times over. Skin and tissue sagged or sloughed off en masse as the water pulled away but regenerative tendon and ligament pulled it back and held it closed. Green light from his eyes lit the cavern. The other hound, now joined by two more and a growing number of undead waited in silence for this one, the first of all that still lived in this world to speak or command them.

Flipping the sleeves on his gold-trimmed red robe, Bomoki walked through them. From behind his spine, the jade sceptre of Orcus spat threats at the other hounds reminding them of their enslavement. Bomoki reached back and scratched at the skin around the sceptre's claws where it dug into his spine at the neck's base. Bomoki paused when he felt the jade head of the sceptre and then patted it on the head whispering for it to calm. Ahead of him, skeletons and undead felt like water, splashing apart and rushing to reform into a throne of eye sockets and gore. On this, Bomoki sat, flipping his sleeves out as the sceptre reformed from his spine to his left hand where his fingers reached over the skull and stroked the nose bridge. From the chair, other sceptres crawled onto his skin, helmeting his head, becoming shoulder armor. Each a complete ram skull and spine, it locked and crisscrossed his body tearing at it as they settled into their host.

"A glorious time comes to us brother," he said addressing the lesser hound. "Unlike the disaster in Ori, we have a time of prophecy and rivers of blood flow through time. The king of Tania is here and his pet gold dragon is with him! Long have I prayed to Orcus that the blood and eyes needed to complete the master's gate would be brought. Too long has the master been locked out of Tehra."

The hound and undead groveled and the throne tittered at the seeming good mood of their ungodly master. "Hound, you must take a message back to Orcus and the waiting hounds. You will tell Orcus the following. Gold dragon eyes will at last complete the artifact we began constructing centuries ago to unlock the gate. I require six hound generals to retrieve the eyes, under my command, my absolute command. I also require the demi-liches, so convey my request for their release to the master."

Under his hand, the sceptre crooned and said, "Orcus will question your timing. Get the eyes first or else the artifact is just another wand. The hound generals will want the eyes before they come. Too risky the price of failure they will think."

Bomoki retained his gaze at the lesser hound and paid the sceptre no attention. "You will tell this to the master with all respect and politeness. Now go. It will take them time to travel here though I need them already. As for you," he turned his gaze to the sceptre. "You forget that time passes *thing*. I have waited eight centuries for a gold dragon to come here. And, here it is. We will take this opportunity."

486

I'd love to hear from you and your thoughts about Malcor. To tell me or to learn more about the Forsaken Isles, please visit me at:

darmalcor.weebly.com

www.ingramcontent.com/pod-product-compliance
Lightning Source LLC
Chambersburg PA
CBHW070857260626
47162CB00007B/2478